Two men stood in ▓▓▓▓▓▓▓▓▓▓▓ armed with Mausers. ▓▓▓▓▓▓▓▓▓▓ rags might once have b▓▓▓▓▓▓▓▓▓▓ and caked mud made it impossible to tell with any certainty. They came toward the car at a trot, spaced across the road and moving in the instinctive half-crouch of men who expect to come under fire. As they came closer, the nun could see the lice moving in their beards, catch a gagging whiff of their stink.

The guerrilla nearest the river went to one knee and began a nervous scan up and down the road; the other hailed the car.

"Who's there? Answer, or I fire!"

Tom's voice replied, in slow ungrammatical French: "Just us serfs, here. Who yaz an' what yo' want?"

"This is the Auvergne command of the National Resistance," the man said; he repeated it as if it were a spell, a mantra against reality. "Food; we need food, medicine, weapons, clothing."

" 'Fraid there's nothin' for yaz here," the ex-Janissary said mildly.

"What—why—"

"Because yaz gonna die, bushman!" The guerrilla was an experienced soldier, but the bull bellow still checked him for the first fraction of a second.

Tom's carbine cleared the lower sill of the window with smooth economy; he fired from the hip, with the forestock braced against the metal of the windowframe.

A plate-sized area of the guerrilla's back fountained out in an eruption of bone-chips, spine and shards of flesh.

UNDER THE YOKE

S.M. STIRLING

BAEN
BOOKS

UNDER THE YOKE

Copyright © 1989 by S.M. Stirling

A Baen Books Original

Baen Publishing Enterprises
P.O. Box 1403
Riverdale, NY 10471

ISBN: 0-671-72077-5

Cover art by Carl Lundgren

First Printing, October 1989
Second Printing, November 1990

Printed in the United States of America

Distributed by Simon & Schuster
1230 Avenue of the Americas
New York, NY 10020

To Dave and Poul,
for their kind words.

And always, to Jan.

THE WORLD OF THE DOMINATION
1948 A.D.

Note: The planet is divided between the Domination of the Draka and the 11 member states of the Alliance for Democracy (headquarters: San Francisco). The Alliance excludes Draka vessels from the Pacific except for coastal waters: the Domination does likewise in the Indian Ocean. The Atlantic is divided.

DOMINATION OF
THE DRAKA

EMPIRE OF
JAPAN

UNITED STA
OF AMERI

San Francisco

INDO-
CHINESE
REP

PHILLIPINES
(U.S. State)

INDONESIAN
FEDERATION

AUSTRALASIAN
FEDERATION

AUSTRALASIAN
FEDERATION

AUSTRALASIAN
FEDERATION

CHAPTER ONE

... enlargement of our standard lines in domestic, supervisory and recreational items for the intending settler in the new territories. Our Agency has had agents on hand for every auction of choice items; stock your kitchens and servants' quarters from the best hotels and restaurants of Europe! And while Settlement Directorate issue may do for field-hands and machine-tenders, when it comes to the strawbosses, interpreters and drivers you will need for your plantation or enterprise, our breaking-and-training establishments are unmatched for price and quality. Why go to the expense of importing your serf cadre from the dregs of the Police Zone?

And amusement? From the snowy blond of Sweden to the olive of Italy, the fruits of conquest are yours to pluck. From peasants to aristocrats, from the illiterate to the ballerinas and university students of Paris, wench or prettybuck, your fantasy is our reality. Whether your desire is sjambok-broken docility or a wild Finn you can tame yourself, Stevenson & de Verre has it! Chemo-conditioning and polygraph testing ensure unmatched reliability for our product, reared in and tailored to local languages and custom, from Seoul to Lisbon! Don't waste precious time and capital training your own;

1

consult our brochures, and contact your local represen-
tative for further information.

> Advertising flier of Stevenson &
> de Verre, Labor Agents, included in:
> Settler Information Kit No. III
> Settlement Directorate, European
> Area, 1948 ed.

LYON, PROVINCE OF BURGUNDIA
REGIONAL HQ, SECURITY DIRECTORATE
DETENTION CENTER XVII
APRIL, 1947

"Pater Noster, qui est in caelis . . ."

"Shut up, slut-bitch!" The guard raked her hard-
rubber truncheon along the bars in frustration, then
stalked off down the corridor.

Sister Marya Sokolowska lowered her head and fought
to recapture the Presence; a futile effort, it could not be
forced. *Enough, prayer is more than feelings,* she chided
herself, while habit droned the sonorous Latin words
and told the beads of her rosary. The words were a
discipline in themselves; faith was a matter of the intel-
lectual will more than subjective sentiment. And the
others relied on her: even Chantal Lefarge the communist over in the corner was joining in; it helped remind
them they were human beings and not animals-with-
numbers, that they were a community, linked one with
the other. Something easy to forget in the ten-by-twelve
brick cube of cell 10-27, under the Domination of the
Draka. Though she was the only Pole here, and the
only religious.

Covertly, her eyes followed the guard as far as the
grill-door would allow. The building had not been designed as a prison; the Draka had taken it over when
Lyons fell, back in '45. Before then . . . a school, perhaps, or some sort of offices. Then the Security Direc-

torate had come, and cordoned off as many square blocks of the city as need dictated; knocked doors and built walkways between buildings, surrounded the whole with razor-wire and machine-gun towers, put in bars and control-doors. It was a warren now, brick and concrete, burlap and straw ticking, the ever-present ammonia stink of disinfectant. Lights that were never dimmed, endless noise. The tramp-tramp-clank of chain gangs driven in lockstep to messhalls or to their work, maintaining and extending the prison-complex. Far-off shouts and screams, or someone in the cell across the corridor waking shrieking from a nightmare. Mornings were worst: that was the hour for executions, in the courtyard below their cell. The metal grille blocked vision but not sound; they could hear the footsteps, sometimes pleading or whimpering, once or twice cracked voices attempting the Marseillaise, then the rapid chuttering of automatic weapons and rounds thumping into the earth berm piled against their block's wall . . .

The nun finished the prayer and came to her feet, putting solemnity aside and smiling at the others. Together they rolled the thin straw-stuffed pallets up against the walls, each folding her single cotton blanket on top and placing the cup and pan in the regulation positions. There was nothing else to do; it was forbidden to sleep or sit after the morning siren. Conversation was possible, if you were careful and very quiet, a matter of gesture and brief elliptical phrases, and it helped break the terrible sameness of each day. Newcomers brought in fresh tidings from the world outside, and bits of gossip passed from hand to hand, on work details or at the messhall . . . not as elaborate as she had expected, there were too many informers and turnover was too high. This was a holding and processing center, not a real prison; a place to sit and wait until they took you away. Terrible rumors about what lay beyond: factories, labor camps, bordellos, medical experiments such as the Germans had done during the Nazi years . . . but no real information. For herself, it was not so bad; she had much time to meditate, and the others to help, and what came after would be the will of God, Who would give her strength enough to meet it, if no more.

Marya crossed herself and moved a careful half-pace closer to the bars. Good, the guard had gone around the corner. She was just a trusty, a prisoner like the rest of them, with no key to open cell doors. She *could* mark an individual or a whole cell down and inform the real guards, the Security bulls and retired Janissaries who ran Block D, Female Section. That could mean flogging or electroshock or sweatbox for all of them, you never knew. But the guard would be reluctant to do that; it was unwise to have more contact with the bulls than you had to. A prayer was not enough provocation; a real racket might be, because then she would be in danger of losing her position and being thrown back into a holding pen, which meant being quietly strangled one night. Seven to one was bad odds.

God forgive them all, Marya thought. *For them too the Savior died.* She herself would probably get nothing more than a whack across the kidneys with the rubber truncheon at mess call.

Not for the first time, she reflected that Central Detention was like being inside a machine. Not a particularly efficient one, more like an early steam engine that gasped and wheezed and leaked around its gaskets, shuddering with loose fittings and friction. But it used the Domination's cheapest fuel, human life, and it was simple and rugged and did its work with a minimum of attention; she had been here six months and rarely even saw the serf guards and clerks who did the routine management, much less one of the Citizen-caste aristocracy of the Domination . . .

There was an iron chung-*chang* from the landing down at the south end of the corridor; the main door to Block D, two stories up the open stairwell. A sudden hush caught the cells along the narrow passageway, an absence of noise that had been too faint for conscious attention, then a rustle as the inmates sprang to stand by their bedrolls. The nun moved to her own and assumed the proper posture, feet together, head bowed, hands by sides. She could feel the sweat prickle out on her palms, wiped them hurriedly down the coarse cotton sack-dress that prisoners were issued. Suddenly the familiar roughness itched against her skin, and she forced her toes to stop their anxious writhing in the sisal-and-wood clogs.

A whimper. Therese; she had never been strong, or quite right in the head since they brought her and Chantal in. A slight girl, dark and too thin, who never spoke and slept badly. The nun had had medical training, but it was nothing physical; the abuse that had made the elder Lefarge sister strong with hate had broken something in Therese. Perhaps it could never be healed, and certainly not here. Eyes met across the cell, and someone coughed to cover the quick squeeze of the shoulder and whisper of comfort that was all they had to offer.

Pauvre petite, Marya thought; then with desperation: much too early for the bulls to be down looking for amusement. And they had never picked cell 10-27. Holy Mary, mother of God, *please . . .*

The guard pelted down the corridor and dropped to her knees by the stairs from the landing. Marya's bedroll was nearest the door; she could see boots descending the pierced-steel treads. Three sets, composition-soled leather with quick-release hooks rather than eyes for the lacings. Draka military issue, the forward pair black and the other two camouflage-mottled. Quickly, she flicked her eyes back to her toes. A Citizen! Could they have found out? Silently she willed the boots to pace by, on down the corridor. Not praying, because this could only mean bad trouble and the only words her heart could speak would be: somebody else, anyone but me.

Marya swallowed convulsively, thick saliva blocking her throat. *Even Our Lord asked that the cup pass from him.* But he had not wished it on anyone *else.* Nor would she.

The lock made its smooth metal sound of oiled steel and the cell door swung open. She could feel the breeze of it, smell leather and cloth, gun-oil and a man's cologne.

"*Bow*, you sluts!" the guard barked, hovering nervously in the corridor. The eight inmates of cell 10-27 put palms to eyes and bent at the waist.

"Up, stand up." A man's voice, cool and amused, speaking French with a soft slurred accent. "Present, wenches."

Marya jerked erect and bent her head back to show the serf identity-code tattooed behind her left ear, one hand holding back the long ashblond hair that might have covered it.

The position gave her a good look at the three men. Their armed presence crowded the cell, even though there was room in plenty with the inmates braced to attention. Two were common soldiers, Janissaries from the Domination's subject-race legions with shaven skulls and serf-numbers on their own necks. Big men, young, thick heavy-muscled shoulders and necks and arms under their mottled uniforms. Both carried automatic rifles; ugly, squared-off things with folding stocks and snail-shaped drum magazines; there were heavy fighting-knives in their boots, stick-grenades clipped to their harness, long machete-like bushknives slung over their backs. Dark men, with blunt features and tight-curled hair and skins the color of old oiled wood; Africans, from the heartlands of the continent where the Domination began. Their people had been under the Yoke for generations, and the Draka favored them for such work; they looked at the women with indifferent contempt and casual desire.

The third was an officer, a Citizen. In the black tunic and trousers of garrison uniform, with a peaked cap folded and thrust through his shoulder-strap; Marya understood just enough of the Domination's military insignia to know he was a Merarch, roughly a colonel. A tall man, leopard to the Janissaries' bull strength. Tanned aquiline features, pale gray eyes, brown hair streaked with a lighter color, a single gold hoop-earring. No more than thirty, with white scar-lines on his hands and face, one deep enough to leave a V in his left cheekbone. A machine-pistol rested in an elaborate holster along his thigh, but it was the weapon in his hand that drew her eye. A steel rod as thick as a man's thumb with a rubber-bound hilt, tapering along its meter length to the brass button on its tip; a cable ran from the hilt to the battery-casing at his belt. An electroprod.

The tip came towards her face. Sweat prickled out along her upper lip as she fought against the need to flinch. Marya knew what it could do; the 'prod was worse than a whip, as bad as the sweatbox. The Draka used it to control crowds; the threat was usually as effective as an automatic weapon, and less wasteful. Too many times and you could start having fits. Applied to the head it could cause convulsions, loss of memory, change you inside . . . She closed her eyes.

Metal touched her chin. Nothing. Not activated. She opened her eyes, and the Draka nodded with approval.

"Spirited," he said. "Sound off, wench."

"Marya seven-three-E-S-four-two-two, Master," she recited, fighting off a flush of hatred that left her knees weak, on the verge of trembling. She would not show it, not when it might be mistaken for fear.

The man in black flipped open a small leather-bound notebook with his left hand. "Ssssa; 34, literate, languages French, German, English, Polish . . ." He raised an eyebrow. "Quite a scholar . . . advanced accounting . . . ah, category 3m73, religious cadre, that would account for it." The electroprod clicked against the crucifix and rosary that hung through the cloth tie of her sack-dress. Made from scraps of wood, silently at night beneath her blanket. "Nun?"

"I am a Sister of the Order of St. Cyril, Master."

The Draka flicked the steel rod against her hip, hard enough to sting. "You were. Now you're 73ES422, wench." He read further, pursed a lip. "Suspicion of unauthorized education? Ah, that was six months ago;

Security must have been dithering whether to pop you off or send you to the Yanks with the Pope and the rest." He shook his head and made a *tsk* sound between his teeth. "Headhunters, typical."

Marya felt herself pale. "The . . . the Holy Father has been exiled?"

Two more cuts, harder this time. "Master," she added.

He turned without answering, scanning the others. "You," he pointed.

"Chantal nine-seven-E-F-five-seven-eight, Master." Marya could see the film of sweat on the other woman's face, and knew it was rage, not terror.

Calm, keep calm, she thought. *Suicide is a mortal sin.*

The Draka stepped over and looked her up and down, smiling slightly. She had dark-Mediterranean good looks, long black hair and a heart-shaped face, a full-curved body under the coarse issue gown. "At ease," he said, and the inmates straightened and dropped their eyes again; the officer chuckled as he watched the dark woman glaring at his boots and consulted the notebook.

"Twenty years, literate, numerate, French and English . . . ex-bookkeeper, member of the Communist Party . . ." He caught the hem of her gown on the end of the electroprod and raised it to waist height, and murmured in his own tongue: "Not bad haunches, but these Latins run to fat young."

Marya understood him, with difficulty; the English her Order had taught her was the standard British form. The Domination's core territory in Africa below Capricorn had been settled by Loyalist refugees from the American Revolution, speakers of an archaic eighteenth-century southern dialect, and it had mutated heavily in the generations since. He paused, let the cloth fall, tapped the steel rod thoughtfully against one boot.

"Shuck down, wenches," he said after a moment.

There was a quick rustle of cloth as the inmates stripped; the prison gowns were simple cotton sacks with holes for arms and heads. Marya undid her belt, pulled the garment over her head, folded it atop her bedroll, slipped off the briefs that were the only undergarment and folded them in turn, stepped out of the clogs and stood in the inspection posture, hands linked behind the head and eyes forward. The dank chill of the place seemed suddenly greater, raising the gooseflesh on shoulders and thighs, making her wish she could hug herself and run her palms down her arms.

When she had been arrested, it was only chance that the secret school was not in session and the children gone. All unauthorized education was forbidden, under penalty of death; they would have penned her and the children together in the room and tossed in a grenade. Alone, she would have died there and then if any evidence had been found. Two of the mothers had been with her, and there was no room in the police van; the green-uniformed Security Directorate officer had drawn her pistol and shot them both through the head as they knelt, to save the trouble of calling in for a larger vehicle. And inside Central Detention there had been no interrogation, no torture; only the cell and the endless monotony spiced by fear, until she realized that her gesture of defiance was not even worth investigating.

There had been a speech for her batch of new inmates. Very brief: *"This is a bad place, serfs, but it can always be worse. We ask little from the living, only obedience; from the dead, nothing."*

Beside her Therese was weeping silently, slow fat tears squeezing out from under closed lids and running down her face, dripping from her chin onto her breasts. Most of the others were expressionless, a few preening under the dispassionate gaze; the Draka nodded and turned to the guard.

"This one and that one," he said, flicking the prod toward Marya and Chantal. "Put the restraints on them."

Marya's stomach lurched as the guard's rough hands turned her around and pulled her arms behind her back. The ring-and-chain bonds clanked, fastening thumbs and wrists and elbows in a straining posture that forced the shoulders back; you could walk in them if you were careful, but they were as effective as a hobble when it came to running. Not that there was anywhere to run; and anything at all might be waiting beyond the iron door. Cell 10-27 *was* a bad place; of cold and fear and a monotony that was worse than either, grinding down your mind and spirit. Now it seemed a haven . . . The one thing you could be certain of in the Domination was that there was always someplace worse.

The guard shoved the two women roughly toward the door of the cell. Marya staggered, turned and bowed awkwardly.

"Master," she said. "Our things?"

"You won't be back, wench," the Draka said, stretching. The Janissaries chuckled; one reached out and grabbed the weeping Therese by the breast, pinching and twisting. She folded about the grip in a futile shrimp-curl of protection, mouth quivering as she sobbed.

"Yo' be needin' us'n, suh?" he said. "Mebbeso weuns stay here fo' whaal?"

The officer laughed, and Marya could feel Chantal quivering behind her. Therese was her younger sister; they had been swept up together for curfew-violation. Distributing leaflets, probably, but they had been clean when the patrol caught them and might have gotten off with a light flogging if Chantal had not attacked the squadleader when he started to rape Therese . . . The nun forced herself between the other woman and the soldiers, pushing her back against the bars, hearing the quick panting breath of adrenaline-overload in her ear and a low guttural sound that was almost a growl. Madness to attack three armed men with hands bound, but a berserker does not count the odds. Even worse madness if by some freak she could hurt one of their captors; that would mean impalement, a slow day's dying standing astride a sharpened stake rammed up the anus. And not just for her; the Draka believed in collective punishment, to give everyone a motive for restraining the wilder spirits. Innocents would die beside her.

The Draka laughed again, reaching out and playfully rapping the Janissary across the knuckles with the electroprod. "Na, no rough work with Security's property," he said. "Besides, I know you lads; once you had your pants down you wouldn't notice even if one of the others pulled the pin on a grenade and shoved it where the sun don't shine. *Then* think of the paperwork I'd have to do."

The dark soldier released the woman and saluted. His officer returned the gesture, then grinned and clapped him on the shoulder. "But no reason you shouldn't hit the Rest Center until we're due; consider yourselves off-duty until . . ." He looked at his watch ". . . 20:00 hours. Report to the depot then. Off you go; I think I can handle the wild French wenches alone."

"Yaz, *suh!*" the serf soldiers chorused. Their clenched right fists snapped smartly to their chests before they wheeled and left.

It had been half a year since Marya last saw the main door of Block D; not since the night of her arrest, when she had been kicked through still bruised and dazed from the standard working-over with rubber hoses that all new inmates received. And she was nearly the oldest inhabitant; the others came and went, swept in off the streets for some offense too petty to merit an immediate bullet, processed through and vanishing to places unknown. A few found the courage to call farewell as they climbed the pierced-steel treads . . . Behind them came Therese's voice, thin and reedy:

"Chantal, don't leave me, come back, *please—*"

Then the welded panels clanged shut, and they were outside. A serf clerk at a desk-kiosk, a saffron-skinned slant-eyed woman in neat coveralls who bowed as she took the papers the Draka handed her.

More corridors, more cells; the electroprod tapped

her on the shoulder, left, right, pointing to crossings. A
harder jab to Chantal's lower back, just over the kidneys. She gasped, stumbled, would have turned her
head to glare if the aching strain of the restraints had
not prevented.

"Walk more humble, wench," the Draka said softly.
"Through there, I think."

A men's section, hairy faces crowding close to the
bars and glittering eyes, silent and intent, others who
looked at her with pity, or away. The nun felt herself
flushing under that hopeless hunger, forced herself not
to shrink back towards the sound of the Draka's
bootheels. Courtyards, and she began to shiver as a
thin drizzle of cold rain fell slick on her skin. Cobblestones, a brief glimpse to a road outside as a convoy of
steam-trucks chuffed in with a new load of detainees,
ragged figures clutching bundles and children as the
guards chivied them into ranks for processing. Overhead, huge and silent, a dirigible was passing, its lights
disappearing northward . . .

Then they were in an office complex. Soft diffused
lighting instead of the harsh naked bulbs, warmth, rain
beating against sound windows of frosted glass. Incredulous, her feet felt carpet beneath, soft and deep; somewhere a teleprinter was chuttering, and the homey
familiarity of the office-sound brought sudden inexplicable tears prickling under her lids. She was conscious of
her nakedness again; not in shame or modesty, but as
vulnerability. Most of those she saw were serfs as well,
but they were neatly clad in pressed overalls and good
shoes, clipboards and files in their hands as they strode
purposefully down the aisles or sat at desks working,
typing, filling the air with a clatter of abacuses and
adding-machines. Their eyes flicked over her and away,
and she could see herself in them: nude and wet and
muddy-footed, rat-tails of wet hair clinging to her shoulders, arms locked behind her. Livestock, beneath contempt to these born-serf bureaucrats, the selected elite

who occupied the management positions just below the Draka aristocracy.

"Hope these'un're house-broken," a voice said, and others chuckled. Her ears burned, and Chantal beside her stiffened and glared. The man behind them evoked more interest: deferential bows, and curiosity. Marya saw a few other Citizens, through the open doors of offices or walking in their bubbles of social space, crowds parting for them; but those men and women were in the olive-green of the Security Directorate, not War Directorate black. The freefolk grew more numerous as they climbed stairs and at the last an elevator to the upper level. There was no bustle here; empty corridor with wide-spaced doors, wood paneling replacing the institutional-bile paint of the lower levels. Names and mysterious number-letter codes on brass plates: "Morrison: infl.77A Relig.delation," "Carruthers: alloc.10F Labor." A larger door still, unmarked, at the end of a hallway.

"Through," the Draka said, tapping them again on the backs of their necks with the 'prod. Hesitantly, Marya stepped closer. The dark oak panel slid aside with a soft *shusssh*, and she stepped through, blinking with astonishment. She had been six months in prison; before that six years in war-crippled cities, on the roads of Europe, in refugee centers and tenements . . . For a moment she lost herslf in wonder.

The room was large, a lounge-office fifteen meters by twenty. Two walls were floor-to-ceiling tinted glass, a view over the tumbled rooftops of Lyon down to the choppy surface of the Rhone, iron-gray under a sky the color of a wet knifeblade. The other walls were murals in the Draka style, hot tawny savannah and herds of zebra beneath a copper sun. A huge desk of some unfamiliar glossy-russet wood occupied one corner, with a sparse scattering of files, intercom, telephone, closed-circuit television monitor. The floor was covered in Isfahan carpets, the furniture soft chairs around a cluster of low brass tables on filigree stands, Arab work.

The remains of a light meal were scattered on one, meats and cheeses, fruit and bread, coffee warming over a spirit-lamp with little pots of sugar and cream.

Marya felt her nostrils flaring and mouth filling. The prison fodder was abundant and adequate; porridge laced with fish and soya meal, hardtack, raw vegetables. Bland, bland; after months of it, years on scrimping wartime rations, the smell of the good food was intolerable. She was used to austerity, would not have chosen a religious vocation if comfort were essential to her, but she could feel her skin drinking in the softness and warmth, eyes flooding with the color and brightness. To feel something besides harsh cloth and stone, to see something that pleased the eye and was not ugly and hurtful . . .

The Draka officer's hand rested on her shoulder, forcing her to her knees beside Chantal. Inwardly, she shook herself as she bowed her head and glanced upward through the lashes; a prisoner could not afford the luxury of distraction. *Focus on the people*, she thought. *Study them. Know those with power*. Knowledge was the only defense of the weak.

There were five others in the room. A man behind the desk; Security uniform, high rank. In his forties but athletic, short, with dark curly hair, blue eyes, tanned pug face and a cigarette in an ivory holder. In the lounger . . . Marya blinked. The woman lolling there was the first Draka she had ever seen not in some type of uniform; she was wearing low tooled boots, loose burgundy trousers, a long blouse-shirt over a stomach that showed the seventh month of pregnancy. Somehow that seemed unnatural, shocking . . . Of course Draka had to be born like other folk, but . . . Tall, hawk-faced, hair a mixture of brown and gold that gave the effect of burnished bronze, one hand holding a cup. A massive thumb-ring, long fingers . . . And beside her a girl of perhaps ten years in a thick silk tunic, playing with a long needle-pointed knife.

The nun frowned, glanced covertly from one face to

another. There were two servants, in dark elegant liveries; one knelt in a corner and played softly on a stringed instrument, the other was a middle-aged black woman standing by the child, probably a nurse. Forget them for a moment; there was something about the Draka . . . All the Citizens she had seen had a certain look, of course: hard sculpted faces, gymnast's physique, the studied grace that came of long training. Even the girl had none of the coltish awkwardness usual on the verge of adolescence; her hands moved the blade with relaxed precision, spinning it up and snapping it closed again around the hilt without looking down. But there was something more . . .

Ah, a family likeness. Pale eyes and long limbs and sharp-featured eagle-nosed high-cheeked faces; the pregnant woman might be the sister of the officer who had fetched Marya from the cell. She licked her lips, waiting.

"Gudrun, yo' said you were old enough to carry a weapon; don't fiddle with it." The woman's voice. Soft, rather husky. The child pouted, flushed and pulled up the hem of her tunic to slide the blade into a sheath on her leg. The blush was very evident under pale freckled skin, copper hair; there were dark circles under her eyes.

The pregnant woman worked her fingers and spoke to the man behind the desk. "An' yes, Strategos Vashon, I've been known to do outlines for mural work; the Klimt workshops have a few in their standard offer book. Not takin' commissions right now, though, what with everythin'." She transfered her attention to the two prisoners.

"So, Andrew, these two are the best yo' could do?"

The voice stirred a memory, elusive; darkness and pain, dust and the hot-metal stink of engines . . . It slipped away as she tried to grasp at it.

The Draka who had brought the women from their cell snapped his fingers for coffee, sinking into one of the chairs with a grateful sigh and hooking the electroprod onto his belt. "More difficult than the manual workers,

sister dear, yo' wanted them spirited and intelligent
. . . troublemakers, in other words. That, these are;
healthy sound stock, as well."

The woman shifted, sighed, rested one hand on her
belly and held out the other.

"The tag," she said, and her brother tossed a strip of
metal; her hand picked it out of the air with a hard fast
slap. "Yasmin." The girl in the corner laid down her
mandolin and rose to take the key. "Take the restraints
off'n them."

Marya kept her head bent as the serf approached,
knelt behind the two inmates. A crisp sound of linen
and silk, a smell of scented soap, a soft hand on her
arm.

"These-heah on way too tight." The girl's voice was
harder to understand than the Draka's had been, the
same soft drawl but a more extreme dialect. "It gowin
hurt." Metal clicked. Thumbs first, then wrists, then
the painful stretch of elbows drawn together behind the
shoulderblades. The fetters had been a burning ache;
agony lanced through muscles and tendons, throbbing
as circulation returned. Then relief through the fading
pain, almost as hard to bear; involuntary tears starred
her lashes, breaking the light into rainbows that flickered like kaleidoscopes as she blinked, as her hands fell
trembling to the rough surface of the carpet. She heard
Chantal's hoarse grunt, and the metal of the restraints
clanking as the serf-girl folded them. When the dark
woman spoke it was in a whisper, barely audible and
spoken downward into the rug so as not to carry.

"Be brave, mah sistahs. Tings bettah soon." Yasmin
rose, laid the restraints on a table with a bow and
returned to her instrument, strumming a faint wander-
ing tune.

Endless moments passed, and Marya became aware
of the Draka speaking among themselves.

". . . nice pair of Danes, but I thought you still had
that Jewish wench, what was her name . . ." the woman
was saying.

"Leja." The officer in black worked his shoulders into the cushions and sipped his coffee. "I do, but I'm out of Helsinki in the field, most of the time. No company while I'm gone, too much work for one when I'm back. Besides, she's pregnant again."

"Why not have her fixed, for God's sake?"

Andrew sighed. "And spoil years of work? She just might not *like* that, you know; even gratitude has its limits. Why do you think I pulled her out of that Treblinka place when we overran it back in . . . yes, '42. *Don't* roll your eyes, I'm *not* going to start another boring war story."

"You don't have to, I remember the pictures you sent. Fuckin' sick picking her out, too, she couldn't have weighed more than thirty kilos." A grimace. "What happened to the rest of them, anyway?"

"Ask our good friend Strategos Vashon here."

The squat secret police officer looked up from his desk and leaned back in the swivel-chair, picking up a ball of hard indiarubber. "Nursed them back to health, every one we could," he said; the ball flexed under the rhythmic squeezing of his hand. "Most enthusiastic collaborators we've got, particularly in Germany."

Alfred nodded. "And Leja was well worth the trouble, to me; six months an' the bounciest wench yo' could want. Saw she had good bones from the start, an' spirit too." He grinned without opening his eyes, as if savoring a memory, a gaunt expression. "Gave her a knife and she went down a row of SS guards we had tied up, slittin' throats. The two I picked up in Copenhagen, Margrethe and Dagmar, they're just nice little bourgeois muffins, pathetically happy to be out of the ruck and terrified of goin' back."

"Why not Finns?"

Andrew snorted. "Almighty Thor, no! When I want to commit suicide, I'll do it decent, with a pistol." He opened his eyes and extended a finger at Chantal. "Those Finns're most-all like Leja, or her; hearts of fire.

Sisu, they call it. Place won't be safe for a decade. You can tell it by the eyes."

He waved his cup toward Chantal. "Speakin' of which, look at that one, sister dear. I didn't save *her* from a gas chamber. Sure yo' want her 'round-about the place?"

The pregnant woman rested her elbows on the arms of the lounger, placed her palms together, tapped fingers, addressed the inmates.

"Look at me, wenches." Gray eyes, impassive. Appraising. "My name is Tanya von Shrakenberg," she said. "Yo' will address me as 'Mistress Tanya'; we pronounce it 'Mistis.' This is my daughter Gudrun; you will call her 'Young Mistis Gudrun.' I have bought you out of Central Detention." A smile. "It may interest you to know that your price was roughly the same as a record player's; the tort-bond I had to put up was considerable larger, because yo' two're classified as potential trouble-makers."

Her head went to one side. " 'This is a bad place . . .' Freya's truth, and you've probably heard rumors 'bout what might happen when you leave; most of them are true . . . breaking rock and shoveling rubble in a chaingang until you died, most likely. Or worse. You've been very lucky indeed; now you're going to be part of the *familia rustica* on the plantation my family is establishing west of here. Household serfs; interpreters, bookkeepers. Possibly in positions of responsibility, eventually. Well fed and clothed, not punished unless you break my rules. Which are simple and plainly stated, by the way." She pointed at Chantal, turned the hand palm-up, crooked a finger. "Come and kneel here by me, Chantal."

The Frenchwoman shuffled forward on hands and knees, wise enough in the Domination's etiquette not to rise without permission. Tanya cupped a hand beneath her chin, forcing the head up. "I've read your dossier, wench. You were picked up for curfew-breaking by an Order Police *lochos;* yo' then tried to brain the monitor with a piece of pavin'-stone. Why?" A tighter squeeze. "The truth, Chantal, not what you think I want to hear."

"He—" A pause. "He tried to rape my sister, she's a child, she's only fourteen, *Mistis!*" The last word was a hiss.

Tanya used her grip on the other's chin to wag her head back and forth. "With the result that you were both raped, repeatedly, then beaten bloody and ended up here, rather than in the factory compound where your family was sent." Another pause. "Have you enjoyed it here? Has your sister? From the report, she's simple-minded now: 'post-traumatic shock syndrome.' How do you think she's goin' to do without you to look after her, here in Central Detention?"

Marya could see the hands clenched by Chantal's sides, quivering. The Draka's voice continued: "Have you *learned* anything from this, Chantal? Besides the fact that the Draka are not humanitarians, that is.

"Hearken to the voice of experience, wench. Where are we?"

"In—in prison, Mistress."

"Beyond that."

"France, Mistress."

The hand shook her head again. "Wrong. We are in the Province of Burgundia, under the Domination; *I* am at home, *you* are an immigrant, ignorant of the laws and customs of the land." A smile. "And a serf, who is new to being a serf. *I* am a serf-owner, born of seven generations of serf-owners; consider who will have the advantage of knowing all the tricks, here.

"Now, here's what I'll do. I will buy your sister Therese, as well as you. She will have a room, light work; nobody will hurt her, and I'll even tell the overseers that she's hands-off." Chantal jerked and made a muffled sound. "Or, if you wish, I will have you sent back to her cell and pick someone else. Your choice. Shall I send you back, or not? *Now,* wench."

A whisper. "No, Mistress."

"Louder. I can't hear you."

"No, Mistress, please."

Tanya chuckled and leaned closer. "Now, that's what you should have learned from the incident that brought you here: the difference between courage and recklessness. Not at all the same thing. Tell me, Chantal, do you know what *in loco parentis* means? Yes? Good; you will be *in loco parentis* for your sister. Only, for you a special rule will be made; when the parent sins, the *child* is punished. Understand?"

She removed the restraining hand, but Chantal did not move.

"Yes, Mistress," she said, in a quiet, conversational tone.

"Oh, ho, what a look," Tanya said, keeping her eyes locked with Chantal's. "Andrew was right; a heart of fire, this one. Maybe we'll continue this conversation at greater length, someday." She brought up finger and thumb and flicked the other's nose. "Back."

Marya let her breath out in a long shudder, only then conscious of holding it, averting her eyes as the other woman crawled back and sank on her heels by the nun's side, panting as if from a sprint. The sight was disquieting; the nun felt a flush of shame rising from breasts to cheeks and bent her head, letting the pale curtain of her hair hide her face and silently cursing the milk-pale skin her Slavic ancestors had left her. The war, the Soviet and Nazi occupations, the long flight westward before the Draka had been chaos, random death, hunger, sickness, running through the cold wet squalor of the refugee centers. Soldiers and police, prison and camps she understood; even the Draka occupation had been merely a harsher version.

This was not a matter of armies and bureaucracies, however brutal; it was a ritual of submission rawly personal, as much a matter of calm everyday routine to her new owners as eating a meal. *Oh, I understand the psychology of it*, she thought; hers had been a teaching Order, and a progressive one. It was still something out of the ancient world, come to impossible life around her.

Tanya turned to her daughter, stroking her hair. "You've been patient, darlin'; now tell me, what do *yo'* think of these two."

"Well . . ." the child frowned and wrinkled her nose. ". . . They seem sort of, well, uppish. Sort of . . . um, shouldn't you punish them, mother?"

Tanya laughed, and tousled the girl's hair. "Gudrun, sweetlin', school can teach any number of useful things. But handlin' serfs is like . . ." She pursed her lips and tapped one thumb on her chin. "Like dancing; has to be passed on, one practitioner to the next. There's never a set answer, not on an individual scale. What did the Romans call their slaves?"

Gudrun's frown relaxed; that was much easier. "*Instrumentum vocale*, mother. The tool that speaks."

"A wise people. But always remember, the tool that speaks is also the tool that thinks, and believes. Watch." She turned her attention back to the two kneeling figures. Fascinated, Marya observed the change sweep over her face; less a matter of expression than of some indefinable shadow behind the eyes, warmth vanishing until frosted silver looked out at her human chattel.

"You, yo' were a nun, eh?"

"Yes, I am, Mistress."

"Were. Now, if'n I told you to sweep the floor, would you do it?"

"Yes, Mistress."

"If I gave you Gudrun's knife an' told you to cut Chantal's throat, would you?" There was a silent pause. "The truth, wench: don't try lyin' to me."

Marya moistened her lips. "No, Mistress."

"Ah." The Draka smiled. "And if I told you to jump out the window?"

"No, Mistis." At the Draka's arched brows: "Suicide is a mortal sin."

The Draka woman laughed softly. "And if I told you that if you didn't, I'd kill Chantal here?"

Marya opened her mouth, hesitated, shook her head. "More difficult, eh?" Tanya chuckled and nodded to her daughter. "Remember this; there is always some order that won't be obeyed. Either don't give it, or be prepared to kill. Human bein's are like horses, born wild but with a capacity fo' domestication. These are old fo' breakin', so it'll be difficult." She turned to the serf-girl with the mandolin.

"Yasmin," she continued, writing and tearing a leaf from a pocket-notebook. "Here. There's a Stevenson & deVerre office on the ground level. Take them down and see to them, there's a good wench. Light cuffs, clothin', tell them the basics. We'll come down when yo're finished."

Yasmin covered her instrument in a velvet case and pattered over to them, signalling them to rise. Tanya levered herself to her feet and approached also, stopping them for a moment with a lifted finger, paused.

"You two are mine now," she continued; neither of the women lifted their eyes from the carpet. "All your choices are gone, except one. Obedience, life. Disobedience, death. That one we can never take from you." Another pause. "But yo've already made it, no?" She shrugged. "I am your fate, then. Yo've decided to spend life under the Yoke; so remember, there's no point kickin' and buckin'. Be good serfs, an' my family will be good masters. Resist, and yo' suffer."

CHAPTER TWO

. . . to defeat an enemy, we must understand him. National myths—and their modern equivalent, propaganda —are perhaps inevitable, certainly useful, but they must not be allowed to blind us to objective reality. Take, for example, the belief, common even among some historians, that the Loyalist refugees who settled the then Crown Colony of Drakia in the 1780's had a secret master plan of world conquest already set out, and that a hidden cabal of Draka aristocrats has been implementing it ever since. Nonsense: a transference to the past of present patterns, as ridiculous as a historical novel showing an 18th-century Englishwoman deliberately seeking a suntan. What is the reality? As usual, a process of cultural evolution that combined blind chance with conscious decisions—many of those falling victim to the Law of Unintended Consequences.

The leaders of the proto-Draka were migrants from the slave societies of the Caribbean and the American South; but their subjects were not the uprooted, demoralized fragments delivered by the slavers of the Middle Passage. Little is known of the pre-conquest cultures of Africa—the Draka shattered them too thoroughly—but the evidence suggests strong, militarily formidable peoples. Breaking them, and keeping them broken, produced an overwhelmingly warlike culture with a built-in

*bias towards expansion; the ideologues and philoso-
phers, Carlyle, Gobineau, Nietzsche, Naldorssen, merely
produced an ideology for a society eager to cast off the
increasingly alien ethos of liberal rationalism. The Draka
aristocracy needed a world-view and belief system which
would make them comfortable with what they were,
and ordinary social evolution produced it. Such developments cannot be forced; they must spring organically
from the human environment. The failed attempt in the
1890's to revive Nordic paganism is an example, producing nothing but a new type of Draka profanity. But
the belief system that did arise among the lords of the
Domination then took on a life of its own, becoming
cause as well as effect . . .*

    *The Mind of the Draka: a Military-Cultural Analysis
    Monograph delivered by Commodore Aguilar Ernaldo,
      U.S. Naval War College, Manila.
   11th Alliance Strategic Studies Conference
     Subic Bay, 1972*

DRAKA FORCES BASE NORDKAPPEN
JUNE 12, 1947
0200 HOURS

It was very quiet in the screen room of the electrodetection center, quiet, and dark. There was the underlying whir of the fans, click and hum of relays, a low
murmur now and then from one of the operators or
floor-officers. Most of the stations in the long bunker
were switched off and under dust-covers, and the projac
map on the north wall was dimmed. The air smelled of
tobacco and green concrete and stale coffee and heating-
duct, a tired night-watch odor. The controllers bent
over the faint green glow of their screens, faces corpse-
sallow in the cathode-tube light, insectile beneath head-
sets and eye-filters, motionless except for minute
adjustments to the instruments; they were in Citizen

Force undress uniform, black trousers and boots and dove-gray short-sleeved shirts.

Operator-first Dickson Milhouse leaned back and stretched, sighed and waved his cup in the air to attract the attention of the serf with the refreshment cart; the pedestal chair creaked as he yawned. Nightwatch sent you to sleep with sheer boredom, and when you came right down to it there was nothing very complicated about holding down a screen. Work for the Auxiliaries, really, except that it still had the cachet of high technology and novelty and so was reserved for Citizen personnel.

He rubbed his eyes. Nordkappen Base outside was just as boring. Morale Section tried hard, films and sports and amateur theatricals, and there was always the bordello, but there was just nothing to *do* here at the northern tip of what had once been Norway; they all had assault-rifles clipped to the top rails of the workstations, but that was merely War Zone regulations. There was still guerrilla activity in much of the territory overrun during the Eurasian War, Europe, Russia, eastern China, but here there was no native population at all, since the Lapps were run out. No game animals to speak of, not by African standards; the long summer days were a novelty that soon wore off, and as for winter . . . he shuddered. The winters here were nothing someone born under the peaks of Mt. Kenia could have believed.

Oh, well, you can always sit on a rock and watch the construction work, he thought sourly. This was an important base, watching the shortest great-circle route connecting western Eurasia and North America, and tensions were already high between the Domination and the Yankee-run Alliance for Democracy. Dirigibles over the Pole, submarines under the ice—round the clock work here, everything from barracks and messhalls to industrial-size fuel cells and electrodetector towers; many of the installations were burn-before-reading secret.

His eyes fell back on the glowing green surface. He blinked, glanced away and back.

Equipment malfunction? No, too definite. Suddenly he was no longer tired, nor bored at all. His finger flicked a relay, and the amber light clicked on above his workstation.

"Let me see it." The floor-officer leaned over him, her fingers tapping the key-pad beside the screen. "Bring it up, two." A pause. "And again, two." Her thumb punched down on the red button. An alarm klaxon began to wail.

"Definitely a bogey," the floor-officer said.

Merarch Labushange grunted in reply, hitching at the uniform trousers that were all he had had time to don; sweat glistened in the tangled hair of his chest, amid several purple bite-marks. He was a short man for a Draka, ugly-handsome in the Mediterranean style, black curly hair, blue jowls, body the shape of a brick and thick arms and legs knotted with muscle.

"Estimate height and speed," he grunted, rubbing at red-rimmed eyes. The operator hid a smile behind a cough as he worked the calculator; the commander's new German wench was supposed to be costing him sleep . . . The results clicking up drove camp gossip from his mind.

"Estimate . . . estimate Mach 2.2 at 36,000 meters, Merarch."

There was a rustle from the other stations, a turning cut short by the floor-officer's glare. Silence, until the operator began another check of the console.

"Forget it," the Merarch said. "It's genuine."

"But sir, *Mach 2?*" the operator said, a cold feeling seeping up from his gut. The Domination had flown its first supersonic jet only a few months ago, and this was nearly half again as fast.

"The Fritz got manned rocket-planes to well over Mach 1, just before the end," the commander said absently, lost in thought. Of course, those had been one-off experiments, air-launched from bombers and not capable of more than a few minutes of powered flight, but . . . "The Yankees must have been workin' hard, produced a surprise. Afterwards they can claim it was a glitch in our equipment, or little green men from Mars." He grinned like a shark. "Trouble is, *we* have some surprises too, an' they can scarcely object to our usin' 'em, on somethin' that don't officially exist."

He glanced around the dim-lit room, and his smile widened. "Of course, it could be headed this way with an atomic . . ." He strode briskly to the commander's dais, sank into the chair and keyed the communicator.

"Alert, codes Timbuktoo, Asmara, Zebra. Get me—"

Echoing, thundering, the darkness of the B-30's cargo pod shook around Captain Fred Kustaa, toning through muscle and bone with subsonic disharmonies. He was strapped almost flat in the crash-couch, imprisoned in the pressure-suit and helmet, packed about with gel-filled bags to absorb the bruising punishment of the experimental craft's passage through the upper atmosphere. Outside the titanium-alloy skin would be glowing, the edges of the huge square ramjet intakes turning cherry-red as air compressed toward the density of steel.

It was the helpless feeling that was hardest to take, he decided, not the physical danger. He had been a combat soldier in the Pacific before he transferred to the OSS in '44, and God knew liaison work with the Draka in Europe in the last year of the War had been no picnic, but this . . .

Experimental, he thought. *Everything's too fucking experimental for my taste. Donovan should have tried the submarines first.* Hell, Murmansk wasn't more than a few weeks on foot through the forest to Finland, although it would be a bit difficult to carry the contents of the cargo pod on his back.

The aircraft lurched and banked, and his stomach surged again; he concentrated on dragging in another breath through the rubber-tasting facemask. Vomiting inside it would be highly unpleasant and possibly fatal. *About as maneuverable as a locomotive*, had been the test-pilot's words; too little was known about airflow at these speeds. Kustaa did not understand the B-30—he would not have been risked over enemy territory if he did—but even just looking at it from the outside was enough to know it was leading-edge work. It didn't even *look* like an airplane, it looked like a flattened dart pasted on top of two rectangular boxes . . .

"*Merde.*" The pilot's voice, Emile Chretien; Kustaa recognized the thick Quebec-French accent. He spoke a little of the *patois* himself, there were plenty of *habitants* scattered among the Finnish-Americans of his home in the Upper Peninsula. "Electrodetection, high-powered scanners."

Kustaa winced. Well, that had been one reason for this mission, to find out for sure just how good the Domination's new Northern Lights Chain was. The dark pressed against his eyes, and he used it to paint maps; their course from the Greenland base, over the Arctic toward darkened Europe. His imagination refused to stop, and he saw more; saw the alert going out below, to bases in Sweden and Norway, alarm-klaxons ringing out over concrete and barracks, flight-suited pilots scrambling to their stations. The blue flare of jets lighting the predawn as the stubby delta shapes of the Draka *Shark*-class fighters rolled onto the launch paths . . .

The B-30 was supposed to be immune to interception; the Domination had the physical plant of the German ramjet research projects, but the U.S. had managed to smuggle out most of the actual scientists and the crucial liquid-hydrogen results. The aircraft lurched again, shook as if the wings were going to peel away at the roots, stooped. One of the Pacific Aircraft researchers had said something about eventually flying right into outer space if they could lick the problem of combustion in a supersonic airstream; damned long-hairs had no sense of need-to-know, shouldn't have been talking like that in a canteen.

"*Tabernac'!* Another ray . . . guidance beam, something's coming up after us!"

Of course, he reminded himself, the U.S. hadn't gotten *all* the German scientists; some had stayed, captives or those who had taken the Domination's offer of Citizen status for themselves and their immediate families. And the Draka army's Technical Section had good ideas too, sometimes; it was propaganda that they stole all their inventions.

"Positive detection . . . *fille d'un putain*, three of them; not manned, not at those speeds. They're closing on us, they must be riding the beam. Hold on, Captain, I'm dropping chaff and taking evasive action."

You mean this battering about wasn't evasive action? Kustaa thought plaintively.

This was as bad as going down the tunnels after the Nips, back on Sumatra in '43, pushing the flamethrower ahead into the cramped mud-smelling blackness. *Japanese, Captain, Japanese,* he reminded himself. Part of the Alliance for Democracy now, they'd be associate signatories to the Rio Pact as soon as Halleck and the Army of Occupation got through restructuring . . . Couldn't call the little yellow bastards monkey-men anymore. His mind skipped, nerves jumping in obedience to a fight-flight reflex that was pumping him full of adrenaline. *And all I can do is sweat,* he thought wryly. He could feel it trickling down his flanks, smell the rankness and taste salt on his upper lip. *Think,* he commanded himself. *You're not an animal driven by instinct, think.*

Unmanned antiaircraft missiles, a typical Draka brute-force solution. Crude engines would be enough, if they were intended to burn out after a single use. The U.S.—he corrected himself mentally, the *Alliance* —didn't have guidance systems small and rugged enough for a missile like that, although they would soon—so the Domination wouldn't either; they were years behind in electronics. But they could put the tracking and electrodetection on the ground, just a passive receptor-steering system on the missile itself, that and a big simple two-stage drive and a warhead.

Christ have mercy, I hope it isn't an atomic, he thought. Probably not—they were still rare and mostly reserved for strategic use—but the Draka would be willing to explode one over a populated area. Populated by serfs, that is.

Jets and atomic bombs built by slaves, he thought. *Insane.* The Domination was madness come to earth; he shivered, remembering his liaison-work with the Draka army, during the misbegotten period of joint action against Hitler. *Gray faces of the Belgian farmers as they prepared to drive their tractors out over the minefields* . . . and the sick wet noises of the one who had refused, seated on an impaling-stake cut out of the little forest; his feet had scuffed around and around as he tried to rise off the rough wood sunk a foot deep into his gut, and blood and shit dribbled down the bark. Some of the Draka dug in at the treeline had laughed, at him or at the explosions and screams in the plowed field ahead.

The B-30 went *thump*, absurdly like an autosteamer going over a bump at speed, and the sensation was repeated. That would be the strips of foil being ejected, hopefully to baffle the Draka electrodetectors. Acceleration slammed him down and to the side; they were climbing and banking, and metal groaned around him as the big aircraft was stressed to ten-tenths of its capacity.

"Still locked on. *Merde.* Coming up on target. Prepare for ejection, Captain." The pilot's voice was full of a tense calm; Air Force tradition, can-do, wild blue yonder . . .

His heart lurched, and his mind refused to believe the time had gone so fast, so fast; it was like the wait between boarding the landing-craft and the moment the ramp went down on the beach. Kustaa wished he could spit out the gummy saliva filling his mouth, as he had running waist-deep through the surf in a landing-zone. Some men did that, some were silent and some shrieked wordlessly, a few shouted the traditional *gung-ho* and a surprising number pissed their pants or shat themselves; you never saw *that* in the papers, but only a recruit was surprised at it.

Damn, start out a Gyrene and end up a paratrooper, he thought. "Acknowledged." His circuit was locked open, had to be with his hands strapped down, but there was no point in distracting Emile.

"Ten seconds from . . . *mark*." There was no point in bracing himself, the harness was as like a womb as the technicians could make it.

Nine, he counted to himself. He had married in '41, right after the Nips had attacked Hawaii; they had planned to wait until he finished the engineering course, but being a Marine private was a high-risk occupation. Aino had spent the war years in San Diego working in a shipyard. They had bought one of the new suburban ranch-style bungalows that started springing up around L.A. right after the Armistice . . .

Eight. The sweating dreams had been bad, waking screaming as the bunker door opened and the calcinated body of the Japanese soldier dropped out onto him, knocking him down in an obscene embrace with their faces an inch apart; Aino had held him and asked no questions, even when it woke little Maila . . .

Seven. She hadn't wanted him to continue with the OSS, especially not when it meant moving back East to New York; the capital was no place to raise a family. She had seen to the sale of the home where she had expected to live the rest of her life, doggedly settled into the Long Island brownstone, entertained his co-workers on awkward evenings when nobody could talk shop and long silences fell . . .

Six. They had been out to a movie, a Civil-War epic called *President Douglas;* the newsreel had been a political piece, film of a serf-auction in Archona. The usual sensational stuff lifted from the Domination's news services, no routine shots of black factory-hands here, ABS-Pathway knew their audience found injustice more titillating spiced with sex and inflicted on white people. A showing of high-cost European concubines in heels and jewelry and nothing else, parading down an elevated walkway; the American film-editors had inserted black rectangles to keep the Catholic Decency League happy. The shabby refugee beside her had stood and begun screaming, pointing at the screen. "*Mein Gott, Christina, Christina!*" Still screaming, climbing over the seats with clawed hands outstretched towards the smiling blond image standing hand-on-hip. He was screaming as the attendants carried him away.

Five. Kustaa's wife had not objected to his volunteering for secret duty after that. He dreamed of the bunker less, now; but sometimes it was the refugee who stumbled through the steel-plate door in the nightmare, and the face was his own.

Four. It was not getting agents into Europe that was the trouble, it was moving them around, harder each month as more and more of the population vanished into pens and compounds. The Domination had leaned on its "allies" to reveal their Resistance contacts during the War, and had been politely refused. Some of the networks still survived, incredibly, but they were useful mostly for small stuff, escape-conduits and microfilm. Virtually impossible to move in equipment, except a few microscopic loads by submarine on wilderness coasts.

Three. His tongue touched the false tooth at the back of his mouth; melodrama, bad Hollywood, but he knew too much. It was lousy tradecraft, sending him in multiply tasked. There were too many contact-names and dates and codes in his head, but what was the alternative? Besides, they needed a survey, an overview of what was going on. If only they could get deep-cover agents into the Security Directorate! It was easy enough to slip in agents posing as Europeans or Chinese, it would be years before a billion individuals could be necked and registered, but every Citizen's identity was established from birth and there were only forty million of them.

Two. Of course, the Draka had probably slipped hundreds through with the vast flood of refugees that had poured across the English channel in the last days of the War, when the Domination's armies were driving for the Atlantic. More would come through with every boatload of escapees, probably many sleepers under deep cover, it was long-term planning and the Draka thought that way, but what could you do?

One. He had seen his daughter take her first steps on his last leave; Aino had looked up, and as their eyes met—

Impact. Blackness.

A yell of satisfaction filled the electrodetection center of Nordkappen Base. The third missile's trajectory intersected the American aircraft's flight-path, and the sound rose to a howl; fell away to a disgusted mutter as it winked out and the blip of the intruder re-emerged. Merarch Labushange ground out another half-smoked cigarette; an attendant had brought his shirt and tunic, but the rims of his eyes were still a bloodshot red.

He rose in disgust, then checked.

"Wait a minute," he muttered. Then: "Cross-patch on that; increase resolution." He leaned forward to watch one screen, then another; swiveled to view a third that received its input from an automatic station in the mountains to the south.

"She's shedding something," he said quietly. "Increase resolution again, maximum. Look!" His finger stabbed out. Half a dozen traces were spreading out from the veering curve of the American aircraft. Smaller, much smaller, curving and falling.

"Is she breaking up?" the floor officer said hopefully, cradling her coffee-cup.

Labushange shook his head. "At that speed? It'd be

over by now. Lose aerodynamic stability at Mach 2 and you'd be metallic confetti; she's maintaining velocity. Increasin', if anything; and turning north."

His head turned to the nearest operator with a gun-turret precision. "Give me a ballistic trajectory on that debris, unguided."

The operator frowned, adjusting and calculating; his fingers danced over the controls while his eyes stayed fixed on the hooded green glow of the screen. "Faint, almost as if they were non-metallic . . . hmmm, if'n they don't change direction after they drop below our detection horizon, central Finland, sir."

"So, so, oh, *clever* little Yankees; force us to show our best defenses, get back with the data, 'n drop good things to the worst troublespot in Europe." Labushange closed his eyes and rose on the balls of his feet, biting his lower lip in thought. Then the orders came, spoken with a triphammer beat.

"Get me a teleprinter patch; East Baltic H.Q., Riga. Route it though to Europe Command in Marseille, and to Castle Tarleton. Copies to Security liaison, all along. Then—"

Kustaa was unconscious as the pod fell, the flexing snap of deceleration striking like a horse's hoof. It needed no guidance, a ton-weight egg of soft curves and dull, nonreflective coating that would make any but the most sophisticated electrodetector underestimate its size. Plummeting, tumbling, then turning to present its broadest end to the earth as weight and drag stabilized it. The shards of the cover that had held it to the B-30's belly tumbled away; *their* inside surfaces were shiny, polished reflectors to draw the invisible microwave eyes that probed through the low clouds. Unpowered, the pod was arching to earth as might a rock dropped by a bird. The bird had been high and fast, and the curve would be a long one.

If there had been a conscious observer aboard, and a port to see, the sky would have darkened as the sun dropped below the horizon and the pod fell from the fringes of space. Below, the gray waters of the Gulf of Finland were hidden by a white frothed-cream curtain of cloud; there were gaps to the east, swelling views of forest and lakes and overgrown fields, a land of dark trees and water reflecting back the moon like a thousand thousand eyes. Lights moved slowly across the land, Draka dirigibles with massive electrodetectors whirling soundlessly inside their gasbags. Then a humming whine, and lean shapes lifted through the clouds, twin-engine Sharks with the moonlight bright on the polished metal of their stub wings; bubble canopies and painted teeth and cannon ports.

Helmeted heads moved in the fighter-cockpits, visual scan added to the short-range detectors in the interceptors' noses, hungry eyes linked to thumbs ready on the firing buttons. But the Alliance designers had done their work well, the vision of humans and machines slipping from the dark skin and smooth curves of the capsule. Kustaa hung in his cocoon of straps and padding, while pressure-sensors clicked softly under the whistle of parted air. The pod dropped through cloud with a long thrumming shudder, and unliving relays determined a preset altitude; for a moment a tiny proximity detector adapted from a shell-fuse pulsed at the ground and calculated distances.

The pod split at its upper point, jerking as the drogue chute deployed; it was barely a thousand feet from the ground, and still traveling fast. The larger canopy followed with a thunder *crack* that echoed over the dark silence of the forest below; the rending crackle of branches bending and breaking followed almost at once. Lines and shrouds and camouflage-patterned cloth caught and tangled, snapping and yielding, but each absorbed a little more of the pod's momentum, until it halted and spun and beat a slow diminishing tattoo against the strong old trunk of a hundred-foot pine, and was still. Night returned, with its small sounds of animal and bird, liquid ripple from a stream falling over a sill of granite below, wind through branches and wind through synthsilk cords and a gentle snap and flutter of cloth.

Kustaa slept.

"He's concussed. Not too badly." A thumb was peeling back his eyelids, and a flashlight shone painfully in the darkness. Kustaa tensed, then relaxed; Finnish, his parents' first language. The guerrillas had found him.

Another voice, deeper. *"Get him down, and those crates."*

Hands unstrapped him and lifted, passing him downward to damp mud-smelling earth. The world heaved and turned; he twisted his head to one side and emptied the contents of his stomach in an acid-tasting rush. A canteen came to his lips, and the American rinsed and spat. There was a clatter from above, as the cargo pod emptied.

"Careful . . . with those fuses . . . delicate," he mumbled. Pain swelled behind his eyes, a hot tightness that threatened to open the bones of his skull. Nausea twisted his stomach again, and he *hurt*, right down to his bones. It was a familiar sensation; this was not the first time he had been knocked out. After the *Robert Adams* was hit by the kamikaze off Surabaya, he had woken up in sickbay, puking and with a head just like this. Absurdly among the shrilling along his nerves he remembered a movie . . . a Western, *Steamcoach*, where the hero took a chair-leg across the side of the head and woke up in a few hours fit enough to outdraw the villain.

So Jason Waggen is a better man than me, ran through him as the Finns lifted him onto a stretcher. *Of course, he had the scriptwriter on his side*. The guerrillas were dark shapes against darker trees, only the occasional low glow of a hooded light showing as they quickly stripped the ton-weight of crates from the pod. Someone put a pill between his lips, offered the canteen, and he swallowed. The pain faded, and the nighted forest turned warm and comfortable. Before the dark closed around

him he heard a rising scream of turbines, howling across
the sky from south to north, horizon to horizon. A
blue-red flare of tailpipes streaked by above, close enough
that the treetops bowed in the hot wind.

"No'much longer," he mumbled.

Waking was slow. He lay for minutes beyond counting with his eyes closed, watching the dull glow that
shone pink through the skin. Soup was cooking somewhere near, and there was a background of voices,
movement, tapping of tools; the air was close and smoky,
with a feeling of being indoors or underground and an
odor of raw cedarwood. He was naked, in a hard bed
laid with coarse woolen blankets. There was a foul taste
in his mouth, his teeth felt furred, and legs and arms
were heavy as lead . . . but the pain behind his eyes
was mostly gone, and the smell of cooking food made
his mouth water instead of turning his stomach.

I'm recovering, he thought, as he blinked crusted
eyelids open. Not as well or as quickly as the time
when his troopship had been hit, but then he wasn't a
new-minted lieutenant fresh from his first battle and
field-promotion any more. *Thirty is too old for this shit,*
he mused. *Sergeant McAllistair was right: in this business it's easy enough to end up with your ass in a crack
without volunteering for it.*

The room was windowless, log-walled, a twenty-by-
ten rectangle with a curtained doorway at one end.
Both walls were lined with bunks made from rough
spruce poles and pallets; there was a small stove made
from a welded oildrum in a corner, and a long trestle-
table down the center. Light came from a single dim
lantern overhead, showing the blanketed mounds of
sleepers in the other beds. Rifles, machine-pistols, what
looked like a breakdown rocket launcher were clipped
to frames beside the bunks; a dozen or so guerrillas sat
at the table, spooning broth from bowls, chewing on
crusts of hard black bread, working on their weapons or
simply sitting and staring before them. One man looked

up from his task and caught Kustaa's eye, then returned to his methodical oiling of his rifle's bolt-carrier; the other parts lay spread before him on a cloth.

Kustaa frowned; he had spent a good part of the last decade in barracks of one sort or another, and this one disturbed him. For one thing, nobody was *talking*. Granted these were Finns, and the average man of that breed made the most taciturn north-country Swede look like a chatterbox, but even so . . .

The American sat up cautiously, ducking his head to avoid the edge of the bunk above him. The blanket slipped down from his shoulders, but he ignored the damp chill, cleared his throat.

"I'm awake," he said.

The man who had glanced at him earlier looked up, nodded, went back to his work on the weapon. It slid together with a series of oiled metallic clicks and racheting sounds; a Jyvaskyia semiautomatic, the soldier's corner of his mind noticed. The Finn thumbed ten rounds into a magazine, snicked it home in the rifle, and rose to lay it on the pegs above an empty bunk.

"We have to talk," Kustaa continued. The other man nodded again, coming to sit on a corner of bench nearer the American.

"Talvio," he said to one of the fighters sitting on a bench, a woman. She rose, filled a bowl of soup and a mug of what smelled like herb tea, set them down on the bed beside Kustaa, and returned to sorting through a pile of blasting detonators.

"Arvid Kyosti," the Finn continued. "Regional commander," and held out his hand. It had a workingman's calluses; the form behind it was blocky beneath the shapeless field-jacket and woolen pants, the face broad and snub-nosed, high-cheeked, with slanted blue eyes and shaggy black hair.

Not more than my age, but he looks older, the American thought. *I'm not surprised.*

"Fred Kustaa," he replied aloud, conscious of the other's slow, considering stare. *At least I've kept in shape*. Kustaa was a big man, two inches over six feet, broad-shouldered and long in the limbs. A farm-boy originally, and a light-heavyweight of some promise at St. Paul Institute, before the war; the slight kink of a broken nose still showed it. The Marines worked a man hard, too, and after the War he had spent some time on Okinawa and joined a *dojo*; the OSS had encouraged him to keep it up . . . A ragged pattern of old white scars showed along one flank and up under the thatch of yellow hair on his chest, legacy of a Japanese grenade.

"The equipment came through all right?" he said, to break the silence.

"As far as we can tell," Arvid replied. "My people are studying the manuals. And there's that." He nodded toward a sealed packet.

The hint of a smile. "Fortunate you survived to explain them. Hard landing. Too close to the firebase. The snakes would have had you, in another couple of hours."

"There's a Draka base near here?" he said, with an inward wince at the thought of being taken prisoner.

A nod. "Regiment of Janissaries, two batteries and an airstrip. Use it as a patrol base, so the complement fluctuates."

Kustaa took up the bowl of soup and sipped. It was thin and watery, a few bits of potato and rubbery fish, but it was hot and filled the hollowness behind his stomach. The Finns looked hungry, too; not starved, but without the thin padding of fat beneath the skin that a really healthy body shows.

"Good intelligence," he said.

Arvid shrugged. "They built it over a year ago," he said. "Used local forced labor; they've learned better since, but we got the layout. Keep it under observation, as much as we can. Managed to make them think we're farther away, so far."

"Well, that's one reason they sent me. We need to know the general situation, and how the Alliance can best help you."

A few of the others looked up; their eyes were as coldly flat as Arvid's. "General situation is that we're being slowly wiped out. Help? Declare war on the snakes and invade," he said coldly.

Kustaa forced a smile. "Personally, I'm inclined to agree we should," he said. "But they've got atomics as well, now." True enough . . . he forced down memory of what Osaka had looked like, when the Air Force teams went in to study the consequences of a nuclear strike on a populated area. The photographs had been classified, to prevent general panic, and New York was *the* target. His mind showed him Aino's skin peeling away with radiation sickness, gums bleeding, blind and rotting alive; little Maila sitting in a burning house screaming for her mother with melted eyes running down a charred face.

"An amphibious task force is a big target, and their submarines are good enough to take out some of the coastal cities, at least. The plan is to deter them, and make them choke on what they've taken. You've been bleeding them here; if we can help you, and help others match your performance, who knows?"

Arvid's face went white around the mouth; with rage, Kustaa realized with a start. Behind him, one of the guerrillas half-raised her weapon, before two others seized her; she hung between their hands, her face working, before regaining enough control to tear herself free and stumble through the cloth door-cover. The guerrilla commander mastered himself and spoke again.

"That was a stupid thing to say, American." He looked down at his hands. "You know how many troops the snakes have in Finland?" Kustaa shook his head silently. "Sixty thousand: three legions of Janissaries, a brigade of their Citizen troops. Lots, no? Want to know why so many?"

Arvid rummaged under the table, brought out Kustaa's kit and tossed him his pipe and matches. While the American's hands made the comforting ritual of filling, tamping and lighting he continued, in an emotionless monotone.

"Snakes made a mistake with us. By-passed us in '43, to deal with the Germans. We had two years, to watch what Draka conquest meant, and to prepare. No point trying to hold the cities or borders. We'd been mobilized since the Winter War with the Russians, in '40 . . . put everyone to work. Making weapons, explosives, supplies. Digging bunkers and tunnel-complexes like this, stockpiling, training everyone who could fight. Then they demanded we surrender."

"And you didn't," Kustaa said softly.

"The cities did . . . so the snakes thought. All the ones who could were out in the forests. We destroyed our machinery, fuel, everything useful; burnt the crops, and all the livestock was already salted down. Some stayed behind in the towns for sabotage; many of the ones who couldn't fight took poison." He paused. "My wife, and our children." Another pause. "After a while, the snakes got sick of time-bombs and ambushes in the cities, so they deported everyone they could catch. The younger children to training creches, the rest to destructive-labor camps. We've heard . . . we've heard they sterilize the camp inmates, and lobotomize the troublemakers." Arvid grinned like a death's-head. "And we Finns are all born troublemakers, no?"

There was a silence that echoed. "I doubt there are half a million people left in the whole of Finland," the guerrilla finished softly. "Most of those Swedes and Danes and Germans the snakes brought in for labor. The documents we've captured say they aren't going to ever try and settle more than a few hundred plantations on the south coast. The rest of the country will be a nature-preserve and timber farm. Right now it's a hunting preserve, and we're the game."

Kustaa looked around the long room, at the men and women sitting at the table, at others lying wakeful on their bunks, at the eyes empty alike of hope and fear.

"Damned dangerous game," he said. "Damned dangerous. More so now that I've brought the new radio, and our little surprises for their Air Force." He nodded to the seal package. "The codes, and directions on how to fit the deciphering wheel."

Some of the cold hostility faded from the faces turned to him. "What if they'd captured you?" Arvid said.

"There's a sequence of four randomly selected sentences you have to use on the first four contacts. One word wrong, and they cut off contact permanently, and then the codes are useless." He shrugged. "Don . . . Donovon . . . the OSS trusted me enough to hold out convincingly long, then give them the wrong word-group. Not necessary, as it turned out; and with luck, we can set up a permanent supply route."

Arvid nodded. "This is bad country for armor, and they don't have enough infantry to spare to really comb us out. We've got plenty of weapons and ammunition, enough food. Their aircraft, though, and the damned helicopters—with an answer to *that* we can cause them even more grief, before we die." Thoughtfully: "There are outposts east of here, in Karelia and Ingria, almost as far as the White Sea; if we could set up a supply line through submarines, then . . .

"The doctor says you'll be ready for action in a day or two. Come along and see your toys in action."

"I'm supposed to make Helsinki as soon as possible," Kustaa said carefully. Then a broad grin split the weathered tan of his face. "Obviously, it'll be impossible to leave before we stomp a few snakes, hey?"

CHAPTER THREE

... no soldier who has bent to scratch and felt the bullet go crack through the space above him can doubt the role of chance in war. The same applies to larger issues; how would the Domination have fared if we had not pressed ahead with the nuclear-weapons research? It was a long shot, after all; another of Tech Section's crack-brained just-in-case projects, in the beginning no more promising than that absurd 150-ton articulated tank, or the caseless-ammunition project that has been "one year" away from success since 1928. And nuclear physics is not our field of choice; we Draka are competent technologists but simply lack the cultural inclination for really first-rate pure science work. But Security swore that Hitler and the Americans were pressing forward with their reactors, and suddenly the implications of atomic explosives sank in. Then it became a priority project. Whatever our other faults, we have seldom passed up a promising weapon, and through great good luck and our initial head start we exploded our first device within months of the Americans. Those first crude bombs proved very useful in breaking the last resistance in Europe ...

Yet it was after the war they proved crucial. Whale and elephant, sea power and land power, the Domination and the Yankee-led Alliance have glared at each

*other under the enforced Truce of the Mushroom Cloud;
now we curse the technological stalemate that keeps us
from the Americans' throats. But in the late 1940's our
conquests were potential strength and present weakness; the defeat of Germany and the annexation of
mainland China left us desperately overstretched, a billion new-caught serfs to pacify, the whole of Eurasia to
guard, while the sheer biological necessity of reproduc-
tion forced us to demobilize the Citizen Force to peacetime levels. The Alliance navies could have struck at will,
with the Domination forced to shift armies through
devastated lands and populations primed to revolt ...
except that we held the nuclear sword over Melbourne
and New York and Rio de Janeiro. Of course, the game
of "what if" can be extended back indefinitely. For
example, "what if" our ancestors had followed impulse
and revolted in 1833 when the British abolished slavery
throughout the Empire? Sober second thought pre-
vailed, and so did slavery under various cosmetic dis-
guises; but the revolt might have happened, and
the infant Domination been crushed in its cradle. For
that matter, "what if" the Netherlands had not joined
France and Spain in war on Britain in 1779, giving
Britain an opportunity to seize southern Africa? The
Loyalists scattering without a new home to welcome
them ... a weak Dutch colony in place of the great cities
of our southern African heartland ... a world without
the Domination, perhaps?*

> *Fire And Blood: The Eurasian War*
> *V. VIII: Conclusion and Aftermath, 1946-50*
> *by Strategos Robert A. Jackson (ret.),*
> *New Territories Press, Vienna, 1965*

LYON, PROVINCE OF BURGUNDIA
DETENTION CENTER XVII
APRIL, 1947

Tanya von Shrakenberg eased herself to her feet,
leaving the half-empty cup of coffee on the table and

gently uncurling the small solid weight of her daughter
into the waiting arms of the nurse. Not so small any
more, either; arms and legs just starting to lengthen
out, she would have the rangy height of the von
Shrakenberg line, even if her coloring took after her
father's maternal ancestors. Tanya looked down at the
fine-featured oval face, already losing its puppy-fat and
firming towards adulthood, and stroked one cheek.

I wonder if I could catch that? she mused, in painter's reflex. Difficult, when so much of an image like this
was your own response to it; that was the weakness and
strength of representational art, that it relied on a common set of visual codes . . . *Oh, shut up,* Tanya told
herself. *Critics theorize, you're a painter.*

The girl murmured without opening her eyes, turning and nuzzling her face into Beth's wide soft chest.
Tanya felt a slow warmth below her heart, and reached
out to draw a light finger down her cheek. *Mother,
painter, soldier, Landholder,* she mused. *All true, but
which is really me, the me I talk to inside my head?*
Knowledge was a thing of words, but you could never
really reduce a human being to description. Still less a
child, whose self was still potential, before the narrowing of choice. She felt a moment's sadness; children
changed so fast, the one you knew and loved reshaping
into someone else as you watched.

"Shall Ah wakes her, Mistis?" Beth asked.

"Let her rest," Tanya replied. Not enough sleep last
night, and then the long drive down; the family gathering in Paris had been enjoyable but strenuous for all of
them, a good thirty adults and more children. The first
opportunity since the War, now that travel was getting
back to normal and demobilization nearly complete,
and most of those still in the Forces able to get leave. A
good deal of useful work, besides the socializing: plans
had been made, political and otherwise, and the dozen
or so younger members who were settling in Europe
had compared notes.

Damnation, Tanya thought, rising and catching herself on the back of the chair. *Balance going again*. Pregnancy always did that to her.

She looked around the office, eager to be gone but reluctant to face the bother of the trip; the air smelled of coffee and food from the buffet and the peculiarly north-European odor of very old damp stone, so different from the dry dust-scent of her birth-province, Syria. At Evendim, her parent's plantation in the Bekaa Valley, the days would already be hot. From her old room in the east wing she could watch the sun set over the Lebanon mountains to the west, down from the snowpeaks and the slopes green with the forests of young cedar her people had planted; over the terraced vineyards in patterns of curving shadow; slanted golden sheets between the tall dark cypress that fringed the lawns behind the manor.

They tossed in the evening cool, the wind down from the mountains faintly chill against your skin while the stone of the windowledge was still blood-warm from the day's sun. Sweetness from the mown lawns, delicate and elusive from the long acres of cherry-orchard blossoming between the greathouse and the main water-channel; sometimes the sound of a housegirl singing at her work, or faint snatches of the muezzin calling his flock to prayer, down in the Quarters.

No use getting homesick, she chided herself. It was probably just this damned depressing city . . . Tanya had been a Cohortarch in the Archonal Guard Legion when she saw it last, back in '45; burnt-out rubble, and the natives sick and hungry enough to eat each other. Things had improved a little, but not enough.

Or it could just be pregnancy, the aches and itches and the continual humiliating need to pee. It was unfair: some women went into the sixth month hardly showing at all . . . Thank Freya this was the third; one more and she could count that particular duty to the Race done. Or no more if it was twins again; her family ran to them. Children were delightful and no particular bother; if anything, between the servants and the eight months a year at boarding school required of all young Draka, you scarcely saw them enough. She glanced over at Gudrun, the bright copper hair resting against Beth's dark breast. Sleep was the only time you saw her still; where all that energy came from was a mystery. But *having* them was something she would rather have skipped; the whole process was stupid and barbaric, like incubating and then shitting a pumpkin. And Almighty Thor knew a Security pen wasn't the most cheerful setting in the world, either; the fear and misery and throttled hatred drifted through the air like smoke. Stimulating, in reasonable quantities, like all danger, but there was a sickness in too much of it. No point in being sentimental about serfs; this sort of place was necessary enough in new-taken territory, but so were terminal wards in a hospital, and who would live in one by choice?

She nodded politely to the Security Strategos. It was courteous of him to expedite matters; a routine request like hers could have been handled at much lower levels, even if Draka did not set much store by proper bureaucratic channels.

"Thank you for your time," she said. "It'll help; stonemasons and electricians and bookkeepers are in demand. I expect yo'll be glad when the other Directorates and the labor agencies get set up proper an' things normalize.

"It'll be good to get back home," she said more quietly, to Andrew. Her brother looked up, unhooking the borrowed electroprod from his waist and smiling.

"The new place is home already?" he asked, lifting one eyebrow. The movement pulled at the scar on his cheek, exaggerating the quizzical gesture.

"Of course. *Chateau Retour*'s mine, and Edward's," —she laid a hand on her stomach—"an' our next will be born there. Evendim stopped being home a long time ago; it's Willie's." Draka law and custom demanded a single heir for an estate, usually the eldest. "We can visit, but that isn't the same . . . I worry about you, brother mine; where's the place yo' can call home?

Officers' quarters in Helsinki? We fought the War, let the next generation do their share. There's still some good landholdings ready for settlement, down in the Loire valley. Yo' should get yourself a mate, stop wastin' all your seed on the wenches, make a place for y'self. The Race has to build, or what's the conquerin' for?"

"Maybe after my next hitch," he said absently, pulling the folded cap from under his shoulder-strap and settling it on his head. "Loki's hooves, I'm barely thirty-odd; still plenty of time, unless I stop a bullet, and good Janissary officers are scarce. An' Finland will be a while bein' tamed. A while, surely." He blinked, and she could see his consciousness returning, pulled back from the forests and snowfields of the Baltic. "Meanwhile, leave the motherin' to Ma, she's been bombardin' me with the same advice since we reached the Channel."

"An' the young fogey should shut up about it, eh?" Tanya reached to stroke her daughter's forehead. "Wake up, sweetlin', time to go down to the cars." To her brother: "Well, doan' forget to visit, before they post yo's back east. Some good huntin', a little up-valley; boar and deer, at least. And we've still got crates of that stuff you picked up, in the attics. Should get it catalogued soon."

Her brother laughed and took the yawning Gudrun from her nurse, tossing her and holding her up easily with his hands beneath her arms; she smothered a smile and responded with an adult glower. "Not too old to play with y'uncle, I hope?" he said, and continued over his shoulder to his sister: "It took a two-ton car to drag the lot you got out of Paris, as I recall."

He turned to the Security officer. "Thanks again, Strategos Vashon."

The secret policeman closed a folder, rose and circled the desk to take the offered hand, give a chuck under the chin to Gudrun as she sat on her uncle's shoulder. "No trouble," he said. "A relief from my other problems, frankly; and I knew your granduncle Karl, we worked together after the last war." Unstated was the fact that Karl von Shrakenberg was now an Arch-Strategos of the Supreme General Staff; there was always an undercurrent of tension between the Directorates of War and Security, the Domination's two armed services. It never hurt to have a favor due. "Nothin' *but* problems; sometimes I'd be glad to be back home, promotion or no."

Tanya nodded to the murals of rocky hills and and plains covered in long lion-colored grass. "There, Strategos?"

He shook his head, fitting another cigarette into the ivory holder. "That's North Katanga, where I was born; I meant Bulgaria. Sofia's home, I worked out of there from 1920 until the Eurasian War started. Probably why they sent me here, similar problems." Thrace and Bulgaria had been the western stopping-point of the Domination's armies in the Great War, a generation before. "Although at least we could terrorize Rumania into sending back runaways who tried to make it over the Danube. Sweet fuck-all luck we've been havin' with the English on that score; good thing the Channel isn't swimmable." He puffed a smoke-ring. " 'Course, they've got the Yanks behind them, their damned Alliance for *Democracy*." For a moment his calm tone became something far less pleasant.

Tanya shrugged. "Ah, Sofia; pretty town, had a leave there durin' the War . . . '43, I think." A grin. "Gudrun here'll take care of the Yanks, eh, chile?"

Brother and sister nodded approvingly as her hand made an unconscious check of the knife in its leg-sheath.

Vashon laughed dutifully. "Maybe our grandchildren," he said with sour pessimism. "If then."

"That ol' stretched-thin feelin'?" Andrew said, swinging the girl to the ground.

Vashon shrugged. "Ah, well, it's only two years since the War ended." He looked out over the city, brooding. "Remember how things looked back in '39? Soviets to the north of us, Germans to the west, Japs to the east? War on three fronts, wouldn't that-*there* have been lovely, now?" A shake of the head. "Then Hitler conquers Europe an' Russia fo' us, exhausting himself in the process; the slanteyes attack the Yanks—who'd have thought we could end up fightin' on the same side of a war as the U.S.? Enormous victories for negligable cost."

"Didn't seem quite so negligible in the Guard," Tanya said dryly, hitching up the elastic waistband of her trousers. "An' the Fritz didn't seem so exhausted, not when they damn' near shot my tank out from under me, half a dozen times. Four years fightin', total mobilization."

Vashon spread his hands in an apologetic gesture. "Negligible in relation to the booty," he said. "Half the earth, an' half mankind; two-thirds, with what we had before. It's *assimilatin'* it that's going to be the problem. We aren't a—"

"—numerous people, and nobody loves us," Tanya said, completing the proverb as she crossed to the windows, leaned her palms against the strong armor-glass. "Doin' my best about that, Strategos. Perceptible improvement here, since I saw it last."

The Security officer scowled. "Partly because so many of the labor-force doan' have anything to do but shift rubble." He stubbed his cigarette out with a savage gesture. "*Damn* that sack! Waste: waste of raw materials, waste of skilled workers, waste of machinery. We could have used it, the Police Zone is still run-down from lack of maintenance durin' the War an' having trouble retooling."

"What's the point of victory, without lootin'?" she said lightly. The clouds were thinning, a good augury for the trip home.

"To take what they make and grow—for which we need them *alive,* and their tools. More important than stealin' their jewelry, no?"

Andrew snorted. "My Legion was in on that sack, Strategos. We took twenty, thirty percent casualties between the Rhine crossin's an' here. Janissaries aren't field-hands or houseserfs; yo' needs to give them proof-positive of a victory. Lettin' them loose in a town, drinkin' themselves wild, pickin' up pretties and riding the wenches bloody is the best way I know. Does wonders for morale, sir; wish there was somethin' equivalent on antipartisan duty."

Vashon composed himself and donned a smile. "At least with yo' settlers gettin' agriculture in order, we won't have to sell much more oil to the Yanks for wheat to feed Europe with . . . how's it going, over there along the Loire, Cohortarch?"

She stretched. "Jus' Tanya, Strategos; I'm in the Reserve now. Well as can be expected, all in all; the French were good farmers, but they pushed the land too hard durin' the war. Shortages of fertilizer and livestock, equipment, horses . . . We're producin' a surplus and it should increase pretty steady-like. Our place is all yo' could ask, on the basics. North bank of the river, just west of Tours; first-rate light alluvial soil, with some hills on the north. Lovely country, fine climate, grow anythin', well kept . . . but Frey and Freya, the way things are cut up! Fields the size of handkerchiefs, little hamlets 'n villages all over the place, goin' take a generation or two to get things in order."

He nodded. "Same on the industrial front, or so the people from the Combines tell me. Overall output about equivalent to ours, or nearly, but the *methods* are so bloody different, it's a mess. Had a fellah in from the Ferrous Metals Combine, actually broke down an' *cried* after doin' a survey; said the Poodles had thirty-six times the number of different machine-tools we did, all of 'em needin' a skilled operator, all split up in tiny little factories. Puttin' together a compound system for the factory-serfs is a nightmare, either dozens of little ones and supervisory costs eat you alive, or you pen the workforce in a few big ones and have to spend hours a day truckin' them back and forth to their jobs. Or consolidate the machines, means losin' months of production . . ."

Andrew raised a brow. "Yo're beginnin' to sound like my distressingly liberal cousin Eric, *he* thinks we should hold off on modernizin' the Europeans, at least the Western provinces, supervise 'n tax them instead." A laugh. "Maybe-so I should report yo' to Security, sir?"

Vashon forced himself to echo the laugh. Eric von Shrakenberg was a sore point with the Security Directorate, but after all, he was Arch-Stategos Karl von Shrakenberg's *son*. And he had never quite qualified for a Section-IV detention, "by administrative procedure." Not *quite*. He sighed, clicked heels:

"Service to the State," he said in formal farewell as the von Shrakenbergs turned to leave.

"Glory to the Race," they replied; the adults, at least. Gudrun put her head back through the door for a brief instant, stuck out her tongue and fled giggling.

They will definitely bear watching, Vashon thought, seating himself again and propping one hand under a chin. *Damn planters should teach their children more respect.* The closed-circuit monitor was still flicking on its random survey of posts important enough to rate surveillance; an indulgence he found restful when he needed to concentrate, even if the system was supposed to be primarily for accessing records from the basement filerooms.

Aristocrats, his mind continued. A relic of the Domination's early years, when wealth meant acres of cotton and sugar and tobacco, and the younger son's drive for an estate of his own had been the motive force for expansion. Oh, granted, the conquered territories' farmland had to be reorganized into line with the Domination's practice, although he had privately thought some sort of large scale state-farm system might be more efficient. But this was not the 1780's, or southern Africa; in these times power grew out of mines and forges, machine shops and steel mills . . . better to concentrate scarce personnel on Security work and getting Europe's industrial machine back into full production: *that* was the real prize of the War, not the vast reaches of Russia and Siberia and China. The Domination and the United States had been roughly equal in GNP before the war, but the long struggle with the Yankee-dominated Alliance would need all the productive capacity that could be had, the Americans grew so *fast*.

He shook his head. His were a conservative folk, where circumstance allowed; even if three-quarters were city-dwellers now, the white-pillared mansion and its fields still had too strong a grip on their imagination. And to be sure, the officer corps was still infused with the planter-aristocrat ethos; most of the Janissaries were recruited from the estates as well; and the Supreme General Staff were no fools, sitting there in their aerie at Castle Tarleton overlooking Archona.

Archon, the title of the Draka head of state; *Archona*, the city named for that office. An old town by the Domination's standards, founded in the 1780's; the first of the string of industrial centers that ran north to Katanga, core of the Domination's strength, mines and hydro-dams, universities and steel mills and power-plants . . .

It was a long time since he had seen the capital, away south in its bowl of hills, where the high plateau began its descent toward the Limpopo river. Not since the victory celebrations; he had had a good seat, in the bleachers erected in front of Transportation Directorate headquarters on the Way of the Armies, a kilometer short of Victory Gardens and the two-hundred-meter stained-glass dome of the Assembly building. A bright summer's day, the sky a blue curved ceiling, light blinking off colored marble, tile and brick and glass, shimmering on the leaves of the roadside trees and massed flowerbanks. He remembered the noise all around him, shouting, crying, laughing. The old, the young, the wounded, who had waited and worked here on the home front, and the first scattering of demobilized veterans. Crazed with release, victory, the return of sons, daughters, lovers, with the memory of the dead scattered from the English Channel to the South China Sea. Himself crying out with them through a throat gone tight and dry, one with the many-throated beast, pouring out its triumph and its grief.

The ground shook beneath him as the tanks of the Archonal Guard thundered slowly by. Filling the air with the burbling throb of their engines, trim in silver and black parade paint, the red bat-winged dragon of the Domination on their glacis plates, its claws clutching the slave-chain of mastery and the sword of death. Black squat beetling shapes of the infantry carriers, with the helmeted heads of the crews rigid in the open hatches; long-barreled self-propelled cannon; other legions of the Citizen Force with battle-honors hanging from their eagle standards; endless cohorts of marching Janissaries expressionless as automatons. Roses and frangipani and streamers of colored paper flung like sprays of summer rain from the sidewalks and the windows of the buildings, the surf-roar of massed voices louder than engines. Thunder overhead as well, fighters and strike-planes, the new jet-propelled models and clattering helicopters, still a dazzling innovation then; the stink of burnt hydrocarbons, flowers, the heavy smell of dense-packed humanity.

The floats had followed, drawn by chained and naked prisoners of war from a dozen armies, decked with captured flags, bearing symbolic booty. Russian furs and grain and timber, Finnish glassware, ingots of Norwegian aluminum heaped about jade Buddhas and katanas and kimonos, Flemish lace like piles of snow-froth, silk tapestries of Lyon, paintings and sculptures, machine tools, crates of priceless vintages, sturdy workers and picked wenches in national costumes or nudity emphasized by silver manacles. Musicians and dancers and tumblers walking alongside, throwing golden eggs into the crowd. Message-eggs with slips of paper that might grant anything, from a bottle of Chateau d'Yquem to a Leonardo plundered from the Louvre to an estate in Tuscany. Last of all a train of older men, bewildered in their dunces' caps and fools' motley, bearing signs on poles listing their ranks and titles: enemy leaders on their way to the ceremonial pistol-bullet through the head on the steps of the Archon's palace.

He sighed; that had been a good time. A time to be at one with the Race, when they could relax from the long years of grinding effort and feel the pride of a great accomplishment. Limitless vistas of power and possibility opening out before them . . . Another sigh. The warriors fought their open battles against uniformed opponents, and when the foreign armies were beaten retired to their estates; he was left with the endless twilight warfare against the enemy within, ferreting out the last *maquisards* in the hills, breaking up sabotage rings, policing the pens and labor-compounds of the administrative Directorates and the industrial Combines. Routine work back in the Police Zone, but it took extreme measures to get any worthwhile effort out of the newly conquered territories.

Strategos Vashon adjusted the controls of the monitor; now it was showing one of the interrogation chambers, belowground in another bow to tradition. A chamber of antiseptic white tile, easy to wash, scattered instruments of chromed steel and wire; a frame for lowering subjects slowly head-first into a vat, the old-fashioned stretch-and-break models. Two Psy-Ops officers in green, with the usual dark bib-aprons, but the procedure was something new, outlined in last month's circular from headquarters.

The subjects were seated facing each other, two Poodles, locals; a father and son, both probably couriers for what was left of the underground. A more important case than most, since their network was suspected of contact with the American OSS, Office of Strategic Services, the Alliance's secret-intelligence and covert operations *apparat*. He leaned closer, adjusted the grainy black-and-white picture until the dark stubbled face of the older man came close, sweat and rolling eyes above the gag; he was strapped naked into a steel chair with electrodes at the classic points, testicles, anus, nipples, ears, toes, wires and copper disks taped to his olive skin. The passive partner. The secret policeman worked the controls to swivel the camera; the younger subject was similary outfitted, with one difference. There was a switch under his right hand, a simple pressure-activated on-off plaque. One of the officers was explaining in slow bored French:

". . . as long as you keep that pushed down, the current will flow through your father. Release it, and it will flow through *you*. The current increases each time you push *or* release the button. When that meter"—he pointed—"goes into the red zone, it will be approaching the killing range. Understand?"

The young Poodle was not screaming, not yet; you could hear the effort it took to force reason into his voice.

"What do you want? What do you want me to *do?* For the love of God, tell me what you want, *please*—"

The Security officer continued: "Current on in five seconds. Five, four, three—"

The boy was shrieking even before the current hit; his father's head was moving back and forth in the padded clamp, a silent *nonononono*. Vashon smiled. The treatment would continue until the passive subject was dead, of course; the Psy-Ops theorists swore that it was more effective at breaking the will than any amount of raw pain, better even than sensory deprivation. Once it was over, the subject *knew*, right down to the subconscious level, that he would do anything, absolutely anything, rather than stay in that chair . . . and then they would bring in his sister and mother, and explain what he was going to do after they released him. The Security Directorate would have another conduit, ready to be activated if the Americans tried . . . oh, to smuggle out more of the captive scientists working for the War Directorate's Technical Section, or to get saboteurs into the plutonium-refining plant at Le Puy. There would be no repetition of that embarrassing affair with

Heisenberg and the rocket-ramjet researchers, in the chaotic period right after the War. Credit where credit was due—this technique was based on German Gestapo research, but it had the malignant beauty of a concealed razor-blade in a melon.

His smile broadened. Perhaps they would get an American. The ancient enemy, the hereditary foe; the Domination had been founded by refugees from their Revolution, its self-evident lie that all men were created equal. Loyalists from Virginia and Georgia and the Carolinas, hounded from their homes and plantations by the vengeful Whigs . . . The smile became a grin as the first incredulous gut-deep grunt came from the speaker, as the subject felt the electricity having its way with him. The Vashons were much the same mixture as most Draka, American Loyalist, Hessian, Icelander, miscellaneous nineteenth-century immigrants. But their male line had been French, originally; émigrés in 1793, one step ahead of the Committee of Public Safety's guillotines.

Liberté, Égalité, Fraternité, he thought with a stirring of almost sensual pleasure at the base of his stomach. *You thought you'd won, you peasant filth; now you're going to pay.* "Ahh, *how* you will pay," he murmured aloud.

He turned down the volume and pulled another file from the in-stack. There was the work of the day to attend to.

In the corridor outside the office Tanya took her brother's arm. "You know, Andrew, I was never particularly squeamish," she said meditatively. "Killed my share in the War, Wotan knows, an' not all of 'em were shootin' at me. We grew up in the New Territories, after all." Syria had been pacified and settled during the Great War, but not officially transferred to the Police Zone, the area of civil government, until 1937. "Is it my imagination, or is Security goin' hog-wild these days?"

He spread his hands as they strolled toward the

elevator, their bootheels scrunching in the carpet. "Necessity, sister mine: if yo' think this-here's bad, you should see Finland. We're applyin' a methodology of conquest developed while we overran Africa, Iron Age barbarians, an' the Middle East, mostly starvin' diseased peasants subjected to *somebody* since Babylon an' before. We killed the native elites an' stepped into their shoes; what freedom did those villagers around Evendim have, before Pa 'stablished the plantation? Not that they just rolled over an' spread—read his journals: plenty of trouble with religion an' wenches an' so forth in the first few years; we're too young to remember it. But once they'd submitted, if anythin' they were better off; higher standard of livin', certainly, better housin' and medical care.

"These West-Europeans, they doan' have that Asian sense of bein' victims of Fate; not yet, at least. They're literate, these were real democracies at least until the Fritz conquered them back in '40. The Russians are damn-sure easier, Stalin cleared the way for us. Breakin' the countries west of the Elbe to the Yoke goin' be a long, bloody business. Three generations, minimum, even after we've wiped out mass literacy; folk tradition can be almost 'z bad."

Tanya frowned, slowing her pace and letting Gudrun and her nurse move forward out of earshot before dropping her voice. "Tell the truth, I'm a little concerned about Timmie and Gudrun, an' the new baby. Wouldn't want any of 'em soft, but watching too much killing and pain too soon isn't good either; serfs are inferior, but they're not dumb beasts or machinery. Think of them like that an' you start underestimatin' them; also . . . yo' can lose something, a sort of basic respect fo' life, I've seen it happen. Then y'lose respect for yo' *own* life, an'—" She stopped, shook off worry as they overtook the others. "Ah, well, take the days as they come."

The wire door of the elevator cage scissored open. "And I miss yo', brother, I really do; it's not just the War and different postin's, we've been drifting apart and yo've been getting too wrapped up in hard an' bitter things. I'm not naggin', leave the future to itself, but drop by after the harvest this fall. The wine's fantastic, the place grows everythin' to perfection, I've got old Cindy from Evendim as head-cook and three of the best chefs in France . . . Nice bunch of neighbors, too, when we get the chance to socialize; three-quarters of the Guard who weren't heirs took out grants thereabouts when they stood the veterans down. Plantations, mostly; construction partnerships, restaurants . . . Hell, the crew of the *Baalbeck Belle* took estates on both sides of me; my gunner spent the War fightin' with my loader and then they went'n married, and the same with the driver an' Sparks. Come down, party a little, hunt, feast, let yore heart have room to breath." A smile and a gentle pinch on the arm. "And you really should get that booty tallied."

"I'll drop by; put those two wenches I found you to work on the loot, if you want, 'n can spare them from bookkeepin'." He winked. "An' bedwenchin'."

Tanya smiled sourly, recognizing the signs of a gentle but firm refusal to pursue a subject further. "Not for me; doctor's orders, nothin' rough or deep. I'm not even sleeping with Edward, much less teachin' a wild mare how to play pony for me. Ah, well, Solange is sweet and willin', but it's a bit like living on Turkish Delight; tasty and nourishing, but after a while you crave meat." A wiggle of eyebrows. "Plenty for you, though; one good thing about this-here inconveniently advanced country, they're not worn-out hags at twenty-five." She laughed. "Edward and I're going to need them, in a year or two, when Timmie hits puberty. Recallin' you at thirteen, y'had half the wenches on Evendim sittin' down careful."

"Ah," he said with a nostalgic chuckle, "nothin' like that first fine flush of hormonal frenzy. Not that you felt that way at the time," he added thoughtfully.

She shrugged. "Gender difference, I suppose. Seems to take males twenty years to learn that personalities are what makes it more interestin' than masturbation. Though," she added, with a mock-malicious smile, "there's women I could name that never did grasp the distinction either. Present company excepted."

"What, never?" he said slyly.

"Weeell, after a battle sometimes, just to remind myself I's alive."

They exited into an internal alleyway, a narrow street closed off when the Security complex was established. Tanya looked up at the gaps of blue sky between the long tatters of cloud and breathed deeply; the chill was leaving the wet air, and some hopeful soul had hung pots of flowering impatiens from the eaves on either side, slashes of hot pink, coral and magenta against the browns and greys of the stone. The alley was lined on both sides with agency showrooms, the Settlement and Agriculture Directorate liaison office, a few restaurants, outfitters. It was crowded to the point of chaos, not least with construction crews making alterations; civil settlement in France was just getting under way and receiving priority as a matter of State policy. Every settler needed labor, even if it was only a few household servants. Planters in soft dark working leathers, bureaucrats in the four-pocket khaki working dress of the civil service, Combine execs in suits of white linen and Shantung silk, serfs of every race and kind and degree pushed through.

Sort of irregular, she thought, as she stopped before the Stevenson & de Verre office, a converted house. That was the largest agency in the Domination, with hundreds of branches. Back—she stopped herself—back near the *old* home, even in a small provincial town like Baalbeck, it would have been much larger. Showrooms and auction-pits, holding pens, workshops, medical facilities; in a major city like Alexandria or Shahnapur, a complex of creches and training-centers . . . Here there were only the offices and catalogs and a simple fitting-out room, with the serfs in the Security cells. Of course, Europe was still too raw for the usual procedures, only recently out from direct military government; still in the initial process-and-sort stage, the mass transfers to the Combines just beginning to hit full stride. Direct sales to private holders would continue until the situation stabilized; for that matter, Tanya and her husband had rounded up the basic labor force for Chateau Retour directly, with only a few *lochoi* of Order Police to help with the culling and neck-numbering and registration.

"Well," she said, stopping on the worn stone steps of the shop. "Take care, brother mine; y'all remember the door's always open."

"An' yo've *got* to see my new white Caramague horse, she's a beauty, Uncle," Gudrun said. "Pa gave me a real Portuguese bullfighter's saddle, with silver studs."

"So yo've been tellin' me for the last week, sweetlin'," he said, stooping for her hug. "Maybe-so I will; been a while since I done any riding."

Tanya embraced him as he straightened, feeling the huge and gentle strength of his arms as they closed around her, the slight rasp of his mustache on her neck, smelling cologne and soap and leather. She dug her fingers fiercely into the hard rubbery muscle of his neck.

"I love you, brother," she whispered.

"An' I you, sister," he replied quietly; stepped back, saluted and strode away into the crowd.

She looked down, to find Gudrun scowling at the unseemly adult display of emotion, took her hand despite an effort at evasion, pushed through the swinging doors. *While I can*, she thought, giving it a quick squeeze. *They grow so quick.*

The waiting room was quiet and dim, walled in rose silk and eighteenth-century tapestries, with lecterns bearing photo-catalogs. The attendant at the desk in the corner was busy with an argumentative exec from Capricorn Textiles who was waving a requisition for a thousand loom-tenders; Tanya idly flipped open one of the leather-bound catalogs, leafing through the front-and-side shots and brief descriptions of skills.

"Ma," Gudrun said.

"Hmmm?" Tanya looked down; her daughter was craning sideways to see the photographs.

"Ma, could I buy a serf?"

"Whatever fo', my heart?"

"Well, for a maid."

"Yo've already got two body-servants, sweetlin'.."

The red brows frowned, drawing a crease between them; Tanya felt her heart turn over with warmth at the gravely serious expression. Gudrun had the innocent greed of childhood; horses had been her latest passion, she would have filled the stables at Chateau Retour if she could . . . but clothes and attendants had been a matter of profoundest indifference, until now. *They do grow up,* she thought wistfully.

"Well, Beth's nice," Gudrun said, reaching behind to pat the nursemaid on the arm, "but I's too grown now to be looked after by a nurse. An' Miriam's good at fixin' up my things, but she's so old, she never wants to do stuff like run or swim or ride or climb things an' it's no fun telling her to."

Her mother winced inwardly; Miriam was all of twenty-two, eight years younger than herself. *Well, to ten a parent is ancient beyond worlds anyway,* she told herself.

Gudrun continued, as if checking off a carefully thought-out list. " 'Sides, Ma, Beth 'n Miriam were gifts; at school, the older girls are tellin' us that we need to learn serf-handlin' with one of our own. I've saved up my allowance, honest."

Tanya controlled a smile. *Why not,* she decided. *Good news should come in twos.*

"Tell yo' what, daughter," she said seriously. " 'S true that a new maidservant's a good idea, but buyin' here isn't; quality's uneven, an' we don't have rightly enough time to check. When we get back to the plantation, we'll go over the young wenches together"—she held up a hand at the beginnings of a pout—"an' when you pick one, I'll *sell* her to yo', right proper an' legal, with the papers and everythin', an' you can take her along to school for the fall term. Thirty aurics. Deal?"

Gudrun considered, nodded. They slapped palms in the countryside gesture for sealing a bargain, and Tanya continued.

"Now fo' some news; yo're moving schools." She laughed at the expression of surprise; Gudrun had been attending back in Syria Province. All Citizen schools in the Domination were boarding institutions, but usually in the same province as the child's home, at least; it was a long trip from the eastern Mediterranean.

"New one being put in, jus' north of us, to match the boy's school down near Chinon." Draka schooling was sex-segregated below the University level. In theory to allow children and adolescents undistracted time for their studies and premilitary training, although she suspected it was just as much a simple case of institutional inertia: the system worked well and nobody had reason enough to push for a change. "Yo'll only be two hours' drive away, close enough to visit home on weekends."

The girl gave a squeal of joy and bounced up to hug her with arms and legs. "Whoa, darlin', I'm not shaped right for that right now!" Tanya picked her daughter up, tossed her in the air, placed her down on her feet and tousled the bright bowl-cut hair. "I'm happy too, darlin'." She sighed. "Well, let's pick up the goods an' get home."

CHAPTER FOUR

... which is not to say that the Domination was totally unique. Like Rome or Macedonia it had its beginnings as a 'marcher' state, on the fringes of civilization, expanding at the expense of wholly alien and less advanced peoples and thus gaining access to population and resources on a scale impossible to the states of the core area. Like Czarist Russia it was essentially imposed from above, using imported technology, organization and in the beginning personnel to impose Western standards of rationality and efficiency on an uncomprehending and hostile peasantry. Established by coercion, it existed primarily to maintain its own armed forces, which in turn maintained and expanded the state; a circular arrangement much like the classical Prussian formula. Indeed, the society that resulted bore considerable resemblance to Prussia: an aristocracy of uncouth militarists ruling a brutalized peasantry of landless serfs. As in Prussia the state was created from nothing by a generations-long act of collective will, producing a political culture that exalted discipline, service to the state, the military virtues, ruthlessness, and a hard, unsentimental realism.

What gave the Domination its relentless dynamism was, essentially, a series of 'accidents.' If the Netherlands had not entered the War of the American Revolution in

1779, southern Africa might not have been available for Loyalist settlement, might even (although this seems unlikely) have remained a backwater for generations. The thirty-year period of the French Revolutionary wars gave the early Draka a period of cultural and partial economic isolation, crucial to their development. Geological accident ensured that the high spine of south-central Africa was a treasure house of gold, diamonds, coal, copper, iron, manganese, with a native population numerous and hardy enough to sustain the shock of conquest and furnish a labor force, yet technically backward enough to be successfully dominated by a small minority of immigrant conquerors with the simple technology of the eighteenth century. If great navigable rivers had been available, nothing more than another colonial export-economy of mines and plantations might have developed; the isolation of the plateau forced the beginnings of the great complex of industrial cities between the Orange river and Katanga which formed the basis of the Domination's power-machine . . .

The Age of Domination
by E.P. Hobsdown
Nicolfield and Weidenson
London, 1987.

LYON, PROVINCE OF BURGUNDIA
DETENTION CENTRE XVII
APRIL, 1947

Therese had been crying when the guard thrust her through the side door of the serf-dealer's office, into the holding-bay.

"Anybody goan' sign for thissere piece a' shitbitch?" he said, giving a final flat-palmed shove between her shoulder blades that sent her sprawling on the floor; she was unbound, but the guard was a hulking man, muscle under fat, a baton in one hand and lead-backed brass knuckles on the other that held the clipboard. His green coverall was faded, and there was no weapon on his webbing-belt.

The room was a four-meter cube with wooden benches along the walls, dusty and empty and dim, silent save for Therese's sobs as she crawled toward her sister. Chantal broke forward and hugged the slight girl to her; Marya sat trembling on the brink of action, suddenly acutely conscious of the slats digging into her naked flesh. Beside her, she heard Yasmin take a long breath and then rise; the serf-girl had only just come in from the main section of the shop.

"I's the one," she said calmly, striding forward, trim in her jacket and skirt. The guard saw her, straightened slightly at the clothes and manner; only slightly, and his smile was insolent as he transferred his gaze back to the nude prisoners and extended the sheaf of documents. Yasmin took it, read, signed, pivoted on one heel and slammed the pasteboard flat across the side of the man's face with a full-armed swing.

Crack. The sound seemed loud as a gunshot in the musty stillness, and the nun felt time slow in gelid coldness as her stomach clenched; the green-uniformed man loomed a head higher than the dark serf-girl, and Marya saw the tension in her back. None of it showed in her voice as she spoke, even when the fist with its glove of spiked and weighted metal pulled back.

"Is that how yo' treats yo' momma? Yo' sistah? Tings not hard enough fo' the po' little wench, yo' big, strong man gotsta make 'em worse?" Marya could make out the angry red right-angled mark of the clipboard as the man paled in rage; it had not done any great harm, but a blow like that carried an unmistakable significance in the world of the Domination.

"Yo, cain' talk to me like that-there, wench! I's Security; yo' blind?" He jerked his chin at the skull markings on his collar.

"Ohhhh, dearie *me*," Yasmin drawled, and Marya could suddenly see the expression of mock-fear even though the girl's back was turned. "Whut *have* I gone an' done? I's jes' *pissin'* mahselfs with fear; watch me throw mahself on mah back 'n spread outa tremblin' respec' fo' yo' awesomeness, chain-dog."

She stepped closer. "Security? Where yo' rank badge? Where yo' *gun*, chain-dog? Security? Yo's a jumped-up strawboss whut ain't talked to nobodies but new-caughts fo' too long." Her other hand dipped inside her jacket and came out with a palm-sized leather folder, snapped it open and held it at eye-level for the man, above her own head.

"Cain yo' read, hmm? See this? This whut *I* is; I gots *Category I* papahs, chain-dog. I's gotta thousand-auric bond posted on me, I's private property—an ol' fam'ly servant, and mah mistis trusts me, *an'* she a von Shrakenberg, *an'* she a Landholder, *an'* my pa a soldier under *her* pa. *Citizens* doan' lay hand to me without they got permission or provocation." She raised the clipboard and slapped him across the other cheek.

His fist snapped up again. Yasmin laughed; a little breathless, but loudly.

"Go 'head, chain-dog. All I has t'do is *say* yo' hits me, an' they trice yo' to the frame an' uses a whip to show the world yo' backbone."

The fist relaxed; the man's eyes dropped from the intimidating identity-card, past Yasmin's glare.

"Jes' doin' my job," he grumbled.

"Yo' job was to brings her heah," Yasmin snapped. "Not to slap her 'round. These wenches is all bought-out now, belongs to the von Shrakenbergs same's me. An' iffn they didn't, 's that any cause to be treatin' 'em rough? Is they fightin', disobeyin'?" She tore the top sheet from the clipboard and threw the remainder into the guard's face. "Ain't tings bad enough fo' us, withouten we makes it worse fo' each othah? Git outta my sight; yo' makes me sick."

Yasmin turned as the door closed, drew her hands across her face and then clenched them together while she struggled to control her breathing; looked up with a smile as Chantal brought her sister to her feet.

"Thank you, Yasmin," Chantal said quietly. Yasmin shook her head wordlessly, then smiled again as Therese stretched out a hand, wiping at the tears on her face with the other and watching the serf girl with wide, astonished eyes. Yasmin took the hand in both of hers, patted it and gave it a gentle squeeze. "Don't worry, little one," she said in slow, careful French. "I look after you now." She leaned forward to kiss the other girl on the forehead, urged her back to her sister's side, then slumped back to the seat beside Marya. The nun turned to study her for a moment.

Yasmin. *Another person it would be better to study carefully,* Marya thought. *Elegant* was the word that occurred to her; pleated blue silk skirt and high-collared jacket with silver-and-lapis buttons, dazzling white blouse, ostrich-skin pumps. Even with a light dew of fear-sweat along her upper lip . . . Young, not more than twenty, small and slender-built, long limbs and long neck, trim-figured, with an oval face that hovered somewhere between prettiness and beauty; the hair *was* beautiful, abundant and coal-black and softly curled. Her features looked European but the skin was darker than Italian or even Gypsy, a milk-chocolate color. The serf identity-tattoo stood out bright orange against that brown, below her right ear.

A trusted servant, though, Marya thought. *Be careful.*

"That was brave," she said.

Yasmin rose again to pace nervously, making an odd rapid up-and-down gesture with her hands and forearms. "Oooo, somtimes I gets so"—she stamped one slender foot—"so . . . so *angry.* Some people! Some people!" She shivered suddenly. "They woulda whupped him iffn he'd hit me, but my face'd still be . . . some people, I swears, give 'em a stick and they acts worse'n Draka, like they was Jesus an' Allah an' the masters' dead gods all put together." She sighed and laughed, relaxing. "Plantation life gets dull, sometimes, but they's a good deal to be said fo' stayin' where everybody knows we. Doan' worry, we home soon an' yo' ain' gonna see no green coats fo' a year at a time."

"Yasmin?" The girl looked up at Marya's voice. "Is that an Arab name?"

"Mm-hm," she nodded. "My momma, she Arab. Druze, really, but that no-mattah; a new-caught, like yo'uns. I's house-born, though; on Evendim. That Mistis Tanya's poppa's plantation, it near Baalbeck." Seeing their blank looks, she continued: "Syria Province; I'll show you on a map, sometimes. Cain yo'uns read?"

Chantal bristled, then relaxed.

"Can you?" she said, then flushed with embarrassment. "Sorry, Yasmin," she muttered.

Marya stepped in hastily. "You're a house-servant, then?"

Yasmin's brows rose. "Does I look like a field-hand?" she said dryly. "I's Mistis Tanya's dresser. Dress*maker*, that is, in charge of all her clothes." A sigh. "Back on the old place, that is. Here I's in charge of a dozen Frenchie wenches 'n bucks, an' you'd think they *craves* whuppin', what with whinin' and work-dodgin' and carryin' on." She sighed again and shook her head. "It goin' age me befo' my time. Hopes y'all has more sense." Brightly: "Well, what do y'all say to a nice hot showah, 'n then we'll get you somethin' to wear? Y'feel bettah clean an' with coverin'."

Marya's eyes met Chantal's in sudden wordless understanding. Cleanliness in the cellblock had meant being hosed-down with cold water under pressure.

Hot water, she thought with a wave of longing.

"Jes fo' now," Yasmin said cheerfully, fitting the light padded handcuffs to their wrists. Therese shrank back with a sound of protest; the dark girl immediately laid the cuffs down and sat beside her, laying an arm around her shoulders.

"It's all right, Therese," she said, in her accented French. "S'all right, really. Just for the rules, understand; just for a little while. I'm here, nobody will hurt you . . ." Coaxing, she stroked the younger girl's arm until it relaxed, then slid the metal circlet around the wrist. "See? It don't hurt . . ."

Chantal jerked her hands apart to the full twenty-centimeter length of the chain, ignoring the pain in wrists still bruised by the over-tight restraints, and again. The serf-girl frowned, concern on her face; Marya stepped close and shook the Frenchwoman by the shoulder.

"Chantal! Save your energy for something useful, and your anger. See to your sister, she needs you."

The communist took a deep breath and turned to Therese, who sat wide-eyed and on the verge of tears again, shrinking from her sister's tension. They were in the dealer's fitting-room, space leased from the Security Directorate by a labor agency and used to process serfs bought out of Central Detention into private ownership; racks of clothes and undergarments and shoes . . . Yasmin had sneered at the quality, but the drab-colored skirt and jacket, blouse and head-scarf and flat-soled brogans felt solid and warm. Good-quality cotton and wool and leather, with metal snaps and fasteners; better than had been available to ordinary people in Europe since before the War started. Marya smoothed her hair back and tied the scarf tightly; there was ample slack in the handcuffs for that if she was careful. It was a relief to have her hair covered again; the full habit of her Order was a physical impossibility, but even this little felt good.

"You've been very kind," she said, fighting down a sudden irrational surge of optimism and vague friendliness; that was merely the effect of comfort, clothing and privacy and the remembered benevolence of hot water cleansing her skin. As to Yasmin . . . Marya reminded herself that her confessor had always chided her for an excessive fondness for beautiful things; not to possess them—the vow of poverty had never been a burden to her (she crossed herself)—but to simply know them. The vestments of the mass, the great Baroque churches of Lwow and Cracow, the plainsong, the crystalline symmetry of a mathematical solution . . .

All good things are good as they reflect God, she reminded herself. Nothing was evil in itself, only as it turned away from the Source of all good; evil was a negative quality, an absence rather than a presence. *I must see the Divine in every thing and person,* she reflected; then she could love God through them. To love any thing for itself was to erect an idol, and destroy the good one saw in it.

" 'T ain't nothing," Yasmin said. " 'Sides, I's not like some I could name, what thinks climbin' the ladder's an excuse to kick down at those below." She frowned. "I's come to all this kinda young, on account this bein' new-taken land, an' they needin' us born-serfs so bad, but bein' one of the upper-servants is a heavy load 'n serious respons'bility." The clear black eyes met hers. " 'Specially here. Tings . . . ." she hesitated. "Tings doan' have to be as bad as they can be, understand me? We born-serfs, we understand hows to make it as best as may be; these-here new-caughts, they-uns like pups, doan' understand nothin', 'bout hows to live together or how to live with the Mastahs. Now, if yo'n goan' be bookkeeper, that a respons'ble po—" The door swung open.

She swung smoothly to her feet, bowing with finger-tips to forehead. Tanya von Shrakenberg leaned her head through the fitting-room door, smiled at Yasmin, ran her eyes over the others as they repeated the servant's bow more clumsily.

"Here," she said, tossing something underhand at Marya's head, turning and leaving without another word.

The nun snatched it out of the air, found herself gripping the scrap-wood crucifix and rosary. Remembered working on it after lights-out under her blanket, carefully, by feel, month after month. Not that it was forbidden, except that everything was forbidden that was not compulsory, in Central Detention. She had named each bead to herself, a private remembrance of

her Sisters. The Order of St. Cyril had not been large
or wealthy, but it had taught children and cared for the
sick and given so many bright and pious girls a window
on the life of the mind . . .

One. Mother Superior Jadwiga. Old enough to remember teaching secret classes in Polish in Poznan, in
Bismarck's time. She had stopped once to show a novice named Marya how to bunch the skirt of her habit
under her knees when scrubbing floors.

1939, when the Bolsheviki divided Poland with Hitler. The day in the little village in Malopolska, mist and
gray mud and the hating eyes of the Ukrainian villagers
who had betrayed them to the Red cavalry. Mother
Superior had told the Sisters to forgive them, they were
simple peasants and had no reason to love Poles, who had
forbidden their language and Orthodox church, which was
a heresy but must be combated with truth, not guns—

"*Spit!*" the Soviet officer had said to the Mother
Superior. "Spit on the cross!"

Marya remembered the thin pockmarked face, cap
with the red star above. Torn mustard-yellow uniform,
a smell of old sweat and cheap perfume, a Russian
smell. Gaping dull faces of the soldiers, and the long
triangular bayonets on their rifles glinting in the rain.
His hand slapped the Mother Superior's head back,
forth; the wimple of her habit came lose, exposing her
cropped gray hair; there was blood on her cheeks, but
she signed herself; he struck again and again, until she
fell and crawled to kiss the carved rood they had carried
from the abbey in Lwow, embracing it where it lay in
the slick churned-up clay and sheepdung of the street.
The officer stepped back, signing to one of his men; the
Cossack grinned, heeled his shaggy pony forward, drew
the long guardless saber and leaned far over.

The honed steel glimmered wetly, a shimmering arc
that ended in flesh . . .

Two. Sister Kazimiera. Slight and nervous and dark,
a lawyer's daughter from Znin, always ill with something.

1941, in German-occupied Mazovia, north of War-

saw; Modlin, that was the name of the town. Some of
the Sisters had objected to hiding the Jewish children,
in the root-cellar below the stable that was their only
shelter; there were Christian youngsters whose need
was almost as great. Sister Kazimiera had looked at
them and quoted, *"Insofar as ye do it unto the least of
these my little ones . . ."*

Marya remembered the bored impassive faces of the
SS *Einsatzkommandos* as they hammered with boots
and rifle-butts on the floors and walls, thrust bayonets
into the heaps of straw and bedding. The nuns had
gone down on their knees and begun to pray. Marya
remembered fighting a sneeze as ancient hay-dust flew
up from the boards of the walkway; it was an old stable,
brick and battered wooden stalls and bright sunlight
streaming through small broken windows and the cracks
in the doors.

All of them kneeling, except Sister Kazimiera in the
cellar, keeping the children quiet. But there were a
dozen of them, some only five or six years old; they
must have heard the shouting in German and been
frightened. One cried, a thin reedy sound through the
boards, then the others. The *Rottenführer* had laughed,
going down on one knee and probing amid the straw
and dirt for the lifting-ring of the trapdoor. Marya had
screamed as he lifted it and pulled the stick-grenade
from his belt, and he had laughed again with the
Schmeisser bouncing against his chest as she lunged
forward and froze with a trooper's bayonet before her
face. Then more of the nuns were shrieking, as the
heavy timber of the trapdoor lifted and the sound of the
children weeping came louder; Marya could see them,
thin black-clad bodies and sidelocks and yarmulkes, the
girls' kerchiefs, the huge staring eyes. Sister Kazimiera's
were closed as she crouched protectively over them;
the SS-man yanked the tab on the grenade, tossed it in
and let the door drop . . .

Marya squeezed the wood of her rosary until her
nails showed white.

Three. Sister Zofia. Fat, so long as they had any food at all. A peasant's daughter, her father had beaten her when she claimed a vocation until the village priest shamed him with valuing a pair of hands more than God's will.

1944. Marya and the others had been looking north, toward Brussels, when it happened. A high whistling in the sky: one of the new reaction-jet airplanes, a thin thread of contrail against the aching blue of a morning sky. Draka; there were almost no European aircraft left. A flash of . . . not fire; light, intolerable, brighter than the sun, a single moment of light so intense that the shadow of a single leaf before the face could be *felt* against the skin. Then hot darkness, absolute, not even the flickers that come beneath closed lids.

Blind, she had thought. *I am blind.* The earth shook, rose up and struck her amid a noise like the laughter of Satan, louder than the world's ending, and the heat; there were screams, and the sound of buildings breaking. Sister Zofia had been inside; she pushed her way out of the rubble and stood looking at the mushroom cloud climbing above the horizon like the wrath of the angry God who turned His eyes on Sodom; had led them stumbling in a line to the intact cellar and sealed it, and bandaged their eyes, and nursed them through the weeks that followed, and gone out to find sealed food and water. Nursed them through the fever and the bleeding gums and the falling-out of hair, and had said when they heard her vomiting in a corner that it was bad food. Marya's eyes had recovered first; the vision was blurry but she had been glad of that, it would have been unbearable to vomit herself at what Sister Zofia's face had become, or shrink from the oozing, ulcerated hands that had saved her life. God had been good; Sister Zofia died quickly, with none of the raving that brain lesions brought to some of the others. Her dosage had been too extreme.

Marya's mind skittered sideways, the focus of remembrance darting away as the hand does from a fire, instinctively. *"No,"* she whispered fiercely, in Polish. "No, I *will* remember. I will remember all of you; always, I will remember."

There were sixty beads, a name for each. She would keep this, or if it was taken from her make another, but nothing could take the memories, and if she was the last of the Sisters of St. Cyril she would keep the Rule. Marya looked down at the scrap of wood and string: a poor thing, the cruxifix and the three greater and lesser beads, the ten sets of five with their dividers, each a mnemonic to a series of meditations . . . and there was a name for each now; perhaps that was bad doctrine, perhaps a sin, but she did not think so. And it was something not issued to Marya 73ES422, it was something of her own.

You do not need a rosary or cross to be near to God, she reminded herself severely as the breath caught in her throat and she stuffed the thing of wood and string into the pocket of her skirt. They walked out behind Yasmin, behind Tanya and the beautiful evil-eyed child in the silk dress, through the outer rooms of the shop that sold people, into the corridors of Central Detention. The guards and clerks looked at her differently. As if they *saw* her now, as if the clothes and the company of the Draka made all the difference, and she had been invisible naked. Part of the process, she judged; strip everything away, then give it back in another pattern. Clothes were part of it, symbolism, psychology, the vulnerability of nakedness; the Draka were *descended* from people with a Christian sense of modesty, even if they were as shameless as rutting dogs themselves.

I am afraid, she thought, as they came out into a courtyard. The rain had stopped, and the clouds were breaking up; the courtyard had been a road, the walls that closed it off on three sides were new concrete block topped with razor wire; the gate was tall panels of perforated steel. There was a work-group sweeping rain and mud into the gutters; the Draka loved neatness, puddles offended them. Gray-faced men in burlap sacks, their feet in wooden clogs. The serf foreman had turned to see the party of Citizens and their servants leave the buildings; he bowed, turned back and swung the long whip at one of the gang who had lagged a little. The whip did not crack, instead the air whistled as it passed and there was a flat smacking sound across the backs of the man's thighs. It hummed again in a whirring circle too fast to see, like a propeller, struck.

They passed the gang, the *scrutch-scrutch* of the straw brooms on the cracked and broken asphalt, and the sound of a man sobbing. The air was warmer, smelling a little of spring and more of wet pavement and motor fuel. There were two cars and a truck with a torn canvas tilt parked by the gate, the draft-fans of their boilers making a gentle hissing. The truck was an Opel of German army make; a coffle of serfs in neck-collars linked to a central chain waited by it, twenty or so. Mostly men, working-class Lyonnaise by their looks, with the dulled skin of people who have not eaten properly in years, dressed in new drab issue-clothing of the same sort she was wearing.

The two cars were large six-wheelers with sides of stamped steel panels colored olive-drab. Marya had always been interested in machinery; in the abbey in Lwow she had been the one who could fix the boiler and the balky electrical system, and later in the War years that had been more than useful, it had meant survival. Now she recognized the type from newspaper photos, from know-the-enemy articles in copies of *Signaal*, the German soldiers' magazine. Two-ton Draka staff utility vehicles, civilianized with hard roofs and windows. Not *very* civilian; one of them had a heavy machine-gun pintle-mounted on a hatch in the middle of the roof.

Two Draka waited by the lead car, a man and a woman in soft black leather trousers and armless cotton singlets, passing the time throwing a heavy medicine-ball back and forth. They had the Draka look, long swelling muscle moving under skin with no padding of fat, blurring-quick speed and a bouncy, tensile physical presence. The man threw, pirouetting like a dancer, the heavy shot-filled leather sack arching across the five-meter distance; the woman leaped, caught it two-handed close to her stomach with an audible *smack* and a grunt, front-flipped in place, a complete forward somersault, landed on her feet and flowed smoothly down into a crouch, coming erect and flinging the ball high. Involuntarily the nun's eyes followed it, a long parabolic curve, a breathless moment hanging where inertia balanced gravity. It fell, a slow instant stretching down into a straight-line drop that went neatly through the roof-hatch of the first car to land with an unseen hollow *tunk* on the floor within.

I am afraid, ran through her again, as the two looked at her and Chantal and Therese. The sensations were familiar, dry mouth and nausea and a lightness behind the eyes. Hard tanned Draka faces, one thin and freckled, one broad and flattish; cold light eyes examining her. Not with hostility, not even the deadly indifference of the Security officer who had arrested her those six long months ago. She was a servant, not an enemy; they were looking at her and wondering whether she would work well or badly, how much trouble she would be to direct.

Odwaga, she thought: courage, in her own language. I am afraid but I will not show it. I am a Pole, we are a small people and poor and backward, we have no frontiers and everyone on earth has taken it in turn to crush us but even when we must hitch ourselves to the plough so that our men may ride the horse to fight tanks we have never lacked *odwaga*. Common sense, yes; luck, yes, but never courage. I am a Pole and a religious and a Sister of the Order of St. Cyril and these I will be until I die, and if this is the sin of pride I cannot ask God's forgiveness because I do not repent it.

Perhaps there would be a priest, though, wherever they were going. It would be good to confess again, and receive the sacraments.

*   *   *

Chantal Lefarge looked away from the Draka. Her eyes fell on the green-uniformed Order Police by the gate, caught the glitter of the chain-slung gorgets around their necks; she turned away, shaking as her mind turned back the months, her mouth dry, hearing—

"*Hold her, Achmed.*" Therese screaming through the muffling of her dress that the *Orpos* had pulled up over her head, thin rabbit-shrieking, running blindly into the wall, dress a blot of dark in the night-dim alley and her body thin and white. The monitor rose staggering with blood running down his brown acne-scarred cheeks and turned to face Chantal; he had ignored her while he stripped her sister and pushed her down. They had all ignored her; she could wait her turn. Ignored her until she picked up the rock, raised it high.

The fist struck her and filled her mouth with the taste of salt. Again, and the world blurred.

Jean-Paul had said that leaflets were essential, to show the workers that the Party still existed. In Lyon the Party was Jean-Paul, who had been a minor cell-leader before the war, and a dozen others. More had survived the war and the Gestapo, but the Draka found them somehow; impaled them all; Jean-Paul said he was still getting orders from Paris, but she had seen him once writing the letters from "headquarters" himself, sitting alone with the papers and a bottle of absinthe, writing and drinking and weeping slow tears. She had backed out silently and said nothing.

The serf policeman stepped closer and rammed his fist into her again, into the belly, and she doubled over with an anguished *whoof* of air, silver dazzles before her eyes, weakness like water running through her arms and legs. A foot kicked her behind the leg and she was down on hands and knees on the garbage-slimed cobbles of the alley. One of them squatted and ripped open her blouse, grabbed at her breasts and squeezed first one and then the other; a milking gesture, saying that she was nothing, a cow. Another knelt behind her and hit her again, a hard ringing cuff to the back of her head. Threw up her skirts and tore her underwear down one seam and let it fall along that thigh. Night air cold on her buttocks, raising gooseflesh.

"Changed my mind, Achmed, yo' kin have that othah little thing," the voice said. Hands gripping her hips, another pain through the dazzle. Then—

No. She shivered back to the present. The coffle were looking at her and the nun. Marya was a good sort despite her absurd superstitions and that air of passive meekness . . . Most of the coffle were just staring, dazed; some with curiosity, others with a sullen burning hostility broad enough to lap over from the Draka onto her and anyone standing near them, all overlaid with a heavy numb fear. Those were her people, she had grown up among them in the shrilling garlic-smelling brick tenements between the two rivers, ancient noisy factories and little frowsty shops and cafes . . . the run-down overcrowded schools which taught her nothing but reading and writing and how to be an obedient drudge for the rich, the Party libraries that had opened a world.

The Draka woman was walking forward; the two who had waited by the car as well, shrugging on jackets of the same soft black leather as their trousers, buckling on gunbelts, slinging assault rifles and the machete-like bushknives; the long whips they swung in their hands. Blacksnake whips, *sjamboks* they called them, tapering cylinders of rhino-hide that could touch lightly in the hands of an artist, touch the corner of the mouth or an eyelid or the groin, or slice a back to the bone; the lashes trailed on the wet pavement, the metal tips making dull chinking sounds on the cracks. The coffle struggled to their feet, bowed, jostling one another in their clumsiness. Chantal watched and felt a taste at the back of her throat, sour, like vomitus after too much cheap Languedoc red wine; it was odd that hatred had a physical taste. The sjamboks cracked suddenly, a volley like gunshots; birds flew up protesting from the walls of the couryard, and a fine mist blew from the wet leather.

"Good." The Draka woman speaking, French this time; nodding as she saw the eyes fix on her. "It is too early for the whip, serfs." A thumb directed towards herself. "I am Mistis Tanya von Shrakenberg; my husband and I are your new owners." She paused.

"You are stonemasons, builders, electricians; we have bought you for our estate, because we need more skilled labor. You will serve me all your days, and your children will serve mine. This is your fate; accept it." A smile. "Pray to your God for rewards in the afterlife, or hope the Yankees will come and rescue you, as you please . . . but on this earth, and in this time, obey.

"You've all been here long enough to learn a little about the Draka; I'll add to it. Think on the fact that we have never lost a war, or given up an inch of earth once we possessed it."

Another pause, and she rested her hands on her hips. "Now, being plantation serfs is about the best thing that could happen to you all, here in the Domination; you've got the added advantage of belonging to the von Shrakenbergs, who do not believe in unnecessary cruelty to underlings." Another smile, this one like a shark's. "*Unnecessary*. You will work, and work well; don't delude yourself that you can play stupid, shirk, break tools, make 'mistakes'; we've seen every one of those tricks a thousand times. Work well, bow your heads in meekness, obey every order as if it were the word of God, without resistance open or secret, and you can live out your lives; you'll have cottages of your own, not factory-compound barracks; permission to marry and raise families; good food, medical care, clothes, even an occasional holiday. Try any stupidity with us"—she shrugged—"and you can spend the rest of your days working in a chain hobble, with your dried balls in a sack around your tongueless head. Do anything *really* stupid, and you'll die on the stake."

"You have a chance," she concluded. "Use it."

Oh, I will, Chantal thought fiercely. *I will, Mistress.*

* * *

Tanya turned her back as the overseers chivied the coffle into the truck; there was a creaking of springs, a metallic clatter as the ends of their chain were reeved through stout eyebolts and padlocked closed. It was difficult, dealing with Europeans. They certainly had weaker stomachs than born-serfs; you could terrify them with even the mildest physical punishment; on the other hand, anything could set them off, something as routine as a cuff over the ear. She shook her head. Then there were others who just collapsed completely, more totally pliable than any but the best house-bred servants in the Police Zone.

Strange, she thought as she walked toward Yasmin. The three local wenches were shaping up nicely; the dresser had them in hand, she was a steady and reliable one, young as she was. Tanya wished there were more like her available, but then, demand was high; millions from the old territories were being drafted in for supervisory work, and even so . . .

Hope these two work out, she thought wearily, studying Chantal and Marya; bookkeeping was a high-status occupation, usually reserved for house-reared serfs or the products of the training creches. She shifted her gaze to Therese; slim, not over fourteen, huddled close to her sister and flinching at every moving shadow or loud noise. Sick dread in the huge fawn-like eyes whenever they strayed to the green-clad *Orpos* at the gate. *Pity about that*, Tanya thought. *Wasteful*. Elite serfs had to have their privileges, of course, and there were good reasons for making the Order Police an object of fear. Gentle ones rarely volunteered for the green coat, but there should be some sort of age restriction on this type of thing. Her father had had a strict rule that no wench was to be touched before her sixteenth birthday, and there was a good deal to be said for that.

"Good work, Yasmin," Tanya said, running a critical eye over Marya and the Frenchwomen. "No trouble?"

"No, Mistis. 'Cept that-there greencoat who brought

Therese up from th' cells. I had a few words wit' him, he bein' rough." A sniff. "They pigs, beggin' yo' pahdon, Mistis."

"No argument, Yasmin," Tanya said. The serf-girl glanced about, leaned closer.

"Ah, Mistis, 'bout Therese, might be good idea, iff'n—"

Tanya nodded. "Already gave the orders." A sigh. "There are times when I wish I were still in uniform," she said.

Yasmin smiled, with a small chuckle. "Not what yo's sayin' right after the War, Mistis, when yo's come home." A sly glance from under demurely lowered lashes.

"Hmmmm, true enough, too busy celebratin'."

She rubbed her back; they had managed to get a competent home-trained masseur for Chateau Retour, thank the gods. "The thing is"—she nodded to the little three-vehicle caravan—"it was easier. Officer has to think fast under pressure, time to time, but mostly war isn't a very complicated business; there's a sort of . . . brutal simplicity to it. Limited number of situations, an' a limited selection of responses; the people on y'r own side are a known quantity, an' all you have to know about the opposition is how they fight. That's one reason command don't require genius, just trainin' and willpower." She shook her head. "Anyways, get these three loaded in the rear car, should be room. Tell the driver standard convoy distancin', and *no* tailgaitin'."

Her gaze turned towards the airship haven; Andrew's flight would be leaving that afternoon; officers returning from leave did not rate heavier-than-air transport priorities. *At least I'm not heading into a combat zone*, she thought. *Luck go with you into the north, brother*.

CHAPTER FIVE

DATE: 11/06/47

FROM: Strategic Planning Board
        Supreme GHQ
        Castle Tarleton, Archona

TO: Merarch Andrew von Shrakenberg
        District III, East Baltic Command

RE: Inspection 16/06/47

        Please to be informed that the Strategic Plan-
        ning Board anticipates a senior officer will be
        visiting your sector as part of our general
        survey of conditions in the European territo-
        ries. No ceremonial will be necessary.

        Service to the State!

DATE: 12/06/47

FROM: Merarch Andrew von Shrakenberg
        District III, East Baltic Command

TO: Strategos Demitria Angelstem
        East Baltic Command GHQ
        Riga, Aestii Province

RE: Inspection 16/06/47

             Look, Dema, I've got better things to do than
             shepherd visiting inkosisanas about. In fact, I
             think we've finally got a handle on Saarinen's
             gang, who've been causing no end of trouble.
             Can't you send them over to van der Merwe in
             District V? The bitch deserves an inspection!

             Service to the State!

DATE: 13/06/47

FROM: Strategos Demitria Angelstem
             East Baltic Command GHQ
             Riga, Aestii Province

TO: Merarch Andrew von Shrakenberg
             District III, East Baltic Command

RE: Inspection 16/06/47

             Sorry, youngling, but they asked for you spe-
             cifically. More of your Friends in High Places, I
             suspect ... although GHQ is unhappy about
             Finland. (Who isn't? After it's pacified, we'll
             finally have something to say to those old farts
             who keep muttering about how everything is a
             picnic compared to Afghanistan.) Bite the bullet.

             Glory to the Race!

             as quoted in:
             The von Shrakenbergs: Two Centuries of Service
             By Strategos Asa Meldrin (ret.)
             New Territories Press, Vienna, 1983

CENTRAL FINLAND, 22,000 FEET
NEAR FIREBASE ALPHA
2ND MERARCHY, XIX JANISSARY LEGION
DISTRICT 3, EAST BALTIC COMMAND
JUNE 16, 1947

Strategos Sannie van Reenan glanced down through the porthole at her elbow as the transport's engines changed their droning note, signaling descent. Sound-proofing could only do so much, and after a while the vibration became like your heartbeat; not something you heard consciously, but a change was instantly apparent. The smudged glass of the window showed the same endless dark-green coniferous forest they had been flying over since Moscow, hours ago, but the lakes and rivers had been growing steadily more numerous. Cultivated fields, too, or the weed-grown spaces that *had* been fields, before the Draka came. Yawning, she rubbed at her face; she had worked and catnapped through the night, cleaning up details of her notes from the Ukrainian and Russian sectors. She made a slight face.

"I hope this is a little less grim," she said to her aide.

He looked up from a file folder on the table between their recliner seats, closing it neatly and tapping it between palms to align the contents. The interior of the transport was fitted as an office with microfiche racks, files, copier and a hot-plate; bunks could be folded down from the walls. The aide signed for coffee and one of the serf auxiliaries brought the pot; he gave her a smile and thanks before she returned to her typewriter and the headphones of the dictorec machine. These were skilled specialists, part of a team that had worked together for years, not to be spoiled by mistreatment.

"Well, from the sitreps and digests, near-like as bad, even if the reasons are different."

His superior yawned again, patting her mouth with the back of her hand. She was a small woman with an air of well-kept middle age, neatly made, trim despite twenty hours without change of uniform. Looking very much what she was, an Archona-born career Intelligence officer of an old professorial family.

"Reasons give mere fact human significance, Ivar," she said. "Russia left a bad taste in m'mouth, to be frank."

The aide shrugged. "We underestimated the Germans," he said; his voice had the precise, rather hard-edged accent of Alexandria and the Egyptian province. "It took a year longer to muscle them back into Central Europe than we anticipated." Another shrug. "We couldn't be expected to spare transport to feed the cities, now could we?" North Russia's industrial centers had been fed from the Ukraine, before the war, and the black-earth zone yielded little grain while the Domination's armies fought their way west across burning fields.

"Hmmmm. Necessary, I know." It was an old precept of Draka ethics that to desire the goal was to approve the means needed to achieve it. "Still, technically, they were Draka cattle as soon as the Fritz pulled out. For all we know, good cattle, obedient an' unresistin'. We made a mistake, thirty million of them died for it."

Her finger flicked open a report. "'With regard to MilRef 7:20a, demographic projections indicate nonpositive . . .' Sweet soul of the White Christ, an' to think I once had pretensions to a passable prose style. Why not 'they're all dead'?" she muttered. "Must be some internal dynamic a' large organizations." To her assistant: "Not to mention the waste a' skilled labor; those that didn't eat each other are too demoralized t' do much good."

"Well, at least the bloody survivors aren't giving us much partisan trouble."

She shrugged in her turn. "Patchwork way of doin' things, Ivar: serfs're supposed to get an implicit promise of work, bread an' protection in return for submission, yo' know. Despair's as like to produce rebellion as obedience, in the long run; let 'em think we're like to slaughter whole populations just 'cause they're inconvenient . . . That famine may be savin' trouble now and causin' us problems for two generations. Patchwork, short-term way a' doin' things."

Sannie closed her eyes, touched fingertips to the lids. "Sometimes I get to feelin' we don't do anything else but, run around all our lives thinkin' up short-term solutions t' problems created by the *last* set of short-term . . . Nevah mind."

Ivar took another sip of his coffee, then chuckled. "One humorous aspect, though, dear Chief." At her raised brow he continued: "Well, most of the machinery is intact, now that transport and power are functional again. We're drafting in industrial labor in job-lots, besides landworkers. And where are they coming from?" he asked rhetorically. "Germany, mostly. They started the war for *Lebensraum*, living room, and now they're certainly getting it."

Strategos van Reenan smiled dutifully before returning her attention to the porthole . . . It *was* an irony. Also Ivar was bright and capable, possibly even a successor on that distant but eagerly-awaited day when she retired. *I'll be glad to get back to the capital*, she thought.

For a moment homesickness squeezed her with a sudden fierce longing. Archona: the time-mellowed marble colonnades of the University, gardens, fountains, broad quiet streets, cleanliness and order. *Damnation, I could be sitting under a pergola at the Amphitheater*. An original Gerraldson concerto this week, his new Fireborne Resurrection opus . . . or visiting the galleries, or her nieces and nephews. Gardening in the half-hectare about the house that had been her parents', or just sitting with a good book and Mamba curled purring in her lap.

Enough, she told herself. Work to be done, and not all of it could be accomplished from a desk in Castle Tarleton. The Eurasian War had left the Domination doubled in size, tripled in population; civil administration, economics, military, all the decision-making branches had critical choices to make by the score, all of them needed information. Not raw data, Archona was innundated with it; they needed *knowledge* more than facts, and knowledge had to proceed from understanding. *We are so few, so few,* went through her, with weariness and fear. *So few, and so much to be done.* The State to be safeguarded, built up, made more efficient, wealthy, powerful. Not as an end in itself, but because it was the instrument of the Race, people and blood and her own descendants.

Still, it would be good to be home. *I'm tired of it,* she realized. Tired of mud and flies and filth, the shattered empty cities. Memories flitted by. Goblin-faced children tearing the rotting meat from a dead horse, not even looking up as the cars splashed them in passing. Janissaries kicking heaps of black bread from a moving flatbed, laughing at the struggling piles of bodies that tore at each other for the loaves; there was enough, more than enough for all, but not much resembling a human mind left in the survivors. The peculiar wet stink of cholera, bodies piled high on the steamtrucks; rag-clad stick figures lining up for inoculation and neck-numbering, staring at her with dull apathy and a sick, brutalized hatred.

Yes, it will be very good to be home. All the nonexistent gods know we're not a squeamish people, but this is getting beyond enough. Sannie sighed. One day there would be an end to it. When all the world was under the Yoke, peaceful; when the Race no longer had to forge each individual into a weapon, or squeeze their underlings so hard for the means of war, and long-tamed peoples gave no cause for fear and the cruelty it made necessary. Then they could rest; scholarship, beauty, simple pleasure, all could become more than something to be fitted into the spare moments . . . She forced herself back to the present; that good day would not come in her lifetime, or her grandchildren's. In the meantime, each day was a brick in the final edifice.

"These Finns are an *immediate* problem, though,"
Ivar was saying. "The number of troops tied down here
is ridiculous, considerin' the relative importance."

"That it is, Ivar," she answered. Below, something
winked from beneath a stretch of trees. *Quartz*, she
thought idly. *Tin can, shell fragment.* Flying was a
humbling experience. In an office in Castle Tarleton,
you dealt with maps, reports, photographs; the accumu-
lated knowledge of centuries at your fingertips, an unmatched research staff, electronic tendrils reaching out
over half the earth. The illusion of control came easily,
there. Out here, flying hour after hour above the living
earth, you realized how *big* it was, how various, how
unknowable.

"Aircraft. Down, everybody *down*."

Kustaa froze in place, crouching, with the other members of the guerrilla patrol that was threading its way
through the forest. The noise swelled overhead, coming
from the south, their own direction. Two planes; not
fighters or strike-aircraft, too high, wrong noise . . .
medium bombers or transports. Ten thousand feet and
coming down.

Ahead of him one of the guerrillas rolled over on her
back and unshipped a pair of binoculars. That was a
risk, although a slight one. There was a pine-seedling not
far from his nose, growing canted beside a cracked slab
of granite rock. The brown duff of needles and branches
was damp beneath his hands and knees, sparsely starred
with small blue flowers and coarse grass. An ant crawled
over the back of his hand, tickling; the air smelled
coolly of resin, wet spruce needles. Wind soughed
through the high branches above, louder than the throb
of engines. Light swayed over the patchwork camouflage clothing of his companions, dapple and flicker . . .

It was unbearably like home. Almost, this might be a
hunting trip with Dad back in the '30's, up in the woods
north of town. Or that time right after the War, when
he and Aino had visited home; everyone sitting down to

Mom's blueberry pancakes, then Dad and Sam and he driving out to the lake and canoeing down the Milderak, finding a good spot under the lee of Desireaux Island and throwing their lines out on water so clear you could see the pike gliding by like river wolves twenty feet below.

No, it isn't like home, he thought wryly. *Home is like this*. Which was why so many Suomaliset had settled there around Duluth and the upper Lakes; it reminded them of the home they had been driven by hunger to leave, let them make a living in the ways they were used to. Lake sailors, lumberjacks, miners, hardscrabble back-clearing farmers.

The woman ahead of him lowered her captured Draka binoculars. "Light transports," she said. "Heading into the snake base."

Circling, the aircraft made their approach to Firebase Alpha. It was laid out in a double star pattern, to give overlapping fields of fire on the perimeter; that was standard. The doubled number of heavy machine-gun nests were not. Nor were the dug-in antiaircraft tanks, the snouts of their six-barreled gatling cannon pointing outward. Sannie's eyes flickered, taking in other details; two batteries of heavy automortars in gun-pits near the center of the base, with top-covers improvised from welded steel sheet; everything underground except the vehicles, and those in sandbagged revetments.

"Well," The Staff officer's aide said again as they banked and began the steep final descent to the pierced-steel surface of the airstrip. "This *is* a bit out of the ordinary. Firepower, eh?"

The Strategos smiled. "If Andrew's put all this in, I'm sure it's necessary. He was always a boy to take pains."

"Yo've known him a fair bit?"

"Unofficial aunt," she replied, sliding the Russian reports into the wire-rack holder by her elbow for the clerical staff to re-file.

"Not one of the Oakenwald von Shrakenbergs, is he?"

Sannie shook her head. Ivar was Alexandria-born, city-bred, and he had spent most of his service in the outer provinces. Nothing wrong with that, of course, that was where the work was, but it was time for him to learn the social background, if he was to operate out of Castle Tarleton. The elite military aristocracy of the Domination were a close-knit group; new names came in on merit but the old ones tended to recur generation after generation.

"No, younger branch. Yo' met Karl an' his son Eric at the reception on Oakenwald, last January, remembah? Andrew's the second son of Everard, Karl's younger brothah; Everard mustered out back in the '20s', took up a land-grant in Syria, near Baalbeck. He's got a sister, cohortarch in th' Guard, settled down in France, near Tours. Married to a fourth cousin from Nova Cartago, near Hammamet . . . complex, isn't it?" A pause. "Used to meet Andrew a good deal, when he was down south visitin'. Good boy, bit too serious. Smart, but quiet about it."

The command bunker was three meters down: sand-bags for the walls and floor, the ceiling layers of pine-logs, earth, and salvaged railway iron. Radios and teleprinters were lined along the walls; short corridors with switchbacks to deflect blast led to other chambers. It was morning, but there was no light here except the overheads, little sound but the click and hum of equipment, the sough of ventilators. It smelled of damp earth, raw timber, leather and metal and oil, faintly of ozone; in the center was a map of the surrounding area, cobbled together from aerial photograps and scrawled with symbols and arrows in colored greasepaints. The officers around it had talked themselves silent; now they were thinking.

The map was of central Finland, their Legion's area of responsibility. Forest, starred with lakes scattered like a drift of coins from a spendthrift's hand, bog, burnt farmhouses and fields going back to brush. Red marks for ambushes; too many of them. Green for counter-ambushes, blue for arms caches and guerrilla bases discovered; far too few.

"Suh?" The word was repeated twice before Merarch Andrew von Shrakenberg looked up from the table. It was one of his Janissary NCO's, Mustapha, the Master Sergeant from Headquarters Century. "Suh, the plane come, radio say five minutes." A reliable man, half-Turk, his father some anonymous Draka passing through a Smyrna comfort station, raised in a training creche. Stocky, hugely muscular, square-faced and green-eyed.

Andrew sighed, returned his salute and stretched. "Take over, Vicki," he said. His second grunted without looking up and continued her perusal of the map. "Corey, we'd bettah see to it. Mustapha, attend."

Corey Hartmann grunted in his turn, throwing down a cigarette and grinding the butt out on the floor of the command bunker. The two officers snapped their assault-rifles from the racks by the exit and pushed past the spring-mounted door, up the rough stairwell and into the communications trench, blinking and adjusting their helmets as they reached surface level. The dank damp-earth smell of the bunker gave way to the dust-bodies-burnt-distillate stink of a working firebase, and under it a hint of the vast pine forests that stretched eastward ten thousand kilometers to Kamchatka and the Pacific.

Four light utility cars waited, amphibious four-seaters with balloon tires; Andrew swung into the second, standing with a hand on the roll-bar, next to the Janissary gunner manning the twinbarrel. It was a fine day, warm for Finland. Warm enough to forget the winter, or nearly. He grimaced at the memory, slitting his eyes in the plume of gritty dust thrown up by the lead vehicle. It was a short ride to the airfield, a simple stretch of pierced steel sheet laid on earth and rock laboriously leveled; the light transport was already making its approach-run.

Twin-Zebra class, he thought. An oblong fuselage, high-winged, two engines, two slender booms holding the tail. He looked for the national blazon; the Domination's crimson dragon, wings outstretched, talons clutching the slave-fetter of mastery and the sword of death. But the shield covering the Snake's midsection was a black checkerboard with a silver roman-numeral II, not the usual green-black-silver sunburst. Supreme General Staff, second section, Strategic Planning. Behind, another dot was circling, another Twin-Zebra. That would be the flunkies, secretaries, comtechs, whatever.

"Well, well," he said. "Staff planes, not Transport Section. A panjandrum indeed." An ordinary Staff inspection would be a fairly junior officer, taking his luck with the transportation pool. There were not many who could command this sort of following.

"Sheee-it. Sir." Corey added.

"Know how y'feel," Andrew replied, with a wry smile. "Still, we always complainin' GHQ gives the Citizen Force more 'n its share of attention, can't nohow complain when they take us at ouah word."

"Outposts here, here, here," Arvid said, sketching with his finger in the dirt. The other half-dozen Finnish officers were folding their maps, giving their notebooks final once-overs before they departed to rebrief their subordinates. There was a ridge of frost-shattered granite between them and the road that speared down from the north and turned west in front of them, enough to give a prone man good cover. The wet earth behind it was an excellent sand-table.

Kustaa watched, aware that much of the information was added for his benefit. Arvid contined: "Marsh through here, and this approach is blocked by the lake; hard for us to get in, but it limits the routes out for their patrols. The main base is out of mortar range for us, so we pepper the outposts now and then; they they chase us, and we can usually count on taking out a few at least. They patrol the roads and sweep the woods at random intervals. Not much contact for the last six months."

"Why?" Kustaa asked, shrugging his shoulder against the prickling itch of the foliage stuck into loops on his borrowed tunic. *I feel like a bloody Christmas tree*, he thought resentfully; they were all in uniforms sewn with loose strips of cloth colored dull-green and brown to break the outlines of their bodies, stuck all over with bits of grass and branch. Very effective for a stationary ambush.

They had stopped well short of the gravel-surfaced road and the cleared zone that extended twenty meters on either side of it. The sun was bright enough to set him blinking after the green-gold twilight of the trees, and the tall grass that had grown up around the stumps waved, spicy-smelling as their feet crushed it, starred with flowering weeds and thistles that clung to their trousers. Nothing remarkable, simply a good two-lane country road through tall pine timber, coming from the north and curving sharply east. There was a whiff of tar—the crushed rock must have been lightly sprayed to lay the dust—but not even the Domination's resources extended to putting a hard surface on every back-country lane.

The squads laying the mines were lifting the rock with swift, careful motions of their trowels and entrenching tools. Hands lowered the heavy round bundles of *plastigue* into the earth as carefully as a mother tucks her child into the cradle. Kustaa watched a woman kneel beside the hole, the hilt of her knife between her teeth as she peeled apart the strands at the end of a reel of wire. Sinewy brown-tanned hands stripped the insulation from the bright copper and twisted the leads to the detonators, pressing the blue-painted rods of fulminate into the soft explosive. Others were unreeling the wire as she worked, trenching the surface of the road and then packing the gravel back in reverse order to keep the darker weathered stones on top; Kustaa could hear the rhythmic tinking of their spade-handles hammering the surface to the proper consistency. The Draka supply convoy was going to get a warm reception.

Good work, he thought. They weren't putting them all in the roadway, either, more along the sides, and homemade directional mines spiked to stumps and concealed by the brush. No trampling that lovely waist-high cover, even though there must be the equivalent of two companies—they'd been joining the march in dribs and drabs. Nobody who didn't absolutely have to be was in view, and those were getting their business done and getting back past the treeline.

"And I'm surprised they don't keep the vegetation down more," he said.

"Not enough manpower," Arvid replied. "Which is the basic reason for the light contact, too. Remember, they're stretched thin, they took thirty million square kilometers in the War. And they're not in any overwhelming hurry; the snakes are like that, long-term thinkers. Cold-blooded."

"Like real snakes," one of the others said with a grimace.

"Finland isn't all that important to them," Arvid continued in a dry, detached tone. "There isn't anything here they need badly enough to make an all-out effort to get. They've swept the civilians out. Just us and the snake military; they're not even trying to run the timbercamps any more. Their aircraft make sure there's no farming going on, and they mostly just wait for us to die, helping when they can. I think the only reason they try to occupy us at all is the resistance we've put up; they're like *that*, too. Aggressive." A sour grin. "Most of our attacks are directed at their supply convoys. Polish hams, Danish butter, French wine . . . it'll be a while before we starve to death."

Kustaa nodded, remembering the storerooms he had seen stacked with cans and boxes, the camouflaged garden plots, nightfishing equipment.

"I think they're afraid, too," the American said. "Right now the Domination's like a lucky gambler, they want to get up from the table with their winnings . . . Sure they're going to send in their air?"

"Oh, yes," a guerilla said. "Policy: they always give a cut-off unit full support. Air strikes, and a rescue column."

Kustaa turned and looked behind him. Two crates of the missiles had come with the guerrillas on this strike. Two units here under camouflage tarpaulins, spidery swivel-mounted tripods with a bicycle-type seat for the gunner, battery clusters, the black-box exotica of the launching system. A pair of rockets for each, one on the rail and a reload, cylinders a little taller than he, a uniform twelve inches through except for the last foot that tapered into a blunt cone. Simple cruciform control fins at the base, and a single nozzle for the rocket; like an illustration for *Thrilling Planet Stories*, the pulp he had hidden folded inside serious reading in his teens. Except that gaunt female guerrilla in faded overalls was nothing like as photogenic as the brass-bra-ed earthwomen who had figured on the garish covers, usually menaced by something with tentacles and a lust for mammalian flesh.

"But I'm up against monsters, sure enough," he whispered to himself.

There were no markings, no serial numbers or manufacturer's stamps anywhere inside the apparatus. Kustaa sneered mentally at the security worldview run amok; as if transistors were something the Finns could cobble together in their bunker hideouts. As if the Fifth Cav hadn't paraded a dozen of them past President Marshall's reviewing-stand on Fifth Avenue last Inauguration Day, with the Draka embassy's military attaché taking notes and snapping pictures. The hastily-trained crews lay beside the missile launchers, going over the manuals again. Well, the mothering things were *supposed* to be soldier-proof—they were designed for infantry use. Skills built into the machinery, anyone who could walk and breathe at the same time capable of operating them.

At that, these old-country Finns had picked up the theory quickly enough, better than a lot of the hill-crackers and ladino peons he'd had to train on much simpler equipment in the Corps during the War . . .

"Ambush in more senses than one," he said to Arvid. The Finn nodded and settled down behind the jagged granite crenel.

"Not long," he replied. "Mines all ready. First action this close to the base since snowmelt, they'll react quickly."

Damn, you never remember how hard the waiting is, Kustaa thought, as silence settled on the stretch of forest. Silence enough for the wind-rustle through branches and occasional birdsong to fill his ears. His mouth was dry; he brought out a stick of chewing gum, stopped himself from tossing the scrap of silvered wrapping paper aside and tucked it neatly in the front pocket of his fatigues. There was no point in giving the Draka an extra clue, it might be important if they made it away clean. *And you never remember how stupid the reasons for volunteering sound in your head, either.*

"God *damn* you, Donovan," he muttered under his breath, sliding the borrowed Finnish rifle through the fissure in the rock before him. Nice sound design, gas-operated semiauto, not much different from the Springfield-7 he'd used in the Pacific except that it had a detachable box clip, and that was an improvement. He'd managed to persuade them to give him a scope-sighted model, too.

"I've given Uncle my share, I'm too old for this shit," he said, continuing the dialogue with his absent superior. "You and that fucking Mick blarney; you could've made a fortune selling suntan oil to Eskimos." Something tiny burrowed up from the grass beneath him and bit him on the stomach; he crushed the insect and rubbed his palm down a pant-leg before tucking the stock of the rifle back against his cheek. It was cool and smooth against beard-stubble grown long enough to be silky.

There was a muffled buzz from above, no louder than a dragonfly humming at arm's-length. A brief flash off plastic and metal and a scout-plane went by overhead toward the south, a twinboomed bubble fuselage on long slender wings with a shrouded pusher engine. Then it banked and turned north again, flying a zigzag pattern less than a hundred feet above the treetops. His stomach felt sour, the same feeling as too much coffee; Kustaa could feel his eyes jumping back and forth across the scene before him, looking for movement with a reflex much stronger than conscious thought.

Hell, I know where they are and can't see them, he told himself. *No way a plane's going to spot anything.*

Sounds echoed back and forth between the trees, motor sounds. Turbocompounds, the Domination's internal-combustion engines of choice for automotive applications. Many, but not really heavy stuff; other noises under that, a vague mechanical hum. This was different from ambushes in Sumatra. The jungle of southeast Asia hid sounds better; the Nips could be right on top of you and walking by before you heard anything. He had always hated having to shoot the pack-mules, the way they screamed. At least there wouldn't be any of that, with a mechanized convoy.

Donovan was wrong, this isn't a job for a veteran, he thought. *This is work for a fucking kid who doesn't believe he can die.* His mind was running through everything that *might* happen. Sergeant Hicks, that was the first casualty he'd ever seen. Hicks'd lived for hours after the bullet went widthwise through his face behind the nose; his eyes had popped out like oysters . . .

They saw the dust-plume before the vehicles, spreading brown-white above the road. Now things were clear, very clear, like the sight-picture that firmed up as you turned the focusing screw of a pair of binoculars. His stomach settled with a last rumble. Then the first Draka warcar was in view, keeping to the right of the road. Light armored car, six-wheeled, a smooth welded oval with a hexagonal turret mounting a heavy machine-gun and grenade launcher; two more behind it, same class, their weapons traversed to alternate sides of the road.

The commanders head-and-shoulders out of the turret hatches: that was good practice, you couldn't see shit buttoned up. He eased his eye forward to the telescopic sight and the first man's head sprang into view. There was not much to be seen, just a line of mouth and square strong hands beneath helmet and dust-goggles. Black hands, black face, a Janissary; a camo uniform, with some sort of shoulder rig for an automatic pistol.

Trucks behind the armored cars, a dozen of them, then three armored personnel carriers; *Peltast* class, eight-wheeled, not the heavy tracked Hoplites the Citizen Force legions used. More trucks, then something military that was hard to make out through dust and engine-induced heat haze. The trucks nagged at him with familiarity . . . yes, German make. *Wehrmacht* Opels, four-ton steamers, but not worn enough to be leftovers from the War. That made sense, it would be easier to keep the production lines going than retool right away, even with the spare-parts problems that would cause. Autosteamers were fairly simple beasts, anyway, low-maintenance. Ten-yard spacing, and they were doing thirty-five miles an hour tops.

The lead car slowed; Kustaa could see the figure in the turret put one hand to his ear, pressing the headset home to improve hearing. The American stiffened, his finger touching delicately down on the smooth curve of his rifle's trigger, resting, waiting.

"Wait," Arvid said. "I think . . ." The whining hum of heavy tires sank into a lower note, punctuated by the popping crunch of gravel spitting sideways under the pressure of ten-ton loads of armor plate.

The whole convoy was slowing, half a kilometer of it, the warcars and APC's first as the radio message reached them and the cargo vehicles responded jerkily. Trucks halted in the center of the roadway, but the escorts wheeled theirs to face the woods, staggered herringbone fashion in alternate directions. The warcars' engines sank to idle, no louder than the thrumming of the

autosteamers' boiler-fans, and there were shouts back
and forth along the line of vehicles.

Arvid swore viciously under his breath in Finnish,
then relaxed as the cab-doors of the trucks opened.
"Rest stop," he muttered. "All the better." He laid a
hand on the Finn waiting with his hand on the plunger
of the detonator box. "Wait for it."

The drivers were climbing down, stretching, walking
to the ditch and opening the flies of their gray overalls to
piss into the ditch; the strong musky odor of urine and
wet earth came clearly across the sixty feet of open
space. Kustaa winced, hoping they would be finished
before the action started. Shooting a man peeing was
like killing him while he picked his nose: the homey
human action made the target too much a person. It
was more comfortable to keep targets as simply shapes
in your mind. You put a shot throught the center of
mass and went on to the next. Targets did not come
back before your eyes while you were sleeping or eating or making love . . .

A file of soldiers came jog-trotting up from the APC's,
dropping off pairs every ten yards; the troopers fanned
out from the road halfway to the trees with their assault-
rifles slung across their chests. One soldier with a cardboard carton over his shoulder walked to unpin the
back flap of the truck closest to Kustaa. He reached up
to help the first of the occupants down, his grin visible
even at this distance.

"Christ, women!" the American blurted in a whisper.

Arvid turned his head fractionally, studied the two
trucks that were shedding passengers. "Whores," he
said flatly. "The snakes rotate twenty or so every two
weeks. Must be busy, there's a thousand men in that
base."

Kustaa slid his eye to the scope. There were ten from
each of the trucks, dressed alike in plain dark skirts and
white blouses. All young, mid-teens to mid-twenties
(although it was hard to judge through the narrow field
of the telescope), wearing handcuffs with two-foot chains.

Mostly white, but he could see a tall statuesque Negro girl and a couple of Chinese; they were milling and chattering, a few bringing out combs and taking the kerchiefs from their travel-touseled hair. The Janissary was talking to a girl with reddish-brown braids done up in Gretchen coils on the sides of her head; she was snubnosed and freckled, a dead ringer for the bobby-soxer daughter of his next-door neighbor back in New York—except for the serf-number tattooed on her neck.

She took the carton from the soldier and opened it, began handing rolls of toilet paper to the other women. They walked away from the truck toward the granite outcropping, the soldier beside them; he was still talking to the Gretchen-girl, laughing and gesturing with his free hand while the right rested lightly on the pistol-grip of his rifle. Closer, closer, Kustaa could feel Arvid tensing beside him, hear that the Janissary and the girl were speaking German to each other. The soldier was young too; the face leaped into close-up in the crosshairs of his sight, shaven-skulled but adorned with a wispy yellow mustache and plentiful acne, the neck-tattoo standing out bright orange against his tan.

They halted ten meters from the rocks, and the girl gestured imperiously to the serf trooper. He laughed again, turning his back on the clump of women squatting in the long grass, dropping to a knee. His rifle rested across one thigh as he scanned the edge of the treeline and reached inside his mottled tunic to bring out a package of cigarettes, flicking one half-free of the container and raising it toward his lips. Kustaa saw the pack freeze halfway to the young man's mouth, sink back, then drop from stiffening fingers. Pale blue eyes went wide in alarm, and the face rocketed past his 'scope as the soldier shot to his feet.

"*Now!*" Arvid shouted, and the man with the detonator twirled the crank-handle on its side and raised the plunger. For a half-second he paused, an expression of utter pleasure on his face, then slammed it down.

Kustaa's finger stroked the trigger of his rifle, and he

felt the recoil as a surprise the way it always was when the aim was right. The blond Janissary pitched back, the *smack* of the bullet punching through his stomach close enough to be heard with the crack of the round firing. *Clack* as the action flicked back, *ting* went the spent brass of the cartridge as it bounced off the stone by his right ear. Then the earth under the lead warcar erupted, a sound so huge it struck the whole face like a giant's invisible hand. Groundshock picked him up and slammed him down again, with the iron-salt taste of blood in his mouth from a cut tongue. Nothing was left of the lead car but a tattered rag of steel crossed by the heavier lines of axles, centered in a circle of burning scraps and fuel.

The second armored car was over on its side, wheels spinning in slow futility. Its crew crawled from their hatches, staggered erect, were caught and shredded in the metallic sleet of fire that raked the column from both sides; another roar and pillar of black smoke came from the rear of the convoy, then half a dozen more along the kilometer length of stalled vehicles, *crash-crash-crash*, ripple-firing in a daisy-chain of high explosive that sprouted like malignant black mushrooms. Trucks were burning, and a pattering hail of wood and metal and human body-parts came down all about them; the heavy oily smell of distillate burning in the open was all around them, and the throat-rasping fumes of burnt propellant.

All along the treeline on both sides of the road arcs of tracer swept out to chew at the convoy's edges from concealed machine-guns. The heavier *snapsnapsnap* of semiauto rifles joined in, and an anvil chorus of ricochets hornet-buzzing from engine-blocks and armor. Kustaa shifted aim, found a Janissary kneeling and firing a light machine-gun from the hip, strobing muzzle-flashes and his mouth gaping pink against the dark-brown skin as he shouted defiance. The crosshairs dropped over his face and *crack* the rifle hammered at Kustaa's shoulder. The Janissary snapped backward with a small hole between just above his nose and the back of his skull blown away in a spatter of gray-pink brains and white bone; he lay still kneeling, his body arched back like a bridge and the kindly grass closing over the shock-bulged eyes.

A whipcrack sound went by overhead, close enough for the wind of it to snatch the cap from his head and brush heat across his forehead. Ice crystallized in his stomach as he wrestled the rifle out of the notch in the granite and swung it to the left; the third Draka warcar was coming towards them, the long fluted barrel of its 15mm machine-gun spraying rounds that whined overhead and blasted spalls and fragments from the stones before them. The stubby muzzle of the grenade launcher beside it made a duller sound as it fired, more like ripping canvas. The two-inch bomblets were low-velocity, almost visible as they blurred through the air. Their bursting-charges were much louder, a *crang* and vicious hum as the coils of notched steel wire inside dissolved into a cloud of miniature buzzsaws; each one cleared a five-meter circle in the long grass, as neat as a lawn-mower.

With angry helplessness, Kustaa forced out a long breath as he steadied his aim on the gunner's vision-block; bullets were already sparking and whickering off the sloped plates of the car's armor, leaving lead-splashes and gouges but not penetrating the welded-alloy plates. The warcar lurched over the rough ground, its six independently-sprung wheels moving with a horrible semblance of life, like the legs of some monstrous insect. A few seconds and that line of fire would walk across his missiles, across *him*. He squeezed gently at the trigger—

—And the shot went wild as a streak of fire dazzled across his vision to impact on the glacis-plate of the warcar. *Pazooka*, he thought, with an involuntary snigger of relief. Actually a Finnish copy of the German 88mm *Panzerschreck*, but never mind . . . A globe of magenta fire blossomed against the armor, and the warcar turned flank-on and stopped as if it had run into a wall. The American's mind drew in the picture within, the long jet of plasma and superheated metal from the shaped-charge warhead spearing through like a hot poker through cellophane, searing flesh, flash-igniting fuel and ammunition. A second of hesitation, and then the turret of the car blew apart with a sharp rending crang; pieces of jagged metal went whirring by overhead, and he dropped back to a prudent knees-and-elbows position.

Now he could see the rocket-launcher team; the backblast had set a grass fire that was a black and orange finger pointing to their position. The gunner rose, letting the sheet-metal tube droop behind him while his partner carefully slid a second round home and slapped his shoulder. They shifted position in a quick scuttling run, moving a hundred yards north towards the rear of the convoy; dug-in guerrillas cheered as they passed.

Kustaa wiped a shaky hand over his forehead; that had been far too close, and he could smell the rank musk of his own sweat, taste the sickly-salt of it on his lips. His eye caught the wristwatch. Only four minutes, and the muscles of his shoulders were shaking. He forced them to untense as he rolled back to look for his original targets; dense black smoke was billowing past, obscuring the view, but he could see one of the APC's past the trucks glowing cherry-red with interior fires, another nose-down in the roadside ditch, disabled by a contact-mine but exchanging fire with the guerrillas. No, another lancing shriek of fire from the antitank launcher, striking high on its flank; the small turret on its deck fell silent.

The women were still visible through the thickening smoke to his front, barely; milling and screaming, some with their underwear around their ankles. No, the big black woman was running among them, pushing them down into whatever safety there was on fire-beaten ground. The German-speaking girl with the braids had dashed forward; now she was dragging the Janissary

Kustaa had shot back toward the road, leaning into it with her hands clenched in the shoulder-straps of his web harness. The American could see her face quite clearly, huge-eyed with terror and speckled with blood now as thickly as the freckles, her mouth flared in a rictus of effort and determination.

From the way the man's head lolled Kustaa thought there was probably very little point, but he had done things as pointless himself, in combat. Overload, no way to take it all in, so you focused on something. Your job, or some detail you could make your job, even if it was meaningless and the only sensible thing was to scream and run, it was still something you could *do*. Better than freezing, or cowering, or panic. *At least, that's my preference*, the American thought, scanning the thickening smoke for a target. As for the rights and wrongs of a slave-whore risking her life to save a slave-soldier, he supposed she was operating on the general assumption that the people shooting at her were not friends. He could sympathize with that, too; the equation "someone trying to kill me = enemy" had a certain primitive force . . .

From their right, from the north beyond the veil of smoke, came a sound like a chainsaw. But far too loud; it would have had to be a Paul Bunyan-sized model. A courier dashed up, fell panting on his knees by Arvid and gasped out a message as he leaned on his rifle; between the breathy gabble and the thick Karelian dialect, Kustaa caught only the English word in the middle of the sentence: "Gatling." Then he heard the engine-sound from the same direction, and saw two horizontal lines of white-orange light stab out of the smoke. Where they struck the edge of the uncleared forest, trees fell, sawn through at knee height in white-flashing explosions that sent splinters flying as lethal as shrapnel. The hundred-foot pines swayed forward, quivered, fell.

One smashed down in front of the forward wheels of the Draka flakpanzer, clearing the smoke like a fan for

an instant before the burning truck next to it ignited
the dry resinous branches. Kustaa recognized the type,
Dragon class, two four-wheeled power units at each
end and a big boxy turret between them: antiaircraft
mounting, originally designed to escort mechanized-
infantry columns. The armament was two six-barreled
gatling-cannon, 25mm; each was capable of pumping
out 6,000 rounds a minute. That was why the vehicle
was so large, it had to be to carry enough ammunition
for the automatic cannon to be useful. Very effective
against ground-attack aircraft coming in low; at short
range, against surface targets, whatever came in front of
the muzzles simply disappeared.

"Shit," Arvid said, listening to the courier and twisting to keep the attacking flakpanzer in view, then rising
to his knees and cupping his hands about his mouth.
"Tuuvo! Keikkonnen!" The rocket-launcher team looked
up from their new blind. "Circle around and take it
out!" he shouted. They rose and went back into the
woods at a flat run, wasting no time on acknowledg-
ments. "This had better be worth it, American," he
continued in a flat conversational voice.

The Dragon's turret moved again, a 180-degree arc;
two seconds of the savage chainsaw roar, and a hundred
yards of forest went down like grass before a scythe, the
twin lines of fire solid bars through the smoke. Then it
lurched forward again, the wedge-shaped bow plowing
through burning timber in a shower of sparks. The
outside wheel-sets were in the ditch to allow the gun-
truck to ease past the burning wreckage in the center of
the road, and the thick cylindrical tubes of the gatlings
were canted up sharply to compensate. Trees were
burning half a kilometer back into the woods, ignited
by stray incendiary rounds and sparks, and he could
hear the pulsing bellow of a full-fledged forest fire
.beginning.

And the volume of small-arms fire from the area
under the iron flail of the flakpanzer's cannon was slack-
ing off noticeably.

Another runner slid into the covered zone, gasping as the shock of landing on her back jarred the crudely-bandaged arm bound across her body.

"There were four trucks more of infantry at the rear of the convoy," she gasped, between deep panting breaths.

"Replacements," Arvid rasped. "Goddam."

"They've pushed us back into the woods on the west side but everything's on fire, we and the snakes are both breaking contact and trying to circle round, it's spreading fast." She glanced back to where the armored vehicle was systematically clearing *this* side of the road. "The antitank teams on the west are out of range and the one you sent back up toward us is gone." The runner gestured toward her bound arm. "Nearly got it in the same burst. Eino's going to try and take out that fucker with a—"

Another roar of autocannon fire. Kustaa swiveled his rifle, in time to see three figures in guerrilla uniform bounce to their feet and race forward toward the Dragon with satchel charges in their hands. *The gatlings can't depress enough to stop them, God damn it, they're going to make it!* went through him with a shock of elation.

The crew of the Dragon reached the same conclusion. Hatches cracked open on the square-wheeled power-units at either end of the long vehicle, and the muzzles of machine-pistols whickered spitefully.

"Shit, shit, shit," Kustaa cursed under his breath, emptying his magazine at the narrow gap between hatch-cover and deck. The machine-pistol jerked and ceased firing, lay slumped for a moment before it pulled back inside with a limp dragging motion that suggested an inert body being manhandled down into the driving compartment. The hatch clanged shut again, and the guerrilla was only ten yards away, his arm going back in the beginning of the arc that would throw the cloth bag of explosives under the hull of the Dragon; the other two satchelmen were down. "Go, go, go," the American chanted under his breath, eyes urging the Finn on as his hands felt blindly for a fresh clip and slid it into the loading well of the rifle.

The hatch opened again, this time only for a second, just long enough for a stick-grenade to come spinning out. It flew in a flat arc, whirling on its own axis, the sharp bang of its detonation coming while it was still at head-height. The Finn stopped and fell with an abrupt finality, as if he were a puppet whose strings had been cut, and the sweep of his arm faltered. Wobbling, the satchel charge fell short, throwing up a plume of rock and soil amid the muffled thump of an open-air explosion. Dust cleared, with a ringing hail of rock on metal; the armored cab of the Dragon was intact, but three of the wheels on the outer flank were shredded ruin, and the fourth was jammed by a twisted steel panel.

"Good," Arvid said. "Runner, get back to Eino; bring some of those trees down on that thing, there're a dozen or so in reach." He looked at her arm. "And then get out to the fallback rendezvous; you're not fit for combat."

A shout from a machine-gun team beside them. "Ahh, thought so," Arvid muttered. "They're going to try and peel us back up here while the Dragon keeps the center of our line busy."

Figures were dodging through the smoke of the burning trucks on the road ahead, behind the clump of women prone in the roadside grass. A sudden scream like a retching cat, and a line of fire streaked out toward Kustaa's position, slamming the cluster of rocks ahead of him with an explosion that sent fragments of granite blasting uncomfortably close overhead. The sound was fainter than it should have been; his eardrums were ringing, overstrained and losing their capacity to absorb the battering noise. Muzzle-flashes and tracer, and the Janissary infantry poured out into the cleared zone along the road, into the waist-high grass and stumps.

A score of them, running, some falling as the Finnish positions swept them. Squads throwing themselves down to give covering fire, others leapfrogging their positions. The American picked a target, fired, shifted to another. Lizard-mottled uniforms, drug-magazined assault rifles, machetes slung over their backs. Bucket-shaped helmets with cutouts for the faces; he could see one's mouth move, a curse, as he broke stride to avoid stamping on a hysterical girl who lay face-down, beating her hands into the earth. A sergeant, bare-headed save for a checked bandana around his gleaming dome of skull. Kustaa's bullet struck his thigh, sledged him around in a circle that sent a cone of tracer into the air from the light machine-gun in his hand. Then he was up again, kneeling, firing from the hip and waving his men on as blood gouted from the massive flap of torn muscle hanging down his leg.

Kustaa slapped another magazine into his weapon, jacked the slide with his right hand; the metal of the barrel burned his palm, overheating from rapid fire. The volume of fire from the Draka infantry was appalling, and damnably well-aimed. He ducked as he reloaded, thankful of an excuse to get out of the way of the light high-velocity bullets that tinked and spanged off the stones before him. He had seen enough combat to know that a firefight was less dangerous than it sounded, it took thousands of rounds to cause a casualty, but standing up in front of that many automatic weapons was still unhealthy.

"We can't hold them!" he shouted to the man beside him.

"Hell we can't!" Arvid said, reaching for a handclasp solenoid-detonator linked to a spreading fan of wires. "This is what I laid the directional-mines for."

Kustaa froze. His mind's eye saw the weapons, curved steel plates lined with *plastique*, faced in turn with hundreds of ballbearings. Like giant shotgun shells, their casings spiked to the stumps and ready to fill the whole space between forest and road with a hail of ricocheting metal. His hand streaked toward the guerrilla's.

"The women—" he shouted. The Finn hacked backward with an elbow, a paralyzing blow into the point of Kustaa's shoulder.

"Fuck them," he said, still not raising his voice. His other hand clenched, and the roar of the fires was cut by explosions and a sound like the whining of a million wasps. "Get your missiles ready, American," he continued. Then he raised his voice to a shout. "Follow me, the rest of you, don't let them rally!"

A leap, and he was over the stones and running toward the road. The others followed him with a deep guttural shout, loud enough to drown out the shrill screaming of the wounded lying among the murdered trees.

The Twin-Zebra slid in, flaps dappling the square wing to shed lift, touched smoothly down with the gentle touch of an expert's hands on the controls, rolled to a stop not twenty meters from the two cars. The ramp dropped, but the first two passengers were down before the further end touched. Bodyguards: Special Tasks Section, General Staff Division.

Ah, Andrew von Shrakenberg mused. *They did send someone important.* Standard camo uniforms, but cut away from the arms, customized assault rifles, automatic pistols in quick-draw Buchliner harnesses across the stomach. The eyes slid over him without pausing, flickering in an endless animal wariness. Special training, careful selection, and there weren't very many of them. Even among Draka, few had the aptitude, and fewer still were the Citizens who could be spared for such work.

Two more figures came walking sedately down the ramp in garrison blacks. Silently, he approved; even out here, fairly near the sharp end, it was a little ridiculous for staff types to travel in field kit and armed to the teeth. He drew himself up and saluted, conscious of the other officer doing likewise.

"Merarch Andrew von Shrakenberg," he said. "Cohortarch Corwin Hartmann. Service to the State."

The leading staff officer removed her peaked cap and nodded; small, slight, gray-streaked brown hair, broad face and snub nose . . . She smiled at the slight shock of recognition.

Tantie Sannie, I'll be damned, he thought, slightly dazed. Sannie van Reenan; Uncle Karl's aide . . . Andrew had been born on Oakenwald, the original von Shrakenberg estate south of Archona; his father a younger brother of Karl, landless until after the Great War. Tantie Sannie had been there often enough when he visited, had taken him under her wing when he was stationed there during his year at the Staff Academy.

"Glory to the Race," she replied formally. "Strategos Sannie van Reenan. Soon to be von Shrakenberg." A laugh; this time his brows had risen appreciably. "Permission to satisfy your curiosity, Andrew. Yes, its offically Tantie Sannie now, not just by courtesy."

"Uncle Karl?"

"Who else, man?" She patted her stomach. "You're due for another cousin, come eight months, too." She turned to Hartmann, saluted. "Combinin' the tour with a litle family business, Centurion." A wave to the other officer. "Cohortarch Ivar Barden Couteaux." A cluster of gray-uniformed auxiliaries were following, secretaries and clerks.

"Ah, mmm, this is rather sudden, Strategos," Andrew muttered, as they walked toward the cars.

"It's breakin' out all over, now the war's—as we jokin'ly put it—over. An' I'm not *that* old, Merarch; bit of a risk, but one can always terminate. About time I did my duty to the Race, anyway."

She stepped into the car, paused standing with one hand on the rollbar, looking about. Andrew stopped beside her, stripping away the veil of familiarity and trying to see it through her eyes. Ugly, of course; vegetation stripped away to leave rutted sand and mud, pavements of gravel and crushed stone. Bunkers, buildings of modular asbestos-cement heaped about with earth berms, a few floating balloon-held aerials. Spiderwebbed with communications trenches, skeletal support towers for lookouts and arc-lights . . .

"You've got a Century of the III Airborne Legion here, I understand," she said, nodding to a section of revetments; the long drooping blades of helicopter rotors showed over the sandbagged enclosures.

"*Ya*, it's unorthodox"—Citizen Force troops were rarely brigaded with Janissaries, and it was even rarer for them to come under the command of an officer commanding a Janissary formation—"but we needed a quick-reaction force pretty bad. Trio of gunboats, too." Nearly three thousand troops inside the wire, counting several hundred unarmed Auxiliaries in the maintenance and combat-support units.

"I wondered why Castle Tarleton would send anyone to Finland," he continued, as the driver twisted the utility-car's fuel-feed. "Back to HQ, Mustapha. We goin' get some organic helicopter transport of our own?"

"Not my department, officially," she said, as the car accelerated with a quiet *chuffchuffchuff* of steam. "Unofficially, no, not fo' while. Bottlenecks in the turbine plants, they tell me, an' maintenance problems. Still a new technology, aftah all. Also, we're givin' priority to convertin' more Citizen Force units to air-cavalry, cuttin' back on the heavy armor."

"An' *we* get the short end of the stick, as usual," he said. Conscious of her questioning look, he added: "Take it this is a general survey?"

"Very general," she replied. "Makin' a swing-through all the way from China to the Atlantic, gettin' an overview, combinin' with the Board's compilation of regular data." She was silent for a moment. "A mess, t' be frank."

"Well, we *did* take a shonuff big bite, this time," he said, absently returning the salute of a Citizen officer as they ate dust down the gravel street.

"Hmmmm, yes. Still, only thing we could do, at the time." A pause. "Long-range strategic situation's what I was talkin' about, though." Sannie reached for her cigarettes, remembered the doctor's advice and settled for a hard candy. "Damn those Fritz, they had to go an' discover tobacco's bad for yo'. Anyway . . . we're just realizin' down in Archona that the progress of the Race is, ahhh, enterin' a new phase."

"How so?" he said, as they reached the headquarters bunker. "Welcome to our humble home." The Strategos looked around, nodded.

"Good to see the real thing, after spendin' so much time in the Castle . . . well, it's the blessin' and curse of atomics, for starters." The maps had been cleared from the rough plank table in the center of the bunker and pinned to a board framework on one wall; Sannie van Reenan absently returned the salutes of the H.Q. staff and poured coffee in a thick chipped mug.

"Gods, I'd forgotten how vile the Field Force brew is . . . Where was I?"

Andrew nodded as they seated themselves at the map table. "Atomic stalemate," he said. "An' a good thing, too, in my opinion."

"Good in the short term; without we had 'em, the Yankees could beat us now. Muscle us out of Europe an' eastern China, at the least." She sighed and rubbed her eyes again, grateful for the cool gloom of the bunker. "Trouble is, the atomics'll still be theah, ten, twenty, forty years from now. Unless the TechSec people pull somethin' completely unexpected, traditional mass warfare is goin' to be, hmmmm, completely out of th' question. Not to mention there's considerable ocean 'tween us and them."

Andrew pulled a cheroot from a box on the table, snipped the end and puffed it alight. "See your point. On the one hand, we get time to consolidate; on the othah, when we're ready we can't attack them. An' it's destabilizin' to have a non-Draka society too close to our borders; these days, the whole planet is close.'"

"Perceptive, younglin', but it's worse than that. We're bein' forced into a new type of competition, an' it's one we're not really suited for." She frowned. "Look at it this way. We started off by conquerin' southern Africa, usin' weapons and techniques developed here in Europe; enslaved the natives, applied European organization to their labor, an' used the crops and minerals we sweated out of 'em to buy more weapons and machinery. Well, that wasn't a stable arrangement, so we industrialized to supply our own military, buyin' machine-tools and hirin' technicians instead of importing finished goods.

"But all propaganda aside, it's always been a spatchcock modernization, pasted on the surface. *Exemplia gratia*, right up till the Eurasian war, most of our exports were agricultural, an' minerals; still are, fo' that matter, oil an' chrome and rubber and so on. Mostly we used the resultin' war potential against really backward societies, the rest of Africa, then the Middle East and Asia."

"We beat the Europeans," Andrew protested mildly, drawing on the dark mouth-biting smoke. *It must be nice to have the leisure to think strategy*, he thought wryly. *So much more interesting than tactics, also safer.*

"Hmmmm, 's much by luck as anythin', they wrecked each other first." A shrug. "Oh, we've got advantages; sheer size, fo' one thing, substitutin' quantity fo' quality. We do some things very well indeed, bulk-production agriculture, mining, mass-production industry: the sort of thing that organization an' routine labor can handle. Our great weakness is the size of the Citizen population, of course—an aristocracy *has* to be small in relation to the total population—but we compensate by concentratin' it where it counts and by specializin'. In war, primarily.

"So yo' might say the Domination's like a lower-order animal, a reptile, that's learned to do some mammal tricks, mimicry. Or a big shamblin' zombie with a smart little bastard sittin' on its shoulder whisperin' orders into its ear."

Andrew raised a brow; of course, there was nobody from Security around . . . that he knew of.

"Fear not, nephew. As I was sayin' . . . we're goin' to

be fightin' the Yankees and their Alliance fo' a *long* time. We can't count on them cuttin' their own throats, the way Western Europe did. I mean, if there's one thing the Eurasian War showed so's even a Yankee couldn't miss it, it was exactly what the Domination is an' what we intend. The Alliance will hold; we may be able to convince a few useful idiots of our peaceful intent, but not enough to matter. Pity. Likewise buyin' outright traitors with promises of Citizen status; that worked well enough with a few score thousand Europeans, but it's a limited tactic. Our traditional tools of brute force, terror an' violence are out of the question. System as centralized as ours is *more* vulnerable to atomics than theirs.

"Which moves the competition onto other grounds. Production, technology, science, not our strong points." Another frown. "This is a little speculative, but what the hell, the Strategic Planning Board is supposed to be . . . Apart from the fundamental fact that they're a society oriented to dynamism while we're committed to stasis, we an' TechSec are gettin' a very nasty feelin' that development is movin' into areas where we're at a *structural* disadvantage. The Domination couldn't have been built without machine technology, but it was the nineteenth-century version. Coal an' iron an' steam; rifle-muskets, railways and hand-cranked gatlings. Then steel an' petroleum, no problem; we're the perfect Industrial Age empire.

"Only, it looks like the balance is shiftin' toward things based on nuclear physics an' quantum mechanics. Rare alloys, ultra-precision engineerin', electronics. Electronics especially, an' they're already ahead; we can steal their research, but bein' able to *apply* it's a different matter. At least we don't have to try an' compete in general living standards; this isn't a popularity contest, thank the nonexistent gods."

"Bleak picture, Tantie," Andrew said, with a frown of his own. A bit vague, but the Draka had always tried to plan for the unlikely. Living on the edge, being con-

scious of having no margin for error, at least made you
less likely to fall into complacency.

"Not as bleak as all that. We *do* have some serious
advantages. For one, the Alliance is a strong coalition
but it's still a coalition, an' a coalition of democracies, at
that. Which means it'll only make outright war if we
push it into a corner, which we'll carefully avoid—unless
an' until we can win quick an' final." She unwrapped
another candy, began absently folding the paper into a
tiny animal shape. "Very democratic democracies;
accordin'ly, they have trouble plannin' as much as a
year ahead. Some of their agencies can, surely; the OSS
are just as smart an' nearly as nasty as our Security
Directorate. But the most of 'em are short-term thinkers; we can use that any number of ways. Example, by
gettin' them to sell us their technology for profit. Yankee civilization as a *whole* may be smarter than ours,
but we're better right at the top—leadership's a scarce
resource fo' us, so we make better use of it.

"No, it's their society in gen'ral we've got to be wary
of. Their dynamism, flexibility, the way they can bend
with the wave of change. Army fo' army, bureaucracy
fo' bureaucracy, we can beat 'em every time. Accordin'ly,
what we've decided to do is to keep the military tension
ratcheted up as tight as possible, indefinitely." A wolf's
grin. "If we can't fight 'em, we can at least force 'em to
tax, to regulate, make 'em security-conscious an' secre-
tive . . . force them onto ground where we've got the
advantage, waste resources."

Andrew grinned in his turn. "Lovely double-bind,
Tantie, but . . . not that I don't appreciate yore takin'
the trouble to fill me in on high strategy. I'm commandin'
a Merarchy of Janissaries; what's the relevance to me?"

She leaned forward, resting her chin on her palms.
"Well, twofold, nephew. Firstly, I'm afraid our 'armed
peace' policy is goin' to make your pacification work
even more of a nightmare than 'tis now. Provokes the
Alliance to strike back in covert style, an' we can't
hardly object too hard, seein' 's we're stompin' on their

toes every chance we get, plus makin' big bad Draka faces at them all the time. Fo' example, we think that alarm a few nights ago was an attempt to get somethin' —agents, weapons, who knows—into Finland." Andrew winced. "It gets worse. Yo've been havin' troubles enough with the Finns *here*; we've got evidence they've been infiltratin' small parties across the pre-War border, equipped for long-term wilderness survival."

"And there's a *lot* of wilderness east of here," he said.

"'Zactly, nephew. More joy . . . y'know that scare we had, few days back? Security's sources in the U.S. say that wasn't just a probe at our Northern Lights chain; they were puttin' in an agent, possible-like with advanced weapons. Might be tryin' to link up with them, set up a long-term supply effort."

"Submarines? No *earthly* way we could guard the whole northern flank of Eurasia in detail."

"'Specially not with all our othah commitments, and seein' as they're ahead in submarine-warfare technique. Hell with it, light me up one of those . . ." She paused to inhale the smoke. "Now, this is confidential, younglin." She looked around; there was nobody within earshot. "Besides the operational problems all this creates, we're a *little* worried 'bout the way this prolonged pacification situation is reboundin' on the Army-Security balance."

Andrew leaned back, puffed at his own cigarillo and grimaced. The Directorates of War and Security were the two armed brances of the State, and their rivalry went back generations; more emphatic the higher you went in the command-structure, as well.

"If we're goin' to be spendin' the next two generations sittin' tight and makin' faces at the Yankees, I can see how it would sort of rebound to the headhunters' benefit," he said carefully.

"Hmmm-hm. Like, they're agitatin' to have more of the Janissary Corps put under their direction."

That brought the younger Draka sitting bolt upright. "The *hell* yo' say, Tantie—Strategos," he amended himself hastily. "Fuck the bureaucratic bunfights, those ghouls *spoil* good fightin' men, I won't have any of *us* put—"

He stopped at the quizzical lift of her eyebrow. "Us?" she murmured. There was a certain detached sympathy in her face as she leaned forward to pat the clenched fist of his hand where it rested on the pine board. "Andy, it's inevitable there should be some degree of identification, when yo' lead men into battle. Inevitable, desirable even, fo' maximum performance. But never, never forget what the Janissary corps was established *for*."

She lifted the cigarillo, considered the glowing ember on the end and flicked away ash with a judicious finger. "'Sides, we in Castle Tarleton basically agree with yo' position. The headhun—ah, Security Directorate are gettin' as many recruits fo' their Order Police as they can handle, in our opinion. Janissary units are useful fo' *both* open-field warfare an' pacification, whereas the Order Police are a militarized gendarmerie, not combat soldiers. Limited usefulness, even in guerrilla warfare, not that the Security people look at it that way."

Sannie shrugged. "On the othah hand, we *do* have to coordinate more closely; the Archon's made it clear, an' the sentiment in the Assembly's likewise gettin' pretty intolerant of jurisdictional squabbles. Remembah, most Citizens just do their three-to-six military service an' leave; they're primarily interested in gettin' the pacification completed in the quickest possible time. Quite rightly, too. 'Service to the State,' hey? Which *we* have to remember, and not confusin' our own particular institution with the State itself—which a certain Directorate I could name but won't is prone to do. We all got spoiled by the Eurasian War an' the run-up to it, bein' free to concentrate on conventional warfare.

"Which brings me to what we have in mind fo' you. Now, yo' made it to Tetrarch in the Citizen Force originally; transferred to the Janissary Corps as per SOP, excellent record since . . ."

Andrew tensed. "Now wait a minute, I've been with this unit since '42, I know them an' they me, they *need*—"

"Policy, Andy, and yo' know it. Next step up fo' you is a Chiliarchy or Legion command, and yo' do *not* get it without rotation back to the Citizen Force." She held up a hand. "Unless yo' were thinkin' of commandin' the 2nd Merarchy, of the XIX Janissary fo' the rest of your career? Which *could* happen, yo' know."

Andrew von Shrakenberg opened his mouth to speak, hesitated. The calm eyes resting on his were affectionate but implacable; loyal to the tradition that put State and Race above any personal tie. Like Pa's, or Uncle Karl's. *How can I leave them?* he thought; braced himself and—

—the radio squawked frantically. "*Mayday, Mayday, convoy one niner, undah attack! Come in, Firebase Alpha, come in!*"

Sannie van Reenan stepped back to one wall and crossed her arms, withdrawing person and presence; it never paid to hinder experts at their work. An alarm claxon was wailing across the base; officers and senior NCO's piled into the command bunker, moving with disciplined haste.

One flipped the map back onto the table, smashing the crockery aside. Andrew took the microphone, forcing calm down the transmission by an act of will. It was obviously a Janissary NCO on the other end, and a young one from the voice. *Not* the commander of the convoy due in today.

"This is the Merarch. Quiet now, son, an' give me the facts."

"Ah, Sarn't Dickson, suh; 4th *Ersatz* Cohort, reportin'."

"The recruit shipment, by God," somebody in the room murmured. "Where's the escort CO?"

As if to answer, the static-laden voice continued, stumbling over itself in haste: "Tetrarch Galdman, he up front, the car jus' blow up, mines suh, front an' rear, we pinned. All thaz warcars done be knocked out, suh.

Mast' Sergeant Ngolu take t' Dragon an' his Tetrarchy 'n try goin' up t'support, lotsa firin'; jus' me an' the replacements lef here back a' the column, suh. Allah, they *close* suh, mus' be near two hundred, I kin hear 'em talkin' bushtalk to each othah in thaz woods, we runnin' short on ammo."

"Report yo' position, soldier."

"Ahhh—" he could hear the Janissary taking a deep breath. "We 'bout thirty kilometers out from yo', suh. Jus' past t'long thin lake, an' turnin' west."

"Right, now listen to me, son. Dig in, an' *hold your position*, understand? Help is on the way, and *soon*. Keep broadcastin' on this frequency, the operator will relay. When yo' hears us, fire flare—yo've still got a flare gun?"

"Yazsuh."

"Good. Recognition code." Red this week, but no need to advertise it to anybody who might be listening; the Finnish guerrillas still had pretty good Elint. "An' stay put, a world of hurt goin' to be comin' down round there."

He handed the microphone back to the operator, turned, orders snapping out as he walked to the map table.

"Sten, get the gridref to the flyboys and they're to boot it, blockin' force behind the ambush, the bushmen will have to retreat through that bottleneck between the lake and the marsh. The gunboats are to give immediate support, and they will *not* cause friendly casualties this time, or I personally blow their pilots new assholes. Same to the Air Force base, max scramble. See to it.

"Vicki, got the position?"

"Sho do. Here, the dogleg." Her close-chewed fingernail tapped down on a turn in the road, just east of the firebase.

"Joy, joy, just out of automortar range, even with rocket-assist. *Damn*, they haven't gotten this close since spring. Corey, ready?"

"Reaction-cohort scrambled an' ready to roll at gate 2, suh," he said; that would be his unit, they were on call today.

"Right. Jimbob, detach two of yo' SP automortars to follow." 100mm weapons mounted in armored personnel carriers, they would thicken up his firepower nicely. "Tom, get the mineproofs rollin', two of them, to lead off. Vicki, my personal car an' a communications vehicle. Yo're in charge while I'm gone; maximum alert, it may be a diversion fo' an attack on the base. Appropriate messages to Legion HQ an' the III Airborne, this is a chance to do some long cullin', let's *move*, people, let's *go*."

Andrew took the stairs two at a time, with the other reaction-force officers at his heels. Sannie van Reenan turned to follow, pausing for a moment as the Special Tasks Section bodyguard put a hand on her shoulder.

"I know," she said, to his silent inquiry. "But I wouldn't miss this for the world; nor is any individual immortal or irreplacable."

"Ma'am, it's our responsibility—"

"—To keep me alive, yes. Now yo'll just have to earn your pay, hey? Let's go find a lift."

"Twenty minutes," Kustaa said, glancing at his wrist.

"Always seems longer, doesn't it?" the Finn beside him said, running through a last quick check of the missile-controls. The American had been a good teacher, but there had been no possibility of a test-firing. "They'll be here soon."

"Oh?"

"Well, it's only a half-hour drive from here to the snake base," he said, running a finger approvingly along one of the control boxes beside the bicycle-style gunner's seat. "Such fine workmanship, so precise and light . . . yes, only half an hour, at high speed. Of course, they can't come barreling down here, that's the oldest trick there is, a relief-column lured into another ambush. They'll have to stop short of here, deploy and come in on foot with their armor backing them up. It's roadbound, you see; a lot of small timber just west of here, there was a forest fire a few years ago. More brush, once the tall timber is down."

Sort of fire-prone around here, Kustaa thought sardonically. The wind was from the south, moving the forest fire north along the road in the direction from which the supply convoy had come; even moving away from them the heat and smoke were punishing, backdrafts of ash and tarry-scented breathless air. By now it had spread out into a C-shaped band a mile wide, moving before the wind as fast as a galloping horse, with outliers leaping ahead a thousand yards at a time as burning branches tossed free and whirled aloft.

"Smokey the Badger will hate me," he muttered, and shook his head at the Finn's incomprehending look. *Only YOU can prevent forest fires*.

The remains of the Draka column smoldered, guttering oily flames still bringing the scorch-stink of hot metal to their position beneath the unburnt fringe of trees. A pop-popping of small-arms fire came from the north where the last survivors were holed up, punctuated by bursts of machine-gun fire and the occasional grenade. Three trucks came back toward them, singed and bullet-holed but still mobile, jouncing as they left the edge of the road and moved across to the missile position. Arvid Kyosti stood on the running board of the first; it stopped near enough for Kustaa to see the neat row of bullet-holes across the door on the driver's side, and the sticky red-brown stain beneath it.

The guerrilla commander waved the other two trucks on, and they disappeared to the southwest as he hopped down; there was blood caked in his moustache, where a near-miss with a blast-grenade had started his nose bleeding. The truck he had been riding slid ten yards into the cover of the trees and halted; half a dozen guerrillas emerged from the bed, and began rigging planks into a ramp up which equipment could be dragged in a hurry.

"Ready?" Arvid said.

"Ready," the American replied. "Motor-transport?" he added, jerking his chin toward the other vehicles disappearing among the tall pine-trees.

"A little. Get the heavier supplies and the wounded well into the woods before the snakes get here. A lot of it can be sunk in the swamp and retrieved later, tinned food and sealed boxes. You can go five, ten kilometers easy if you know the way; then we pack it out. This one's for your missile launchers, when we need to move fast."

Another pair of the ex-German, ex-Draka Opels passed them. "We got some useful booty, too. Snake rocket-guns." Kustaa nodded; those were shoulder-fired recoil-less weapons, a light charge throwing a rocket shell out twenty meters before the sustainer-motor cut in. Very effective antiarmor weapons and good bunker-busters. "Good to get *something* out of this."

He offered the American agent a package of cigarettes. Janissary army-issue, in a plain khaki-colored package. Kustaa inhaled gratefully; they were good, nice light mild flavor.

"You killed a fair number of them," he said.

Arvid lit one himself and sat on the running board, heedless of the sticky remains of the driver still pooling there.

"We lost thirty dead, killed maybe that many Janis-saries," he said with the flat almost-hostility that Kustaa had grown accustomed to. "It takes them, what, six to eight months to train a Janissary, from induction to posting. Replacements with this convoy, they were mostly Europeans. Germans, Czechs, Croats, some Swiss. The Janissaries are volunteers, you know? They get more than they need. We destroyed some equipment, too." He nodded to the Dragon; four trees had fallen across it, and the crew had chosen to burn alive inside rather than emerge to face the guerrilla bullets. The turret had peeled open along the lines of its welds when the ammunition blew, but the armored cabs were outwardly intact save for scorchmarks. The screams had stopped long ago.

"They have their own industry and all Europe, all Asia to replace that. As easy for them as replacing the drivers and whores."

"Those are people you're talking about," Kustaa said quietly. "Have you thought of asking them if they want to join you?"

The guerrilla smiled without humor. "The snake secret police would just love that, an opportunity to get agents among us. We've had enough problems with that, American; my family killed themselves so they couldn't be used as levers against me."

Fanatic, Kustaa thought, chilled. Then: *And who's to blame him?* He tried to imagine Aino giving Maila a cyanide pill crushed into her milk, raising one to her mouth with a shaking hand and tears runneling down her cheeks, pictured them lying together cold and twisted with blue froth on their lips . . .

That's what I'm here to prevent, he thought. The guerrilla was speaking again.

". . . probably killed one, two Citizens at most. And a couple of Janissary senior NCO's, they're harder to replace than the cannon-fodder." He glanced up. "The survivors got a message through to their HQ, the aircraft should be here any minute." Most of the guerrillas were already fading back into the woods, to let the counterstrike fall on empty ground. "It's up to you to make this worthwhile, American."

A faint *thupthupthup* came blatting over the trees from the west, louder than the crackling roar of the forest fire. And a turbine howl, growing.

"Helicopters," Arvid said bitterly. "Damnation, I was hoping for jets . . ."

They ducked beneath the chest-high canvas with its load of shoveled pine-duff, crowded with the angular metal tubing of the launcher and the half-dozen guerrillas who would help him operate it. Arvid's field-glasses went up, and Kustaa followed suit. Three droop-nosed shapes coming in low, two thousand feet, narrow bodies and long canopies tilted down under the blur of the rotors.

"Gunboats," Kustaa muttered. He was tired, with the swift adrenaline-flush exhaustion of combat; the sound flogged him back to maximum alertness. The Alliance hadn't put as much effort into helicopters as the Draka, and the Domination had captured most of the German research effort as well. A question of priorities: gunboats and assault-transports were more useful for antipartisan work, and the Alliance had little of that, thank God. Their choppers were mostly for casualty-evacuation and naval antisubmarine . . .

"Damn, air cavalry as well," Arvid said. A broad wedge of troop-transports followed the ground-support craft, but behind and much further up, tiny dark boxy shapes. "Can you take the transports?"

"No. Not unless they come a lot closer and lower. The operational ceiling's four thousand, and—" The transports broke east and south, sweeping in a long curve that took them away from the missiles waiting crouched by the road. Arvid's eyes followed them.

"Must be trying to get behind us at the lake, bottle us up," he said quietly. "Most of us will get through, they don't know that area as well as they think. A pity they're not coming here, ten Draka in every one of them. The gunboats have Citizen pilots too, of course. Don't miss."

"I don't intend to," Kustaa replied, and turned to the crews. The missile launchers were spaced ten yards apart, for safety's sake; the reloads well back, in case of a misfire. "Ready," he said. "Remember, second team *waits* until I've fired. These things track thermally, we don't want them chasing each other. Fire from *behind* the target only, you have to get the exhausts. *Do not fire until the lock-on light comes on and the signal chimes*. Then fire immediately." Repetition, but never wasted. "Now, get the tarps unlaced, and be ready to pull them off *fast*."

A flare rose from the north end of the convoy, popped into a blossom of red smoke. The gunboats circled over the dug-in Janissaries, then peeled off to run straight down the road at nearly treetop height. *Whapwhap-whapwhap* echoed back from the forest; the blades drove huge circles of smoke and ash billowing into the forest, fanned the embers on charred trunks into new flickers of open flame. Kustaa buried his mouth in the crook of his arm to breathe through the cloth, blinking pain-tears from his eyes and keeping the helicopters in view. They had their chin-turrets deployed to either side, firing the gatlings in brief *brap-brap-brap* bursts; one sawed across the wet ground in front of his position, the sandy mud spattering across the camouflage tarpaulin. Machine-guns spat at them from the ground, carefully grouped away from the rockets to attract the Draka gunners' attention.

The firing ceased as they swept south past the head of the convoy and banked, turning 180 degrees like a roller-skater grabbing a lamppost. Kustaa worked his tongue inside a dry mouth and reflected that even without insignia it would be obvious to anyone watching that the craft were Draka-crewed, the hard arrogant snap of the piloting was unmistakable. They were nearly back level with him—

"Now!" he shouted, sliding into the gunner's seat. Strong hands flipped the tarp back, pumped at the hydraulic reservoir to maintain pressure, and the launch-rail swung smoothly erect. The helicopters were going by in line, six hundred feet up; they wouldn't notice, not with the smoke . . . Ring-sight up, just a gimbal-mounted concentric wire circle, adjust for range, *there* they were past, lay the wires on the two exhaust-ports of the last gunboat's turbines, *clench* left hand. The electronics whined and his feet played across the pedals, keeping the whole frame centered on the blackened circles and heat-shimmer of the exhausts.

Come on, come on, he thought. God, not a vacuum tube failure, he'd tested every component individually when they assembled them, *when* were they going to get everything solid state, the Draka had to notice any second, even with the launchers behind them—

Ping. Pingpingping—the idiot-savant sensor in the rocket's nose announced it had seen the thousand-degree heat source moving away from it. Someday they would have something smaller, more reliable, but for now . . .

"Clear, firing!" he shouted, and his right hand clenched down on the release. The solid-fuel booster of the missile ignited with a giant *sssssSSHHHHH* and a flare that flash-blinded him even from the side; *that* they were going to notice for sure. No need to shout for a reload, the crew were heaving the long cylinder onto the rail. Out of the corner of his eye he could see that one of them had a jacket shredded and smoldering. He had *told* them to stand clear of the backblast.

But his focus stayed on the line of white fire streaking away from him, across the dazzled, spotted field his abused retinas were drawing on the sky. Spear-straight, one second, two, and the flight-lines of the helicopter and the rocket intersected. The explosion was an undramatic *thump*—the warhead was smaller than a field mortar—but the result was spectacular enough to satisfy the most demanding taste. The tail-boom of the last gunboat vanished, and the shock-wave of the detonation slapped the rotors from behind. Unbalanced, the helicopter flipped nose-down, and the blades acted like a giant air brake, killing its forward momentum. Killing more than that. For a fractional second it seemed to hang suspended, and then it slid two hundred yards straight down into the road.

Vision ended in a hundred-foot fireball, as fuel and munitions burned. The shock-wave struck hard enough to rock the launcher on its outspread pads, drying his eyeballs with a slap from a soft hot invisible hand.

"Wait, wait!" he barked to the other team, as the orange fire-globe cleared; the next helicopter was pitching and yawing across the sky as the pilot fought to regain control. Even as he shouted, the dragon-hiss of the other launcher sounded. Kustaa watched with angry fatalism as the missile arced neatly toward its target, dipped, and crashed itself into the burning wreckage of the one he had downed; that was hotter than the exhausts, and more consistent.

"Ready," the reload team gasped, and he felt a hand slap his boot.

"Keep the pressure up," he rasped, working with heel and toe to control elevation. The second helicopter was traveling straight and level again, impressive piloting to regain control after getting tumbled flying low and fast like that. Extreme range, two thousand yards, dark fuselage against the black smoke of the forest fire . . .

Ping. This time he scarcely noticed the heat of launch, too focused on slitting his eyes to follow the flare. Four seconds to impact, three, *Christ, I hope they don't have rearview mirrors*, two—

"Shit," he said. The Draka helicopter waited until the last possible instant, then pulled up in a vertical climb that turned into a soaring loop. Less agile, the missile overshot and began to climb; then the sensor picked up the unvarying heat of the burning trees and began its unliving kamikaze dive. "They learn fast."

The seat almost jerked out from underneath him as the Finns hurled themselves at the frame, ten strong backs lifting it in a bend-snatch heave that clashed it down on the bed of the truck with a vigor that brought a wince to Kustaa's face; electronics were just too sensitive for that sort of treatment. Suddenly he was conscious of Arvid pounding him on the back, the hard grins of the others.

"Not bad, American!" The Finn's face was black with soot and dried blood, a gargoyle mask for white teeth and the tourmaline blue eyes. "One hit for three shots, a gunboat and two snake Citizens dead!"

Kustaa grinned in reply and fisted the guerrilla on the shoulder. "Where've the other two gone, that's what I'd like to know," he replied. Neither helicopter was in view. *Run away?* he thought. Quite sensible, in

the face of a new weapon of unknown qualities, but
unlikely. If the Domination's elite warriors had a military fault, it was an excess of personal aggression. Nothing in the smoke-streaked blue of the sky ahead and to
either side; he shook his head against the ringing in his
ears and concentrated. Yes, the thuttering of helicopter
blades and engine noise . . . getting louder, but *where*?
The Finnish crew were taut and ready by the four
outrigger legs of the second launcher, the snub nose of
the missile tracking a little as the gunner's toes touched
the pedals.

Not worth the disruption to go and take over, he
thought.

Arvid tensed and broke into a sprint. "Behind you!"
he called to the missile team, running toward them,
pointing frantically back into the forest. Kustaa had just
enough time to twist and see the shadow of the gunboat
flicker through the trees as it dove toward the ground at
a near-vertical angle. It ripplefired its rocket pods nearly
above his head, and the blast as they impacted on the
waiting missile was behind him. He felt it as pressure,
first on his back and then as if his eyeballs were bulging, pushed from within his skull; the impact as he
struck the tailgate of the truck came as a surprise,
something distant in the red-shot blackness.

Vision cleared almost at once; Kustaa could see as the
Finns hauled him in beside the frame of the launcher.
See clearly, as if through the wrong end of a telescope,
things small and sharp and far away, too far away to be
worth the effort needed to move a body turned warm
and liquid. There was a crater, scattered about with bits
of twisted metal and softer things; the treetrunks and
rocks that had absorbed much of the force, still settling
and smoking. And a figure was probably Arvid, that had
to be Arvid, though it was difficult to tell since it was
burning. The man-thing took a step, two, fell forward;
its back was open, and things moved in there, pink and
gray-cooked and charred. Then the far-off scene was

vanishing, into shadows and movement and somewhere the sound of weeping.

The bodies moved. Both the Special Tasks gunmen had their pistols cleared and slapped three rounds each into the topmost corpse before Andrew could react, swinging in to put themselves between Sannie and the stirring in the jumbled pile of wood and flesh.

"Wait," the Merarch said; the staff Strategos echoed it, and soldiers all along the line of smoldering wrecks that had been a convoy came out of their instinctive crouches. There was still firing from the southeast, an occasional popping and the crackle of Draka assault-rifles as the Janissaries mopped up the guerrilla rearguard. Here the loudest sound was the protesting whine of engines as the recovery vehicles dragged wreckage to the side of the road; mine-clearance teams were sweeping the verges with infinite caution, marking their progress with fluttering banners of white tape. The burial details were busy too, an excavator digging a mass trench for the dead drivers and other auxiliaries, prefab coffins for the Janissary casualties.

I hope the ceremonial does them some good, wherever, Andrew thought wryly. Actually, the flags and banners at the Legion's homebase cemetery served the same purpose as any funeral, to comfort the living and remind them that the community lived even when its members died.

He hooked off the top layer of dead partisans with his boot; *their* heads would decorate stakes around the firebase, after somebody collected the ears. There were flies already; he looked up, noticing almost with surprise that the sun was still bright on a summer's afternoon, still high above a horizon that had darkened no further than twilight. A haze of smoke obscured it, and that was the smell; smoke from burning wood, metal, fuel, explosive, rubber, bodies. At least it covered the usual stink of death, stunning his nose so that he could barely smell the liquid feces that streaked the uniforms.

There was another stirring; he reached down and grabbed a jacket, heaved.

"Take him," he snapped, and two troopers grabbed the Finn, pinned his arms and searched him with rough efficiency. Andrew resumed his measured pacing along the line of burnt-out trucks and armored vehicles. A cutting torch dropped sparks amid the tangle of alloy plate that had been an APC; melted fat was pooled beneath it, overlaid with the iridescent sheen of petroleum distillate.

Corey Hartmann was walking towards them from the head of the convoy. "That's where the whatever-it-was was located," he said, pointing east to a crater just beyond the cleared firezone that edged the road. "I've got my people cataloging and bagging the fragments, but the gunboat didn't leave much."

"Can't say's I blame him," Andrew said dryly, taking a look back at the much larger crater where one of the helicopters had crashed.

"There were two of them, we're thinkin'," Hartmann said as they turned through the burnt grass. "Seems they got the othah 'way in a steamtruck."

"Interestin'," Sannie van Reenan mused, narrowing her eyes. "They must've backpacked it in; we didn't think they could build 'em that light an' portable."

"They? The Yankees?" Andrew asked sharply.

"Who else? Fo' sure, the bushmen didn't cobble it together in their caves. We couldn't make somethin' that small an' capable, but the Alliance is ahead of us on miniature stuff."

They came to another line of bodies in the black stubble; scattered women with gunshot wounds or the flesh-tattering multiple punctures of directional mines. One of the females lay sprawled beside a dead Janissary, her hands still gripping his harness. *Young*, Andrew thought, studying her face. Probably quite attractive too, before her hair burned. Another of the women sat beside her, cradling her head in her lap and rocking back and forth with a low ceaseless moaning; the live girl's hands were swelling with their burns, skin cracked and glistening with lymphatic fluids.

"Medic, we need a medic ovah here!" he called sharply.

"Comin', comin'!" the nearest called; a Citizen doctor, overseeing the auxiliaries who were inserting a plasma-drip in a Janissary whose legs were mostly gone below the tourniquets. She stood as they eased him onto a stretcher. "Priorities heah, yo' knows."

Andrew wheeled sharply, lighting a cigarette with a needlessly aggressive snap of the Ronson. "Corey," he said flatly. "These were the replacements fo' the Comfort Station, weren't they?"

The Cohortarch nodded. "Out of luck, po' bitches," he said, glancing up from a clipboard someone had handed him.

"Well, soon's our wounded're out, have 'em lifted to Legion HQ as well an' tell the duty officer to find somethin' for them to do when they're patched up," he said. The other Draka nodded again.

"Only fittin', seein' as we were supposed to be guardin' them," he said with a grimace.

Andrew flicked the half-smoked cigarette to the ground, lit another. "Yo' . . . Sergeant Dickson, right?"

A young Janissary with junior NCO's stripes made an effort to straighten to attention; it was difficult to see his expression, since half his face was bandaged.

"Suh," he said dully.

"Good work here, son. I'm puttin' yo' down for a month's furlough, an' a 'recommended' on yo' promotions record."

"Suh." The reply was almost as dull, then a more enthusiastic "Suh!" as the words sank past pain and exhaustion.

"Dismissed," Andrew continued; he saluted, and the Janissary began a snapping reply, winced and completed the gesture slowly but in regulation wise before wheeling and marching off.

"Now," the Draka commander said, turning his attention to the two troopers who held the prisoner. The Finn was reviving, bore no obvious wounds beyond the battering to be expected; an adolescent, with a shock of flax-colored hair and gray eyes. No noticeable difference in dilation, so any concussion would be mild.

"You," he said in Finnish, pidgin but understandable. "Where they go? How many?"

The partisan tried to spit, but his mouth was too dry and his lips still too numb; it dribbled down his own chin, cutting a track through soot-grime.

Andrew lowered his bunched fist, hearing the slight *click* as the metal inserts in his gloves touched each other. Too crude, far too crude. His eyes went to the Janissaries holding the guerrilla: Dieter, yes, one of the new replacements. German, might even have fought on the other side; they had been taking them young, toward the end. Quiet, did his work and kept to himself, very little in his personal file. The other was . . . Ecevit. Turk: there were a lot of volunteers from those provinces; hook-nosed, hairy and thick-bodied, enlisted before the War. Capable but too impulsive for promotion beyond squad leader, and—

"Ecevit," he said musingly.

"Sar!"

"As I recall, yo've something of a taste fo' blond boys." The trooper straightened, suppressing a hopeful grin. "This one looks as if he'll wash up nicely. Bring him to Interrogation tomorrow, alive, able to talk, and in a more cooperative frame of mind. Understand, soldier?"

"Yaz, *sar!*" the soldier said. "Many thanks, effendi!"

The Finn must have understood some English too, because he began to scream as the two Janissaries dragged him away.

"Rough an' ready, but effective," Sannie van Reenan said with in a dry murmur. "Perhaps Intelligence work was yo' callin', aftah all."

"I'm . . ." he paused to look at the wreckage about them—"somewhat annoyed," he finished. "And maybe it is, Strategos, I couldn't fuck it up worse'n I've done this, could I?"

"Spare me the guilt, such a bourgeois emotion," Sannie said, with a snap in her tone. More softly: "Actually, your jungleboys did quite well, heah."

"That *they* did," Andrew said, meeting her eyes. "Yo' know, they really don't care much fo' that particular nickname." A slow drag on the cigarette hollowed his cheeks and cast the harsh planes of his face in outline; for a moment, you could see the skull behind the flesh. "An' frankly, neither do I."

"Point taken," Sannie said with a nod. "Now, about that proposition I was speakin' of, before this little *shauri* started." She waited with hunter's patience while his mind fought back past the last two hours; he was the sort of man who concentrated with his whole being—a valuable trait if controlled. "We're thinkin' of formin', hmmmm, specialized *hunter teams*, to deal with . . . certain types of problem. Fo' example, Yankee agents formin' links with bushman groups. We have some information on this particular one, an' expect more. There'll have to be a coordinatin' officer, and a fluctuatin' unit structure; part Intelligence work, part bushman-huntin', part liaison. Security will have to cooperate closely, of course."

Or present its behind for the appropriate political shrapnel, went unspoken between them.

"Ahhh, an' this *particular* case would be a trial run?" Andrew asked.

Sannie smiled at the interest in his voice. "Indeed, it would, nephew mine. Indeed it would."

CHAPTER SIX

Chateau Retour: Touraine Province, Loire valley west of Tours. Est. 1945, National Highway N17. On Val d'Anjou Wine Tour route. Winner, Plantation Garden Competition, 1968; Regional Estate Management prize, 1958, 1964.

Area: 3,000 hectares
Population: free 8–12, serf 976

Notable features: Established immediately after the Eurasian War, as part of a group settlement by veterans of the Archonal Guard Legion. This plantation is noted for flowers, early vegetables and its wines, principally a light and almost perfumed red made from the Cabernet Franc grape. The manor is a modified pre-war Chateau of Renaissance date; the village is largely purpose-built, but there is an interesting small Gothic church on the grounds. Viewing by arrangement only.

Proprietors: Edward and Tanya von Shrakenberg. Edward von Shr. is of the Nova Cartago branch of that family, while Tanya von Shr. was born on the original

*von Shrakenberg estate of Oakenwald, south of Archona,
and raised in Syria Province.*

Plantations of the West: A Guide (1970 ed.)
Landholders League Publications
New Territories Press
Orleans, 1970

**LYON, PROVINCE OF BURGUNDIA
DETENTION CENTER XVII
TO:
CHATEAU RETOUR PLANTATION,
TOURAINE PROVINCE
APRIL, 1947**

The car was not crowded, even with seven and an
assortment of bags and parcels; the interior was open,
folding metal seats in the rear and two bucket chairs at
the front, a view through the front windows to the
coffle of serfs huddled on the floor of the truck ahead.
Marya crossed herself and waved to them as she climbed
through the clutter to her seat, composing herself neatly
out of long habit, feet and knees together, skirt folded
about them and hands clasped in her lap. The car
smelled of machine oil and leather, wickerwork and a
stuffy heat that brought a prickle of sweat to her upper
lip.

The driver was a thin-faced Frenchman in overalls,
wearing a cap pulled down over his eyes and cuffs with
a long chain looped through the steering wheel; the
man beside him was uncuffed, with an automatic shotgun
across his knees and a leather vest full of loops for the
fat shells. A serf, European, a thin strong young man
with a dark face and old-looking green eyes; a Jew,
Marya thought, Polish or Lithuanian or from the Ukraine.
She ventured a smile; he looked her up and down with

cold disinterest and turned back to the front, his right hand stroking lightly across the receiver of his weapon.

The women sat in the rear, with the other serf: a big man, even sitting down with his kettle belly spilling into his lap; African-dark, wide-featured and wide-shouldered, the arms below his shortsleeved cotton shirt thick and corded with muscle. Grizzled tight-curled hair and muttonchop whiskers, shrewd black eyes with yellowed whites. A rifle was resting upright by his side. Not the T-6 assault rifles the Domination had used in the Eurasian War; this was a full-bore semiautomatic model, dark wood and blued steel and a look the nun recognized, of machinery that is old but lovingly cared for.

He smiled with strong square yellow teeth as they *chuffed* into motion, but he did not speak; there was a moment of backing and circling as the convoy lined up for the gate. The engine had the silence of automotive steam, but the heavy vehicle still quivered with the subliminal feeling of life, rocked slightly as a uniformed figure hopped up on the running board. A woman's face leaned in the window, green military-style uniform and cloth-covered steel helmet; a Citizen officer of the Security Directorate's internal-security troops. Order Police; Therese buried her face in her sister's shoulder, and the other serfs covered their eyes and bowed. There was another rocking as she stepped down, a brief sound of boots on pavement.

Marya could hear a murmur of voices, then Tanya's weary drawl:

"No, Tetrarch, I *don't* have clearance papers fo' two armed serfs. I'm violatin' the law and armin' *all* my fieldhands. Didn't we go through this all three hours ago? Or didn't the duty officer log it?"

The nun raised her head and craned to see through one of the windows. The Security officer saluted and returned a file-folder through the opened door of the other car. A *lochos* of green-uniformed troopers behind her, shaven-skulled and neck-tattooed; the Domination

did not waste elite troops on that sort of duty. The
Tetrarch shouted, and one swung up the barrier while
two more threw their shoulders against the steel gate.
It groaned open, and the light seemed to brighten as
the cars accelerated smoothly and turned into the road
outside.

Yasmin shivered and shook her shoulders. "Doan'
like that place," she said. "An I *sho'* doan' like them
chain-dogs. They look at yo' an' they gotta impalin'
stake in they eyes."

The middle-aged man beside her brought the rifle
across his knees, slapped in a magazine and jacked the
action with a metallic *wrick-clank*. "Headhunters," he
said in agreement, turned and spat out the open window behind him. "Greencoats, *tloshohene* dogs; stay
clear of 'em." He looked up at the women across the
body of the car, and grinned broadly. "Name's Tom,"
he said. "Late o' th' 15th Janissary, an' father to thisshere
uppity wench, fo' mah sins. Listen to what-all she say,
this time. Usually nohow good for anything but sassin'
and bed-wenchin' with her betters."

Marya nodded warily, with a shock of alarm, feeling
Chantal stiffen beside her. Therese was paying no attention, eyes dreamy, humming under her breath. Better for her that way.

Janissary, Marya thought with distaste. Serf soldier.
Volunteers—she could understand why many would
choose such a way out of the dull drudge's life of a
Draka factory- or plantation-hand . . . though not the
courage with which they fought. And they had a merited reputation for relentless brutality. She shivered
inwardly. They would be confined with him for hours;
they were bound and he was armed. Although . . . she
glanced at Yasmin. Her father? And even a Janissary
could hate the green-coated secret police troopers.
Remember the publicans, she reminded herself. Roman
tax collectors had not been well regarded in Judea in
the Lord's time on earth, either. *Hate the sin, love the
sinner.*

She nodded in return, swiveling to watch the city go by. Much had changed, in the six months of her imprisonment. Central Detention had been a fortress then, wire and firing-trenches and dug-in armored vehicles; all that was gone, save for two concrete machine-gun bunkers beside each gate. The road outside the wall had been repaired, and the cleared firezone beyond was being converted to a park by labor-squads and construction machinery; piles of earth and sand, benches of brick and marble, fountains, pavements, a flatbed steamtruck loaded with young trees, springing up from burlap balls of root and earth. The city beyond was changing, too. There had been a fair amount of street fighting when Lyon fell two years ago; more damage after the surrender, when the Domination turned its troops loose for a three-day sack that killed more than the artillery and air-bombardments.

Marya forced that out of memory: days spent crouching thigh-deep in a sewer, furnace-hot air roaring overhead as the buildings burned, and the fever the filthy water brought . . . No, consider what this meant. Less Resistance activity, obviously; that was bad, very bad that it should happen so quickly.

Now the ruined buildings and rubble were mostly gone, cleared gaps where they had been and new structures going up, buildings in the low-slung gaudily-decorated Draka style. There were more Citizens, walking on the streets or driving little four-wheel runabouts, many in civilian dress; armed, but from what she had heard, Draka always were, even in their homelands. The native French were less numerous than she remembered, fewer of them in rags, more in grey issue-overalls or the sort of warm, drab outfit she had been given in the serf-dealer's rooms. That might account for much; it had been years since rations were enough to still hunger, even to sustain health.

The man's voice broke in on her thoughts. "Not a bad-lookin' town, pity I's too ol' an' useless to git in on thisshere war, git me some lootin'."

"Oh, poppa," Yasmin said in resigned exasperation. "That ain't nohow polite, these folks is from around hereabouts."

She pulled up a wicker basket from under her seat and began to open it. "Who's fo' somethin' to—" The ex-Janissary's hand shot into the basket, came out with a sandwich made from a split loaf of French bread; pink ham and onions and peppers showed around the edges. "—eat," Yasmin finished.

Marya had absorbed the byplay in silence. The food brought an involuntary spurt of saliva to her mouth, and she could feel her ex-cellmates stirring beside her. Yasmin tucked a careful linen napkin into the high collar of her silk jacket and began unloading the basket; sandwiches and slices of thick crusty bread with real butter, tart cheese, olives and tomatoes, sugar-dusted biscuits and real fruit, a thermos of coffee and a bottle of the violet-scented wine of Bourgueil. The dark girl coaxed a peach into Therese's hand, laughing at the little sound of pleasure she made as she bit; they were a country-orchard variety, small, tart and intensely flavored. Chantal put a hand on her sister's shoulder and leaned back into the padded wall of the vehicle.

"You are a soldier, sir?" she asked slowly in her careful English. "Or do you also belong to the von Shrakenbergs?"

Marya could read the expression of polite interest; Chantal was Gathering Intelligence, in the recesses of her own mind. *Carefully, carefully*, she thought; but it was a sign of something more than rage born of despair, at least. You could come to know someone well, after four months together in a crowded cell. A wave of pity overtook her; at least her own faith was not so tied to the fortunes of war. God promised no victories over material enemies, His Kingdom was not of this fallen earth . . . but poor Chantal had given her heart to a prophet who promised a tangible paradise. The Marxist heresy was sinful and godless, but the Frenchwoman's belief had been deep and sincere, rooted in love of the poor who Christ also had held dear, her hatred a hatred of injustice as well as simply of the rich.

Be cautious, my friend. It was ironic, here a Pole was being the calculating and rational one, cautioning a Frenchwoman against romantic gestures . . .

"Doan' need to 'sir' me," the man replied, his voice a slow deep rumble. "Yaz 'n no. I's Janissary. Born on Oakenwald, that Mistis Tanya's pa's place, down in th' Old Territories, way south. I go fo' Janissary back in, Allah, that be 1911, '12. Masta Everard, Tanya's pa, he officer in mah legion, th' 15th."

He flipped the rifle up, holding it out by the barrel to show a small ivory inset near the buttplate; the head of a hyena, biting down on a human thighbone.

"We the Devil Dogs, th' *bone-makers*," he said proudly. "Thisshere mah original piece; fight all through th' Great War, beatin' the rag-heads; Syria, Persia, Bulgaria. Aftah that, we'se in The Stan." He paused at his audience's blank looks. "Afghanistan. Hoo, 'deedy; we make our bones *theah*, sho'ly did." His smile slid away. "Left plenty bones, too. Damn few come out what went in, damn few." More softly: "Damn few, sho'ly."

"Well," he continued brightly. "That where I loses th' foot." He shifted his right leg, knocked it against a strut with a hollow sound. "Step onna landmine, 'n lemme tell yaz—"

"Oh, poppa, not more of yo' war stories," Yasmin broke in, rolling her eyes and turning to the others. "They *disgustin'*."

The man grinned slyly and glanced sidelong at his daughter: "Hell, jes' losin' a foot not so bad. I's rememberin' a sergeant, supply sergeant that was, rag-heads caught him, and we found him with his—"

"*Poppa!*"

He laughed again, and reached out one huge hand to stroke the knuckles gently down her cheek. "Alright, sweetlin', jes' jokin'."

"So," he continued, taking a meditative bite of the

sandwich, "coulda took retirement, laak a twenty-year man. Didn' seem mucha life fo' a young man, though. Done seen too many old Janissary, nothin' to do but drink an' knife each othah over cards 'n whores down at the *caserne*. Yo' can go home, though. Janissary always belong to th' State, cain't never be sold, or whupped 'cept by our own officer, but iff'n yo' volunteer, they rent you back. As guard, foreman, like that-there. Masta Everard, he settin' up Evendim, that his place in Syria; he younger son, 'n Masta Karl gettin' Oakenwald. I go with Masta Everard, he know me, y'see?

"I's settle down nice; get me a wench, Fatima." An affectionate sadness. "She got no sense, but she a good woman, I doan' want no other while she 'live. She die birthin' back befo' this new war come; mah boys gone fo' Janissary too—they in th' 15th now too, out east fightin' down the slope-eyes, someplace called *K*orea. Yasmin heah mah las' chile, 'n she go with Mistis Tanya, so I comes too. Yo' Frenchies got lotsa book-learnin', but yo' needs us t'learn the Draka. Some folks here is pretty sensible—got me a nice little widow-wench 'n cottage—others altogethah useless 'n triflin'.'"

He shifted his grip on the rifle, holding the heavy weapon by the stock and prodding the driver lightly in the back of the neck. "Like Jacques here; I's got mah *eye* on yo', boy. Doan' forget it." The rough voice went cold for a moment, and then he flicked the rifle upright beside him and relaxed once more. "Issac—th' skinny boy with th' bird-gun—he a smart one. Doan' talk much, though."

"Like yo', poppa," Yasmin said dryly as she repacked the basket, handing him a bottle of dark German beer. Her father snorted amusement, flicked the cap off with one horn-hard thumb and turned sideways to watch the passing scene, the rifle cradled in the crook of his arm.

"*I*," the girl continued, fastidiously wiping her hands on her napkin and then using it to clean Therese's chin, "am second indoor servant."

It was said with a slight unconscious preening; the

ex-Janissary's glance was fond and proud. *Even slaves must have their accomplishments*, Marya thought. Then: *be careful, this is real power, here and now.*

"Iff'n yo' got any questions, come right to me." She sighed and tossed back the loose black mane of hair. "Sometimes doan' know rightly how to start, with yo' Frenchies. *Doan'* sass back; doan' sulk or disobey. There's ways 'n ways of gettin' around the Mastahs, but goin' straight up agin' they will ain't accomplishin' nothin' but grief fo' us all. Remembah all us serfs is family; talk as y'wants, *do* as y'wants iff'n yo's the only one to suffer, but *doan'* do anythin' what gets us all traced up to the whuppin' post or worse. Iff'n yo' finds someone's doin' a crazy, like tryin' to hide weapons or sneak off to the bushmen, come tell me an' we'll decide amongst ouahselfs what to do."

Yasmin smiled and nodded toward the cuffs. "Soon's we gets back to Chateau Retour"—she pronounced the French words carefully—"we'll get those-there off; the Big House doan' cuff or hobble on the plantation, 'cept as a punishment. Now," she continued briskly, "the overseers, Masta Donaldson, Mistis Wentworth"—she shrugged—"they overseers, whats cain I say? Not too bad, 'n the Mastah 'n Mistis keep a close eye on 'em. Mistis Tanya, she downright easy goin', fo' a Draka, long as yo' doan' cross her. Masta Edward, her man, he pretty much the same 'cept when his head painin' him."

One brown finger tapped an eye. "He gets a head-wound in th' war; lose an eye, headaches real bad sometimes; gets pretty testy when one comin' on, yo' sees it, stay outta his way. Other times, doan' talk to y'much." She giggled. "Not so bad in bed, either, iff'n y'likes it, not rough, anyhow. 'Cept sometimes he finish too quick, but yo' be findin' out that fo' youselfs." An ironic eye at their flinch. "Call it work, call it play, doan' make no nevah-mind to them, dearies. Honest, the things yo' new-caught get upsets about, it beyond me."

Chantal cleared her throat, spoke in genuine wonderment: "Are . . . you content with your life, then?"

There was silence for a moment, a thrumming as the car swung onto the bridge over the Rhone. Light flickered by as they passed through the shadow of the girders, winked back from the surface of the river below; Yasmin wound down a window, and the stream of wet silt-smelling air poured in, ruffling the black curls around her face. She brushed them back with one hand, craning her neck to see a train of coal-barges passing below.

"Pretty river," she said quietly, turning back to them. "Yo' thinks there's somethin' wrong with lookin' at it?" She paused, pursed her lips in thought. "My life? It the only life I's got, or is goin' get; iff'n I ain't content with it, then I ain't goin' get much contentment, eh?"

A spread of the hands. "Ain't sayin' as everythin's the way I'd put it, were I God, but that-there position's filled, last time I looks. Plenty good things in my life; pretty things"—she touched the buttons of her jacket—"'joyable things, like m'work, which I's good at an' getting better, my music,"—she touched the case of her mandolin—"'n my fam'ly an' friends. Someday I's have children of my own, maybe-so a steady man. Iff'n I doan' take no pleasure from all that-there, who it hurt? Me, that who. Somebody else hurt yo', that fate; hurt yo'self, that plain ignorant; troubles enough in anyone's life, withouten yo' go courtin' 'em. I ain't hongry, ain't sickenin' to die, never been whupped; plenty folks worse off than me, I saves my pity fo' them, doan' waste it on myself.

"Look," she continued gently, "I knows y'all not born an' raised to this." She touched her identity tattoo. "But this-here the only life yo' has to live, likewise same's me. I's not sayin' nothin' bad doan' happen, but"—she gestured helplessly, as if trying to pluck words out of the air—"not *everythin'* is bad, unless yo' makes it so. The Draka?" She shrugged. "They's like the weather, they's jus' *there*. I's known folks, rather cut off they foot than 'commodate to the mastahs; they-all end up churnin' they guts with hatin'. Hate enough, it make *yo'* hateful;

it jus' ain't worth the trouble, to my way a' thinkin'."

Earnestly: "Yo' sees, the Draka can make yo' obey, but they can't make yo' miserable. Well," she amended "not unless they sets out to, which the ones which owns us doan', speakin' general-like." A tap on the head. "They orders, but *we* can say what goes on in here, eh? I's do my work, takes the days one at a time, doan' hurt nobody, helps those I can; when I's got to do somethin' I doan' like, I does it an' puts it outa my mind, soon's I can."

She smiled, trailing a hand out into the airstream. "Yo's looks like sensible, wenches, y'all will learn."

For a moment Marya's gaze touched Chantal's, and they knew a rare moment of perfect agreement; an understanding so complete it was almost telepathy.

Never.

> "*Beads of sweat glisten—*
> *Ai!*
> *In the undergroun' lights—*
> *Wo-hum*
> *Where a million lifetimes go—*
> *Wo-hum*
> *All our lives gone,*
> *Wo-hum*
> *Lost down the mineshafts . . .*

The car lurched and slowed, and Marya jolted out of a dreamy semi-sleep; the day had turned warm, and she and the Lefarge sisters had dozed, lulled by the comfort and food and even a single glass of wine, after so long without. And the music, strange quiet folk-songs in Yasmin's fine husky contralto, rhythmic minor-key laments. *Odd how sad music can make you happy*, she thought, stretching and rubbing at her eyes. She looked up, her ears ringing as the rush of air gave way to a pinging silence.

Wind blew through the opened windows, and the sound of earth-moving equipment, clanks and the sharp *chuff* of steam pistons, a turbine hum and the burbling growl of a heavy internal-combustion engine. The cars had halted before a roadblock, a swinging-pole barrier set across the two-lane road; a pair of armored cars flanked it, light four-wheeled models with twin machine-guns in hexagonal turrets. There was a fence along their left, running down the eastern flank of the road, steel mesh on thick reinforced concrete posts three meters high; razor wire on top, and thin bare copper threads held away from it by insulated supports. Electrified, then.

And signs wired onto the mesh: PROHIBITED AREA. ENTRY FORBIDDEN ON PAIN OF DEATH.

Marya glanced the other way, south and east to the direction they had come. That was where the activity was, broad weed-grown felds littered with wrecked and rusted war-machines; German models, *Panzergrenadier* half-tracks and Leopard tanks with their long 88mm guns swiveled every direction in silent futility. Broken, peeled open like fruit by the explosions that had wrecked them, still blackened by the dark oily soot of burnt motor-fuel; armor crinkled around the narrow entry-holes of the penetrator-rods, lighter vehicles like soup-cans stamped on by cleated boots.

Workers were swarming over them, cutting-torches laying bright trails of sparks; others were winching the carcasses onto flatbed trucks. A recovery-vehicle was dragging the most difficult cases out, the ones whose weight had half-buried them in the light volcanic soil. The turretless tank bellowed, its broad tracks raking stones and dry-smelling dust into the air, the hook dangling from the jib of the crane on its deck shaking; black fumes quivered from the slotted exhaust louvres, and she could see the bare head of the driver twisting in the hatchway as he rocked the treads. Elsewhere gangs ripped out vegetation, leveled and pounded earth, spread crushed rock.

The nun lifted her eyes. They were in a high plain bordered by hills, shaggy fields and copses of trees bright-green with the late spring, the Auvergne mountains beyond blue and hazy in the distance. A glint of metal over them, approaching. It swelled into a circle, then a shape; long slender squared-off wings, a bulbous nose-compartment that was all curved transparent panels save for the metal supports of the pilot's seat and the console, a pusher-prop engine in a tubular cowl slung between the twin booms of the tail. It passed overhead, ghost-silent, wheeled and returned: observation plane, muffled engine. Slots and flaps opened on the wings as the undercarriage came down. The little aircraft slid down at an angle, as if hitched to an invisible rope, bounced lightly and rolled to a stop ten meters from contact on a finished section of the landing platform.

Marya dragged her attention back to the road outside; her owner was there, stretching and rubbing her back and talking to an officer as they strolled back from the lead car.

". . . better than 'copters for scouting," the man was saying. Mottled camouflage uniform, black-edged rank-badges, paratrooper wings. Citizen Force, of course, the elite military, and the airmobile arm were picked volunteers within the Citizen Force. Marya looked west, toward the area behind the fence. That would be the town of Le Puy, and there were rumors of what had been done there, during the war and since. Atomics. She shivered, and listened.

"Doan' have anywhere near enough landing-grounds," he continued. "Everythin' short, as usual; just got things under control out east and they move us back." He jerked a thumb over his shoulder, towards the fence and the minefields behind it. "We're refitting after China, overseein' thisshere construction work fo' our permanent base, and doin' antipartisan work in the hills, and watchin' *that*."

Tanya nodded thoughtfully, looked at the wrecked war-machines. "The Guard went down from Paris to Tours, but some of my friends were through here; the Fritz held hard." She shrugged. "Well, not exactly the

Fritz; by '45 it was all odds and sods. Spaniards, these were, iff'n I remember. Chewed up two Janissary units, and held the VI Cartago fo' three days; tryin' to keep us off until got their atomics goin'." A shudder. "Wouldn't *that* have been jus' lovely."

The airborne officer nodded, watching the observation plane. The transparent egg around the pilot had folded open, and a fuel cart had pulled up beside the three-wheeled runabout that was unloading the cameras.

"Natural place fo' it," he agreed. "Hydro power, lots of water, remote, not too far from their uranium mines; that's why Tech Section took it over: even damaged, the equipment was useful." He grimaced. "Wotan's spear, I's glad they didn't blow the reactor."

"Sho'ly am myself," Tanya said. "Praise be to Hitler's ghost; even after the little bastard died—when was that?"

"December of '42; I's in hospital then."

Tanya nodded. "Poland, myself . . . anyways, his memory kept the other Europeans from unitin' against us until it was too late. Even as it was, we used too many of the atomics breakin' through into Spain. I considered settlin' in Rousillon, down near the Pyrenees, but on second thoughts, no. Not that I doubt Tech Sec's infallible judgment 'bout it bein' safe, but I wanted to stay as far up-wind of that hell-garbage as possible."

The officer spread his hands. "It was a long war, we-all was tired, everybody wanted to get it over an' go home." He looked into the rear car; Marya averted her eyes, but the man's gaze was on Tom's rifle. "By Frey's cock, a T-5! Couldn't yo' get him a Holbars?" He slapped the T-6 assault rifle slung across his chest.

"I prefers whut I's trained on, mastah," Tom rumbled respectfully.

Tanya snuffled laughter. "Tom's bein' polite; s'far as he's concerned, a T-6 is a 'girl-gun.' He's damned good with that old big-bore monster, though. Hell, we conquered half of Asia with them; a weapon's never obso-

lete iff'n it'll kill someone." She extended a hand. "Glad
to have yore assurance the route's safe," she concluded.

He gripped hers. "Pretty well," he answered. "There
may be a few bushmen left, but we've been huntin'
hard." A sigh. "Most of this mountain country was
swept clear by Security—plan is to put it all back into
forest—but I wish they'd get the cultivated portions
settled an' modernized; hard to keep these little peasant farms from slippin' supplies an' information to the
holdouts."

Tanya shrugged. "There's only so many of us, Cohortarch, an' we can't *all* be Landholders." She patted her
stomach. "Take a generation or three to get it all
covered."

"Oh, sweet Mother of God, let it be food," the guerrilla whispered, flexing his fingers on the grip of the
machine-gun. The muzzle trembled, shaking the screen
of leaves and blurring the view of the winding road in
the gorge below; the soft whisper of wheels and engines
echoed, but the vehicles were still hidden by the hill-
shoulder to the left.

"Shut up," his partner hissed savagely, but his mouth
filled at the thought. He adjusted the ammunition belt
with trembling hands. German ammunition, 7.92mm;
there was little of it left. Little of anything; he could
smell the new-bread scent of starvation on both of
them, under the rankness of unwashed bodies and the
sap-green of crushed leaves.

"Shut up," he said again, wiping his hand across his
mouth, and wincing as it jarred one of his few remaining teeth. The belt was lying smooth, ready to feed; his
rifle was by his hand, and the single precious stick-grenade.

"Shut up," he repeated. The enemy had stopped
convoying all vehicles through the Massif Central a
month ago, while the *maquis* were hiding in their winter caves; there were only a dozen men left in their
unit, but that should be enough. One of the survivors
from Denard's group had told of the single truck they

took two months ago. Cans of food, ammunition, medicines. "Of course they will have food."

If nothing else, meat.

The gorge was drowsy with the afternoon heat as the convoy dropped through, down from the plateau and into the winding valley the Loire had carved through basalt and limestone. The road was rough, only sketchily repaired; the underbrush had been cut and burned back twenty meters upslope and down, but the angles above the way were steep enough that greenery overhung them as often as not. Young and turbulent with spring, the river bawled and tumbled below them to the left. At two hundred meters Marya could still hear the deep-toned rumble as the water poured oil-smooth over curves and then leapt in manes of white froth from the sharp rocks. It send drafts of coolness buffeting up from the river surface, the smell of wet rock and silt.

Ahead of her Issac's head was bent over a portable chess-set, carved wood with peg-holes for the pieces. He moved, slipped the knight he had taken into the inside of the box, snapped it closed and turned to hand it to Tom. He was stretched over the back of his seat when she heard the sound.

Crack. Familiar: rifle bullet. A starred hole in the window ahead. The Jew pitched forward as if slammed by an invisible giant's hand, the thin face liquid with shock and only inches from hers, the chess-set dropping from fingers that spasmed open in reflex. He bounced back, and she could see the dark welling crater of the exit-wound in his shoulder. Then he slumped between the twin seats, left hand pawing feebly at the wound. Blood welled between his fingers, bright primary red in the dusty sunlight. Marya felt herself darting forward, braced her hands under the Jew's armpits, heaved to haul him back into the body of the car. The smell of blood was in her nose and mouth, raw salt and iodine, like the scent of the sea.

He stuck briefly as the shotgun caught in the seat,

then slid free. The cab was full of noise and confusion as the driver wrestled with the wheel; the car slid out toward the ravine, turned, skidded sideways with its length perpendicular to the road. The nun's hands were moving automatically, ripping at the wounded man's clothes for pads to block the holes, shifting him to lie flat and applying pressure. She could feel the vehicle sway, pause sickeningly on three wheels, jounce back down on all six and give a brief spurt of forward motion; then they clanged into the boulders on the hillside verge of the road.

Marya lurched, spreading her knees and fighting to keep position beside her patient. One hand was beneath his shoulder, spread flat with the palm up; her other bore down on the exit wound. Boxes and wicker crates swayed about her, buffeted and bruised. Her fingers grew slippery.

Plasma, she thought. *Clamps, stitching, sulfa powder. More plasma, whole-blood typing, transfusion. Sterile gauze.* The techniques she had been trained for, before the War as a nurse's aide. In the long years since by experience, in true hospitals and tented field-medic camps, hundreds of hours of observation and reading and the sort of personal instruction harried doctors could give, enough to make her an M.D. of sorts herself. Now all she had was the knowledge and her hands and the memory of too many dying as she tried to help.

Not this one, she thought. The flow of blood was slowing; skin gray-tinged but not clammy or cold, unconscious or semi-conscious, rapid shallow breathing beginning to slow . . . and the blood *was* tapering off, praise to the Mother of God and His Son and all the saints, not nearly enough lost to kill if shock didn't take him off, *but I don't dare move or the hemorrhaging will start again . . .*

Sweat rolled into her eyes. Another rifle shot, and something pinged off metal. She looked left, toward the rear of the car; Chantal crouched, her fingers white on

the lip of the window, her head craning to scan up the
cliff-face above them. Therese on the floor, crying again.
Crouched over her protectively was Yasmin, cradling
the French girl's head. Tom also at a window, the rifle
held easily in one hand below the metal body of the
car, binoculars to his eyes. They moved in tiny, precise
movements along the slope outside, rock and scrub oak.
A ripple of automatic-weapons fire, machine-gun; she
recognized a German MG38, an experienced gunner
tapping off short bursts. Then Draka assault-rifles, and
the savage hammer of the 15mm twin-barrel on the
lead car, echoing around the curve of road that hid it.

A click. She turned her head, looked toward the
driver's seat. The driver, Jacques; he had not spoken
half a dozen words that whole day. Now he lay twisted
across the seat, one arm through the wheel to give the
other room; the chain stretched taut between his wrists,
and she could see blood beneath the cuffs. His right
had reached the shotgun and held it between the bucket
seats, pointing back into the cab. Marya's vision was
suddenly very clear, the blued steel muzzle of the gun
wavering uncertainly, fear-sweat and desperate tension
on Jacques's face as it craned over his shoulder in the
unnatural posture his bonds and position forced.

"*Out of the way, Sister,*" he hissed. "Let me get a
shot at the Janissary, that is the *maquis* out there, the
Resistance, move, *please.*"

The moment stretched as she felt the slowing ooze of
blood past her fingers, as her mind sketched the narrow
space behind her. If she flung herself forward and down
she might be out of the cone of fire; the muzzle of the
shotgun was only a hand's-breadth from her face. Then
the wounded boy would die, of course. The shotgun
would empty its six-round magazine as quickly as Jacques
could squeeze the trigger, and recoil would slam the
barrel back and forth in his awkward grip, would fill the
rear of the cab with the heavy mankiller double-buckshot
rounds. Therese huddled wide-eyed on the floor, Yasmin

stroking her hair with her body between the French girl and unknown gunmen, Chantal.

And if Marya did not move, and Jacques fired, the first round would tear off her face.

The nun kept her eyes on the driver's as she straightened and leaned forward, as far forward as she could without relaxing her hands on Issac. The cold metal of the gun-muzzle brushed millimeters from her throat, and she could feel the skin crinkled into gooseflesh at the wind of its passing.

"Do what you must, my son," she said. Her mouth was very dry, her tongue felt coarse, like soft sandpaper. She began to shape the prayers.

"*Please—*" Jacques screamed.

A blur past her eyes and a clang of metal on metal; the buttplate of Tom's rifle, lashing down on the barrel of the shotgun. Jacques screamed again, in pain this time as the triggerguard dislocated his finger. The shotgun fired once, into a wicker crate full of some dense-packed cloth that absorbed sound and shot both. Marya looked back; saw Tom raise the rifle again, held like a spear at the balance-point above the magazine, and all his teeth were showing in a grin that had nothing to do with laughter. Chantal was reaching for him, until Yasmin snatched the chain between the Frenchwoman's wrists and braced a foot against the seat.

"Yo' *stop* that, now," she snapped. The other woman reared back, struggling and shouting; Yasmin straightened her leg and pulled with all her strength, and Chantal went to the floor with a squawk and a flurry of limbs. "*Damn* yo' hide, wench, I's saving your worthless *life*." The serf buried both hands in the other woman's hair, gripped tight and bounced her head on the floor with a hollow booming sound. And turned to her father:

"*Doan' kill him, Poppa!*"

The rifle stayed poised, but something flickered out in the black eyes. A flat hardness, a total intensity of focus; his attention switched to the nun for an instant.

"Please," she said.

He nodded at her, a brief jerk of the head. "Owes yaz one," he said. "Now duck." The rifle flashed past her ear, to where Jacques lay cradling his wounded hand and moaning, between the front seats. The butt cracked down on the back of his skull and he slumped into boneless silence.

"He woan' die," Tom said grimly. "May wish to, 'fore I's through with him." His eyes were back on the road outside; one hand stroked Yasmin's hair. "Yo's too soft-hearted for y'own good, girl. I's promised yo' momma to look after you." For a moment his voice softened, speaking to a memory: *"I is very sorry, Fatima . . ."*

The fire from the lead car had died down to an occasional burst, less loud than the screams and pleas and moaning of the coffle chained to the truck in the middle of the convoy. Tom scanned the slope again and laid the binoculars down carefully; he twisted to face the road behind the car and the cliff-face above.

"They not shootin' much, pro'bly short of ammo," he said conversationally, half to himself. "Just tryin' to pin the lead car, then . . . haaa, here they comes." Marya could see the huge brown hands close more tightly on the smooth wood of the stock, and his thumb flicked the safety off with an oiled metallic *snick*. "Everybody shuts up, hear?"

Yasmin crawled to the nun, rummaged under the driver's seat for the aid-box; Marya took the bandage and ointment thankfully, and for moments there was only the work of her hands. Applying the bandages; gauze pads, tape to immobilize the arm, it would do for now. Then tip of a shadow fell across the window, and she looked up from the wounded man.

Two men stood in the road behind them, armed with Mauser carbines. Wild, bearded figures; their rags might once have been uniforms, but patches and caked mud made it impossible to tell with any certainty. They came toward the car at a trot, spaced across the road and moving in the instinctive half-crouch of men who expect to come under fire. Closer, and she could see the marks of hardship on them; scabs, weeping open sores clumsily bandaged, the slack-skinned gauntness that comes when the body has drawn down all its reserves of fat and begun to cannibalize the muscle beneath. They were strung about with a motley collection of string-tied bundles and sacks; as they came closer, she could see the lice moving in their beards, catch a gagging whiff of their stink.

The guerrilla nearest the river went to one knee and began a nervous scan up and down the road; the other hailed the car.

"Who's there? Answer, or I fire!"

Tom's voice replied, in slow ungrammatical French: "Just us serfs, here. Who yaz an' what yo' want?"

"This is the Auvergne command of the National Resistance," the man said; he repeated it as if it were a spell, a mantra against reality. "Food; we need food, medicine, weapons, clothing."

His comrade called from the verge of the road. "And ask them if there's any wine."

The first guerrilla was turned to the other with a rebuke ready when Tom spoke.

" 'Fraid there's nothin' for yaz here," the ex-Janissary said mildly.

"What—why—"

"*Because yaz gonna die, bushman!*" The guerrilla was an experienced soldier, but the bull bellow still checked him for the first fraction of a second.

Tom's rifle cleared the lower sill of the window with smooth economy; he fired from the hip, with the forestock braced against the metal of the windowframe. Even with the muzzle outside the the car, the blasts were deafening. Marya's ears rang as she watched the guerrilla slap backward, and the hot brass of an ejected cartridge-case bounced unnoticed off her forearm. Tom had fired three shots at less than ten meters range; all of them had struck the guerrilla in a patch over his breastbone no larger than the palm of a hand. They were standard load, 7.5mm jacketed hollowpoint rounds that mushroomed inside a wound; a plate-sized area of the *maquisard*'s back fountained out in an eruption of bone-chips, spine and shards of flesh. The corpse went back, eyes bulging with hydrostatic shock, then fell limply.

The other *maquis* fighter was up, turning and shouting. His first round went over the car with a vindictive crack, and then he threw himself flat behind a boulder to work the bolt of his carbine.

Tom fired twice more, and the bullets bounced off the sheltering rock in front of the guerrilla with sparking whines.

"Shee-it," he muttered. "Gettin' old an' slow." One broad hand dove into the satchel at his feet, came out with a stick-grenade. A quick yank pulled the tab; he brought it up across his chest, counted three and threw it out the window in a flat spinning arc toward the rock. The guerrilla was up and running toward the river-side edge of the road before it landed. Tom's first two rounds kicked up dust and stone-shards at the running man's heels, the third sledgehammered him over the verge of the road an instant before the grenade's blast struck. The guerrilla's rifle pinwheeled free as he toppled over the retaining wall, metal twinkling in the afternoon sun, then clattering on the rocks below.

"Shee-it," Tom said again. "Three rounds, *slow*." He reached up, pulled a lever and swung the roof-hatch open, kicked a box over to give himself a platform to stand on. Head and shoulders out of the hatch, he turned to the cliff-face above them. "Yo' wenches stay down now, hear?"

Marya drew a long breath and wrenched her attention down from the blocky torso filling the center of the car. Chantal was lying with her head in her hands, muttering; Therese lay beside her, eyes wide and frightened. The air smelled of burnt propellant and the sour sweat of fear; the nun started with nervous tension as Yasmin touched her arm.

"I goin' back to take care of the chile," she whispered, jerking her head toward Therese. Marya nodded. The younger woman's brown skin had gone muddy-pale around mouth and eyes, but there was no quaver in her voice. Yasmin hesitated for a moment, then squeezed the nun's shoulder reassuringly.

"Doan' worry," she said in an obvious attempt to comfort. "Poppa woan' let the bushmen get us."

When the attack came, Tanya von Shrakenberg had been paging through the *Landholder's Gazette*, mildly annoyed that the workstock breeding programs were still behind schedule.

Dammit, they should let us use tractors, at least temporarily, she thought. There were sound reasons for the limits on mechanization, both social and economic, but a little more flexibility . . .

The first burst tore into the thin metal of the car's hood, ripping and dimpling the sheet steel; the second pinged and hammered at the thicker side-panels. Instantly her mind snapped back three years, plantation-holder's reflexes yielding to the instincts of a Guards tank-commander. The driver had frozen, eyes round as circles and whipping back and forth; he was reliable enough to go unchained, being very fond of his wife and children, but prone to panic. The car was losing power, a swift *sssssssss* of high-pressure steam and a mushy slowing-down feeling, but there was a fall of flat rock only twenty meters ahead, right side, by the cliff.

"The rocks!" she shouted, wrenching the wheel in the right direction and clouting him over the back of the head to break the grip of fear. "Pull us in by the rocks." That in French, it would penetrate better. Her hands were stripping the machine-pistol out of its clamps over the dashboard, an elbow to pop out the window beside her and look up the tumbled face of the cliff. Halfway between a cliff and a very steep hill, yes, muzzle flashes—

The twin-barrel cut loose above her head in a continuous blast of noise, double streams of tracer in economical two-second bursts. The familiar bitter chemical stink of burnt propellant, and the sound of the 15mm rounds on stone, like thousands of ball-peen hammers on a boulder. Sparks and splinters and dust from the target, a ledge up near the summit; a bush falling, cut through. *That* would keep their heads down: the heavy rounds could chew through brick walls and cut down trees . . . The car lurched as it left the road, skidded in the gravel shoulder and fishtailed to a halt in the shadow of the rocks; they were two meters high, enough to cut the body of the car out of the guerrilla machine-gun's sight-picture.

Tanya pushed at the driver's head. "Down, *stay* down," she said, pulling the radio receiver from the dashboard and punching the send-button. It was a powerful set, predialed to the Settler Emergency Network.

"Code one, code one: 10-7 von Shrakenberg, main road two kilometers north of Vorey, bushmen. Do yo' read, ovah."

"This is 1st Airborne, Le Puy. Say again, 10-7?" A young voice, bored; from what the officer at the roadblock had told her, it had been months since there was any activity this close to the air-cavalry base. Ambush on a main road was inconceivable; she recognized the tone of one resisting information because it violated mental habit.

The sloppiness was intolerable. "*Damn you, puppy, I'm bein' shot at!* Three-vehicle convoy, under fire from automatic weapons in the gorge three klicks south of Chamalieres. *Ovah.*"

"Ah . . . code seven, scramblin', maintain tone-transmission fo' location; ETA—" a pause—"16:10."

Tanya glanced at her watch: ten minutes, quick work. "Good work, 1st. I'm stalled on a C-shaped curve, northbound. My car first, a truck right on the bend, other car out of sight to the rear. Steep slope to the river on my left, an' a 80-degree forested cliff to my right. From the volume of fire, I'd judge one MG and possible six–twelve riflemen."

"Rodge-dodge, A.K."

"A.K.," she acknowledged grimly, leaning out the window and firing a short burst one-handed over the rock outside, aiming off-hand toward the muzzle flashes that winked out of the sunlit bush. No practical chance of a hit, that was four hundred meters, but it would help keep their heads down.

"An' hurry it. I've got two overseers, two armed serfs, a child an' me; an' I'm not up to much just now." She pressed a button. "Switchin' to tracer." The signal would broadcast steadily now, for the triangulator stations to produce a guide beam that the reaction-squad aircraft could ride.

She levered herself up and squeezed back between the seats into the open body of the car. *Damn this belly*, she thought. Gudrun was at the rear doors, craning eagerly to see with her knife in one hand; she yanked the girl back by the hem of her tunic.

"Gudrun!" she snapped, swiveling her around to where the terrified nurse was huddling in a corner with one of the French housegirls. "Protect the serfs, and stay out of the line of fire. That's an *order*, understood?"

Damnation, she thought. *I would run into the last holdouts in central France with Gudrun along.* She pushed the anxiety down below conciousness; there was no time for it.

"Ogden," she continued, turning to the overseer at the twin-barrel. "Can you get them?"

As if in reply, a fresh burst from the hillside machine gun hammered at them. It dimpled the roof panels behind her, where the rear and riverward flank of the car extended beyond the cover of the rocks. Wasp-buzz sounds, and the unpleasant pink-*tinnnnnng* of ricochets: rifle fire. She felt obscenely exposed in this unarmored soup-can, after all the years in a Hond battletank; acutely conscious of the quickened infant beneath her heart. Not that individual riflemen were much of a threat, objectively speaking; it took thousands of rounds per hit on average. But statistics were uncomfortably abstract when high-velocity metal was keening by.

"Na," the overseer said. "Have to be dead lucky, Tanya. Bushmen got a nice firin' slit between two boulders, an' heavy cover. Best I can do is keep they heads down."

"Shit." Tanya looked over at Sarah, the other overseer; she knelt by the rear-door windows with her assault-rifle at the ready, scanning the bush along the road-verge with the x4 optical sight. That was where they would come, and soon; the *maquisards* would know as well as the Draka that a reaction-force would be headed this way. There was a crackle of rifle shots, the slow banging of bolt-action carbines, a quick blast of semi-auto fire, and a grenade from around the curve to the south, where the truck and the other car were stalled on the narrow road. The guerrillas might have assumed the rear of the convoy was soft meat, but Tom was teaching them otherwise.

"Right," she continued. "Ogden,. Sarah, get ready to bail out an' tickle 'em. I'll cover yo' on the twin. When the airborne come in, *get back down*. Fast."

"A.K.," Ogden said, stepping down from the meter height of welded-steel platform beneath the gun and pulling his own Holbars from its clip beside his seat.

Tanya replaced him, blinking in the bright vertical sunlight as she came head-and-shoulders out of the roof hatch. Her hands went to the molded twin spade grips of the weapon, warm from the sun and Ogden's skin. Infinitely familiar, steel and checked *marula* wood against her palms, thumbs falling home on the butterfly pressure trigger. The twin-barrel was swivel-mounted on a ring that surrounded the hatch; she braced her elbows, laid the cross-wires of the sight on the bullet-scarred patch halfway up the cliff, and waited. There was no way they could get out of there without being seen. A very good spot for covering the road, but just a little too low to rake the right-hand verge where the car had run in . . . *Yessss,* right there, a V-shaped slit between the big round grayish rock and the triangular pink one—

"And a very good thing they don't have a mortar," she muttered to herself. The black flared muzzle of the enemy machine-gun slipped through the notch, stick-tiny at four hundred meters.

"Now!" she shouted, and thrust down on the ridged steel of the trigger. The massive weapon shuddered in her hands, a vibration that pounded into her shoulders and hummed tight-clenched teeth together; it was strongly braced, but the yoke and pin that held it to the ring-mount could not completely absorb the recoil. Blasting noise and twin streams of tracer arching away from the muzzles, solid light as they left, seeming to slow and float as sparks before the heavy 15mm rounds dropped home. Spent brass tinkled down across her stomach and into the car, hot enough to sting through the thin fabric of her shirt. Short bursts, push *wait* push. The air over the fluted steel barrels was already quivering with heat; she could feel it on her forearms and face.

Above her the rocks dissolved behind a cloud of dust and chips and sparks. She raked across the top of the two boulders that hid the machine-gun, to discourage any idea of standing up and firing down from the hip, then began working the edges of the opening. It was just possible she might be able to bounce a few rounds in, and it did not take many of the thumb-sized slugs to put a machine-gun crew out of action. Also it would keep their heads down, when they could be moving their weapon to a new firing position.

Behind her the rear doors of the car slammed open. From the corner of her eye she could see Ogden's squat form catapult out and dive into the roadside bush, a blur of black leather and metal. Sarah followed, a running leap from the back of the passenger compartment that took her three bodylengths out into the road, half the distance to the center truck. Then she backflipped, once, twice, dropped flat behind the truck and spider-

crawled beneath it on palms and toes, a quick scuttling
movement. A second's pause, and then the rapid *brrrt-
brrrt* of a Holbars set for three-round bursts.

That will keep their heads down, she thought, and
depressed the muzzles for an instant to rake a burst
across the cliff face below the machine-gun nest. Not *too*
far below, Ogden would be hunting there . . .

There was a sudden choked scream and a body catapulted from the scrub-covered slope five meters up; it
flew through the air with arms and legs windmilling in
an arc that ended in a crunching impact on the pavement. Broken, the guerrilla lay for a moment and then
began to crawl toward the roadside verge. His comrades in the bush-covered rock of the cliffside were
firing at the center truck, trying to silence the automatic rifle beneath it. Bullets pocked the thin metal of
the cab and ripped through the canvas tilt; the screaming of the chained serfs within was louder than the
gunfire, and their scrambling rocked the vehicle on its
springs.

"Come *on*, come *on*," Tanya whispered fiercely as
she walked another burst back up the hillside and across
the two bullet-scarred boulders. This was *not* good, a
blindsided firefight against odds. "Come *on*, you knights
of the air."

Chantal retched as she awoke, and Marya's hand
pressed her back to the floor of the car. The nun briskly
pulled up an eyelid and checked the pupil. "No concussion. You were unconscious for a little; keep quiet and
keep down." In a whisper: "*And there is nothing we
can do except die to no purpose.*"

Marya kept her eyes resolutely below the level of the
windows, down among the tumbled bundles and baskets. It could not have been long since the ambush, the
hot metal of the flashtube boiler was still clicking and
pinging. Danger stretched time, drew the seconds out,
it seemed like hours. The sensation had become familiar in the war years, but the long changelessness of

Central Detention had dulled the memory. Blood pounded in her ears, so loud that for long moments the *thup-thup-thup* sound outside seemed no more than her own heartbeat. Then Chantal dropped her hand from her eyes and looked up questioningly.

"What *is* that?" she asked. It grew louder, a steady multiple whapping with a rising mechanical whine beneath.

Tom answered, looking down from the roof-hatch above them. "Those-there newfangled helicopters," he said, with satisfaction in his voice. "Not too soon, neither."

Chantal and the nun exchanged glances and crawled cautiously to the outside windows, raising their eyes to the lower edge and peering south. A line of dots was visible through the long gash of the gorge, swelling as they watched. Six of them in staggered line abreast, under the whirling circles of their rotors. Closer, close enough to see the rounded boxy fuselages and long tail-booms, then the gaping twin mouths of the turbine intakes. The noise grew, shrilling and pounding; the fire from the hillside increased, no careful conserving of ammunition now, a panic-striken crackle.

The helicopters rose slightly, to perhaps four hundred meters above the level of the gorge. Marya peered upward, blinking. Their speed was apparent now, as they snapped by with the bright flicker of tracer stabbing out from their flanks. The nun could see the door-gunners standing to the grips of their weapons, the troopers crouching behind. The face of the slope above the road erupted in dust and the chittering whine of ricochets; Tom ducked down as gravel and twigs and branches pattered onto the roof of the car. Then the flight passed beyond the cliff-edge, the sound of the rotors changing as they came in to land.

"Look." Chantal tugged at her sleeve.

Marya turned west; two more aircraft were approaching from the other side of the river, not more than fifty meters apart. A different type, approaching slowly in a

straight line toward the rock face above the road. Helicopters like the others, but slender rather than boxlike,
with stub wings and droop noses. Long flat-paned canopies above the nose and she could see the figures of two
crewmen in each, one sitting behind and above the
other. Both craft had multibarreled gatling-cannon in
small domed chin-turrets beneath their prows, and she
could make out the pitted cones of rocket pods under
their wings.

"Sharkmouth markings," she whispered, mostly to
herself. Gaping red-and-white grins painted on the metal,
with clutching hands and screaming faces drawn between the teeth. At Chantal's quick glance she continued: "Draka fighters and ground-attack aircraft have
them."

The gunboats halted over the middle of the Loire.
The nun had seen a few helicopters before—both sides
had been using them by the end of the War—but it still
seemed somehow unnatural for objects to hang in the
sky like that. She swallowed through a dry throat; in
the cockpit of a helicopter one of the bulbous helmets
moved and the gatling beneath followed it, tracking
with a blind, mechanical malevolence. The noise was
overwhelming as the war-machines hung above the water, the pulsing wind of the rotors thumping against the
side of the car and raising a skidding ground-mist of
dust, leaving circles of endless ripples on the surface of
the river. A howling like wolves in torment echoed
back and forth between the stony walls.

Above, on the cliff, the *maquisard* machine-gun spat
at the Draka helicopters. A burst sparked off the armorplate nose of the left-hand vehicle; its neighbor turned
slightly, corrected back.

"Down!" Marya cried, dragging the French girl with
her as the first dragon-hiss and flash of rocket fire
caught her eye. The flare of ten-round pods being ripple-
fired stitched a line of smoke between the warcraft and
the stone; and where the line met granite, the side of
the cliff exploded. She was deafened and dazzled for a

moment; the steel beneath her shook, and a section of the cliff-face slid free onto the road. Rocks hammered down, starring the high-impact glass of the car and denting its metal; there was a fresh chorus of shrieks from the truck ahead as jagged fragments tore through the bullet-weakened canvas. Marya looked up through the windshield as another piece the size of a piano toppled away, hit a crag and split with a *tock* sound exactly like that of a pebble dropped on flagstone multiplied a thousand times.

One fragment bounced high, hung twirling at the apex of its curve, and dropped straight down to crush the truck's engine-compartment with a *crang* of parting metal. Thick distillate-fuel spilled down from the ruptured tank, then caught from some edge of hot steel and burned with a sullen orange flicker and trickles of oily black smoke. The other half of the stone was pear-shaped, wobbling through the air toward the car and missing it by a handspan before bounding down the gorge. Silence fell, or so it seemed as the rockslide ended. Shots, screams, the roaring thutter of the gun-boats' engines as they soared by overhead with slow insolent grace . . . Then true silence as they landed and the fighting ceased.

Draka airborne troopers were dropping down the face of the cliff from rock to rock in an easy bounding scramble; she could hear them calling to each other, yipping hunting-cries and laughter that sounded harsh and tinny to her battered ears. She looked at them and blinked the grit out of her watering eyes, turning to Issac and checking the bandages, hoping there would be no prisoners.

"We got about eight of them," the Tetrarch said to Tanya. South along the road there was another hiss as the extinguisher sprayed foam on the smoking hood of the truck; the oily stink of burnt distillate and over-heated metal was in the air, the universal scents of machine-age war.

The Tetrarch was Eva von Shrakenberg; a cousin, daughter of Tanya's father's eldest brother. A mild surprise, but their family was old, prominent, and had always produced more than its share of officers. The Draka were not a numerous people, the Landholders even less so; you were always running into familiar faces. Eva's sister Ava was the tetrarchy's senior decurion; twins ran in the family too.

"Interrogation?" Tanya asked.

"Oh, we'll keep one or two. Up to the headhunters, really." A lochos of Order Police had flown in with the airborne troops.

They were walking back past the wrecked truck; Ogden and Sarah had unreeved the coffle's common chain from the eyebolts and pulled the serfs out to sit in the vehicle's shade. The Polish nun was working on the wounded, with the Airborne medic standing by. Tanya's nose wrinkled at the familiar smell; the flies were there already, the gods alone knew where they all came from; there were even a few ravens circling overhead or perched waiting in the trees. Chains clanked as the serfs saw her and stirred.

"How many did we lose?" she asked the senior overseer.

Ogden looked up. He was leaning against the tailgate and honing a nick out of a long fighting-knife, the ceramic whetstone going *screet-screet* on the steel. There was a nostalgic smile on his face; Ogden had been with her husband during the War, a reconnaissance commando.

"Three kilt daid," he rasped in his nasal north-Angolan accent, and jerked a thumb over his shoulder at the shrouded bodies in the truck. "Two like to die. Woulda been mo', but that towhaired wench got 'em patched quick. Saved Issac's ass, too."

"Marya?" The nun looked from her work; she had a tourniquet around the man's thigh, and a plasma drip in one arm. "We goin' lose any more?"

Marya nodded toward a still figure. "That man, yes. Shattered spine, multiple perforations of the intestine, spleen and liver. He is in coma. Even a good surgeon and a hospital could do nothing; I have given him morphine and prayed for him.

"This one—" She looked down. "The bullet entered above the hip and ran the length of the thighbone. Multiple compound fracture." He was unconscious, and better so: blood oozed from the sodden trouser leg, and the exit-wound above the knee was cratered, vivid red flesh, white fat, pink shards of bone. "He needs immediate hospital care, and even so I fear the leg must go."

Tanya looked over to the Draka medic; he nodded. Ogden walked over, wiping the long clip-pointed knife on his leather-covered thigh; his jacket hung from one shoulder, and he tested the edge on one of the sparse reddish chest-hairs that curled through the cotton mesh of his undershirt.

"That's our plumber," he said. "Not much use, a one-legged plumber. Kill him?"

The nun looked up sharply, her eyes going wide. Tanya looked at her for a moment, and then to the woman who sat cradling the man's head in her lap, stroking his forehead with a slow regular movement that set her wrist-shackles chiming. Young, under the cropped hair and grey prison pallor. There was blood on her hands. She must have clamped the leg herself; the wounded serf would have bled out otherwise.

"*Vôtre marié?*" the Draka asked.

The woman looked up. "*Oui, maîtresse,*" she said. "My Marcel. He is a good man, my Marcel." She blinked, forced a trembling smile. "He will work well for you, *maîtresse*. Always a good worker, Marcel; he never drank his wages, or fought or . . . his skill is in his hands, fix anything, I will help him—"

Tanya signed her to silence. "No," she said to the overseer. "A plantation isn't a prison-mine, Ogden; yo' can't kill 'em offhand like that."

He shrugged. "Yo're the Landholder." His knife slid into the boot-sheath. "Best Ah see to the lead car, might be fixable, anyhows."

She turned to her cousin. "Favor, coz?"

The officer nodded. "*Pas de problème*, as they-uns say hereabouts." She turned and whistled for a stretcher, and Tanya nodded to her other overseer.

"Unshackle me two bearers, here, Miss Wentworth." To the woman beside the wounded man: "They're taking him back to Le Puy; there'll be doctors for him there, and a place on Chateau Retour if he lives." A frown as she clung doubtfully. "If I was going to kill him, I'd say so; don't push your luck, wench."

Gudrun had come up while her mother and the others spoke; walking briskly, but pale even by a redhead's standards. Tanya put a hand on her shoulder and steered her a little away. "Your first time under fire and yo' did right well, daughter." She could feel the girl straighten pridefully into an adult's stance, hand on hip, and gave her a quick squeeze around the shoulders.

"Pity about losing the serfs just after we bought 'em, Ma," she said, returning the pressure with an arm about her mother's waist.

"In more ways than one, younglin'." At the girl's frown she continued. "Gudrun . . . these are cattle, but they're *ours*. Ours to use, an' ours to guard; we domesticated them, an' when you tame somethin' you make it helpless. Like sheep, or dairy cows. Lettin' the wolves at 'em is a failure of responsibility. Yo' understand?"

She nodded slowly. "I think so, ma . . . Suppose it'll make it harder to tame them proper, if they don't think we can protect them."

"Good," Tanya said. *Well, something of that lecture on the Tool that Thinks sunk in, at least.* "We want these to be good cattle, submissive, hard-workin' and obedient even when they're not bein' watched. They have to fear us, but that isn't enough. Yo' have to make them *depend* on us; that's one reason we make the world outside the plantation bounds so rough fo' serfs. Reminds them, *masterless serf, lost soul.*'"

Gudrun smiled. "I know that one, Ma. Carlyle." A

laugh. "Why don' we keep some of those-there bush-men around, then?"

Tanya joined the child's chuckle for a moment. "We did, sweetlin', back in the old days, in Africa. A few runnin' wild in the woods or mountains . . . made for good huntin', too. That's too risky here, for a lot of reasons." She looked up at the cliff-face, spoke more softly, as much to herself as her daughter. "We'll import leopards, later. Bring back the wolves, give the field-hands reason to be afraid of the dark . . . danger-ous. That's the blood price of mastery, child; we take the freedom for ourselves, the wealth, the power, the pleasure, the leisure . . . we get the danger and the responsibility, too, all of it."

The guerrilla prisoners came up then, stumbling along with their elbows tied roughly behind their backs, prod-ded forward by bayonets whose points were dripping-dark. Gudrun wrinkled her nose at their stink; the green-coated Security troopers slung their rifles and two gripped each *maquisard*.

"Phew, Ma. An' they're so *ugly*."

"I've smelled 'most as bad, sweetlin'; sometimes there's no time to wash, in the field." A quick appraisal. "These look like they've been dyin' by inches fo' a while, too."

A working-party came out of the roadside scrub with poles over their shoulders and their bush-knives in hand. Tanya turned and clapped her hands for Yasmin, and the serf scuttled up with her head bowed, glancing nervously over her shoulder at the soldiers.

"Yasmin, take Gudrun and, hmm, what's-her-name, the halfwit wench—Therese—an' walk a ways up past my car. Ahh, on second thoughts, take Tom with you too. Don't get out of Mister Donaldson's sight, but don't come back 'lessn yo're called. Understand?"

"Aw, Ma, why can't I stay an' watch?" Gudrun said with a trace of petulance. Tanya gripped her chin firmly and tilted the head up to meet her eyes.

"Because yo're too young. This is necessary; it's also an ugly thing. It's *not* for entertainment—that's a sickness an' I won't tolerate it. Were it possible, I'd kill them clean; so would yo', I hope. Understood?"

"I reckon, Ma." A glower at the prisoners. "But they tried to *hurt* you, Ma!"

"So they did; an' yo', sweetlin', which is worse. But it's 'neath us to hate them for it; we kill 'cause it's needful, not for hate, that hurts yo' inside. Remember that . . . and scoot!"

Tanya walked over to the coffle. "Look at me, serfs," she said, jerking her chin back at the airborne troopers and their prisoners. "That bushman offal tried to attack the Draka; they ended by attacking you. It's always that way, we've seen it a thousand times. Now watch how we protect our own, and punish rebellion."

The working party were hammering in the stakes by the outer verge of the road, swinging their entrenching tools and wedging the bases with chips of rock. She could feel a shiver and murmur run through the seven *maquisards*, and turned to watch their faces. Fear, but not real belief, not yet; that was familiar, it was not easy to really believe that there would be no rescue, no reprieve. And these were brave men, to have remained starving in the mountains for . . . years, probably. A glance; the squad monitor was walking down the row of waist-high poles, kicking to check their set. He nodded, and the troopers began trimming the points, fresh-cut white wood oozing sap. Their task finished, the airborne soldiers scattered; some standing to watch the serf police at their work, others beginning the climb back to their vehicles.

One of the guerrillas shouted, some sort of political slogan. The Security NCO finished wiping his bushknife, slid it over his shoulder into the sheath as he walked back to the man, grinning. A flicking backfist blow smashed teeth and jaw with a sound like twigs crackling; the impact ran through the watching serfs with a ripple and a sound of breath like wind soughing amid dead grass.

"This one wants to sing," the monitor said. "Him first. Mboya, Scaragoglu."

The troopers lifted the man easily, each with a hand on shoulder and thigh, carried him out to the first length of sharpened wood. He began to fight then, kicking and twisting wildly; the serf policemen ignored his flailing and lifted him higher as they turned to face him in toward the road. Liquid feces stained his ragged trousers, and urine spread dark on their front. The sudden hard stink carried across the five meters of road, mixing incongruously with the smells of vegetation and river.

"Shit," said the younger of the Order Police.

"Every time," the other grunted, with a frown of effort. Shuffling their feet, they arranged the Frenchman carefully, spreading his legs over the point. "Raaht, let's put a cork in him. Not too far."

They pushed down. The scream came then, long and hoarse and bubbling. The monitor waited until it died down, replaced by a desperate grunt as the guerrilla's feet scrabbled on tiptoe, moving in a splay-legged dance. He strained, trying to drag himself off the six inches of rough timber shoved up through his anus into his gut. Inevitable futility; the rock-tense muscles of his calves could only carry his weight for a few moments. He sank down on his heels, and the scream rose again to a wailing trill as the point went deeper inside. Then a series of tearing grunts; the sound of the wind was louder, and the noisy vomiting of one of the coffle.

Strolling, the monitor paced down the line of prisoners, tapping the knuckles of his right hand against his left. A block-built man with broad Slavic features, he was wearing warsaps, and the steel inserts of the fingerless gloves made a *tink-tink* sound. Then a thumb shot out to prod another guerrilla in the chest.

"You. C'mon, sweetheart, yo've gotta date with the Turk."

The troopers dragged him past Tanya; she could see that this one had gone limp, hear him sobbing with a bawling rasp. This one believed now, yes, *knew* that the dirty unspeakable impossible thing was happening to *him*.

Ugly indeed. That's the point, she thought, watching the wide, staring eyes of the coffle. Nobody died well on the stake, or bravely. It had the horror of squalor, death robbed of all dignity, all possibility of honor.

There are so many of them, she thought. *So few of us*. A kick inside her womb; she put a hand to her belly and looked back at the row of stakes with a chilly satisfaction. "So, so, little one," she whispered. There had been times in the War when she felt a detached sympathy for the men she killed. Not here, never here. This was *home*.

Another kick. "I'll keep yo' safe, doan' worry, child of my blood." Tanya looked at the coffle once more, a sudden fierce anger curling the lips from her teeth, bristling the tiny hairs along her spine. *Remember*, ran through her. *Remember, all of you, make this worth it. Remember this forever, tell your children and your children's children*. It was the ultimate argument. *When you think submission is impossible, remember this. This is what raising your hand to one of the Race means*.

The executions continued at a measured pace, until only two of the captured *maqui*-fighters were left. The monitor stood before them, tapping a finger on his chin; their eyes were wild, and they trembled in the strong hands that gripped them.

"Well, well. One for Abdul the Turk's lovin', one for the interrogators back in Le Puy." A stretching moment. "Yaz the one."

His finger stretched out, slowly, to touch the man on the nose. The Frenchman's head reared back, spittle running down his chin, until the touch. His companion was shaking with hysterical relief, giggling and weeping.

Then the first man slumped, boneless, as the serf policeman's fingertip touched his face. Laughing, the monitor pushed back an eyelid.

"Allah, fainted," he said, shaking his head. "Well, no

point in takin' a sleepin' man to the Turk." He turned
to the other. "Yo' luck's out, sweetheart."

Tanya ignored the last impalement, watching the two
women she had bought in Lyons instead. Chantal was
standing with her hands pressed over her face, the
fingers white as they pressed into her forehead. Marya
. . . Marya was glaring at the execution, face pale and
rigid, eyes alight with . . . *no, not hatred*, the Draka
judged. *Anger*. A huge and blazing fury, held under
tight control, and the more furious for all that.

Her cousin touched her shoulder. "Yore transport's
on its way," she said, then followed Tanya's gaze,
blinked. "Got somethin' interestin', there."

"Yes," Tanya said. "But is it an interestin' plow, or a
landmine?" She sighed. "Ah, well, the work to its day."

CHAPTER SEVEN

Unlike many of my colleagues at the Sorbonne, I never held that structural-functionalist anthropology was incompatible with a historical approach. The Draka proved a fertile field for study ... far closer study than was comfortable! They proved a perfect illustration of how a society exists as a balanced stasis of forces, each furthering its overall functioning. But here one must take a historical perspective. We often hear that the Domination is an outgrowth of Western civilization; this is both true and profoundly untrue.

Any detached settlement is a fragment of its parent society. It may not contain all the elements of its parent, and even if it does, their balance may be different; so will be the environment. Thus the United States is not England; nor is Brazil Portugal, nor Argentina Spain. Yet these differences are of degree, rather than kind. It was different for the Domination; the ancestors of the Draka were a fragment of the slave-plantation society of the South Atlantic-Caribbean, itself an eccentric fragment of the western European expansion. Elsewhere, every remnant of that social formation was scoured out of existence by the forces of the nineteenth century bourgeois triumphant. In their African isolation the Draka were

*free to develop without the constraints, the balancing
forces, to which the parent society was subject; without
the humanitarian phase of the Enlightenment, without
the softening rule of the middle classes, without the
Romantics. What developed was almost a caricature of
Western civilization; the rationality, the worship of technique, the Faustian power-lust . . . so much was obvious
from study. The conquest brought me into personal
contact with ruling-caste Draka, and it was immediately
apparent that these were aliens. Their very faces and
movements showed it; even their war machines, constrained by the universal laws of nature, were unmistak-
ably different.*

> *Secret journal of Dr. Jules Lebrun*
> *Chateau Retour, 1947.*

CHATEAU RETOUR PLANTATION, TOURAINE PROVINCE
APRIL, 1947

It was sunset when the vehicles reached the boundaries of the plantation. They had been driving along the
north bank of the Loire, on the road that ran along the
embankment of the levee. Tiredness dragged at Marya
like water, a band of weariness over the brow weighting
her head, and still the scene brought her out of herself.

The river lay to their left as they drove westward past
ruined Tours, broad and slow and blue, long islets of
yellow sand like teardrops of gold starred with the
green of osier willow. It was mild, with the gentle
humid freshness of spring in the Val of Touraine; the
sun was on the western horizon, throwing the long
shadows of cypress and poplar towards them, flickering
bars of black against the crushed white limestone of the
road. Clouds drifted like cotton-puffs in a sky turning
dark royal blue above, shading to day-color and the
flaming magenta shade of bougainvillea on the horizon.
Down the bank to the river was long grass, intensely

green, broken by clumps of lilac in white and purple;
on the narrow strip of marshy ground along the base of
the embankment were willow trees leaning their long
trailing branches into the slow-moving water, over carpets of yellow flag iris.

I am so tired and so afraid, Marya thought, sliding
the window down and breathing in. Forty kilometers an
hour, and streamers of hair the color of birchwood
flicked out from under her kerchief. *But this minute is
the gift of God; He is here, so here home is.* The
fleeting scent of the lilacs, a delicate sweetness, the
heavier scent of a flowering chestnut tree. Country
smells, warmer and more spicy than her native Malopolska.
She smiled and sighed, ceasing to fight the weariness.
How had Homer put it, in the mouths of those fierce
bronze-sworded Achaean warriors, so long ago? *It is
well to yield unto the night.*

Chantal raised her head from her hands, breaking the
silence that had kept her crouched and swaying with
the motion of the vehicle for hours past.

"Are you so happy, then, nun?" she asked. Black
circles lay under her eyes, like bruises. She should be
hungry, sleepy, but there was only a scratchiness beneath her eyelids and a sour feeling in her gut that left
a bitter taste at the back of the mouth. This was her
first time so far from Lyon, if you did not count one
train-trip to Paris before the War, when she had marched
in a Party youth-group delegation for May Day.

The Pole smiled at her. "For a moment, Chantal, for
a moment. Life is a distance-race, not a sprint. Tomorrow I may be in terror, or in pain, so now I take a
minute of joy to strengthen myself." A chuckle. "Or as
the kitchen-sister used to say when I was a novice, you
only need to wash one dish at a time." Grimly: "God
made the world, we humans make its horrors. Let me
enjoy a moment where our handiwork has not marred
His."

The communist snorted and turned sideways in her

seat, looking out her window. *Humility*, she thought.
The opiate of the people.

Although there would be few people here, few of her
sort. The fields were turning dark, and there was a
deafening chorus of field-crickets, nowhere a light or
sign of man. She shuddered; this was the country, and
she a child of streets and buildings. Empty, the home
of the brutal rurals, the quadrupeds, as the Party men
called peasants. Unfamiliar noises echoed; birds, she
supposed, and shivered again at the thought of woods
and animals and emptiness with no sustenance or hiding place. Insects crawling through everything, dirt,
shit from animals lying about. Pigs and cows and horses,
sly-faced farmers and beaten beast-of-burden women;
all that and the Draka too.

She shivered and hugged her shoulders. *I can face
death*, she thought. It was dying that was the problem,
the way of it.

Marya turned back to the window and sighed again.
Anger so fierce was like vodka; one glass at the right
time could give you the strength of a bear, too much or
too often and it ate you out from the inside. Anger
demanded a direction, an expression; if you could not
turn it on the ones who aroused it, your mind turned it
on yourself, turned hatred to self-hatred and self-
contempt. *Such is the nature of fallen man*, she thought.
Also, anger and hatred gave an enemy too much grip on
you. The emotions locked you to them, and in hatred as
in love one took on the lineaments of the mind's focus;
only God and His creation, and mankind in general,
were safe targets for such feelings. Pity was safer,
charity, the unconquerable Christian meekness off
which an oppressor's physical strength slid like claws
from glass.

Your way is hard, Lord . . .

They turned left and north off the main road, between two tall pillars of new fitted stone, with a chain

slung between them at three times head-height. She read:

Chateau Retour Plantation
est. 1945
Edward and Tanya von Shrakenberg, Landholders

Beyond were the remains of a small village, an old Loire river-port of white tufa-stone cottages and shops. It was being . . . not destroyed, disassembled; she could see piles of salvaged windows, doors, piles of stone block chipped clean of mortar, flat farm-wagons piled with black Angers roof-slates. A few workers were about, stacking tools and clearing up for the next day's labor; they paused and bowed as the cars passed. Marya looked a question at Yasmin.

"Port-Boulet," she said drowsily, straightening up and rubbing her face with a handkerchief dipped in icewater from a thermos-flask. "Ahhh, tha's bettah. Port-Boulet; we knockin' it down to build the Quartahs." Seeing the look of puzzlement, she continued: "The fieldhands' quarters, the village, the mastahs doan' like folks livin' scattered about, wants 'em all near the Great House. And fo' buildin's, smithy and barn and infirmary and suchlike. Even puttin' up a church, bringin' it piece by piece from over t' Chouze-sur-Loire, a bit west of hereabouts."

The nun nodded. It made sense; a pattern of great estates worked from a common center made for concentrated settlement, just as small single-family holdings often meant scattered farmsteads.

"We's not long to home, now," Yasmin said, looking over to her father where he slept stretched out with his rifle by his side and his greying head on a folded coat. "Poppa," she called softly, nudging him cautiously in the foot. "Poppa, almost there. Ten minutes."

He stirred, touched the weapon, then levered himself up, yawning hugely. "Ahh, *gutgenuk*," he said; the nun filed it away, another of the dialect-words that sprinkled his English. That one sounded Dutch or German. "Nice t'be backs under m'own roof."

Home, Marya thought, and fought a new shiver of apprehension. A stopping-place at least.

She forced her eyes back to the darkening fields outside; they were driving north now, away from the river and into the flat alluvial *vienne* of Bourgueil. There was a line of low hills ahead, five or six kilometers, visible in glimpses between the lines and clumps of trees that cut the horizon. Already those were shapes whose upper branches caught blackly at the light of the three-quarters moon. The open ground was still touched lightly with the last pinkish light; a big field of winter wheat to their left, bluish-green and already calf-high. Her countrywoman's eye found it reassuring; flourishing, this was a fat earth. Potatoes to the right, neat rows well-hoed, about twenty acres. Marya could see the marks of recent field-boundaries within the standing crops, lines and dimples brought out by the long shadows of evening.

Smaller fields thrown together, she thought. Then they turned west, onto a narrower lane bordered on both sides by oaks, huge and ancient. Into a belt of orchard; the convoy switched on its headlights, bringing textures springing out in the narrow cones of blue-white light. Swirling horizontal columns of ground-fog rising with the night, rough-mottled oak bark and huge gnarled roots, trefoil leaves above their heads underlit to a flickering glow. The apricot trees beyond with their pruned circular tops, bands of whitewash on their trunks, a starring of blossom and a sudden intoxicating rush of scent. Then through darkened gardens to a gravel way before the looming gables of . . . not a house, not a castle, really.

A chateau; Marya had a confused view of towers round and square, patterned in alternate blocks of white limestone and dull-red brick, before the vehicles swung over a gravel drive that crunched and popped beneath the tires. They halted in a glare of floodlights before the

main doors, and the silence rang in ears accustomed to
wind-rush. The door of the car opened and she stumbled out onto the drive, staggered slightly with bone-
heavy weariness and the stiffness of a body confined far
too long. People were bustling about, servants in dark
trousers or skirts and white shirts, lifting parcels and
bundles with shouts and scurrying. The coffle was un-
shackled from the flatbed truck and led away; the vehicle followed, driven down the lane to some garage or
storage area.

The nun blinked again beside Chantal, trying to flog
her mind into alertness. Stretcher-parties were taking
Issac and the lightly wounded serfs from the truck.
Beside her Tom was stripping the magazine from his
rifle, handing weapon and bandolier to another servant;
that one joined four more staggering under the dismounted twin-barrel from the front car, all shepherded
off by the overseers. To an armory, she supposed, although the ex-Janissary kept the fighting-knife in his
boot, and two steel-tipped sticks rested in his gear-bag.
The cars reversed and moved away as the crowd melted
into the house with their burdens.

A woman shouldered her way toward them against
the movement, waving and calling with a wide smile.
" 'Allo! 'Allo, Tom!" A Frenchwoman in a good plain
dark dress, with a baby on her arm and a boy of four or
so walking by her side. The child sprinted ahead and
leapt at Tom, was caught in the thick arms, swept up
laughing and seated on a shoulder. Towhaired, but the
six-months babe in the woman's arms was as dark as
Yasmin; the Frenchwoman was in her thirties, well-
preserved with a robust village look about her, big-
breasted and deep-hipped. She embraced Yasmin's father with her free arm, was kissed with surprising
gentleness.

" 'Allo, Yasmin," she said, as the younger girl took
the baby, who was looking out from a cocoon of blanket
with wide dark eyes and a dubious expression.

"How y'all, Annette?" Yasmin replied, cooing and

blowing at the infant, who replied with a broad tooth-less smile, waving pudgy fists and drooling. "And how my little sister? Eh? Eh?"

"I am well," Annette replied in slow, careful English. "Justin is well; little Fleurette is well." She stepped back from Tom and glared.

"I am happy also to see that my husband is well. After an *affaire* of shootings, such as he promised me was behind him; at his age one expects a man to act with some sense, *non?* But of a certainty, no: they are all little boys who must play with their toys, *n'est pas?* One man already I have lost with this soldiers non-sense." She crossed her arms on her broad bosom. "Do I ask too much that the second refrain? Or perhaps consorting with all the courtesans of Paris and Lyon has restored his youth?"

Tom grinned, reached up to tug on the boy Justin's hair and hand up a rock-candy, then spread his hands in a placating gesture.

"Sweetlin', it weren't nohows my doin'." He fished in his pocket, came out with a velvet case. "An' Paris, that where I gits this fo' yo'."

"Hmmmp." She opened it; pearl eardrops. "Hmm-mmp." A sigh. "Ah, well, *d'accord*, there is perhaps a ragout waiting on the stove." She turned to Yasmin, took in the two new house-servants with an incline of her head.

"You will join us, daughter?"

Yasmin shook her head, handed the baby back to its mother with unconscious reluctance. "Thanks kindly, but I's got things to do; settle Marya and Chantal here down, 'n Mistis may need me. Mebbeso tomorrow 'round lunchtime?" A grin. " 'Sides, ain't nice to separate man 'n wife after they's been apart two weeks."

" 'Sho 'nuff," Tom laughed, and swung a hand that landed on Annette's buttocks with a sharp *crack*. She jumped, squealed, and dug a sharp elbow into his ribs.

"For that, my old, perhaps you sleep on the floor and learn manners." To Marya and Chantal, in French:

"*Mesdames*, you will be weary from your journey. Another time we will speak: we have a cottage not far from the manoir, you must visit, I will introduce you to others of us." A smile. "You will find us all very much *en famille* here on Chateau Retour, it is needful."

Yasmin watched as the four moved off, the adults with their arms about each other's waists, boy seated astride Tom's neck. A fond look touched her eyes.

"Annette good fo' Poppa," she said. "After Momma die, he get old faster than needs." Shrewdly: "Good fo' her, too. Her man die in the War, an' there widows aplenty: three wenches for every buck. Annette she, hhmmmm, kinda *practical* 'bout things, like yo' French mostly is; do y'all good to listen to her, she talk sense. Set her cap for Poppa, land him a year ago, get things fixed up regular with a preacher an' all." A sigh. "Pretty weddin': Mistis Tanya set store by Poppa. Well, time's a-wastin'."

She put a hand under their elbows and moved them off toward the steps; Marya felt blank, as if her mind was storing information at a rate beyond her exhaustion's capacity to sort it. The family of the master and mistress were still grouped by the doors; the three serf women halted just in earshot and made obeisance, waiting. Marya glanced up under lowered lids, examining the man who also owned her; he and Tanya were standing face to face, both hands linked.

Tall, even for a Draka. Light khaki trousers and shirt showed a broad-shouldered, taper-waisted silhouette; muscled arms, and a sharp V of deltoid from shoulders to neck. His face had a cousin's similarity to his wife's, a masculine version; dark tan, set off by the wheat-colored hair and grey eyes. Eye, rather: the left socket was covered by a leather patch and thong. Scarring below and above, deep enough to notch the bone; his little finger was missing on that hand, and there were more scars up the back of it and along the arm. A boy of perhaps nine beside him, a younger version but with the mother's brown-and-bronze hair.

". . . worst problem was the baby tryin' to get out and kick the bushmen to death, leastways that's what it felt like," Tanya was saying. She turned her head. "Ahh, here's Yasmin with the two bookkeepers. The light-haired wench here's the one I told yo' about, has medical trainin' as well, saved Issac's life."

"Yo' could always pick them, my love," the man said. Deep voice, slightly hoarse; the three women stepped forward and the new arrivals made the hand-over-eyes bow they had been taught.

"Up, look up," he said to them. "We save that for formal occasions, here in the country."

He rested his right hand on the holster of his automatic pistol as he turned to them; not a menacing gesture, simply habit. The other hand gripped his wife's; he was still smiling from the reunion as he looked them over with swift care, turned Marya's head sideways with a finger.

"Slav?" he said.

"Yes, Master," she answered. "Polish." *At least he isn't looking at our teeth*, she thought. Of course, he had access to dental records.

"That was swift thinkin' and nerve, savin' Issac in the ambush. Good wench." He turned to Yasmin. "These two look exhausted, settle them in." A grin. "Yo' worn down from travelin' too?"

Yasmin smiled back from under her lashes. "Wouldn't say so, Mastah," she murmured.

Tanya laughed outright and tossed a key to Yasmin. "This for the 'cuffs. And since yo're not tired . . . when you're finished unpackin', collect Solange and attend upstairs to help with our celebration; 'bout eleven, or thereabouts." The Landholders turned toward the stairs, and Tanya ruffled her son's hair; he hesitated a moment, watching the two women with his head slightly to one side before following his parents.

"The blond one isn't very pretty," he said, glancing back at his mother. "Her face is square an' her legs are short."

His father smiled, dropped a hand to his shoulder and shook him lightly, chiding. "That was unkind, Timmie, an' she's done good service. Remember what . . ." The doors closed.

"Wake up."

"Mmmmmph," Marya said. A hand shook her shoulder, gently insistent. She blinked awake, then shot bolt upright in shock. No siren, no pallet; the air smelled of cloth and wood and greenery, not the wet stone and disinfectant reek of Central Detention. Warmth, and sunlight on oak floorboards, the bright tender light of early morning in springtime, and birds singing.

Yasmin stepped back in an alarm that faded quickly. The nun rubbed granular sleep out of her eyes, looking about the room she had not seen when she tumbled into bed last night. Plain. Up under the eaves of the chateau, with a sloped roof and a dormer window; three beds, for herself, Chantal and Therese, dressers, mirrors, chairs. The furniture was plain but sound; there was a rug on the floor, and the beds had clean sheets and sound blankets. She crossed her arms on her shoulders, feeling at the thick flannel nightdress, warm and new. Luxury, compared to Central Detention; more comfort than the mother-house of the Order, in Lwow before the War.

The serf girl yawned prettily and patted her lips with the back of one hand; *she* was wearing a belted satin robe. "Solange," she called over her shoulder. "Y'all got their stuff?" To the three newcomers: "Thisshere Solange, Mistis Tanya's maid."

"Yes, *cherie,* I have it," a voice from the corridor outside answered Yasmin's question. A woman's voice, soprano, mellow and beautiful.

"*Viens, Pierre,*" it continued.

A man backed into the room, dragging a wooden crate, straightened with a grunt and left. Solange edged past and stood at Yasmin's side, looping a companionable arm over her shoulders.

Parisian, Marya thought; not just the accent, every-thing. Managing to make the midnight-blue pajamas look like a chic lounging outfit. A little past twenty, but she looked younger in the overlarge clothes; long sleek black hair bound up in a Psyche knot at the side of her head, big violet-rimmed blue eyes heavy with a tired satiation. Straight regular features and small-boned grace, a dancer's movements.

"Well, well," she said, gesturing with her free hand. Cigarette smoke lazed from the tube of dull-gold in its ivory holder, a green musky herbal scent that was not tobacco. "Open your present, there's good children."

Chantal looked up; she had been beside her sister, who was smiling shyly at the newcomer, warmly at Yasmin. There was no warmth in Chantal's eyes; Marya could read the thought directed at Solange: *collaborationist bourgeois slut*. And Solange's answer: *blowsy, over-blown gutter tart*.

The nun knelt by the box and undid the rope fasten-ings. A scent of camphor and sandalwood greeted her; the crate was full of clothes, carefully packed in thin transparent paper. Silk underwear and stockings, blouses, skirts, dresses. Unconsciously, her hands caressed the fine cloth. Chantal came and knelt beside her, running an experienced hand through the stacks; she had not grown up among textile-workers and the sweated sewing-trades for nothing.

"This is beautiful work," she said appraisingly. "Pre-War." She stiffened. "Clean but not new, a lot of it." She looked up, full lips compressed. "This is loot!" Her hands wiped at her nightgown, as if to remove a stain.

Solange drew on the cigarette holder, held the breath for an instant, exhaled with slow pleasure. "But yes, my child; the plunder of Paris. I sat in a truck and watched them drag it from shops and apartments. And sack the Louvre; Renoirs and Manets, mostly, for our owners the von Shrakenbergs. The fruits of victory, my old, even as you and I are."

Yasmin reached up to give a warning squeeze to the

hand on her shoulder. "C'mon, darlin', be nice. Why doan' I meets yo' at breakfast?" After the Frenchwoman had left, she yawned again and set a foot on the edge of the box.

"Should be enough's to get yo' started," she said. More sharply, to Chantal: "An' no foolishness, hear?" She looked about, an unconscious reflex of caution. "Ahh . . . 'bout Solange. She friendly enough, once yo' gets to know her; bit snooty, on 'count her poppa a *pro*fessor befo' the War." An aside: "He nicest ol' man y'wants to meet." Pursing her lips. "Solange . . . she an' the Mistis ain' just like *that*"—she held her index and forefinger together horizontally—"they like *that*, too." She crossed the fingers, and sighed at their incomprehension. "She tells the Mistis everythin'. Watch what yo' talks, 'round her." A shake of the head. "Ain' no harm in likin' yo' Mastah, if they merits it. Lovin' 'em"—she shrugged—"bad fo' everybody, in the end."

More briskly: "Anyhows, it six o'clock. Showers down the hall, bottom of the stairs; shower every mornin', that the rule. Those as doan' keep clean gets scrubbed public, with floor-brushes. Evenin' bath iff'n yo' wants to. Breakfast in th' kitchen, six-thirty; work starts seven sharp, that the *general* rule fo' House servants. Midday meal at one, half hour. Supper at seven, two hours fo' yoselfs, then lights out." A laugh. " 'Lessen yo' bed-wenchin', like we was last night. Sees yo' at table."

The kitchens were a bustle, a long stone-floored chamber dimly lit by small high windows; the whole looked to have been part of the Renaissance core of the chateau. The walls were lined with stoves, fireplaces, counters, plain wood, brick, black iron; above hung racks of pots, pans, knives, strings of onions and garlic. About forty were eating at trestle-tables that could be taken up later; a makeshift arrangement, Yasmin told her, until proper dormitories and refectories could be built. An upper table for the chefs and senior House staff.

The servants were wildly mixed. A dozen or so were

like Yasmin and her father, from the old African and Asian provinces of the Domination; there were a half-dozen Germans, a scattering from as far east as China, the rest locals, mainly girls in their teens. They chattered, in French and fragments of their native tongues, and here at the upper tables mostly in the Draka dialect of English.

Ah, she thought. *Cunning*. The imported serfs would turn to English as their *lingua franca*, and the other house-servants gradually pick it up from them, the more so as it was the language of the serf elite, the bookkeepers and foremen. The young girls would spread it in the Quarters, since most of them would marry fieldworkers and move back into the cottages. Of course, it would help that such education as there was in the Domination was in English only; writing in other tongues was forbidden on pain of death. Without a literate class French would decline into a series of mutually incomprehensible regional *patois* . . . Two generations, and it would be the despised tongue of illiterate fieldhands; a century or so, and there would be a scattering of loanwords in a new dialect of Draka English, and dusty books that only scholars could read.

She shivered and turned her attention to the food, crossing herself and murmuring a quick grace. Bowls passed down the tables, eggs and bacon and mushrooms, fresh bread and fruit; the Draka must have imposed their own Anglo-Saxon habit of starting the day with a substantial meal. Coffee as well; she was surprised at that for a moment, until she remembered where Europe's sources had been before the War. The Domination's coffee planters would be anxious to restart their markets. Marya ate with slow care, a respect born of a decade of rationing and hunger, remembering grass soup and rock-hard black bread full of bark, the sticky feel of half-rotten horsemeat as she cut it from a carcass already flyblown and home to maggots. Food was life; to despise it was to despise life itself, and the toil of human hands that produced it.

An old man limped in, sitting carefully beside Solange; she gave him a perfunctory peck on the cheek and returned to pushing her eggs around her plate with moody intensity. He nodded to Yasmin and the others, addressed Marya and Chantal:

"Ah, my successors." One of the cooks put a plate of softboiled eggs in front of him, and a bowl of bread soaked in hot milk.

"A little cinnamon, perhaps?" he asked the server, and sighed as he sprinkled the bland mush and began to spoon it up. "The infirmities of my digestion," he said to the nun. "One of the reasons you have been purchased to replace me." He extended a hand that trembled slightly. "Jules Lebrun, late professor of anthropology at the Sorbonne, and bookkeeper for this estate. And my daughter, Solange."

Marya's eyes widened in involuntary surprise; she would have sworn that this man was eighty at least . . . *No, look at the hands and neck*, she thought. The hair was white and there were loose pouches beneath the watery blue eyes, but that could be trauma; the limp and hunched posture due to internal injuries. He chuckled hoarsely. "Yes, yes, not so old as I look." The chuckle turned into a cough, and Solange turned to touch him on the shoulder.

"Père?" she asked anxiously. "Are you well?"

He shook his head, wiped his mouth with a handkerchief, patted her hand. "I am dying, child; but slowly, and it's in the nature of things. You should be more concerned with your own health." To Marya and Chantal: "*Mesdames?*"

They rose; the nun and the communist exchanged a swift glance and stationed themselves on either side, ready to support an elbow. Lebrun rapped his cane on the flags.

"I am not dead *yet*, ladies," he said. A raised eyebrow. "You, I presume, are Sister Marya?" She noticed that he caught the pronunciation, difficult for a French-speaker. "And Mademoiselle Lefarge, who I believe was a member of the Party. I find that I need little sleep, these days, and spent some time getting the records in order for you."

They walked through the kitchen doors, into a central section of the house. Workmen's tools lay scattered about; partitions had been pulled down, doors removed; the air smelled of old dust, plaster and dry wood, and the early morning light streamed in through tall opened windows. Lebrun waggled his cane to either side and spoke in a dry lecturer's tone.

"You see here the eighteenth-century additions to the chateau. A square block of three stories above the cellars; that was when the moat was filled in. Observe the changes the von Shrakenbergs are making; very much in the Draka taste. Fewer but larger rooms, you will notice. More light; marble floors, eventually. The stonework is sound—local tufa limestone—but structural reinforcements in steel are to be made." He walked slowly, and Marya put a hand beneath his elbow in concern.

"I have some medical training," she said quietly. "Is there—"

Lebrun glanced about, stopped for a moment, continued more quietly. "Your solicitude is appreciated, Sister, but the doctor tells me there is nothing to be done."

"How were you hurt, sir?" Chantal asked; she had the serious, self-improving worker's respect for learning.

He shrugged, a very Parisian gesture. "Cancer," he said. "It started while I was in New Guinea on a field trip, then started spreading more recently. Surgery, remissions, but it is beyond that now. Exacerbated by injuries sustained in the sack of Paris." A mirthless smile. "A tetrarchy of Janissaries were amusing themselves by kicking me to death, while they raped my wife and daughter; this was at my offices in the university, you understand. Mistress von Shrakenberg stopped them, as she was looking for some books at the time and the sight of them burning my library annoyed her.

I survived, with some difficulty, as did Solange; my
wife did not. It is debatable which of us was luckiest,
n'est-ce pas?"

He resumed his walk. "Now, ahead of us is the oldest
section of the manor; fifteenth-century. Most interesting; when you see the outside you will note the checkerboard effect, red brick and white stone. Two round
towers of four stories facing south, with conical roofs of
black Angers slate; on the eastern side, two square
towers, one three stories and one five; and the rear of
the house, looking out on the wine-cellar and the chapel.
The most thoroughly renovated section, begun two years
ago when the von Shrakenbergs took up their land-
grant here; fascinating to watch it change. The master
tells me they plan to put a whole new wing in there, on
the north side, when the more utilitarian parts of their
building program are done. 'Decent baths,' was one of
the phrases he used, by which a Draka means something rather Roman. Ah, here we are."

They had passed into a corridor in the family apartments, the area renovated in the Draka style. Smooth
glowing-white marble floors under soft indirect lighting, doors in lustrous tropical woods a dark contrast.
The walls were mosaic murals, done in iridescent glass,
copper, coral, gold; scenes of hunting, harvest and war.
A pride of lions at bay amidst tumbled rocks, against a
background of thorn trees and scrub grass; horses reared
amid a tumult of huge black-coated dogs, and the lances
of the shouting riders glittered. They turned a corner,
and were amidst a landscape of cool hills green with
clipped tea-bushes and neat rows of shade trees, with a
mansion's red-tiled roof and white walls half-hidden
among gardens. Workers in garish cotton garb plucked
leaves and dropped them in wicker panniers slung over
their backs.

"Ceylon," Lebrun said. "The von Shrakenbergs have
relatives there. The Draka took it from the Dutch in
1796; their ancestors, rather—they were still a British

colony then. And here is one the mistress did the drawings for herself—"

A German farmhouse burning under a bright winter sun, the pillar of black smoke a dun club in the white and blue arch of the sky. Dead cattle bloating in the farmyard, torn by ravens, one crushed into an obscene pancake shape by the treads of a tank. Skeletal trees about the steading, their branches like strands of black hair frozen in a tossing moment of agony; a human figure hung by the neck from a branch, with snow drifted into his open mouth. Self-propelled guns were scattered back across the fields, the long barrels elevated, their slim lines broken by the cylindrical bulkiness of muzzle-breaks and bore-evacuators, the vehicles half invisible in mottled white-on-gray camouflage. In the foreground a group of figures, Draka soldiers bulky in their white parkas and flared bucket helmets.

They were grouped about the bow of a Hond battletank, under the shadow of its cannon. The detail was amazing for a medium as coarse as mosaic; the nun could make out the eagle pommel of a knife, duct-tape about the forestock of a rifle, a loop of fresh ears dangling from a belt. And recognize faces: Tanya von Shrakenberg rested her palms on a map spread over the sloping frontal plate; her bulbous tank-commander's communication helmet weighed down one corner. Marya stooped to peer at the other figure, a man who tapped a finger on the map and pointed with the drum-magazined assault rifle in his other hand.

"Master Edward?" she asked.

"*Exactement*," Lebrun replied. "Note that there is a caption." The two women stepped back to view the cursive script below the mural: *The Progress of Mankind.* Lebrun laughed with a rattle of phlegm. "Our owners' sense of humor," he said, and led them into a stairwell that was old stone and new wood, stained and polished.

"Observe; we are on the ground level, behind the lesser tower of the east wall. Behind there is Mistress Tanya's bedroom; not to be entered without permission."

He began climbing the spiral staircase, slowly and with pauses for breath. "At least I will no longer have to climb these stairs . . . the second floor; library. Not to be entered unless you have the privilege. And here— the office."

The door swung open, and they blinked into bright daylight. The office was a room fifteen feet by thirty, the last ten jutting out onto the final stage of the square tower that formed the southeast corner of the manor. It had originally been open between the rectangular roof and the waist-high balustrade; the renovations had closed it in with sliding panels of glass. They had been pushed back, and a pleasant scent of cut grass and damp earth was blowing in. Bookcases and filing cabinets lined the walls; two desks flanked the entrance, neatly arrayed with ledgers, blotters, adding machines, pens, telephones.

"Where you will work," Lebrun said. He walked forward to the tower section. "The owners' desks; Mistress Tanya uses this as a studio, as well; she says the light is good." His cane tapped on the smooth brown tile; he settled himself with a sigh on the cushioned divan that ran beneath the windows.

Marya stepped up to look at the canvases on the walls: landscapes, several portraits of a dark-haired Draka girl in her teens. Two paintings were propped on easels. One was completed; it showed a man standing nude beside a swimming-pool in bright sunlight. *Master Edward*, she thought. *But younger.* Younger and without the scars, water beading on brown-tanned skin and outlining a long-legged athlete's body of taut muscle, broad-shouldered and thick-armed without being heavy. The other was three-quarters complete, a watercolor nude of a female figure lying on a white blanket beneath a vine-trellis of pale mauve wisteria. The treatment was free, the brush-strokes almost Impressionist, sensuous contrasts of dappled sunlight, flesh-tones, hair.

"My daughter," Lebrun said, pointing with his cane. "I am, I fear, something of a disappointment to her, hard as she wheedled to get me this position. She *will* persist in believing that I will live another twenty years; only natural, in one who has lost so much." He peered shrewdly at Chantal. "Ah, Mademoiselle Lefarge, you are thinking that there is not one of us who has not lost much. Remember, if you please, that each of us has his breaking point, the unendurable thing."

He waved a hand at their expressions, shaking his head and settling his head back into the cushions, eyes closed. Then they opened, rheumy but sharp. "Please, *mesdames*, no pity." Slowly: "I have regrets enough, myself, but no complaints . . . I was born in 1885, did you know? In Paris; ah, Paris before the Great War . . . they do not call it *la belle. époque* for nothing, it was truly a golden age—not that we thought so at the time!" Another shake of the head. "Every generation thinks its own youth was a period like no other; mine had the misfortune to be right." Silence for a moment.

"We were very arrogant . . . we believed in Reason, and Democracy, and greatly in Science (or machinery); together they would abolish war and poverty, unlock the secrets of the Universe, exempt us from history." A dry laugh. "Indeed, history has come to an end, but not as we imagined. Not as we *could* imagine. I was born into the pinnacle of Western civilization, and I have lived to see it fall—by its own folly. When I was a young man, the Domination was no more than a cloud on the horizon, an African anachronism that had somehow acquired the knack of machine-industry."

His hand tightened on the head of the cane. "Our god Progress would destroy them, we thought. Which it would have done, of a certainty, had we not committed deicide; here in the heartland of enlightenment we made the Great War, and Hitler's war which was nothing but its sequel. *That* was what let the barbarians inside the walls; we were undermined from within; we conquered ourselves, we Europeans. And so I will die a slave, and my child and my grandchildren after her." He paused. "The Draka . . . they are an abominable people, in the mass if not always as individuals. But do

not blame them for what has happened; blame us, us
old men. *We* deserve our fate, although you do not. I
have seen a world die, and while watching this new one
being born has a certain academic interest"—he rose,
his gaze going to the door at the rear of the room—"I
can see what it must become, and have no desire to live
in it."

Louder, in English: "Good morning, Mistress. I trust
you slept well?"

Tanya von Shrakenberg yawned as she padded into
the room on silent bare feet, feeling a pleasant early-
morning drowsiness. She had never been able to sleep
past sunrise, no matter how late the night before. *Six
hours is plenty*, she thought, as the two new wenches
made awkward attempts at the half-bow of informality,
and she took another bite at the peach in her right
hand.

"Mornin', Jules," she said. "Slept well enough, when
I did." Tanya finished the peach and flicked the stone
across the room with a snap of her wrist. It struck the
metal of the wastebasket with a *crack* and pattered
down to the bottom in fragments; she pulled a kerchief
from one sleeve of the loose Moorish-style *djellaba* she
wore to wipe hands and mouth.

What I really want is bacon and hominy, she thought.
And another two cups of coffee. And a cigarette. That
would be against the doctor's orders, though; cut down
on the caffeine, no tobacco, restrict the fats and salts,
limit the alcohol . . . *Shit, the things I do for the Race*,
she thought. *Can't even ball with my husband.* She
grinned and rubbed a red mark on the side of her neck:
there were some remarkably pleasant alternatives . . .

Tanya walked past the elderly Frenchman and leaned
a knee against the divan. There was lawn below, and
then low beds of flowers where the ancient moat had
been filled in a century before. She squinted against
the young sun beyond, as it outlined the beeches and
poplars of the gardens that separated the manor from

the first belt of orchards; light broke through the leaves with a flickering dazzle, a nimbus about shadow-black trunks and branches, and the birds were loud. She had spent some time learning them, the hollow cry of hoopoes, golden orioles fluting or giving their distinctive raucous cat-screams. Tanya laid a hand on her stomach. *Someday I will bring you here, little one, and teach you how to read the birds' songs*, she thought.

To work. She turned to the serfs. "Relax," she said. "Yo're goin' to be livin' under my roof the rest of your days; get used to talkin' to me. Relax."

The nun already had, a schooled implacable calm that would waste no energy. *Twenty-seven*, she thought. *Probably too old to ever be completely tamed.* A pity; she was brave and intelligent, the most difficult type to train, but the most valuable if you could. Chantal was easier to read and would be easier to handle, in the long run: a fiery type full of hatred. Tight rein and rope, spur her and let her break heart and spirit against it. Tanya considered her more carefully, and called up memories from the inspection at Lyon; sullen pouting mouth, full dark-nippled breasts, tucked-in waist; round buttocks and thighs, and a neatly thatched bush. *Lush little Latin bunch of grapes*, she thought consideringly; at the best age for her type, too—the bloom went quickly. *And just the sort of filly Edward likes to ride. I'll remind him when she's had a few weeks to rest up; a little regular tuppin' and a few babies could be just what's needed to get her tamed down and docile.*

"Well," she said. "Jules here understands the workin's well enough; just doesn't have the energy for it. He'll stay to show you the books for a week or two; an' yo' can come to me or Mastah Edward with problems. Here."

She walked to one side of the room, where bamboo-framed maps were hinged along one edge to the wall, and began flipping through them like a deck of cards.

"These are overhead maps of the plantation, done up from aerial photographs an' the old French survey-maps; shows all the field-boundaries, crops, buildin's, an' so forth. An' this"—she swung open the stack to expose one in the middle—"is how it'll look in fifteen years, when we've finished. The ones in between are year-by-year plans for the alterations." They clicked by, movement like a time-exposure photograph. Fields flowed into each other, and new hedgerows ringed them, arranged into a simpler pattern of larger plots. Internal roads snaked out from the manor and its dependencies; watering-ponds and stock dams; the scatter of farmsteads and hamlets vanished, consolidated into a large village to the southeast of the Great House, except for a tiny clump at the north end of the map, where low hills marked the boundary of the property.

"Bourgueil," she said. "That's the old winery an' the caves they used for storage. Those hillsides are the best fo' quality vines."

A quick riffle past the maps. "So, with these we can tell what's to be planted, where, at any given time, what buildin' projects are to be completed when, an' so forth. Now, these show the manor, Quarters and outbuildings; as they were when we arrived, then at six-month intervals, up to completion in five years or so. Thisshere is an overall view of the Loire Valley, from Decize to the sea, markin' the boundaries of the plantations and where the towns and cities will be." It was an emptier landscape than the present, the scatter of smaller towns gone, the woods spreading farther.

"Over here," she continued, "are the personnel files. Complete personal records on every serf, updated monthly or as needed. This set with the combination lock contains the passes serfs have 't carry off the property. These are the supply ledgers . . ."

Marya sat and strained to absorb the information; it would be best to be efficient. The accounting system was well organized, easy to understand. Very routinized, designed to function almost automatically once the decision-makers had set a policy.

". . . an' these-here are the inflow-outflow ledgers," Tanya concluded. "Mostly from the Landholders' League, that's the cooperative agency; we send them bulk produce, they process an' market it; we order supplies an' tools, they deliver. Debits an' credits're automatic 'n itemized, sent round from League regional HQ in Tours. Over time, we'll most likely have other outlets; estate-bottled wine an' fresh produce direct to restaurants an' suchlike." She sketched in the other equipment: the photo-reducer to prepare microfilms for storage and the appropriate governmental agencies, the teleprinter, the brand-new photocopier.

"Now," Tanya said, "I, my husband, or one of the overseers will generally be spendin' a few hours a day in here, but you two'll be doin' most of the routine work—I may buy another clerk if it piles up. The headman down in the Quarters has two bookkeepin' staff of his own, an' they'll be coordinatin' with you. Detailed check by one of us once a week, and the League audit is twice yearly. You work eight to seven, half-hour for lunch—it'll be brought up—five days and a half-day Saturday with the usual holidays; as long as the work gets done, we're pretty relaxed."

A smile. "If it *doesn't* get done, there are punishments rangin' from bendin' bare-ass over a chair fo' a few licks with a belt to things yo'd really rather not know about." She pointed a finger at Marya. "Yo're in charge; that makes yo' respons'ble for errors by Chantal as well as yore own. Chantal, remember your sister; both of you, remember that you could be scullions or fieldhands." A warmer expression. "That's the pain side; if things go well, plenty of, hmmmm, incentives. Not least, smooth-runnin' plantation easier for everybody, serf an' free alike."

As she turned to go, Marya spoke.

"Mistress?" The Draka stoped glanced her way. "What is that?" She pointed; a plinth, waist-high, covered with a white cloth.

"Ah, one of mah attempts at sculpture. 'Bout finished."

The Draka pulled the cloth free. Beneath was the model of a tank, about a meter long. Painted clay, the nun assumed, although it had the authentic dull-grey and mottle sheen of armorplate in camouflage markings. A Hond III, a squarish rectangle of sloped plates with a huge oblong cast turret—one of the midwar models, judging by the sawtooth skirting plates protecting the suspension; a commander's craft, from the extra whip antennae bobbing above the turret. A very good model. Detailed down to the individual shells in the ammunition belts of the machine-gun pod over the commander's hatch, cool brass gleams. And it showed combat damage, one of the forward track-guards twisted and torn, gouges, mud and dust spatters on the unit insignia of the Archonal Guard, and . . .

The nun's face went white with the shock of recognition. Tanya's was fluid with surprise for an instant, and then she stepped forward to pull off the Pole's kerchief. Snapping it through the air she held it over Marya's head, imitating the wimple of a nun's habit.

"Almighty Thor," she said wonderingly, shaking her head. Marya stared at her with mute horror. "We've met. Ahhh . . . '43, late summer. That village—"

CHAPTER EIGHT

... very different from the precocious—perhaps even precious—early landscapes of the Syrian Meditations exhibition, with their brilliantly executed but rather stereotyped pastoral and Classical echoes. Better even than the Alexandra Portraits; the delicate treatment and range of color could scarcely be bettered, but the subject— young love—is a strictly limited one. Shadow of the Horsemen *represents a new departure. Bombarded as we are with works on the theme of the Eurasian War, this may seem a paradox. But the* Shadows *collection is sui generis, and likely to remain so amid the flood of painterly veterans that threatens to drown the galleries for the next generation. The flat, static—one might almost say hieratic— treatment, the avoidance of the usual pre-coded combat themes with their pre-packaged emotional responses, all argue that something important has happened to this artist. For the most part the treatment of color also lacks the lushness characteristic of the* Portraits *and* Meditations *groups, and the compositions themselves are less consciously structural ... a second Archon's Prize for von Shrakenberg is definitely*

*in order, if only to remind our other painters that
realism does not necessarily mean a conventional approach.*

> *Shadow of the Horsemen:* a review
> by Phyrros McKenzie
> *Central Gallery Magazine*
> Archona Press, 1947

KALOWICE
MAZOVIA, GOVERNMENT-GENERAL OF POLAND
AUGUST 17, 1943.

Warsaw was burning. The cone of it was a ruddy
glow on the darkening eastern horizon, matching the
huge copper disk of the setting sun in the west. Even at
this distance the firestorm gave a smoky taste to the
wind, a hint of that sulfur-tinged darkness, the taste of
death. The flicker and rumble of artillery were faint, no
louder than the hiss of grainstalks against the steel
flanks of the Draka armor hull-down on the low crest
overlooking the village. Four dozen of them, squat
massive shapes in mottled green-yellow camouflage paint
with the mailed-fist symbol of the Archonal Guard Legion stenciled on their bows. Their engines thrummed,
the roar of free-piston gas generators blending with the
power-turbine's hum. Air quivered over the exhaust-
baffles on their rear decks, and the whip-antennae swayed
erratically in the breeze.

Loki take the heat, Cohortarch Tanya von Shrakenberg
thought, and rubbed a gloved hand over the wet skin of
her neck. She glanced back over the rear of the command tank, through the narrow gap left by the hatch
cover poised over her head like a steel mushroom-cap.

Behind them trails stretched two kilometers south to
the woodlot where the unit had last paused. Broad
parallel stripes where the treads had pulped grain and
stalk into the earth, arcs and circles across the rolling

plain showing where the fighting vehicles had maneuvered. Ten minutes of combat, and the taste of it was still in her mouth, salt and iron and copper, acid in the stomach, ache in the muscles of neck and back. Training helped, *prahna*-breathing and muscle control, the simple knowledge that the job had to be done whatever the state of your emotions . . . and still, every time, you knew a little something was gone. A little of whatever it was that kept you functioning while you waited for the armor to buckle under the brute impact of an antitank shell and send spalls flying like supersonic buzzsaws, for the millisecond flame of exploding ammunition, for the slower trickle of burning fuel as you hammered at a jammed hatch. You survived, and lost a little of yourself from within, and knew that one day if you kept coming the well would be dry . . .

The German armor was scattered back there among the ruined corn, burning with the sullen flicker of diesel oil in circles of blackened straw, or frozen with only the narrow entry hole of a tungsten-carbide penetrator rod to show reason for immobility. The *pakfront* of Fritz antitank guns had been dug in along the crest of this . . . not really a ridge, more a gentle swelling.

The Cohortarch shook her head; they were expecting to lie low as their armor pulled back past them to the village, then hit the Draka tanks as they pursued, no doubt. A good trick, but one she had met before; the Fritz were like that, fine tacticians but a little inflexible. Artillery to suppress the antitank, then a slow advance to force the Fritz armor to engage at ranges where Draka APDS shot would punch through German tanks the long way. Bodies lay hidden in the tall grain or draped around shattered half-tracks; her infantry had hunted them down from the turrets and firing-ports of their combat carriers. Two Draka Hond III's remained, victims of shells fired point-blank through the thinner armor of flank and rear, the blanket-shrouded corpses of their crews showing victory could kill you as finally as defeat.

Moisture trickled out of the sodden lining of the communications helmet as Tanya turned from the wreckage to her rear and made a slow scan of the wheatfield ahead.

The thick armor of a Hond soaked up heat like a sponge under direct sunlight. There was a lot of that in the Polish summer, and she would swear firing the main gun racked up another five degrees with every round. The ventilation fans continued their losing battle; the *Baalbeck Belle* had been buttoned up for more than ten hours, in the line for over a month with scant time for anything but essential maintenance. The inside of the tank was heavy with the smells: lubricant, burnt propellant and scorched metal, old sweat; an empty shell-casing off in one corner of the turret-basket was half full of urine with a couple of used menstrual pads floating in it . . . She ignored it, as she ignored the salt-itch of her unwashed uniform and the furry texture of her teeth and the ground-glass feeling under eyelids from too little sleep and too much exposure to abrasive fumes.

It could be worse, she mused, glancing down at the swivel-mounted map tray on the left arm of her reclining seat, past it into the white-painted gloom of the tank's interior. There was not much open space; the huge breech and recoil-mechanism of the main cannon cut the turret's interior nearly in half, flanked on either side by the coaxial machine-gun and grenade launcher. Dials, gauges and armored conduits snaked over every surface; the gunner lay to the right of her weapon, nearly prone on a crashcouch that raised her head just enough to meet the padded eyepiece of episcope and sights. Behind the gunner's head was the sliding armorplate door that blocked off the ammunition stored in the turret bustle, ready to the hand of the loader on his swivel-seat below.

Economy of space was the formal term; it took considerable training to move even in a stationary tank

without bruising yourself, and there was barely enough
open space to tape snapshots of her husband and children below the vision blocks of the commander's cu-
pola. Still, better than the infantry . . .

*Could be much worse; the Fritz could be using nerve
gas again.* Which would mean everybody into those
damned rubber suits, and *that* would mean casualties
from heat-prostration, even among Draka.

She rapped the heel of one hand against the pressure
plate beneath the vision-blocks, and the hatch cover
snapped upright with a sough of hydraulics. The lift-
brace-step motion that left her standing on the turret
deck with boots astride the hatch was nearly as unconscious as walking, after two years in the field. Wind
blew into her face as she raised the field glasses, warm
and dry, dusty and much, much cleaner than the air in
the tank; the sodden fabric of her overalls turned cool
as the moving air let sweat evaporate.

Still alive, she thought. On a fine summer's day, in
the odd alien beauty of the Baltic twilight, like a world
seen through amber honey; and it was good to feel the
faint living quiver in the sixty-ton bulk beneath the
soles of her feet.

Reliable old bitch, she thought affectionately. The
Belle had carried her a long way since the spring of '42.
North from the Caucasus, over the Don, west across
the Ukraine, through the murderous seesaw winter battles around Lwow. Wherever the Supreme General
Staff thought the Domination's best armored Legion
was needed . . . Eighteen months, a long lifetime for a
tank, even counting weeks in the Legion repair-shops
and a complete rebuild; there were scars and gouges on
the sloped plates of the armor, two dozen victory-rings
on the thermal cover of the long 120mm cannon, a
Fritz skull still wearing its SS helmet on a spike welded
to the fume extractor.

The reverse slope to the village was gentle; this part
of the Vistula valley was water-smoothed, sandy alluvial

loam. Ripe wheat, a big field of it, fifty or sixty hectares, bordered by a row of poplars; more of those lining the country road or serving as field-boundaries beyond. The grain was overripe, gold turning brown in spots and the overburdened stalks falling in swales, and the field was scattered with wildflowers and thistles.

Damned waste, a Landholder's corner of her mind noted. *Lost if it isn't harvested soon*. Three thousand meters to the north a white dirt road crossed the river that wound tree-bordered through the dry summer landscape, and the junction had spawned a straggling farmtown. Trees, unpaved streets lined with fences and gardens and whitewashed log homes, barns, a few brick structures around the flamboyantly painted stone church. Past it . . . heat haze and dust cut visibility, so did the long shadows of evening; woodlot, could be a manor house, hedges and gardens. Beyond were more fields, patches of forest, vanishing northward into the dusty horizon.

Hmmmm, question is, was that half-hard feint their idea of a rearguard, or is there more in the village?

Orders were to consolidate once she met solid resistance. Then the Janissary motorized infantry would pass through and establish a perimeter; the serf soldiers were good enough at positional warfare, and the Citizen Force legions were supposed to save themselves for shock and pursuit. It was a big war, too big to be won in a single rush; you got weaker as you advanced away from your bases, and the enemy stronger as they fell back on theirs. The Fritz had been soundly beaten east of the Vistula, but without Hitler to order senseless last stands they had withdrawn in good order, their mechanized forces screening the foot-infantry's retreat; von Mehr, the German commander of Army Group Center, was a master at luring an attacker to overextend and then catching him with a backhand stroke. It was time to halt, refit, bring up supplies for the next leap.

It never paid to underestimate the Fritz tactically,

either; Germans tended to fight by the book, but the one they used was excellent, and there could be anything ahead. Tanya tapped a meditative thumb against her lower lip, then returned attention to the hum and crackle of voices in her ears; habit strained it out, unless her call-sign came through. She keyed the intercom circuit:

"Call to Bugeye, Sparks," she said. A click, a warble, then the sound of an airplane engine.

"Check, Groundpound to Bugeye, that's negative on movement, over."

"Affirm'tive, Groundpound. Nary nothin' but dead cows an' that-there wrecked convoy I spotted earlier, over."

And the convoy had been moving away from here, northwest toward the Fritz hedgehog around Chelmno, when the ground-strike aircraft caught them.

Worth it, she decided. Plaster the village with HE, cut in with a pincers movement, then halt. The low ground along the river would make a good stopzone. *Damn, I wish I wasn't so tired*, ran through her. Hard to make proper decisions when body and mind and soul together whined for rest; harder still when the lives of friends and comrades depended on it. *No tremendous hurry*, she reminded herself. The village looked deserted, no human movement at all, which meant everyone there had already gone to ground. She blinked again, fascinated for a moment by the quality of the light, the wash of a . . . *faded gold?* Bright, but aged somehow, as if the view had been worn down by the impress of too many eyes. Tired light.

Back to the work of the season, she thought. No point in getting too fancy, but just in case . . .

"Command circuit," she said. That would cut into the headphones of all her officers. "Orders, mark." She flicked up the mapboard hanging from her waist, glanced at it, sideways at the turretless observation tank with its forest of antennae and episcopes; they would be in constant touch with the fire-support tetrarchy. "Century A . . ." she began.

The village was thick with smoke, smoke from burning thatch and chemical mist from the 160mm mortars; high-explosive rounds were mixed in, shrapnel, cluster rounds full of miniature antipersonnel bombs that spread and bounced and exploded to mix their shards of notched steel wire into the lethal stew of the air. The ground quivered under the bombardment, shook from the hundreds of tons of tread-mounted metal moving through the laneways, cast itself up as dust and fragments; the sounds of lesser weapons were a counterpoint, machine-gun chatter and the ripping-canvas sounds of grenade launchers spewing out their belts of 40mm bomblets.

The explosions were continuous overhead, seven rounds a second from the Flail automortars four kilometers to the south. Their proximity fuses blew them at an even six meters above the ground, the rending *crang* of explosive and overpressure thumping like a drum against the sternum. Tanya kept her mouth open to spare her eardrums and ignored the occasional sandblast rattle of fragments against the armor of the *Belle*; the odds of something dangerous flicking through the narrow gap between the turret deck and the hatch cover over her head were too small to be worth the effort of worry.

Besides, if you let yourself think of danger in a situation where it was everywhere and inescapable, you froze. And that *was* dangerous.

The Draka fighting vehicles ground down the street in line, tanks and Hoplite personnel carriers alternating; a fairly wide street, mud mixed with cobbles—more mud than cobbles, and those disappeared under the treads with a tooth-grating squeal of metal on stone. Tanya kept her eyes moving constantly, probing the dense gray-white mist for movement; anybody waiting with a *Panzerfaust* was going to have to stay under cover until the last minute, or be scythed down by the mortar rounds; and at ground level, their visibility would be even worse than hers. The *Belle* had a round of *wasp* up the spout of the main gun, like a giant shotgun shell loaded with steel darts, but the twin-barrel 15mm machine-gun in its servo-controlled armored pod beside her hatch was better for this work.

Flickers, adrenaline-hopping vision, presenting each glimpse as a separate freeze-frame. Roof collapsing inwards, sparks and floating burning straw. A crippled pig, shrilling loud enough to hear as a tread ground it into a waffle of meat and mud. A square of ground lifting and spilling dirt off the board cover of a concealed foxhole, a man coming erect, blond hair and gray uniform and white-rimmed eyes stark against dirt-black face.

And the tube of a rocket-launcher over his shoulder. "Target, six o'clock, *Panzerfaust*," she rasped, her voice too hoarse to carry emotion. Her hand was twisting at the pistol-grips on the arms of her seat, and the twin-barrel pivoted whining above her head; she walked the burst toward him, the heavy 15mm slugs blasting fist-sized craters in the mud. Too slow, too slow, she was close enough to *see* his hand clenching on the release . . .

CRACK. The main gun fired, and sight vanished for a second in the flash. The whole weight of the tank rocked back on its suspension as the trunions and hydraulics transmitted the huge muzzle-horsepower of the cannon's recoil through mantlet and hull. There was a whining buzz as the flechette rounds left the barrel, like their namesake wasp magnified a thousand thousand times. The Fritz infantryman vanished, caught by sheer chance within the dispersal cone. Not ten meters from the muzzle, blast alone would have killed him; the long finned spikes left nothing but chewed stumps of legs falling in opposite directions, and hardly even a smear on the riddled wood behind him, a circle of thick log wall turned to a crumbling honeycomb by the passage of the darts.

The *Panzerfaust*'s bomb had already been launched. Deflected, it caromed off the slope of the sow-snout mantlet that surrounded the tank's cannon, the long jet of flame and copper reduced to plasma gouging a crackling red trough along the side of the turret rather than spearing through the armor. The blue-white spike hung in afterimage before her eyes, blinking in front of the sullen red of the wounded metal.

That was a brave man, she thought. The Fritz would make magnificent Janissaries, once they were broken to the yoke. A brave man who had come within half a second of trading five Draka lives for his own. *Odd, fear really does feel like a cold draft.* A flush like fever on the face and shoulders and neck, tightness across the eyes, then cold along the upper spine. Deliberately, she suppressed the memory of burn victims, of calcinated bone showing through charred flesh, and equipment melted onto human skin. No practical thickness of steel could stop a square hit from a shaped-charge warhead.

"Nice," she said over the intercom, forcing an overtight rectum to relax.

"Th' iron was just pointin' right," the gunner drawled.

"Load—" Tanya began.

"*Shit!*" The voice came tinny through her earphones, override from Century A's commander back on the ridge. "There's somethin' still firin' from in theah, and whatevah it is, still goin' too fast over my head! Permission to return fire on the muzzle flash."

"—load APDS," she continued on the intercom circuit, and switched to broadcast. "Permission denied." That would be *all* they needed, a hail of armor-piercing shot at extreme range from their own guns. Below her came multiple chunk-clank sounds: she glanced down to see the round slide into the breech, a two-inch core of copper-tipped tungsten carbide, wrapped in the circular aluminum sabot. "Sparks, general override circuit." She heard the radiotech's voice calling for attention, and spoke into the hissing silence.

"Groundpound talkin'. Support battery, *cease fire.*"
Silence, as the noise dropped below the level she could
hear through ears ringing with blast and muffled by the
headset. She looked to either side, at the burning log
huts; down the empty curving road that lead to the
straggling green along the river and the only substantial
buildings in this mudhole of a town. Mist curled, patchy
as it caught the gathering evening wind, touched with
gold in the long slanting rays of a northern-hemisphere
twilight.

"Everyone in the village, back yourselves into some
cover. Tetrarch de la Roche," she continued. Tanya had
brought a Century of mechanized infantry with her;
four Tetrarchies, a little over a hundred troopers at full
strength.

"Yo, ma'am?"

"Johnny, un-ass your beasts and scout the square.
Look-see only, I think there's something big, mean an'
clumsy there."

There was a series of muffled *thungs* as the powered
rear ramps of the personnel carriers went down, and
she could see helmets bobbing into the fog. Only six
from the Hoplite behind the *Belle*, when there should
have been eight; every unit in the Cohort was under
strength, casualties coming in faster than replacements
. . . She reached down and flicked a cigarette out of the
carton in the rack beside her seat, lit, drew the warm
comfort into her lungs. There had been very little in
the village by way of resistance, probably no time for
the Fritz commander to set it up. Whatever was firing
at Century A up on the ridge had been left behind,
waiting for her to advance downslope, and had been
unable to reorient enough to engage the Guard's tanks
as they came in from each flank under cover of smoke.

A *Jagdpanzer* then, a limited-traverse antitank gun in
the bow of a turretless tank. The Germans used them
extensively; they were less flexible than a real tank but
well suited to defensive action and much easier to man-

ufacture, a quick cheap way to get a heavy well-protected gun onto the battlefield. This was probably one of the bigger ones, a waddling 70-ton underpowered monster mounting a modified antiairship gun.

A typical Fritz improvisation. She snorted smoke and patted the armor of the *Belle* lovingly; TechSec had taken the time to get this design *right.* Of course, Hitler hadn't come to power until 1932, not much time to prepare for war, and even then had not dared squeeze the German people the way the Domination could the rightless chattel who made up nine-tenths of its population. Occupied Europe could have made the difference, if the National Socialists had waited a generation or so, but no, they had to throw for double or nothing . . . *At least the Race knows enough not to bite off more than we can chew. I hope.*

"Johnny here," the infantry officer's voice replied.

"Yo." She snapped alert and flicked the cigarette out between hatch and turret. An infantry backpack radio, you could tell because the receiver let through more background noise than the shielded microphone of a commo helmet.

"Got as close's Ah could. There was lookouts, we went in and took 'em out quiet. Three big buildin's in a row, north side over from the church, look-so maybe brick warehouses; rooflines cut off the view of the ridge we jumped off from. Holes in the walls, treadmarks comin' back to a common point from all three; whatever it is, it *heavy.* Big smeared place where the tracks meet."

"Good. Pull back now, meet me here."

Tanya pinched thumb and forefinger to the bridge of her nose, concentrating. An *Elefant* for sure, the only Fritz vehicle with firepower and protection in the same class as a Draka Hond III, but limited by the lack of a rotating turret, painfully slow, even more painfully difficult to turn in tight quarters. The three buildings formed the base of a triangle, covered fire positions

commanding the open country south of the village. By
backing out to the triangle's apex the *Jagdpanzer* could
switch quickly without having to do more than a quarter-
turn; her respect for the probably deceased commander
of the certainly defunct German battalion increased. He
had had the sense to use the *Elefant* as a self-propelled
antitank gun, rather than as a fighting vehicle, which its
designers had intended it to be and which it most
manifestly was not. If she had simply blasted through
the first line of antitank guns up on the ridge and come
straight down the hill, there would have been a *very*
nasty surprise waiting.

· Now, what would the *Elefant*'s commander do? *Run
away, as Montinesque said any rational army would*,
she thought wryly.

That was easier said than done, though, in something
that could do maybe forty kph on a good level road;
also, their back was to a soft-bottomed river. That was a
problem Tanya von Shrakenberg could empathize with
wholeheartedly; the Hond III had range, it had speed,
it had broad tracks and a good suspension that let it
cover any ground firm enough to hold a footsoldier's
boots, but the only bridges that could carry it safely
were major rail links or the Domination's own Combat-
Engineer units. The *Elefant* would be even more of a
pain to move any distance, and across a soft-bottomed
riverbed . . .

There had been a *lot* of rivers to cross, coming west.

Better to catch him while Century A back on the
ridge kept his attention; that *Jagdpanzer* was nothing to
meet head-on at point-blank range in one of these
laneways. She looked up again, whistling soundlessly
between her teeth and wishing she had not thrown
away the cigarette, wishing the *Belle* was not best
placed, less than two hundred meters from the church.
Not that anyone would doubt her courage if she sent
someone else: a coward would not have achieved her
rank; the Draka had a firm unwritten tradition of seeing
that such did not live long enough to breed and weaken

the Race. The trouble was that they had an equally firm
tradition of leading from the front . . .

The infantry Tetrarch came trotting back up the
laneway, keeping to the side beside the fence with his
comtech at his heels; he bounced up onto the glacis
plate of the *Belle* without breaking stride and vaulted to
the turret with a hand on the cannon.

Tanya popped the hatch to vertical and handed him a
cigarette. "Don't suppose yo' could tell which of those
three buildin's the *Jagdpanzer*'s in now?"

"Not without we send in a *lochos*'r two, or they move
position, Tanya." He puffed meditatively. "Could try
an' get a rocket gun team in close, likely to cost, though."
A grin. "Prefer to let yo' turtles butt heads with it.
Fuckin' nightmare, eh?"

"Isn't it always," she replied with a sour smile. There
was little formality of rank in the Citizen Force, and
anyway they were old friends. Both from Landholding
families as well—all Citizens were aristocrats, of course,
but there was still a certain difference between urban
bureaucrats and engineers and schoolteachers and the
Old Domination, the planters and their retainers. Many
younger gentry favored the Guard for their military
service, since it was kept at full strength in peacetime
and saw more action. There were five hundred troopers
in the Cohort; counting families, that represented a
million hectares of land and a hundred thousand serfs.

Tetrarch John de la Roche was two years younger
than her twenty-five, but he no longer looked like a
young man. Not just the weathering and ground-in oily
dirt and caked dust; there was something, a look about
the eyes, a weariness that no amount of rest could ever
completely erase. A familiar look; she had grown up
seeing it in the men of the older generation. *Pa had it,
sometimes. Seeing it in the mirror more than I like,
lately.* They had met back in the '30s, when he was
posted to her *lochos* as a recruit; she had been a Monitor then, sub-squad commander. Her father had known

his in the Great War, he was smart and quick and learned well, was handsome in a bony blond way. They had become friends, she had gone to hunt lion on his family's sprawling cattle-and-cotton spread in equatorial Kasai, he had visited her father's plantation under the Lebanon range and chased gazelle in the Syrian desert. They had made love a few times, once in a sandwich with a serf wench, that had been amusing . . . friends, they had all been friends when it started. Comrades now, the ones who were left, and the replacements all looked so *young*.

By the White Christ, were we ever that young? she thought briefly. The infantry officer lit another cigarette from his and handed it back to his radio-operator; the comtech followed him to the turret deck, a short dark-haired woman careful to keep the set within arm's reach of her commander.

"Ride me in, Johnny," Tanya said. "As near to the brick buildings as you can"—that would give her a chance to take the *Jagdpanzer* with a flank shot as it backed out—"and I'd like to be inconspicuous." Which was difficult if you knocked down houses. "But don't forget to dodge out when we get there."

He snorted laughter and rang the back of his hand against the turret. "Surely will," he said. "These movin' foxholes attract the eye."

She touched the microphone before her mouth. "Sparks, command circuit." A click. "Noise, everybody; rev the engines and move in place." Another click. "Sammi, yo' take the western approach to the square behind the buildings. Mclean, yo're north, we'll all three go in together, that ways somebody should get a good flankin' shot."

"Groundpound to Century A," Tanya whispered, and cursed herself for the tone; nobody was going to hear a voice over the racket. The *Baalbeck Belle* was only one house away from the green, a house whose caved-in thatch was still smoldering; the *Elefant* would be there, under cover, still facing south for its inconclusive duel with the tanks of Century A, hull-down on the ridge . . . Three Draka tanks would advance into the square where they could pound the German vehicle cover or no; hers from the east, two more from north and west, any more and there would be too much chance of a shot going astray. Point-blank range, no place to be on the wrong end of a Hond's 120mm rifle.

"He's in the center buildin'; commence firin', HE," she continued in a normal speaking tone. The Century of tanks back on the ridge to the south opened up; she could hear the whirrrrrrr*crash* of high-explosive shot bursting along the fringe of the village. Her teeth clenched; now she would have to move, out into the open . . . *Almighty Thor, but I don't want to do this,* she thought. Not fear, so much as sheer weariness and distaste. The pictures of her children caught her eye, there down below the vision-blocks. Solemn in their school tunics, red-haired Gudrun with a mask of sun-bred freckles across her face, Timmie tanned dark under his butter-yellow curls; she had promised them she would come back.

If I have to kill every living thing between here and the Atlantic to do it, she thought grimly, took a long breath and spoke:

"Sammi, Mclean. Now!"

The engine howled behind her, and she felt the tank lurch as the driver engaged the gearing, rocking her shoulders back against the padded rear surface of the hatch. The *Belle* accelerated smoothly, then slammed into the thick log wall, the bow rising as the tread-cleats bit and tried to climb the vertical surface. Her braced hands kept her from flinging forward as sixty tons of moving steel clawed at the wood, and it gave with a rending, crackling snap. The tank lurched again, rocking from side to side as the torsion bars of the suspension adjusted to the uneven surface. A brief glimpse of tables and beds vanishing beneath tumbled logs, and a shuddering *whump* as the surface caved in a few feet; a clash of epicyclic gearing and the engine snarled again, a deeper sound under the turbine's whine.

The front wall burst out from the *Belle*'s prow in a shower of fragments, and she ducked her head as a last surf of broken wood came tumbling and rattling up the glacis plate and over the turret. Splinters caught on the shoulders of her uniform. The tank pivoted left and south, the turret moving faster than the treads could turn the hull; to the north and west the other two Honds were grinding into the churned mud of the square. The muzzles of their cannon moved like the heads of blind serpents, questing for prey. Tanya scanned the center building: that had to be it. Two stories of brick, square windows, a gaping hole where the main door had to have been. The roof had settled, sagging in the middle; but it was the entrance that mattered, there where the trackmarks emerged. Nothing, and—

An explosion. Not loud, a sharp cracking from the northern edge. Her head turned: the center tank of the trio had lost a track. It pivoted wildly, the intact loop of metal pushing it in a circle as the broken tread flopped to lie like a giant metal watchband on the mud, curling and settling as gravity and tension unlooped it.

"Shit, mines! Mclean, bail out! Sammi, back under cover." *Shit, shit, they must've turned the Jagdpanzer around to face north; the donkeyfuckers outthought me!* Tanya's mind ran through a brief litany of disgust as the *Belle* slammed to a too-swift halt, nosed down and rocked back. The engine bellowed, and the driver reversed along their own tracks with careful haste; it did not take a large charge to snap a tread, and a stationary tank was a deathtrap.

Mclean's *Sofia Sweetheart* stopped, and the hatches opened. "Coverin' fire," Tanya rasped. Two dozen automatic weapons opened up on the buildings across the square and the whole facade erupted in dust and chips and sparks, slugs punching holes through the brick and gnawing at the wall, like a time-lapse film of erosion at work. Then the infantry weapons, assault rifles and the white-fire streaks of rocket guns. From the ridge south of town came a multiple whirrrrr*crash* as the reserve-Tetrarchy opened up with high-explosive shell, most falling well short. Then a shadow moved within the black openings of the building, a long horizontal shadow tipped with the bulky oblong of a double-baffle muzzle brake.

"Sue, can you take him?" Tanya asked, voice carefully controlled. Somebody else was trying; she could see the cannon of a Hond moving, then the flare and crack.

"Mought." Mclean's crew were crawling back into the shadow of their crippled vehicle, two of them dragging a third. "Tricky." The main gun moved in its gyro-controlled cradle, a faint humming whine as the mantlet moved, the breech riding up smoothly.

The *Belle*'s commander slitted her eyes against the flash of the main gun. There was a metal-on-metal sparking from the darkness where the *Elefant* waited, a high brief screech of steel deforming under the impact of tungsten travelling at thousands of feet per second.

Tanya opened her mouth to speak, but before the words passed her throat there was another crash; louder than the Draka tank-cannon, less sharp, a lower-velocity weapon. But the German antitank round was still moving fast enough when it struck the *Sofia Sweetheart* at the junction of turret and hull. The Draka tank lurched, and the turret's massive twenty-ton weight flipped backward like a frying pan. Tanya watched with an angry foreknowledge as it dropped straight down on the two crewmen hauling the wounded driver. A leg was left sticking out from under the heavy steel, and it twitched half a dozen times with galvanic lifelessness.

"Century A!" she barked. "Target the center building an' knock it down, HE only. Everybody here in the village who's got a vantage, load APDS an' stay undah cover." The *Elefant* would have to come out sometime, or be buried under rubble. Thick armour on the front, heavily sloped, good protection; too good, as long as it had cover. Out in the open . . .

Just a stay of execution, Fritz, she thought grimly.

Senior Decurion Smythe saluted as she came up to the *Belle*. Tanya had been leaning back against the scarred side-skirts of the tank, looking with sour satisfaction at the burning hulk of the German *Jagdpanzer;* she came erect and returned the salute. Smythe was like that, a long-service regular. Forty, old enough to have started her military service back before women were allowed in combat units; green eyes in a leather-tanned face, a close-cropped cap of grey-shot black hair.

"Ten fatalities altogether since morning rollcall, Cohortarch," the NCO said, in a faintly sing-song accent. Ceylonese, Tanya remembered; her family were tea planters near Taprobanopolis. "Fifteen wounded seriously enough for evacuation. Three tanks and two APC's are write-offs . . ."

The Cohortarch cursed fluently in the Arabic picked up from serf playmates as a child; there was no better language for swearing. Smythe shrugged.

"We took out better than two hundred of them," she added. "A complete armored battalion."

"The usual odds and sods?" Tanya asked.

"Mixed *Kampfgruppe*, accordin' to the prisoners; SS, 3rd Panzer, bits and pieces from here and there." Tanya nodded; the battles that broke the Fritz's Army Group Center east of the Vistula had left shattered units scattered over hundreds of kilometers, and far too many had made it back to the German lines through the Domination's overstretched forces.

"Put in to hold us up whiles they pulled they infantry back," Smythe continued. "Oh, Cohortarch, about those prisoners?"

Tanya paused, clenched the fingertips of her right glove between her teeth and stripped the thin leather off. The sun was still throwing implausible veils of salmon-pink to the west, and the breeze was cool on the wet skin of her hand. She removed the other glove, slapped them into a palm, looked at the enemy fighting-vehicle half-buried in the ruins of the building her guns had brought down on top of it. The saw-toothed welds had come apart along their seams, and the six-inch thickness of armor plate was twisted and ripped like sheet-wax. Melted fat had pooled under the shattered chassis, congealing now with a smell like rancid lard.

"How many?" she asked.

" 'Bout twenty, mostly wounded."

"Hmmmm." Tanya looked again at the wreck of the *Sofia Sweetheart*. Then again . . . "They fought well, hereabouts. We'll have to keep two or three fo' the headhunters; yo' pick 'em. Give the rest a pill, do it quick." Army slang for a bullet in the back of the neck, and utter mercy compared to the attentions of Security's interrogators. She tucked the gloves into her belt, yawned, continued:

"Legion HQ's word is to get out of the way, the Guard's to freeze in place; the VII Janissary is movin' up into the line north of us, an' the Fritz are still tryin' to break contact."

"We're goin' to let them?" The decurion *tsked*.

" 'Bout time. We should've done bettah today; the troops are tired an' they need rest. Remembah, we've got to win the war, not just beat the Fritz, a victory yo' destroys yo'self to get is a defeat. Anyways, that fo' Castle Tarleton to decide. Meantime, we set up a perimeter an' wait until they can spare transport to pull us back, minimal support till then. Prob'ly refit 'round Lublin, they've got the rail net workin' that far west by now."

She yawned again, nodded toward the little stream that ran behind the churchyard half a kilometer north.

"Call TOE support, get the scissors forward." That was their bridging equipment, a hydraulic folding span on a tank chassis. "We'll laager on that-there clear spot just north of the river, less likely to be unpleasant surprises waitin'. Standard perimeter, no slackin' on the slit trenches."

"Consider it done, Cohortarch. Ahh . . . L&R?" More military slang: Loot and Rape, a parody of the official Rest and Recreation. The troops' right by ancient custom, as soon as military necessity was past.

"Loot? *Here?*" Tanya straightened and glanced about at the straggling village, burning thatch, splintered log walls, tumbled brick. "No pokin' about until it's cleared, nothin' here worth stepping on a mine fo'. No takin' wenches off in a corner, either, same reason; wait 'till we've got the civilians sorted." She wrinkled her nose slightly; what followed would be rather ugly, and she had never found fear a stimulant. Certainly not from some cringing peasant one couldn't even talk to . . . Still, it was probably the only thing worth taking, for those so inclined.

Smythe nodded. "I'll need 'bout four sticks," she said: twenty troopers. "Church'll be best for the pen, seein's how the walls're still standing, an' solid," she continued, settling her helmet and clipping the chinstrap. Her tone had the same bored competence Tanya remembered from that time back in the Ukraine, when infiltrators had tried to overrun Cohort HQ in the night; Smythe had counterattacked with the communications technicians.

You're an odd one, Tanya thought. You got to know people quickly in combat, *needed* to. Smythe was an exception. Always polite, never a laugh, nothing more than a smile. No close friends, no lover, not even any letters from home, and she had never mentioned her family. The Guard were quartered in Archona in peacetime, in the Archon's Palace when they weren't fieldtraining on one of the military preserves. A senior NCO rated a small apartment; Smythe had kept to hers,

except for the informally-obligatory mess evenings, nobody there but three servants she'd brought with her
from Ceylon back in the '20's. *Model non-commissioned
officer*, Tanya mused. *Soul of efficiency, but not a
martinet. And something like burnt-out slag behind the
eyes; wonder if I could capture it . . .*

"Johnny?" she called. The Tetrarch looked up from
the circle of his soldiers, rose. The others stayed, kneeling or squatting, leaning on butt-grounded assault rifles.

"Need a detail; decurion an' two sticks from yo',
get Laxness on the blower an' tell off the same from 2nd
Tetrarchy. Pen the locals."

CHAPTER NINE

. . . your congratulations on the promotion reached me at last, but I almost wish I was back in the bad old days, before women were allowed to hold combat-commands. Yes, I know, the Merarch and the Chiliarch are sending in glowing reports, the work is getting done. Still, every time we're in action I can't help feeling the losses are my fault, that we could have done it cheaper if I'd avoided some mistake. Otherwise, things are going fairly well; Warsaw should surrender fairly soon, what's left of it. We're getting ready for [DELETED BY MILITARY CENSOR]. Nothing much worth stealing left, more's the pity. Between Stalin, Hitler and us, that's been the story all the way west from the Kuban river—those icons from Kiev and Zhitomir excepted. We're all quite looking forward to Germany and the West, provided we don't have to hammer it flat taking it. There's been some trouble with the locals, more behind the lines than at the front; that's increased from east to west, too. The necessary measures of repression have been fairly unpleasant, although luckily the Guard hasn't had to do much in that line. It's a perfect illustration of what you used to tell me, that the owner can only be mild when the serf's obedient. These Europeans are supposed to be

highly educated, you'd think they would realize it on their own, but no.

Of course, if you look at it from their point of view . . . I know, Pa: "We cannot afford to look at it from their point of view." Still, I wish the civilians wouldn't try to keep fighting after we beat their armies. As much for the effect what we have to do has on us as for their sakes.

Anyway, Edward and I send our regards to everybody there at home. (I haven't seen him for three weeks: a recon-commando might as well be in a different Legion.) Tell Ma to get well, immediately—a new-minted Cohortarch decrees it! A hug to Mammy Khaloum, and thank her for the socks. (Honestly, Pa, doesn't she realize I'm not six any more?) A good long kiss to Yasmin, plus one from Edward, and tell her we're both looking forward to seeing her again. And Pa, some advice? You fought the Great War, and spent a generation battening down what we took then. Running the plantation and rear-echelon work is enough! Stop trying to "get into it"! You and Ma've done your duty by the Race; let the younger generation handle this one, there are five of us, after all.

> Letter from Tanya von Shrakenberg to her father
> Written near Lodz, July 1943
> From: Postwar Artists
> by Dion Andrews
> New Territories Press, Paris, 1979

CHATEAU RETOUR PLANTATION
TOURAINE PROVINCE
APRIL, 1947

"Yesss, it's comin' back. The Fritz, that was like a hundred other skirmishes," Tanya said. "But yo', now that's a different matter, not very often somebody hands me two kilos a' *plastique* under a loaf of rye." Her smile was slow and broad, as she looked the nun up and down. "Y'haven't changed much, eithah, would've recognized yo' earlier, 'cept the penguin-suit's missin'. An' the last I saw of yo' was yo' rump, goin' away." She laughed, a rich sound full of amusement, bracing her hands in the small of her back. "Who says Fate doesn't have a sense of humor?" The grin turned wolfish. "We really should talk it over, see how our recollections differ. Might be interestin'. If yo' remembers, that is."

Chantal and Lebrun were glancing from Marya to their owner, bewildered. Tanya was more relaxed than ever, if anything. The Pole's naturally pale complextion had gone a gray-white color; she closed her eyes for a moment, lips moving. Then they opened again, and she planted herself on her feet.

"Yes, I remember," she whispered.

KALOWICE
MAZOVIA
GOVERNMENT-GENERAL OF POLAND
AUGUST 17, 1943

Sister Marya Sokolowska crossed herself with her right hand and held the weeping child closer to her with her left. The cellar beneath the church was deep and wide, lined with brick; bodies crowded it, huddled together in the shuddering dark. Two dim lanterns did little more than catch a gleam on sweat-wet faces, stray metal, the sun-faded white of a child's hair tufting out from beneath a kerchief. Their smell was peasant-rank, garlic and onions and the hard dry smell of bodies that had worked long in the sun; the noise of their breathing, prayers, moans ran beneath the throbbing hammer-blows of the shells. *Remember their names*, she reminded herself. *Wojak, Jozef, Andrzej, Jolanta*. Her father had been a blacksmith in a little village like this, though far to the east.

There was a new burst of shells above, three in quick succession, a bang of impact on the roof, then a *thud-*

CRASH as the next two burst in the enclosed space of the nave and on the floor itself. The whole cellar seemed to sway as the lanterns swung crazily, and fresh dust filled the air. The child hugged himself against her side, as if to fold himself inside her; Marya looked down into a wide-eyed face wet with tear-tracks and trails of mucus from a running nose, and reached into her sleeve for a handkerchief.

Damn them, she thought with cold hatred, as she wiped him clean and settled down with her back to a wall, setting the child on her lap and rocking gently. *Damn all the generals and dictators, all the ones who sit at tables and make marks on maps and set this loose on the people Christ died for.* These folk were poor, they raised wheat to sell for cash to pay rent and taxes and ate black rye-bread themselves, and lately there had been little enough of that. The church was the grandest building in the village and the best-kept, because its people gave freely; Wojak the mason had spent two days on the roof only last month. If their own cottages were bare enough, God's house had light and warmth and beauty, and images of His mother and the holy saints, who stood between them and the awful glory of the Imminence . . .

She shook her head and glanced over at the German soldiers. They were different, controlling their fear with a show of nonchalance; she could smell them too, a musky odor of healthy young meat-fed male bodies. A dozen of them strong enough to walk, a few wounded. Most of their injured too hurt to move had suicided, a custom of the SS if they could not be evacuated.

Poor lost souls, she thought. Self-murder was certain damnation. It was hard, doubly hard for a Pole, to remember Christian charity with the hereditary enemy and oppressor. What was it Pilsudski had said? "Poor Poland: so far from God, so close to Germany and Russia." *They did not ask to be sent here.*

"Politics makes strange bedfellows, sister," their officer said loudly, more loudly than the artillery demanded.

At least, most of them did not, she thought, looking at him with distaste. An SS officer, what was his name? *Hoth*, yes; a *Hauptscharführer*, the equivalent of a Captain, born near the frontier in German Silesia and with a borderer's hatred of Poles. There was alcohol on his breath, not enough for drunkenness, but too much. In daylight, his face was ten years older than his true age.

"War makes strange alliances, you mean," she replied in crisp Junker-class Prussian; the Order taught its members well. "So does defeat." *Calmly, calmly*, she told herself. Wrong to take pleasure in another's downfall, even an evil man's. Vengeance was the Lord's, He would judge.

Marya felt the SS-man's tremor; rage, not fear. "A setback," he said. "We still hold everything from here to the Atlantic, and Europe is rallying to us."

There was a hard pity in the nun's voice. "Your man-god is dead, and his promises are dust," she said. "Now that you need us, no more *slawen sind sklaven*, no more *slavs are slaves*, eh?"

That was still a dangerous thing to say. Officially the regime in Berlin was still National Socialist; officially, Hitler's death had been from natural causes. In fact, the generals ruled the Reich now, and German Army Intelligence had killed Hitler. For good military reasons: his attack on the Soviet Union had left the Wehrmacht overextended, and his crazed refusal to allow retreat had left whole armies to be encircled and destroyed when the Draka entered the war. Now the SS were barely tolerated, only the hapless and powerless Jews still left at their mercy.

The soldier gripped her shoulder, bruisingly hard. "Is your Jew-god going to protect you, sow?"

"No," she said, looking down at the hand until he removed it. "His kingdom is not of this earth. And *I* am going to protect *you*, Herr Captain." She turned her head and called sharply: "Tarski!"

A shock-headed peasant came shouldering through

the press, with a dozen armed men at his back; there was a German pistol thrust through the belt of his sheepskin jacket. The others grew back, and the man smiled through broken brown teeth and spat on the floor near the SS officer's boot.

"You want me to get rid of this manure, Sister?" he asked.

She shook her head. "You know the new orders from the Home Army," she said: that was the underground command. Not that they were in a position to enforce orders, but Tarski was a good man, devout and well-disciplined. Also tough and resourceful, or he would not have stayed alive in the resistance during the last three years of German occupation.

"Get them out," she continued. "Through the tunnel, then into the woods and northwest to the front lines. Everything is still in motion, it should be possible. Leave a force at the tunnel exit, north of the river, well hidden. I will try and rejoin them there, if God wills."

"Is it really needful to help these swine, sister?" Tarski said dubiously in Polish. The German soldiers glowered back at him, helpless; without the Pole they would fall into the hands of the Draka, and that meant immediate execution if they were fortunate.

"Yes, it is. Now, the tunnel."

The SS man showed his teeth again as Tarski groped behind the blackened coal-fired heating stove. "So that was where you hid it," he said.

The heavy metal swung back.

"You aren't hunting partisans now, German," she said. He glowered, then turned and led his troops into the dark hole. The man was a killer and a brute, but an experienced soldier, and every one of those was precious. The peoples of the west would not fight for Hitler, even against the Draka; now they were flocking to enlist: even an ending that left a Prussian *junta* in control would be paradise compared to a Draka victory. *And the remnants of the SS will fight for civilization and the Church*, she thought. *So the Lord God turns the evil that men do to good, though they will it not.* Even this Hoth was a human soul, and no soul was tried beyond what it could bear. Perhaps there was a chance of salvation even for such as him.

It had been so long, this war. So much was wrecked and broken; impossible even to imagine what peace might be like.

She turned to the others, lifted her hands and voice. "Good people," she said, in a clear carrying tone. The murmur and rustle died, leaving the earth-deep *crash-crashcrash* of the shells. *This is work for a priest, it isn't my place,* she thought for a helpless second. Then: *Take up your cross, Marya Sokolowska, and follow Him.* There were too few clergy left in Poland, too few religious of any kind. Nation and Church had always been intertwined in this land where the Madonna was Queen; the Germans knew it, and they had been unmercifully thorough.

"Good people, have courage." *We are all going to need it. Especially those of us who have to make a diversion, risking Polish lives so that those Germans can escape.* "God is with us, God is our strength. Let us pray."

"Out, out, everybody out!" Then, as if realizing the futility of English in this Polish village, the voice switched to rough pidgin-German. "*Raus*, out! Against the wall, *Hande hoche*, hands up. Move, move, *move!*"

Marya stood, spat to clear her mouth of the dust, shook her head against the ringing in her battered ears. The shelling had been over for half an hour now, and she had been waiting for something like this since the last crackles of small-arms fire had died down. She blinked up the stairs at the helmeted silhouette and leveled rifle, raised her skirts slightly in both hands, and climbed. "I am coming," she called in German. "Do not shoot."

The Draka soldier backed into the center of the church

as the Poles emerged, fanning them against the wall with the eloquent muzzle of her rifle. Another stood closer, prodding air with his bayonet.

"Over against the wall, face to the wall, go, go," he barked, and caught her by one arm. Marya jerked against the hold, felt a prickle of cold at a grip as immovable as a machine's. Coughing, blinking, the surviving villagers climbed the stairs and filed through into the central nave of the church. What had been the nave; there were gaping holes in the ceiling, whisps of smoke from the rafters, more holes in the walls, and the stained-glass windows had been sprayed as glittering fragments over rubble and the splintered wood of rood-screen and pews. The hand released her with a shove that sent her staggering, and Sister Marya walked through debris that crunched and moved beneath her feet, toward the cluster of Draka soldiers by the door.

Draka. She had never seen one . . . pictures, of course. A few reliable books, but it had been a long time since anyone with any sense believed what they read in newspapers and magazines. They were standing spread about the shattered doors, helmeted heads scanning restlessly back and forth, quartering the ruined interior of the church. Mottled summer-pattern camouflage uniforms . . . helmets like shallow round-topped buckets with a cutout for the face, flared. Automatic rifles hung across their chests by assault-slings, most with machete-like blades in sheaths across their backs. She stepped closer, out of the spreading crowd along the south wall, and the heads moved toward her with a motion like gun-turrets. Marya swallowed dry fear and continued, movements carefully slow and non-aggressive.

Four of them. One with chevrons on his—no, her arms.

"*Halte*," the woman said. To her companions: "Check if thissun's carryin'."

One of the troopers swung behind her. A hand gripped the heavy fabric between her shoulderblades, lifted her effortlessly into the air. The nun closed her eyes and forced herself limp as another frisked her with brisk efficiency.

"Nothin' but penguin meat under here," he said. "Haunches like a draft-horse."

Marya barely had time to stiffen her legs as the soldier released her; she landed staggering. The Draka decurion had removed her helmet to reveal a sweat-darkened mop of carrot-colored hair, cropped short at the sides and back; salt ran in trickles down into the narrow blue eyes that blinked thoughtfully at her. A pair of dust-caked goggles hung loose around the sol-dier's muscled neck; her face was pale and freckled across the eyes where the rubber and plastic had cov-ered it, coated with streaked dirt below. A flower had been painted around one eye, incongruous yellow and green . . . The nun could see the cords in her forearms ripple as she flicked a cigarette from a crumpled pack in the web lining of her helmet.

A finger stabbed out to silence Marya, and the Draka looked up to the gallery that ran about the interior of the church, four meters up.

"Y'all finished?" she called to the two troopers.

"Ya, nothin', dec," one called.

"Down."

The Draka soldiers walked to the railing of the gal-lery and casually over it. One landed facing the Polish villagers along the wall, rifle ready; the other grunted slightly as the thirty-pound weight of the rocket-gun across his shoulders drove him into a half-crouch.

The NCO turned to Marya, spoke something in a horribly mangled Slavic that sounded as much Ukrainian as anything else.

"Your pardon, ah, sir," she replied, in precise British-accented English, keeping her head and eyes down. There was a string of . . . yes, *ears* hanging from the woman soldier's belt. Dried and withered, some still fresh enough to show crusts of blood. Danger, hideous danger, and to her flock as well. Marya had only been in the village a few months. Most of that in hiding, until it was clear whether the new German regime's offer of amnesty was genuine, but they were *hers*, both as the only representative of the Church and agent for the Home Army.

"It talks," the Draka said, in mild wonder, drawing on the cigarette. There was a short high-pitched scream from behind Marya, from the Poles. The NCO looked up sharply, and walked past the nun with a brisk curse as Marya spun on one heel.

The soldier who had landed facing the villagers was pulling a girl out of the line by her hair. Walking out, rather, with one gloved hand locked in the tow-colored mass spilling out of her kerchief; a toddler ran after her, beating small fists on the soldier's leg and yelling red-faced. The trooper grinned, scooped up the child and dumped him in another woman's arms.

"Hold the brat," he said.

The mother screamed again as his hand gripped her dress at the neck and pulled, the heavy coarse wool stripping away like gauze as the Draka worried her free of the homespun. There was a growl from the villagers, and the other trooper standing near swung her Holbars back to quiet it. Then the decurion was behind the would-be rapist.

"Goddamit, Horn-dog!" she shouted, and swung her boot in a short arc that ended in a solid *thump* against his buttocks. The man spun, snarling, then straightened as the NCO continued the tongue-lashing.

"We're here to pen this meat, not hump it. Freya's *tits*, Horn-dog, yo' keep thinkin' with yo' dick an' we all gonna get *kilt*. Y'wanna ride that pony, come back an' get it after we're stood down."

"Ah, dec—" The Polish girl scuttled past him, weeping, rags of her dress held over her breasts.

"*Shut the fuck up, dickhead!*" She shook her head, muttering: "Men, all scrotum an' no brain." To Marya: "All right, penguin"—the nun puzzled at the word, then remembered the black-and-white of her habit—"what's down in the crypt?"

"A few sick and wounded. German soldiers, but they are unarmed and—"

"Good," the Draka grunted. She drew a grenade from her harness, a stick-grenade with a globular blue-painted head, and tossed it spinning underhand to the woman who stood by the door to the cellar. That one caught it out of the air with a quick snapping motion, pulled the tab and dropped it down the stairs. She kicked the heavy trapdoor down with a hollow *boom* that almost hid the thump and hiss of the detonation below.

"Shee-it, be mo' *careful* with them-there things," she added nervously to the section-leader.

"It heavier than air," the decurion replied, and continued to Marya: "Nerve gas."

The nun started with shock, and missed the next few words. Her mind was with the helpless men below, the sudden bone-breaking convulsions, death like a thief in the dark.

". . . Find the rest." The decurion stepped closer and slapped her across the face, hard enough to start her nose bleeding. "Wake up, bitch. Ah said, is this lot all of 'em?"

"No . . . no, sir. There are others, many others; they have dug shelters under their houses."

"Sa. Can yo' talk 'em out? We's sure not goin' down lookin'." Unspoken: *Otherwise we'll blast or gas anything belowground.*

"Yes! Yes, please, they are harmless people."

"People?" the Draka grinned. "Wild cattle, masterless an' fair game. Yo! Meatmaker!" The woman who had gassed the cellar raised the muzzle of her assault rifle in acknowledgment. "Take Horn-dog 'n this wench, check with the Tetrarch, 'n then talk the rest of the meat out of their holes. She can translate. Get 'em all back here. Iff'n she starts fuckin' around, expend her an' the locals both. Speakin' a fuckups, Horn-dog, remember this is still combat even if they ain't shootin'."

The decurion jabbed Marya in the stomach with her

own weapon. "Yo' hear?" A nod, and she gave the nun another slap across the face, stunning her and wheeling her half around. The gunshot sound echoed through the ruined church, amid a dead silence broken only by the naked girl's sobbing.

"Yes, sir."

"Bettah. Tell these-here t'sit, facin' the wall. Hands on heads. Anybody moves, we kill 'em; any resistance, we kill 'em all. Do it, bitch."

"What's that?" the one called Horn-dog said.

Marya turned with the basket in her hands, willing the fluttering in her stomach to quiet. This was the last house, a Jewish merchant's before the War; the cellar had been crowded. And the stores had been there, just enough time to get what she needed, passed to her in the dark and confusion.

O Jesu, O Maria, she thought. *I had to set the timers by touch*, please *let them be right*. Mechanical timer, improvised, needing only a strong shake to start its count-down.

"Food," she answered. "Fresh bread, from this morning. Cheese, sausage, vodka. For your officer."

"Hnnn," he said, reaching under the cloth and pulling out a small round loaf of bread, tearing at it with square white teeth. His other hand closed on her breast, kneading and pinching at the nipple through the heavy serge cloth. Marya clenched her teeth to endure the pain passively, the anger like the flush of fever; the man had been putting his hands on her all through the hour it had taken to clear the village, her thighs and buttocks and breasts would be covered with bruises tomorrow. And he would have thrown her down and taken her if the other soldier had not been present to hold him to his work.

Fear seasoned the rage. He was a big man, two inches over six feet and twice her weight, but that was not all; she had seen him open doors by slamming a fist through solid pine planking, kill a resisting villager by crushing in his head with the edge of one palm. Stronger than any man she had ever met, and more than strong, quicker than a cat and as graceful. She knew that Draka were trained to war virtually from babyhood in military boarding schools, but meeting the results in the flesh was something else again. Compared to these the Nazis were nothing, cheap reproductions from a cut-rate plant, a child's flattery, a slave's imitation.

The other soldier came back into the kitchen, kicking a splintered chair aside through a rutching of shattered crockery. She sneezed at the dust; the air was heavy with it, murky with the dim twilight; a basket of eggs had smashed in a corner some time ago, adding its tinge of sulfur to the reek.

"Right, all clear," the woman soldier said. Her hand blurred, and came away with half of the bread the man had been eating. "Now we report." She looked at the hand mauling the nun's bosom. "An' no, we cain't take time off until we do. Shitfire, Horn-dog, y'got laid jus' last night, wait half an hour, hey?"

"Some's need it more than others," he said, releasing Marya and shoving her toward the door. "Yo' gets it by killin', Meatmaker."

She shook her head. "Yo' check the basket?"

"Shorely did."

"Well," she continued amiably. "Horn-dog, yo're as good a fightin'-man as any of us in the Tetrarchy—when somebody's shootin' at yo'—an' yo've been in it from the start, an' yo's *still* a private. Gotta learn more self-control, my man, iffn' yo' wants to make monitor. Sides, thissun isn't even good-lookin'."

"Never had me a penguin before," he said. They walked through into the gardens, feet sinking into the sandy dirt and sparse grass.

"Just another wench, when yo've gotten her stripped an' spread." She kicked Marya lightly in the leg. "Hey, wench. Yo' been tupped any?"

The nun clenched her hands into fists inside the voluminous sleeves of her habit. "No, sir," she ground out.

"So, Horn-dog: mutton this old, still virgin, she'll
have a cunt like concrete an' a cherry made a' rhino-
hide." A section of Draka came trotting down the
laneway. Meatmaker hailed them: "Bro's, seen Tetrarch
de la Roche?"

"With the Cohortarch, sis. North a ways; past the
jungleboys' bridge a bit, laager. Cain't miss it."

The vehicle park had been established just north of
the little stream, in a stretch of green common. A
sprawl of more substantial houses lay to the north,
probably the homes of the little town's professionals, a
few traders, perhaps a doctor and notary; the manor of
the local landlord beyond that. The heat of the day had
faded to a mild warmth, and the soft pink glow on the
tops of the poplars was dying; the wind blew in from
the northwest, smelling of green and dust, spicy. The
first stars were out, over toward the east; the glow of
burning Warsaw was brighter, its smoke a black stain
spreading like an inverted triangle against the constella-
tions.

"Odd how long the light lasts after sunset, Johnny,"
Tanya murmured. After ten, and still not full dark.
"Might like to try an' paint it." They had been switched
down to Inactive status, ready-reserve and available in
a crisis, but otherwise only expected to guard their own
perimeter. The High Command would move them back
when the transport situation improved.

She called down past her crossed legs into the interior of the tank: "Sue, the camera, hey?" A protesting
mutter; the gunner, for reasons of her own, preferred
to sleep on the reclining couch beside the weapon. The
heavy Leica was tossed up through the hatch and she
snatched it out of the air, a little resentful of the care-
lessness. Barring some Russian icons, this was the best
piece of loot she had come by in the last year, taken
from the corpse of a Fritz military correspondent.

Sue might be less surly about it . . . Of course, it was
a private matter, and so outside rank. *Ah, well, at least*

in the Citizen Force I'm not expected to hold the troops' hands while they get ready for bed. Janissaries had to be watched over constantly.

Tanya stood, focused, quartered the horizon in a swift *click click click* until the roll was finished. Then she laid the instrument aside, relaxed, tried to open herself to the scene; the record could never be more than a prompt, to help the heart see again and the fingers interpret. Even now they itched for the feel of the materials, worn brushes, smooth nubbliness of canvas, her nose for the smell of linseed-oil and turpentine. But first you had to get out of the way, let the moment just *be,* a perfect thing out of time. It proved difficult, even once she had let her mind sink out of the iron analytical command-logic mode.

"Sort of a shimmerin', these summer evenin's," the infantry Tetrarch said, leaning one elbow back against the barrel of the coaxial grenade launcher. He twisted his face back up over his shoulder to look at her, a pale glimmer of blond hair and teeth in what was quickly becoming full dark. "Good subject . . . Plannin' on another Archon's Prize?"

How to paint it, ahhh . . . Sunsets had always been a favorite of hers; there was an inherent sadness to them, a melancholy. But this was different, without the harsh-edge sharpness of the Levant where she had been raised. *A long way from home.* Memories intruded, of other evenings. Home, Syria Province, sunsets so different, swifter, more . . .

. . . *dramatic, yes, that's the word.* Images flitting. School, that had been an old monastery up in the Lebanon range, renovated after the conquest. That evening with her first lover, Alexandra . . . Freya, was that a decade ago now? So alien, that creature-self of fifteen years. Just a day like so many others, yet still unbearably vivid with the intensity that only great happiness or perfect despair can lend to recollection. Bright dust and sweat in the palaestra, back to the baths and companionable gossip among their classmates, then a ramble hand-in-hand through the nature-preserve outside the walls, winding tiny wild hyacinths into each other's hair.

Memory: the room, and the pale blue flowers against a foam of dark curls, that javelin leaned carelessly by the windowledge, a loose thong casting a black shadow on the cream silk coverlet. Laughing amber eyes in the tanned young face, pale rose-colored wine in the cup they shared, the taste a little too sweet, fingers touching on the cool glass. Through the window, the huge slope of the mountains in tawny-gold rock and pine and greengrey olives, falling away beyond to a sea like a dark-purple carpet thread-edged with white surf. The sun hovering, a giant disk of hot gold at the head of a flickering bronze highway on the water. Smell of lavender and bruised thyme . . .

Damn. She should be thinking of *new* subjects. And too much nostalgia verged on self-pity, a despicable emotion.

Tanya paused a moment, shook herself back to the present, made a dismissive gesture. "Oh, the Prize," she said. "Baldur knows, all *that* thing does is ruin yo' reputation with everyone worth listenin' to; yo' should *see* the crowd a' antiquated fuzzles on the panel of judges." *Long surging roar from the crowd and the hard prickle of the gold laurel wreath*—"I'm thinkin' of givin' up pure landscape anyways. Worked out. Contemplatin' a series on the War; not battle scenes, just, ahhhh, things that have the *essence* of it, eh? Direct experience—" She stood and stretched. "Speakin' of which, yo' bunkin' alone tonight, Johnny?"

"Mmmm, 'fraid not. Sorry."

She shrugged; it was no great matter. *Anyway, should be able to wangle a visit with Edward when we're pulled back into Army Corps reserve.*

"I suppose we should push a patrol or two a little north, it's part of the built-up area an' our responsibility." She blew a smoke-ring.

"On the othah hand, the jungleboys seem to be fresh an' full of beans," she added, looking to the noise and light from the bridging team a thousand meters upstream to the east. They were combat engineers from the VII Janissary; the prefabricated steel sections were in place, but the sappers were shoring and reinforcing even as the bulk of the legion pounded across. Welding torches blinked, trailing blue-white sparks, concrete mixers growled, a low tracked shape dug its 'dozer blade into the earth and bellowed. The combat elements were pouring over the river, a metallic stream of headlights snaking up from the south, speed more important than the unlikely chance of a Fritz air raid; there were antiaircraft cannon dug in around the bridge, but that was just doctrine. Six-wheeled *Peltast* APC's full of serf riflemen, or towing heavy mortars and 155mm gun-howitzers with the barrels rotated back and clamped over the trails.

"Bettah them than us," she said. The other officer nodded; any fighting north of here for the next few weeks would be a toe-to-toe slugging match, absorbing the Fritz counterattack. High casualty work: artillery was the greatest killer on any battlefield, and positional warfare made you a fixed target for the howitzers to grind up. Just the sort of thing the serf legions were recruited for . . .

As if to point the thought, the sky growled behind them to the south. Soldier reflex tensed muscles, sent a few of the troopers working on vehicle maintenance or just strolling flat on their bellies. Then training identified it, outgoing fire from the Guard's own heavy-support batteries, keeping the enemy occupied while the Janissaries pushed forward and dug in. Bombardment rocket, a single long streak of white-orange fire across the bowl of the sky and a lightning-flicker northward where it impacted.

"Ranging round," her companion said.

A Citizen Force armored legion included fifty mobile launchers, each an eight-tube box on a modified tank chassis firing a 200mm round. One or two to establish the fall of shot, and then . . . The sky above them lit, a

rippling magenta curtain that howled like the Wild
Hunt, a huge moaning that drowned all other sound
and left retinas blinking with streaked afterimages. Thirty
seconds of it, as four hundred rockets ripple-fired at
quarter-second intervals. Then the northern skyline lit
with the impacts, a strobing flicker that threw lurid
orange shadows on the smoke-plumes, and a bitter
chemical scent drifting downward.

"There must be some natural law that war has to
smell bad," Tanya said, when the ringing had died a
little from her ears. "And damage yo' hearin'. Those
yours, Johnny?"

She nodded toward three figures walking toward them
through the parked vehicles. The Tetrarch peered and
nodded.

"Must've got the rest of the locals rounded up an'
penned," he said. To the troopers, as they came to the
scarred skirt-plates of the *Baalbeck Belle:* "All done?"

The woman of the pair nodded. "Ya. Sent those
Tetrarchy D types back to they mommas, 'n corraled
the last lot a' the meat ourselfs. No problems."

The man prodded the figure in the tattered nun's
habit forward. "Thissun got a present fo' yo', suh.
Somethin' in the way of fresh food."

Tanya puffed a smoke ring, and John de la Roche
snorted amusement; these Europeans never seemed to
learn that they had nothing to bribe their conquerors
with, since all they had including themselves belonged
to the Draka anyway. Still, it would be welcome. Out
here at the sharp edge not even the Domination's armed
forces could maintain a luxurious ration-scale; there was
plenty of transport but the roads imposed an absolute
limitation. Ammunition first, then fuel, then food and
medical supplies, that was the priority; the food was
standardized ration-bars mostly, unless they could plug
into the local economy.

The nun stepped closer, offering the bundle with a
curious archaic gesture, one hand beneath and one in
the shadowed basketwork. The infantry officer leaned

down to take it, handed it up to Tanya where she lay beside the commander's hatch. "Here, yo' artists need to keep up yo' strength."

"Excuse me, please, respected sirs?" The Draka turned to look at the Polish nun, and she braced herself visibly under the cool carnivore eyes. "Please, what is to happen to my . . . to the people of this village?"

Well, this one has spirit, at least, Tanya thought. There was a small pivot-mounted searchlight by the hatch; she toed the switch and turned the light down onto the other's face with her foot. The bright acintic light washed the flat square Slav face, and a hand flung up to guard her eyes from the hurting brilliance. The delicate colors vanished from its cone, left black and white and gray stark and absolute. *Might as well answer,* the Draka mused. Impertinence to ask, instead of silently awaiting orders, but it would be unfair to expect a Pole to know serf etiquette. Yet.

"That depends, wench," Tanya said. She rummaged in the basket; the nun tensed, then relaxed as a length of sausage emerged. "If the front moves on quick, they'll probably be left to work the land fo' a while; saves on transport space an' such. Until the Security people arrive, an' the serf-traders an' settlers, after the war. Does the fightin' last long, the able-bodied'll be rounded up fo' work on 'trenchments an' such, the rest culled an' killed, saves feedin' 'em." A bite at the kielbasa. "*They* aren't yo' concern, wench; put yo' mind to y'own fate. Life, most like, short of interpreters 's we are."

The other's hand dropped as she slitted her eyes against the searchlight and glared back at the Draka. Tanya knew the nun could see nothing, nothing but a black outline rimmed in hazed white. And the hulking scarred steel presence of the tank, so much more massive than its mere size, intimidating as few other things on earth were. Yet there was little fear in the slow nod, more as if the Pole were confirming something to herself. The trooper beside her started to call to his officer, and then the sky lit again with the whistling howl of dead metal racing to bring death to living men, an agony impersonal and remote, touching everything beneath with a limning outline of orange fire.

"—She's useful, Horn-dog, so doan' do anythin' permanent," the Tetrarch was chuckling when she could hear again.

"Hey, give me a hand, Meatmaker, hey?" the soldier said, an ugly panting rasp in his voice.

The other trooper laughed indulgently. "Well, y'saved mah life just last week, an' I swore I'd pay yo' back," she said, and gripped the nun, spun her around, tossed her staggering back to the man.

Tanya drew meditatively on her cigarette as she watched the two Draka toss the Polish woman back and forth through the puddle of the searchlight's beam. Another bite of the kielbasa, tough and stringy and heavy with garlic; she dug at a fragment stuck between her teeth with a fingernail. *Still not panicking,* she thought with interest; openly afraid now, but fighting to stay on her feet and dodging for what she thought were openings, her cries involuntary gasps of effort and not screams. Meatmaker's face, halfway between boredom and a cruel laughter directed as much at her companion as their victim. The man's . . . his mouth caught the light, open and wet, teeth shining liquid. Curling with the same dreadful sidelong desire that left no thought behind his eyes, flat and hot and sick, the eyes of a rutting dog.

Satyriasis, Tanya thought. *Godawful thing to be stuck with.* Although she remembered reading somewhere that most males were like that for the initial year or so after puberty set in, hormones five or six times an adult's level. And of course a few never got over that thirteen-year-old's first wild realization that they were in a world of serf women who could not tell them no, fantasy become reality. Of course, even then, most households wouldn't tolerate this sort of crude field-expedient, a certain degree of privacy was expected . . . A scream, short and breathless; the two troopers had the nun's habit up around her neck and over her head in a floppy black bag, pinning her arms; Meatmaker was whirling her like a top, while the other's hands tore at the odd clumsy undergarments with scrabbling haste.

And most wenches back in the Domination didn't kick up this sort of fuss, either; willing to please, or meekly submissive. She remembered walking into her father's study once, looking for a book; it had been a rainy October's morning, the water pattering down the long windows in streaks that blurred the tapping of branches. The housegirl's giggles and sighs scarcely louder than the crackling of the burning cedarwood in the fireplace; they had been standing in front of it, Pa behind her with his face in the angle of her neck and shoulder, and his hands just lifting her breasts out of her blouse. He had not seen her, but the wench had. Smiled at her as she stroked the master's thinning blond hair, and Tanya had backed out soundlessly, humiliatingly conscious of her burning cheeks.

Odd, how the memory seems so shocking, she thought. *Still, I was twelve, girls get flighty and fanciful around that age.*

Down in the churned dirt by the treads of the tank Horn-dog put his hand between the nun's shoulderblades and pushed. She lurched, stumbled, fell forward and caught herself on her shrouded hands; Meatmaker stepped forward and planted a boot on the bundle of cloth, pinning it to the earth.

"C'mon, wench," she said, and leaned forward. "My friend's got somethin' fo' yo'." Her hands closed on the other's waist and jerked her forward, leaving the Pole standing bent double with her hands between her feet.

"All right, Horn-dog, can't no friend do better for yo' than that," she continued jovially, with a slap-pat on Marya's buttocks. "Go to it."

Tanya folded her arms and flicked ash off her cigarette, moving the searchlight with her toe to cover the two soldiers. *Thick legs*, she thought idly. Broad bottomed, as well, peasant build. The genitals were rather pretty, unstretched and neatly formed like a teenager's, nestled in curling dark-blond hair.

"Best-lookin' part of the human anatomy," de la Roche said, as if to echo her thought.

Below her she could hear the clink and rustle as the infantryman undid the clasps of his webbing belt; and hear his breathing, hoarse and rapid. *What an absolutely impoverished erotic imagination he must have*, she thought with mild contempt. Pursuing a little dry friction and a few seconds of second-rate pleasure as if it were the Grail . . . *Freya knows, men tend to be creatures of reflex, but this one is a caricature. Thank the nonexistent gods I was born the right gender.*

He stepped up behind the nun and opened her vulva with a brutal drive of paired thumbs; she screamed then, a shrill sound loud enough to hear through the muffling cloth. *An exquisitely uncomfortable ten minutes ahead for you, wench*, Tanya thought. Wasteful way to treat a serf, of course. Raw brutality was a crude tool of domination, only occasionally useful unless you were planning to destroy the individuals in question. Besides . . . how had Pa put it? *"The whip is more effective as a threat than a reality; and don't forget, using it changes you, too."* She bent to pick up the basket, rummaging for the bottle of vodka; a drink would do no harm, even though they were not far enough into rear-echelon to risk getting drunk. A pity, it would be good to completely relax. There was a click and buzz from the radio within as she stooped over the hatch, a ticking—

Ticking?

"Down, down, everybody *down!*" she shouted, as her hand swept the wicker container forward over the north-pointing prow of the tank. Dropped flat as it left her fingers, ignoring the projections that gouged and bit, to hug herself close to the steel, gloved fingers scrabbling. De la Roche shouted as it whipped past his ear, turning fast enough to blur in the beginning of the leap that would take him to the ground, infantry reflex

to seek the safety of soft earth. Tanya's eyes followed
the arching parabola of the bomb, glaring and helpless;
her grip on the handle had been light, no time to firm it
up . . . the basket turned slowly as it flew, shedding
bread and sausages, wedges of cheese and a square
bottle. Hesitated at the top of its arc, dropped. Down,
accelerating, dropping below the slope of the *Belle*'s
glacis plate and—

WHUMP.

A huge, soft sound, then an invisible hand lifted her
and slammed her down again on the unyielding metal,
bouncing, the adrenaline-rush slowing the involuntary
movement of her head until she could feel the movement of her neck swinging up, flexing down again,
impact and the sagging pull on muscle and skin as
inertia tried to strip them from her skull and spread the
soft tissues like a pancake. Watching de la Roche caught
in midair by the blast, the pillow of compressed air
slapping the precise leopard-curve of his jump into a
thrashing fall that ended in a landing with one arm bent
beneath him at an angle that made her mind wince
even then. There was a moment of sliding, as if time
were a film that had slipped the sprockets of the projector and now it was catching again.

De la Roche forcing himself to his knees, to his feet,
hand clamping an upper arm where bone-fragments
pushed through his uniform, white about the mouth.
Horn-dog rolling on the ground, clutching at genitals
his fall had driven into the dirt. The other trooper lying
on her back, blood showing glistening in her hair where
skull had met track-link. Tanya blinked, and felt particles of grit turning under the lids where the explosion
had sandblasted them into her eyeballs. Saw the nun
moving north in a desperate blind scrabbling crawl, up
on her hands and knees as her head emerged from the
cocoon of fabric, then running with the skirts around
her waist and white legs twinkling in the dark.

"Alive!" she shouted; the reaction-squad was already
pounding up, and one had swept his Holbars to his

shoulder. "Alive, I want answers, *alive*." They dashed forward, skirmish-spread, overhauling the fugitive as if she was standing still. Then muzzle-flashes low to the ground, the flickers of light showing figures rising from concealed rifle-pits, dirt cascading off the covers. One of the Draka infantry stopped as if she had run into an invisible wall, flopped boneless to the ground. The others dove to earth and returned fire, and the turret whirred and began to turn under her.

CRACK as the world broke away from the axis of the main gun, afterimages strobing across her retinas. Her hand stabbed through the hatch, jerked the microphone free of its clamps; she spat blood from tooth-cut lips.

"Two an' three, move forward in support; all other units, *no firin' except on confirmed targets*." Too many other Draka units moving around, it would set Loki himself to laughing if they started shooting each other up now. Her thumb pressed the hold-button down, and she raised her head to shout to the infantry. "Wait for support, no chargin' off into the dark!"

Tanya hawked and spat blood, felt the iodine taste and stream pouring from her nose. She keyed the mike again: "Senior Decurion Smythe, report to me immediately."

". . . dead meat by the time we got 'em," the monitor said, and kicked the body of the Pole at his feet; bone snapped with a moist muffled crunching. "Never saw hide'r hair of the penguin."

Tanya grunted; it was less painful than speaking. A starshell went off overhead with a slight *pop* and bathed the cohort's laager with its blue-white metallic glare; the Senior Decurion looked away to preserve her night vision. Tetrarch de la Roche was leaning against the *Belle* as a medic set the fractured humerus of his arm; *his* eyes were closed, face expressionless as fat drops of sweat trickled down his face.

Meatmaker raised her bandaged head from her knees,

where she sat before the body of her squadmate. "Yo' wants a patrol, search the houses, maybe-so get a few ears fo' Horn-dog?" she said, in a hopefulness muffled by gauze.

Tanya inserted a cigarette between her lips with care and glanced northward herself, shaking her head. *Pointless*, she thought, forcing down a sudden rage that left a twist of nausea in her gut. Pointless to risk Citizen lives in this sort of scuffle. Reprisals pointless; it would be nothing but killing to soothe her injured self-esteem, and a von Shrakenberg did not lie to herself that way. Likewise interrogation of the villagers—the Guard was not trained for it, the only language they had in common with the remaining peasants was mangled fragments of German . . . waste. Let the specialists do it. Frustration tasted like vomit at the back of her throat.

"Senior Decurion," she began, forcing the words clear and crisp through the pain of torn lips.

"Cohortarch?"

"At first light, put in a tetrarchy with support to flush those buildings to the north."

"Yes, Cohortarch."

"Notify all troops: no natives within the perimeter an' nobody but assigned guards outside durin' darkness. No group smaller than five in daylight, fully armed."

"At once, Cohortarch."

"An' get on the blower to Legion. To Centurion De Witt. *Security* Centurion, Antipartisan liaison section. My compliments to the Centurion, an' tell him"—she threw the cigarette to the dirt, ground it out with a savage twist of her bootheel, looked around—"that Sector VI-b may now be considered . . . *active.*"

"Are you all right, Sister?" the partisan whispered anxiously.

Marya nodded, one hand covering her mouth and the other gripping the bark of the tree beside her. She nodded, heaved, stumbled around the tree and fell to her hands and knees. Vomit spattered out of her mouth, thin and sour from an empty stomach; she coughed, spat, wiped her mouth and spat again, clung to the rough surface of the tree as another spasm gripped her. The nun pulled a handkerchief from the sleeve of her habit and wiped at her face, conscious of the sick-sweet stink of the vomitus spattering the ground. Another smell added to the sweat and dirt and fluids ground in from days spent crouching in the cellar and tending the sick . . . The thought of a bath beckoned like salvation.

Seconds, she thought, trying to control the cold shaking in her arms and legs. A few seconds earlier and she would have died, torn to tatters of raw bone and meat by the explosive charge. Fresh pain lanced up from her crotch as she dragged herself erect along the trunk of the pine, and she could feel hot wetness trickling down the insides of her thighs from her ruptured hymen. A few seconds later and she would have died with the Draka pumping inside her, lubricated with blood, bent double and blinded in the stifling tent of her habit.

Marya recalled the man's eyes as he had torn at her clothing, the blank shallowness of them, like chips of blue tile. To die like that, a thing used by a thing, a knothole and an animal . . . her body heaved again. Then she found herself gripping the wood hard enough that blood and feeling left her fingers, glad of the distraction. Hate was a different nausea, shrill-sick and twisting under the ribs, making her head throb. Visions from the *Inferno* and Hieronymus Bosch moved behind her eyelids, eternal torment for the evildoer, burning, flaying, rotted with insects crawling through immortal diseased flesh—

Shuddering, she forced a different picture into the forefront of her mind, the Savior on the cross. *Lord, they flogged you until the ribs showed, beat nails through your hands and feet, stabbed you in the side with a spear, and when you cried out for water they gave you vinegar to drink. As you died you called out to the Father to forgive them.*

"Your way is hard, Lord," she whispered to herself.

"I will try." To the guerrilla whose concern she could sense through the near-absolute darkness of the nighted woods: "I can walk, my child, but turn your back for a moment, please."

He obeyed, moving off a few paces with an embarrassed mutter. Marya fumbled up her skirts, improvised a pad from the handkerchief and the rags of her undergarments to absorb the flow of blood. She winced again at the pressure of cloth on the bruised, torn flesh, and distracted herself with the prayers the Rule prescribed when it was necessary to touch the private parts; the words served well enough to take the mind off pain.

"Come," she said, forcing discomfort down into the dark well where she kept fear and loneliness and despair, waiting until there was time to deal with them. She looked up, hunting stars to confirm the map in her mind. "We've got a fair distance to cover and shelter to find before dawn."

CHAPTER TEN

Riots in Mexico City [NPS] President Marshall confirmed today that Federal troops would be called out at the request of Miguel Perrez y Ayala, newly-elected Governor of Anahuac, who announced earlier this morning that anti-immigrant rioting was continuing in Hispanic areas of Mexico City for the fourth day. Governor Perrez conceded that state and local police were unable to quell the violence, although they had confined it largely to the older residential portions of the city. The troubles are believed to have been sparked by the Senate's authorization of funds for a new settlement of European refugees in the Mexico City metropolitan zone, and by housing shortages caused by the rapid influx of English-speaking migrants attracted by the area's booming electronics and aircraft industries.

"There are legitimate grievances behind this unrest," the governor said in his radio broadcast. Conceding that Anahuac is now the northernmost state with a Spanish-speaking majority, he deplored the exploitation of ethnic tensions by irresponsible demagogues. "Violence will accomplish nothing; our language and heritage must be preserved through peaceful economic and cultural development, for which the Democratic-Progressive party has

*always stood. Anahuac cannot remain a backwater, and
growth means increased immigration from out-of-state.
The alternative is a return to the conditions before the
New Deal, when our sons and daughters were forced to
migrate to Chicago and Havana to seek employment."*

*In related news, the Supreme Court today upheld the
12th Federal Circuit Court's judgment that Guatemalan
state law cannot require literacy in English or Spanish as
a qualification for the franchise. "The Fourteenth Amend-
ment is unequivocal," Chief Justice Fineberg stated, de-
livering the majority judgment. Republican sources in
Guatemala have denounced the move as partisan, citing
statistics showing most of the unilingual Indian-speaking
communities of the highlands would vote overwhelmingly Democratic-Progressive if the franchise restrictions
were lifted.*

*New York Times
April 16, 1947*

CHATEAU RETOUR PLANTATION, TOURAINE PROVINCE
JULY, 1947

"Must we do it today?" Chantal LeFarge asked, shifting the ledger restlessly from one arm to another.

"It will do you good to get out of doors," Marya
Sokolowska said firmly. The other woman had been
losing weight and sleep . . . The nun forced herself not
to think of the real reason: it was not something she
could alter, and bringing it up would help neither of
them. "Besides, we've done as much as we can without
instructions. This way."

They turned right from the south-facing main doors,
between tall beeches that threw dazzling leaf-blinks of
sunlight in their faces. The gardens to the east of the
Great House were warm and softly murmurous with
bee-hum, drowsing in the early summer afternoon. Further out they grew shaggy, where fields had been en-

closed for future care. Labor and time were still too short for much to be spent on adornment, and the von Shrakenbergs had merely transplanted sapling trees where avenues and groves would be. Sheep grazed there, keeping the grass mowed short and starting the process that would end in dense velvet-textured lawns. Lately they were joined by a group of dikdik, miniature antelopes four inches at the shoulder; by peacocks and red deer and flamingos.

One of the huge black-coated hounds the Draka kept ambled over to the two women, nosing at Marya's hand; she ruffled the beast's ears, which were nearly at the level of her chest. *Lion dog indeed*, she thought. That was the Draka name for the breed. For their size, and the thick manelike ruff the males grew. And because they were used in catsticking, putting lions at bay for mounted hunters with lances. It wagged its tail, sniffed suspiciously at Chantal, who was holding herself rigid with control. Lion-dogs were also used to hunt runaway serfs, and they had both seen the scars on a man who had tried to make the Channel, soon after the plantation was founded; he had been kept alive at considerable trouble, as an example.

"It's only a dog, Chantal," Marya said. "Touch it, go ahead." The younger woman extended a hand, which received a perfunctory sniff; it wagged its tail and trotted away, nails clicking on the bricks. They continued around a screen of bushes, past a dry fountain, its link to the water-main not yet finished.

Marya stopped at an open manhole cover; the man sitting on the edge beside a wheeled tray of tools stubbed out his cigarette and made to rise, removing his flat cloth cap.

"No, Marcel," the nun said. "How is the leg? I thought you had permission to rest a while yet." *Although he's making a good recovery*, she thought critically. Still drawn and underweight, but it had been only three months since the ambush in the gorge, and it was excellent progress for such a serious injury, followed by major surgery. Of course, the Domination's medical corps had a matchless fund of experience in dealing with wound-trauma.

He laughed with a slightly sheepish expression and slapped the cap against the stainless-steel prosthetic that replaced his left leg above the knee. "A good afternoon, Sister. Don't worry, I'm not walking far on it yet, I sit on the cart and young André here"—an adolescent popped his head out of the hole, nodded to Marya and Chantal, and returned below to the accompaniment of a metallic clanking and banging—"pushes me about. He's a good apprentice, but he needs direction. I only work where I can sit, *vraiment* . . . and I was getting bored, sitting in the cottage and annoying Jacqueline, she has her own work to do. Believe me, Sister, it does a man good to get out in the fresh air and feel he's doing something useful. Very interesting system of piping they've put in here, extruded aluminum where we'd've used cast-iron."

He yawned, paused to look down. "No, no, the *number three connector*, imbecile!" To Marya: "And is it true there's to be a holiday, Sister?"

Chantal answered, running her hand through her uncombed hair. "Yes. The next generation of tyrants is a month old."

The air was warm, scented with tea-roses and freshly cut grass, but a chill seemed to touch them. "Now, that was a very stupid thing to say, Mademoiselle LeFarge," the plumber replied softly. "Very stupid indeed." Down the hole, where the noises had ceased: "Continue, André, and keep your ears shut."

Chantal glared at him through red-rimmed eyes; the pipefitter had belonged to the Catholic trade union, before the War. *Class-traitor*, she thought: just the sort one would expect to turn out a collaborationist. "You were expecting a song of praise for our owners, perhaps?"

"*Chantal!*" Marya whispered sharply.

"No, Sister, let me reply."

Marcel picked up a wrench and spun the adjusting

screw, but his eyes never left Chantal's. "I heard a great deal of that sort of thing before the War," he said. The nun looked at his hands, broad and battered like any workingman's, but also scarred across the knuckles. "Union jurisdictional disputes" in Lyon had meant more than handing out pamphlets, she suspected.

"In the Army, too, after I was called up; that was in '40, before the Nazis attacked Russia. The Party men were always going on about how it was a war for the rich only; after we lost, they said right out we should collaborate. I know, I spent three years in a German prisoner-of-war camp and they let copies of *L'Humanité* circulate. Then when we were released I fought again as a volunteer against the Draka, in Belgium, and I escaped because a Flemish peasant saw a rosary in my hand when he found me lying wounded in the woods. And it was a Frenchman who shot off my leg.

"So now, *comrade* LeFarge, I have my work, my garden, a child on the way and a wife who I do not intend to leave alone again. That is *all* that concerns me. About what used to be, I try not to think at all; I have fought enough. Too much to be pushed by someone like you, the type who lost us everything. Now if Father Adelard, or the good Sister here, tells me to do more, I would consider it . . . As for you, *comrade*, endanger yourself if you must. *But not me or my family!* Or you may suffer an accident. You understand me?"

The Frenchwoman's eyes slid away from his. He nodded to the nun. "A beautiful day, Sister, isn't it? As pretty a place to work as any, as well." A shaky smile. "Better smelling than most a man in my trade gets."

Marya nodded, and decided not to rebuke the man for the threat. Besides which, he was right; it was pure folly to take risks without need or hope of results. Sinful, even; *prudentia* was a virtue, and God had not given the gift of life to be spent recklessly.

"Indeed it is, Marcel," she replied gently; he was sweating, struggling to control his breathing and put on an appearance of calm. There were so many with memories too hurtful to bear, on this wounded earth. She glanced around. "Beautiful, today."

Here, closer to the manor, the changes were more extensive, old plantings with alterations in the Draka taste; French gardens were too formal and close-pruned to suit them. Pathways in tessellated colored bricks salvaged from ruins and towns, ponds and watercourses, a few fine pieces of statuary in bronze or marble, mostly loot as well. And flowerbeds, bush and trellis roses, young hedges of *multiflora*, banks of purple violets, impatiens in mounds of hot coral and magenta, geraniums nodding in trembling sheets of pale translucent lavender. She had seen Tanya's watercolors of what the grounds would look like when the plans were complete; this was merely a foreshadowing.

Well, at least they use their stolen wealth for something *besides tanks and bombers*, she thought wryly.

"I'm sorry," Chantal said, beside her. "It's just—I—"

"I know," Marya said, putting an arm around her shoulders. She could feel a quiver under her palm. "I understand, child. Do you want to go back? I can give the mistress her summaries myself."

"No, no." Chantal drew herself up. "You do more than your share already."

The pergola was set in the middle of a maze, the young hedges only knee-high as yet, with tall beeches and poplars left standing from the pre-War gardens. The inner passages opened into a lawn; centered within was a low U-shaped platform of dark red-veined marble, facing west. Three-meter pillars of Italian alabaster around its edge supported a low dome of chiseled bronze openwork, and continued in a freestanding colonnade to the entrance. There a dancing nymph poured water from a vase into a seashell, and a little stream chuckled down a carved stone bed through the risers of the stairs. Climbing roses twined through wooden trellises between the columns, over lacework arches above them, through the verdigrised metal flowers of the dome; for a moment Marya thought of blood-drops on a sheet of crumpled green velvet. Music sounded over the quiet plashing of the water.

"Solange," Chantal said. Marya nodded; the instrumental portion was a recording but the voice of Tanya's body-servant was unmistakable, a soaring mezzo-soprano, beautifully trained. Solange had spent two years in the *Conservatoire* in Paris, and practiced faithfully since.

"Delibes," Chantal continued. The nun nodded, startled at another flash of the scholarship the girl from Lyons occasionally showed. "Delibes' *Lakme*, the *Fleurette à deux*.

"Quite good," she continued. "Not meant for a solo, but quite good." It was spoken grudgingly: there was bad blood between the two.

The two bookkeepers entered, made their obeisance; Tanya von Shrakenberg signaled them to wait with an upraised palm.

Marya looked at her, then transferred a fixed gaze to the edge of the pergola above, blushing furiously. The mistress of Chateau Retour was reclining on a lounger covered in white samnite, wearing an undergarment that seemed to be made of nothing but two triangles of silk. *Shameless*, the nun thought. *I should be accustomed to it, but I cannot.* She herself was dressed in an ankle-length skirt and a high-collared blouse that buttoned at the wrist; she wiped sweat from her upper lip and suppressed a moment's envy at the cool comfort of the long body resting in the dappled shade. *Indecent*. The Rule of her own Order forbade even bathing without at least a shift.

Of course, it could be worse: at least Tanya was a woman; Draka men were equally careless. Grimly she forced her eyes down again, aware that her ears had turned a bright burning pink and that her owner would see and be amused. The Draka was lying with one arm behind her head, the other resting on a table beside the couch that bore a Carries coffee service and a bowl of strawberries beside a tall glass of clotted cream. Beyond that was a wheeled stroller with her month-old twins;

one was looking around with the mild wide-eyed wonder of any infant, the other suckling at the breast of the wetnurse who sat beside the carriage.

That did not embarrass her; it was something you saw every day in a Polish village. *Madonna and child*, she thought with a brief warmth. A real thing, and also the representation of a Mystery, the first icon of compassion; even the heathen in the days before Christ had made the Mother and Babe a symbol of holiness. Marya watched the wetnurse as she smiled and stroked the baby's cheek; remembered hearing that Draka women almost never breast-fed their infants, and wondered how they could bear not to.

Lovely, Tanya thought, as she watched Solange sing. The piece: French music had reached its absolute peak in those two generations before the Great War. The voice: it had a smooth purity like mercury on dry ice, soaring without the slightest hint of strain, and enormous range. Solange herself: living disproof of the old operatic convention that singers had to be barrel-built.

She stood beside the needle-player in a long white gown and embroidered vest, head thrown back and eyes closed in the transport of her craft. The early-afternoon sun was filtered onto her face through the green and crimson of the rose-vines, moving in shimmering patterns of light, shade, color. Leaf-tinted light on white silk, an onyx ripple on the long cascade of black hair, salmon-pink glinting on the pale fine-grained skin of her neck and shoulders. A classic French face, oval beneath a broad smooth brow, short straight nose, a delicate cleft in the small squared-off chin, and a cupid's bow mouth with a long upper lip; she had a dancer's figure, slender limbs and curves more subtle than opulent.

The music ceased and Solange stood for a moment outlined against the sunlit falling water of the fountain; then her sooty lashes fluttered open to reveal the strange violet rims around the iris of her eyes, strange enough to be a slight shock every time they were seen.

Exquisite, Tanya thought, with a moment's helpless frustration; she would never be able to capture that on canvas. *Exquisite, like a piece of jewelry by Fabergé, or a Fragonard painting*.

"Exquisite," she breathed.

Solange smiled, nodding to Marya and Chantal before switching off the player and coming to kneel gracefully beside the lounger.

"I'm pleased you like my adaptation, Mistress," she said demurely, peering up from the curtain of her hair.

It drifted along Tanya's flank, and she shivered slightly at the ghost-feather touch, running her fingers through the cool strands. They smelled of *sambuc*-jasmine perfume, mingling with the pleasant natural odor of clean sun-warmed skin.

Solange sighed. "Mmmm . . . It really needs a live orchestra and another singer, for the original."

"Well, the music, yes. Must get a recordin' made, next time we're in Tours. *Mais je parle d'toi, ma douce*," Tanya continued, as her free hand dipped one of the strawberries into the sugar-dusted cream. She took it between her lips and leaned forward; Solange giggled, held her hair aside with one hand and propped herself on an elbow to meet the Draka. They nibbled inward from opposite sides of the berry until their lips met; Tanya smiled through the kiss, and chuckled as Solange delicately licked the juice from her chin.

"Just thinkin'," she said. The serf completed the task with a linen cloth from the table and knelt back, resting her cheek on Tanya's stomach. The Draka stretched, feeling the slow warm movement of the summer air over her skin, the soft resilience of the samnite beneath her, the butterfly brush of Solange's lashes; savoring the mingled tastes of strawberry, cream and the mint flavor of the other's mouth.

"Of what, *maîtresse?*" Solange said, sighing and throwing an arm across the other's body.

"Just thinkin'," Tanya continued, "that these are the fabled hardships an' trials of the pioneer life." She stroked the serf's hair, feeling her silent smile through the slim muscles at the back of her neck. Briefly she remembered Paris and the screams that had made her kick open the office door; Solange had been crawling and choking over the garbage-strewn floor of her father's office, face battered into a puffed oozing mask, her skin bruised and marked by fists and boots and teeth.

"Also that it's a damn' good thing I was the one who got yo'," she mused. "Absolute sacrilege to think of yo' fallin' into the hands of someone who couldn't appreciate you. Like usin' a da Vinci as a dishrag."

"*D'accord, maîtresse!*" Solange said.

"Did I tell yo' Jimbob Claremont tried to buy yo' again? Offered two thousand aurics."

"It is a great deal?" she said, propping her chin on a palm.

"Unheard of, sweet. Especially these days; it'd be extravagant fo' a racehorse, much less a wench. Forty times what a fieldhand costs."

"Ah. Pleasant, to be appreciated."

"That's not the half of it; he offered to throw in an original Degas when I turned him down."

"A temptation, *certainement.*"

Tanya laughed and fed the serf a berry between thumb and forefinger. "Not much. Besides, he has hairy fingers. Couldn't bear to think of it."

Marya cleared her throat, and the Draka looked up.

"Patience. There are cushions over there, pull some up an' we'll go over the figures."

". . . and these are the estimates from the League for the construction crew, Mistress," Marya finished. A team of specialists, hired out for heavy building work; they had left last week, and the nun was glad of it; they had created no end of noise and confusion.

"Hmmmm." Tanya flipped through the last of the

account sheets. "Excellent work, Marya, yo've got a talent fo' administration . . . ouch." She folded the contractor's bill. "Piracy, even if everybody *does* need them. Oh, well, we can always take out anothah loan. Anythin' else?"

"A circular from the Transportation Directorate. They are moving one of their labor camps into the area, the gauge-standardization project." The Domination's railways ran on a 1.75-meter gauge, wider than the European system, and tens of thousands of kilometers had to be relaid. "They would appreciate any bulk foodstuffs available, to save transport. We have several thousand kilograms of potatoes surplus to projected requirements, mistress."

"By all means, sell 'em."

"And a cablegram for you in this morning's mail, I think concerning the naming-day celebrations for your children."

Tanya ripped open the flimsy. "Probably Tom and Johanna," she said. To Marya: "Third an' first cousins, respectively; they have a place down in Tuscany." A snort of laughter. "Johanna, all right. Askin' why I've had the infernal bad manners to pup at such an inconvenient time, with grape-harvest comin' on. Says can't I count to nine, or have I jus' forgotten what activity results in babies? Hmmm, that's them, their two children an' six staff. Flyin' up in their Cub. How many so far?"

"Thirty-seven Citizens who will be staying at least overnight, mistress, with about twice that number of servants. Where are we going to *put* them all, mistress? The new wing is just a shell."

"Pavilions, of course. We have a couple around *somewheres*. We'll set them up in the cherry-orchard just south. Serfs can double-up. Then we'll have to find room for the namin'-gifts, as well." A sigh. "Just because I *paint* pictures, everyone assumes I *want* pictures, 'sides everyone havin' loot comin' out they ears. I'm goin' to have to open a gallery." She reread the cablegram. "Ahhh, no, second thoughts—Tom and Jo-hanna are comin' up in *two* Cubs. They two were in the Air Corps, they've got pull, an' I suspect they're goin' to be giving one to us. We'll have to buy another mechanic. Hmmm, we might be able to pick up an ex-Auxiliary from the Forces."

"I will make a note of it, Mistress." A piece of meadow had been marked off as a grass-strip runway for those guests flying in, but she supposed something more permanent would be needed if the plantation was to have an aircraft of its own. Cubs were small six-seater runabouts, but the waiting-list was long. "And I've received a telephone message from Tours, the thousand kilos of oranges you ordered have arrived, the steamtruck will be here Thursday."

Tanya opened her eyes in alarm. "Wait a minute, isn't the cold-storage room out of order?"

"Yes, mistress; Josef tells me it will take a week to repair once the parts arrive . . . and they are overdue." The Landholder's League had just established a sched-ule of per-capita citrus consumption, to get the export trade from the Domination's old territories going again. It was more convenient to buy in bulk and issue from storage, but the oranges would not keep without refrigeration.

"Shit. Burn up the wire, try an' get the parts. Issue every household a big sack, an' hunt up mason-jars, we'll put up preserves an' marmalade. No use tryin' to send them back, those League bureaucrats would rather eat their children than muss the paperwork. Damn waste."

Tanya rose, yawned, put her hands together back-to-back above her head, linked the fingers and bent back-ward. She was not bulky, but for an instant the long smooth swellings of muscle jumped out into high defini-tion, like a standing wave beneath her skin. Frowning, she probed at the curve of her stomach where it scal-loped in under her ribs. "Damn, bettah put in another couple of hours, today; still too slack. Last thing we need is fo' me to get six months punitive callup fo' bein' unfit-for-service."

Solange rose and slid the Draka's white-striped black caftan over her head, tied the belt and knelt to fasten her sandals. The wetnurse had taken the infant from her breast and had it on her shoulder, patting gently at its back until a small, surprised belch indicated success. She wiped up the results and Tanya held out her hands for the wiggling pink form, taking it in an experienced head-and-fundament grip.

"They always look like piglets at this age, don't they?" she asked the air, chuckling and swooping the child around in a circle. It gurgled and waved its arms and legs with a gum-baring smile; Tanya brought it close and fluttered her lips against its stomach. A hand stuck tiny fingers into her nose as wide infant eyes looked down uncertainly, deciding whether to laugh or bawl. They settled on sleep instead; heavy eyelids blinked down, and the Draka settled her child in the stroller beside its twin.

"Hush now," she murmured, pulling up the light coverlet. "You two don' know it, but the whole clan, the neighbors an' half creation are comin' to give you toys." A smile, soft and amused. "Give yo' momma and poppa toys in your name, really." The baby gave a small half-cry and then dropped off with the abrupt collapse-in-place finality of infant sleep. "Don' you worry though, little ones. Momma an' poppa are goin' give yo' the whole *world* fo' a toy."

"Come on, Marya," she said as she straightened. "Few mo' things we need to talk about, might as well do it on the way to the palaestra."

Chantal sat staring dully as the Draka left, watching with blank indifference as Solange hopped up onto the lounger and leaned over to pour herself a cup of coffee.

"A cup, Chantal?" she said, using the silver tongs to drop two of the triangular lumps into her own. "Or some of these strawberries? Really, they are very good, just picked. One doesn't appreciate what freshness is until one lives in the country; a shame to waste them." Sighing with contentment, she spooned some of the cream over the fruit and sank back against the rear of the lounger, cross-legged with the bowl in her lap.

The other woman looked up, the blank apathy leaving her narrowing eyes. "You are *disgusting*," she hissed. "A disgusting *whore*."

"Ah." Solange dipped the long slender spoon into the bowl, picked up a berry and considered it a moment before eating. "I will spare you, *cherie*, the obvious retort that far from being disgusting, I am a beautiful and accomplished whore . . . and instead merely point out that nobody is paying money for my favors; one should use words with precision, no? 'Kept woman,' perhaps, or 'concubine.' Furthermore, *you* have been called to the master's room fairly often of late. In fact, last night—he was with the Mistress, you understand, and I sleep at the foot of her bed—I heard him express great satisfaction with you. Particularly the way you squeeze your—"

The other jumped to her feet with a strangled sound; Solange dropped the spoon and spread her hands in a placatory gesture.

"I am sorry. Truly, that was cruel, and I should not have said it. Accept my apologies, *ma soeur*."

Chantal dropped back to the stool, let her face fall forward into her hands and wept with a grinding sound, hopeless and disconsolate, misery past all thought of privacy or control. Solange turned on one side, busying herself with the cup and saucer in embarrassment until the other woman had command of herself once more.

"I suppose I deserved it," Chantal said at last, blowing her nose and wiping at her eyes with a handkerchief. "I am no better than you, after all."

The serf on the lounger sighed in exasperation and clinked the stoneware down on the marble table slightly harder than necessary.

"LeFarge, it is not a matter of better or worse, but of

less or more foolish. This grows rapidly more tiresome, my old, this martyred pose of yours. If the von Shrakenbergs took you seriously, there might already have been grave happenings. Some . . . friends have asked me to speak with you." She shook her head at Chantal's quick suspicion. "No, not the masters; Mistress Tanya does not, I fear, think of me in connection with such practical matters. Some of the other servants; you are becoming a somewhat dangerous person to be about. Not Sister Marya either . . ." A pause.

"The good Sister is, as one might expect, something of an innocent. She would sympathize, but say you have nothing to reproach yourself for, as one who submits passively to superior force." She kept her eyes on Chantal's, until they dropped again. "Which we both know is not *entirely* the case, *n'est-ce pas?*"

"Say what you have to," Chantal replied in a mumble.

A sigh. "Did you ever see the Bastille Day parade in Paris, Chantal?"

"No," she replied with surprise, startled out of her thoughts. "May Day only."

"A great pity, the spectacle was beautiful. I remember well, I was about six, so this must have been '32 or '33, the first time my father took me. He was just back from a field trip, burned dark as an Arab, with a most dashing beard; he held my hand as we walked to our seats in the reviewing stand where others with the *Croix du Guerre* would sit, and I was very proud of him. Maman," she continued, smiling dreamily, "Maman had the most lovely hat, with flowers; she put it on my head and it fell right over my eyes and I pushed it off again because it was very important to see everything. Poppa put me on his shoulder when the soldiers went by; there were hussars in red cloaks, and cuirassiers in shiny breastplates, and Foreign Legionnaires in white *kepis* and epaulets.

"I was a little frightened, they looked so fierce and the horses were so large. But Poppa explained that these were men from all over France, who would fight to keep bad men from coming and hurting me, as he had fought the Germans in the Great War; he showed me the President of the Republic, who I could tell was very important because of his frock-coat and sash, and told me how he would command them. I felt very safe, then; my Maman was with me, and Poppa was the strongest and handsomest man in the world, and now there were all these others who would look after me, so there was nothing that could hurt me."

Chantal blinked at her, astonished and sadly envious. Remembered *her* father stumbling home smelling of cheap sour Midi wine, and his fumbling hands; remembered hiding in the closet too frightened to cry while her parents screamed at each other outside and then the slap of a fist on a face and the tinny crash of kitchenware. Wondering, she studied Solange, trying to see the child with the starched pinafore and the ribbons in her hair, perched on the laughing bronzed explorer's shoulder. *Watching the soldiers*, she thought bemusedly. For *her*, soldiers were the men who came and broke strikes, or the way her eldest sister picked up a little extra cash for drink after the bottle got to her.

Solange was frowning slightly in concentration, her lower lip caught between her teeth. *Well, I'll listen*, Chantal thought resignedly. *My god, how did the little princess end up here? Perhaps I was wrong to envy; at least I was never allowed to think I could rely on anyone but myself.*

"There is a point?" she said.

"Well, we're neither of us little girls any more, are we, Chantal? Nor are you the only one to have suffered," Solange said with a shrug. "The past is gone, and everything it held, as well. Why should we fight, you and I? Because of things from before the War, politics, classes? It's absurd; that world is *gone* and this one of ours is all we have.

"I remember the War," she continued. "Better, because I was old enough to understand and be frightened. We stayed in Paris when the government fled to Bordeaux. Maman wanted to go but Poppa said it would be safer staying than on the roads. When the Germans came, my father went out to watch them parade down the Champs Elysées. Then he came home and got drunk, the first time I can remember that happening, he was already ill and his hands trembled, he just kept raising the glass and wouldn't listen to me, as if Maman and I weren't there, that frightened me even more. Later, we'd be crouching in the cellar of our building with the other families, listening to the English robot bombs overhead like . . . like bees in the sky, waiting for the engine to stop and the bomb to come down and kill us with nerve gas, and he was afraid too, there was nothing he could do."

"Then the Draka came?" Chantal asked gently. A corner of her mind noted how much of a relief it was, to have the arrow of attention dragged around from its unrelenting focus on the pain at the center of herself.

"Yes." Solange looked down at her hands. "You heard?" The other woman nodded. "The Janissaries picked my father up and threw him into the glass shelves with his souvenirs and kicked him and kicked him, and they . . . they were killing me, there were too many. Big men, crazy drunk, stronger than horses, I knew I was dying, could feel my life flowing away, I was only eighteen and I *didn't want to die*—"

She stopped for a moment, dabbed at her cheeks with the back of her hand, took a deep breath. "Then Mistress Tanya came in, I could see a little still. They had guns, they were many; she just told them they were baboons out of . . . order, I think, and to go. Stared at them, and they shuffled their feet and went away, she picked me up and"—a shrug—"I woke up in a hospital, swathed like an Egyptian mummy. It gave me a great deal of time to think. The mistress came and visited once or twice, but I had a good deal of time, once the pain was less. Time to consider my decisions carefully."

"Decisions?" Chantal asked. "You weren't in a position to make choices, surely?"

"Oh, one always has some choices to make. *Par example*, the mistress offered to find me another owner, if I would rather not stay with her. My decision . . . I decided to give up, Chantal. To surrender absolutely, to submit, to make the best of whatever came. Which, you must admit, could be much worse. We could be whoring in a Janissary brothel, or spending the rest of our lives between a factory and a concrete barracks. Or anonymous lobotomized lumps of flesh in a labor camp. Instead . . ." She waved a hand around at the pergola.

"Actually, I find myself unable to complain even a little," Solange continued more brightly. "Here I am, *safe*, after all. Protected. Unless the Americans drop their atomic on us, or the world ends, of course. Safe, pampered, given every luxury and pleasure, hardly required to work at all, indulged, treated—"

"—like a pet animal!" Chantal snapped.

"No, like a pet human, *cherie*. With affection, valued for my talents and beauty and skills; the mistress is quite proud of me. I'm not treated as an equal, of course, but then we aren't their equals, are we?"

"Are you so convinced of their superiority, then, this *master race?*" Chantal said, quietly but with an ugly rasp below the surface of her voice.

"Superiority?" Solange made a moue. "Is the wolf superior to the deer? Superior at what, my dear . . . singing, perhaps? By that standard, *I* am the superior one on this estate; except perhaps for Yasmin, and she is stronger on the instrumental side. Mistress can paint in a superior fashion; you are superior to me in mathematics. Master race? They *are* a race of masters, that is plain fact, Chantal. Also that they are stronger than we; that is a better word than 'superior.' Stronger in their armies, of course; stronger in their wills and bodies, as well. They are *here*, are they not?

"That," she continued, lying back and linking her hands behind her head, "is what I meant when I said that I had surrendered, Chantal. I don't try to fight, or pit my pride against theirs . . . There's a curious freedom to it, really. No more tension, no more struggle or fear. Like stepping off the high diving board, everything's out of your hands and all you have to do is . . . let go. I just let . . ." She paused, quirked her lips. "No, I *helped* them change me, inside." She tapped her temple. "Like surgery in here, you see? The scars still ache a little, now and then, but that is fading. Once you've stepped through that wall you find they're not so bad. Even kind."

"Kind?" Chantal came to her feet. "Leaving aside the War—"

"—which they did not start," Solange interjected.

"—Leaving that *aside*, I said, leaving aside what is happening to *me*, what about the people they *killed*? Here, on this land they call theirs."

Solange sighed. "A pity, but those three attempted armed revolt, Chantal. If you lift your hand to the masters, you die. Everyone knows that."

"What about Bernard, then? In the stables? *They cut off his balls.* And made everyone watch!"

"Chantal, he tried to burn down the house"—she jerked her head back at the towers of the chateau—"at night, with *forty people* inside, most of them locked in their rooms! I would not have been so merciful." She cocked an eyebrow. "We become somewhat abstract, my dear. Let it suffice to say these people suffered because they resisted. Once you have said in your own heart, 'do with me as you will,' the suffering ends, *n'est-ce pas?*" Her tone became dry. "One might add, at least you are not required to learn a whole new set of . . . ah, *habits*, shall we say." Chantal flushed, and Solange giggled again.

"Actually, it's a bit like those revolting-sounding Normandy dishes we ate in Montparnasse when I was a student, you know, tripe cooked in cream with calf's brains. Horrible to think about, you have to close your eyes the first time, quite nice once you're used to them." A smile. "She could see I was trying hard, and was very . . . patient with me, very gentle. Besides, there is a certain enjoyment to be had from making another happy, is there not?" She sat up on the lounger and moved down, closer to the other serf.

"Let's get to the heart of it, Chantal. You feel that you are a person, and are being used like a . . . like a convenience, isn't that it?"

"Yes, that is it," she replied bitterly. "I'm surprised at your insight."

"Now, now." Solange paused, and bit her lip. "Look, I've slept with him too, you know." At Chantal's surprised glance: "He asked her, she asked me, I agreed . . . why not, after all? He's not a bad man, once you get to know him. Have you tried talking to him?"

"What for?" Chantal said wearily. "What could I say?"

"Because, my old, if you want to be treated as a person, well, people talk, things don't. I talk to the mistress a good deal, you know: I amuse her, she . . . terrifies me, fascinates . . . What to say to him? 'Isn't it a nice day,' or 'how did you get that scar,' or ask him what he'd like you to do . . . They're perfectly willing to treat you as a person, Chantal, *on their terms*. After all, he doesn't want as much from you as the Mistress does from me, just a certain degree of . . . ah, cheerful complaisance. Why not give it a try?"

"No."

"Why not?"

"*No!*" She looked up; there was no anger in her face, only the translucent blankness of someone looking within themselves for knowledge of their own soul. "I am too afraid."

"Afraid of what?"

"Afraid of becoming like you."

"Well," Solange said, stopped herself and threw up her hands, then leaned forward and patted Chantal on the shoulder. "So was I, before I did it. I'm a different person now, and happy . . . Ah well, I've done my best for you. If your pride means that much to you, well, just don't drag anyone else into your suffering." She stood, the violet eyes lidded. "Because you *are* going to suffer, you know, until they break you or you die. Until dinner, *cherie;* I'm supposed to see Father Adelard about the choir."

She bent to strap up the player and walked out into the sunlight past the fountain of the nymph. Her kid-skin slippers scuffed across the grass, and already she was singing.

Tanya von Shrakenberg watched the stroller being wheeled off to the main entrance of the manor, her head to one side. It was very quiet, the loudest sound the wind through the chestnut trees above them; somewhere children were playing, an axe sounded on wood; far off and faint came the long mournful hoot of a steam locomotive's whistle.

"Ahh, children," she said. "One of the better things in life. Once yo've pupped, that is, as my cousin so elegantly put it: conceivin' them is nice, too. *Bearing* them is an insufferable nuisance, but then, life is like that."

Marya made a noncommittal noise as they walked along the path at the foot of the chateau's east wall. The sun was just behind the high bulk of the towers, leaving a strip of shade for the brick path; outside it, to their right, the gardens shone with the cruelly indifferent beauty of nature.

No, the nun thought. *The pathetic fallacy. Nature is merely indifferent, it is the heart of fallen man that is cruel.*

"I would not know, Mistress," she said in the flat, calm tone she found best for dealing with the masters.

"Yes. Pity you're sterile, shame to lose your heredity." Marya started. "Haven't read y'own file?" the Draka continued, surprised. "Radiation overdose." Her face grew somber for a moment. "I wish t'hell we hadn't invented those things, I surely do."

The Pole blinked aside memory of the intolerable flash and searing heat. "I am sworn to chastity, in any case, Mistress," she went on.

"So?" To the plumber and his apprentice, shifting into French: "*Ça va, Marcel?*"

Marcel smiled cautiously and bowed in place; the younger man rose from the manhole and made a more formal obeisance. "It goes well, *maîtresse*," he said. "The fountains should all be working for the celebrations. Also the standpipes in the Quarters are all completed." He shook his head. "You were right about the total input, *maîtresse*."

"Water-borne sewage systems are hungry beasts, that's why we put in a 20% margin." A smile. "You've been doing good work, Marcel," Tanya said. "Don't overstrain, now: I want you healthy. Jacqueline and her baby?"

This time the plumber's smile was more genuine. "Very well, *maîtresse*; there is some sickness in the mornings, but the women tell me that is to be expected."

Tanya nodded, and patted her own stomach. "Inconvenient process . . . Anyway, I'll be sending the midwife by, and I've told the kitchens to send down anything special she recommends. Jacqueline looks like hasn't been eating as well as she should these past few years, so we don't want to take any chances."

"Thank you, *maîtresse*," Marcel said with a worried frown. "She is tired, but will not rest as much as I would wish."

"I'll mention it to the headman. Keep well."

They came to what had been the north side of the chateau, where the new construction began; the old east-west I-shape had been turned into a C by adding a three-story wing to each end. Reinforced concrete frames, Marya remembered, and prestressed panels for the walls, exterior cladding in a stone and brick checkerboard that matched the older part of the chateau without trying to imitate it. Tall windows looked in on echoing empty space, but the ground outside was already comely with fresh sod and transplanted trees; Tanya stopped and nodded to a group transplanting creepers along the base. They were girls in their early teens, mostly, and Chantal's sister Therese. She had been giggling and talking with the others, fell no more silent than they as the mistress halted.

"Good work," Tanya said, and patted Therese casually on the head.

"How is she?" the Draka asked Marya as they continued.

"Somewhat better," Marya replied, keeping her eyes carefully forward. "She speaks more freely, particularly to young people; she remembers a little, although all from her earlier childhood, mostly before the War. But she is still easily frightened, particularly around men, and the nightmares continue." She frowned in thought. "Essentially, she is stabilizing in a regressed state. Very delicate . . ." she hesitated.

"Spit it out," Tanya said.

"Mistress, in Lyon, you, ah, intimated that if Chantal were to misbehave—"

"That Therese would be punished for it?"

"Yes, Mistress. I must advise you that further mistreatment could easily drive her into catatonia, and—"

"—and you're afraid Chantal might do somethin' stupid and Therese would suffer fo' it," Tanya finished.

Marya stopped, wheeled and confronted the Draka; her face was calm, but her hands were clenched and shoulders braced, as if she leaned into a storm.

"Mistress, with all due respect, Chantal is on the verge of a nervous breakdown. The abuse to which she is being subjected—"

"Stop."

Marya jerked slightly, with a prickling consciousness of danger running over her skin like the feet of ants; she forced herself to remember what Chantal's eyes had been like, the last time the summons came. Tanya's were unreadable, the clear pale gray of snow at sunset; her lips were slightly parted, impossible to tell whether in amusement, anger or anticipation.

"Marya," Tanya said softly, taking the long ash-blond braid of the nun's hair and switching her lightly on the cheek with it. "Marya," she continued, with another admonitory tap, "on this plantation we don't starve our serfs, let them get sick, beat them for pleasure or rape their children. Any of those would be abuse, perfectly within our rights, but grounds fo' complaint. Chantal isn't bein' abused, just used. As a bookkeeper, like you; and fo' pleasure. Fucked, to be blunt, and occasional sexual intercourse is no inherent problem to a healthy wench her age, particularly if she lubricates properly, which I'm told she does. If she chooses to find it unpleasant, that's *her* problem. As fo' yo' worries about Therese, fo'get them."

"But—"

"I lied." Tanya gave a wolf's grin. "Never had any intention of makin' her a hostage. Now, as fo' a 'breakdown,' breakin' Chantal down is one of the reasons I mentioned her to Edward. Saw it in her background, the way she fought up out of the guttah, got an education, that sort of thing; took spirit, determination an' a strong sense of self. All of which need to be . . . rechanneled. She's just gettin' what you might call a graphic demonstration of her own helplessness, on a level impossible to ignore or deny. All she has to do is *accept* her own weakness, dependence an' so forth. Lucky we didn't decide hunger or physical pain would be mo' efficient."

Another grin. "Mo' fun fo' my husband this way, too." Her head went to one side. "Why, Marya, sometimes I think yo' disapprove of me." A laugh. "Nice stone-face, an' yo've got good voice-control, but when yo're really upset or angry, yore ears turn a brighter shade of red. Wouldn't be a problem iff'n yo' were wearin' a wimple an' coif, of course."

Marya snatched down a hand that had flown to the side of her head from reflex, and spoke in a voice whose steadiness brought her a small guilty spurt of pride, even now.

"It is not my place to approve or disapprove of you, Mistress," she said. To herself: *That is God's prerogative, and be assured that He will, you murderer, blasphemer, corrupter of innocence.*

"Marya, words cannot *express* mah utter lack of concern fo' yo' opinions, 's long as yo' are reasonably polite about expressin' them . . . Just to clarify, though, we are not tormentin' Chantal fo' its own sake, or because we enjoy seein' her suffer. Draka have two professions, basically: we fight wars—beatin' down open, organized opposition an' enforcin' political obedience—an' we manage serfs, doin' the same thing on a *personal* basis. Obedience isn't enough, in the long run; the objective is domestication. Her sufferin' is incidental to what we do enjoy, the feelin' of another's will breakin', leavin' obedience and humility. Pain is just another tool we use fo' the process, like a hammer; we take it out when necessary, then put it away. Analogous to trainin' a horse to the saddle."

"We are, then, not human in your eyes, Mistress? Animals?"

"To the contrary, we never fo'get yo're human, that's exactly the point. It'd be mo' accurate to say we don't consider *ourselves* human in the usual sense; we're higher up the food chain. In terms of culture, if not biology, though the eugenics people are workin' on that. Or to be blunt again, yo' farm the earth an' we farm yo'. Domesticated humans are much mo' profitable and rewardin' than plants and animals, although much mo' dangerous and tricky, of course."

A blink, followed by laughter. "And if serfs weren't human, we'd all be guilty of bestiality, no? I'll have to tell Edward that one. Well . . . little Chantal's education is goin' to continue until she learns her lesson, after which it'll be recreation instead. I might take that pretty pony fo' a trot myself, when she's properly tamed down, don't much like it unless there's . . . interaction . . . on a personal level, as well. Men do, of course, but"—she made an offhand gesture—"men, well . . .

lovely creatures at their best, very satisfyin' at times, but their nerve endings are a little crude, difficult fo' the poor dears to appreciate the subtleties of the amatory arts. Prisoners of their hormones, really . . ." Another shrug. "If Chantal comes to yo' fo' advice, consider givin' her Solange as an example of successful adaptation."

Marya coughed to cover the lump in her throat and waited a moment. Curiosity as much as anger drove her to speak. "Mistress, in my opinion—my professional opinion, that is—Solange is mentally ill."

Tanya laughed as she turned to walk on, giving the nun's braid a tug to bring her along. "Marya, Marya, I expected better than that, from an intelligent and well-educated person like you. Sanity is always socially defined." She stopped to pick a flower and tuck it behind one ear.

"Among Romans of the late Republic, fo' example, overt sadism was the normal personality type. Mass masturbation in the stands of the Coliseum while they watched people bein' burned alive or torn apart by wolves. I'm familiar with the technical terminology yo' might apply to Solange; masochism, fo' example, learned helplessness, regression, transferal, identification with the aggressor. All addin' up to a perfectly functional response to this environment, even if it would have been neurosis before the War. Fo' that matter, what was that Viennese fellow, Englestein, we studied him in introductory Psychological Manipulation—claimed women were inherently masochistic. Nonsense among us Draka, of course, but perfectly sensible among outlanders, where females are slaves anyways."

Marya opened her mouth, considered certain doctrines of the Church and closed it again; futile, to try and explain the difference to a Draka. *Yet a woman was Mother of God*, she reminded herself. *Beside that, even being Pope is very little*.

"Actually, Solange—well, she's the finest piece of loot I acquired in the whole War. Beautiful, of course; intelligent, well educated as far as cultural things go, good conversationalist, playful, wonderful singer, first-rate amorist . . . and charmin', simply charmin'. Pleasure just to contemplate, and an inexpressible pleasure to own; like havin' one of those magical jeweled birds in the Thousand and One Nights, all fo' myself. Fun just to pet an' pamper, she *enjoys* things so much."

A sigh. "An exotic luxury; I spent five years in that stinkin' tank, figure I deserve it. Also"—she paused for words —"difficult to convey to someone outside the Race—the emotional twining . . . that particular combination of adoration, fear, desire and willing, total submission . . . It does somethin' fo' a Draka. An intoxication, like bein' a god, one of the more disreputable Greek ones." She glanced aside at Marya's face. "Ah, shocked yo' a little, eh?"

Tanya released the nun's hair, and they walked in silence for a moment; the Pole was white-faced, her hands pressed together to control their shaking. "It . . . disarms us, too," the Draka mused, almost to herself. "Like a wolf stops fightin' when its enemy rolls over on its back an' shows its belly. Operates below the conscious level, just as pride an' defiance arouse our aggression." She spread her hands. "Practical reasons, as well. Notice that I don't allow Chantal access to the nursery; won't, either, fo' a good long while."

The nun looked up, the breathing-exercise learned as part of meditation giving her back control enough; her mind felt detached, washed in a white light of anger and revulsion. "I notice that you place no such restriction on me," she said huskily, the liquid Slavic accent stronger. "Have you some program to break my spirit? Am I so tame, then, Mistress?"

"No, I think yo' are incapable of harmin' a helpless infant," Tanya said amiably. "Chantal might, in a fit of temper, though she'd probably flail herself with guilt afterwards. Such a grubby bourgeois emotion, guilt . . . Solange wouldn't hurt a child, but she'd quite probably *neglect* one." A shrug. "Marcel back there, still another case of tolerable adaptation. Even better in a few years, nothin' like a family to teach a man caution an' humility."

They had come to the north end of the new wing, a glassed-in shell with a flat second-story roof ringed by a balustrade of red porphyry. Through the windows they could see climbing bars, mats, ropes, wall racks for weights and weapons, suits of padded unarmed-combat armor, machines of springs and balances. Behind would be the steam-baths, soaking tubs and massage-rooms; not so well-equipped or elaborate as it would become, but what the von Shrakenbergs considered a good beginning. The outdoor cold-water plunge was an embellishment of nature, a stretch of slough and marsh dredged into several acres of artificial lake; trees, gardens, walkways and lawns bordered it, and an island held a grove and pergola. Not entirely a luxury, since it also served as the main reservoir, with intakes below taking off the filtered water.

Most of the fringes were tawny-gold sand brought up from the Loire, but here near the palaestra was a half-moon beach of gently sloping marble; Marya remembered coming across the indent-order for it while organizing the files, forest-green serpentine stripped from a bank building in Tours. The paved space between building and water held potted trees, stone benches and tables, some shaded by trellis-work, others by ornamental hoods of stained glass on wrought-iron frames. Water quivered under the breeze like ticklish skin, shot fifteen meters skyward from a fountain amid the lake's waters, arching up in a sunlit cloud of spray. The sun turned the flat surface into a sheet of silver-gilt and blue for an instant, making her blink back tears with its eye-hurting brightness.

Father Adelard was sitting at one of the tables with Solange's father, playing chess on a board inlaid into the granite surface. The two old men looked up as Tanya and the nun approached, down again when they halted out of earshot.

This too God made, Marya thought, glancing out at

the water and heartening herself to look back at her
owner. *Despair is a sin*, she reminded herself. *Hope
one of the cardinal virtues*. And still meeting the pale
gray gaze made her remember what Dante had said,
that one of the worst torments of the damned in Hell
was having to look daily on the faces of the infernal
Host.

"So, no," Tanya continued, untying her sash. "I'm
not under the impression yo're tame . . . hold this."
She tossed over the cloth belt and began pulling the
robe over her head. "And this . . ." adding the caftan
and putting a foot up on a bench to unlace the sandal.
"Plain to see, your soul belongs to your God, your
Church an' possibly Poland. Irritatin', in the abstract;
obviously, there are orders we can't give yo', if they
conflict with those. Yo' don't have the sense of bein'
defeated that, say, Marcel does, either. That turn-the-
other-cheek nonsense; it's irritatin' as well, makes dealin'
with yo' like punchin' a pillow.

"On the other hand," a shrug as she kicked her foot
out of the leather and began on the right, "we can't give
every fieldhand the sort of detailed attention necessary
fo' tamin' a wild-caught houseserf. Surface obedience
has to be enough; find the levers and keep a close eye
on 'em.

"Same with yo', Marya. After all, we don't want yo'
fo' either a bedwench or a whip-wieldin' bossboy; we
want an accountant an' administrator. The medical skills
are a bonus, and as. fo' actin' as a wailin' wall, buckin'
people up an' so forth, just nuts and cream to us. Yo'
work hard and conscientiously—if I'd known nuns were
so well trained, I'd've bought mo' of them. Christian-
ity's a good religion fo' slaves; of course, it has serious
drawbacks, but we'll cure that, in time. Re-edit it."

"*Will you! Will you, you—*" Marya shouted, and then
stopped, appalled. The priest and Professor Lebrun
looked up, shocked. The nun swallowed and braced
herself; Tanya straightened up from untying her last
sandal and came closer, eyes narrowing slightly.

"Yes, we will," she said softly. "In time, and we have all the time there is. Examine the Koran we allow our Muslim serfs compared with the original, fo' example." A thin smile. "We've had a nice talk, Marya: yo've learned somewhat about me, which helps yo' to serve bettah, and I've learned more about yo', which helps me. But that last outburst was a little beyond the line. Yo' realize that?"

Marya nodded. "Yes, Mistress," she whispered. You did *not* shout defiantly in a master's face; Tanya allowed frankness, you could even state opinion fairly openly, but there was an etiquette, forms of respect. And she had broken the forms, before witnesses at that. *Our Lord was scourged,* she told herself. *It can be no worse than that. Thank you, Lord, that I may share Your wounds.*

Tanya smiled and patted her on the cheek. "But I was pushin' yo', too. No sjambok; pointless to feed your desire to be a martyr, anyways. Finish foldin' my clothes, then come here an' hold still."

Marya laid them neatly on a table; caftan, cloth belt, underwear, sandals with the thongs together in a bow.

"Yo' realize I'm not doin' this because I enjoy hurtin' yo?" Marya nodded; that was true, in a sense. "Believe it or not, Marya, I'd prefer yo' were happy here. Try acceptin' this in the right sprit, and it might be a first step . . ." A sigh. "No, I suppose not. Speak the proper words, wench."

"This serf is ignorant and insolent. I beg forgiveness, Mistress."

Crack! An open-handed slap across the side of the nun's face, with a hand that felt like a board wrapped in cloth. Hard enough to jar her head around and sting, but not to injure.

"Thank you, Mistress."

Crack.

"Thank you, Mistress."

Crack.

"Thank you, Mistress."

"That's that, then." They walked over to the table, and Tanya leaned over the chess game, studying it in silence for a full minute.

"Knight to queen's pawn four?" she said to Professor Lebrun. He cleared his throat, glanced at Marya, back down at the board.

"Perhaps, Mistress," he said after a moment. "Though perhaps . . . ?" He indicated a complex of strike and counter-strike.

"Hmmmm. That's the conservative approach; still, yo' goin' to be down another castle in three moves." She indicated the sequence. "So it's probably worth the risk. Still, suit yourself."

Shifting into French: "Priest." Father Adelard looked up, carefully averting his eyes. "About that request for a school you and Marya made. It's granted." A smile. "Don't look so surprised, priest; we do need mechanics and clerks, after all. You can start this winter; no more than thirty pupils, give us a list of names. Marya, can you get me a list of everything necessary?"

"Ah, that is, yes, Mistress."

"Good: by Monday, then. Oh, and look up Solange on your way back—tell her to attend in the massage room in two hours with my riding clothes."

She nodded in return to the men's bows and walked down to the water's edge; ran the last two steps, sprang, and hit the surface in a clean flat racing dive. The sleek head broke surface ten meters further out, and she began a quick overarm crawl toward the opposite shore.

"This arrived," Jules Lebrun said, sliding the folded slip of rice-paper out of his sleeve. It was only a few letter-number combinations on a liner from a carton of cigarettes; a cheap mass-produced brand, issued to semi-skilled Class IV serfs in ten thousand canteens across the Domination. His back was to the lake where the mistress of Chateau Retour was methodically swimming her kilometers, and the paper could be disposed of in an instant.

The nun came to herself with a start. He peered at her through the upper lens of his bifocals, squinting against the blur and the colored light that filtered through the glass overhead. *Not hard enough to stun her*, he thought. As beatings went, it had been mild, more a symbol of humiliation than real punishment. Something else had struck at her, a blow on the mind or heart. *Name of a dog, but this fading eyesight is inconvenient*, he thought irritably. *One does not realize how much of a conversation depends on seeing the details of another's face.*

"Thank you," she said, curling her fingers around the scrap of stiff liner and letting her eyes drop to it without moving her head. Her face turned, and her hand seemed to brush casually against her mouth; the Frenchman could see her throat work silently. Overlapping handprints stood out redly on her square firm cheeks, but the animation was trickling back into her eyes as she turned them to him.

"It's an acknowledgment. They know that Chantal and I have been moved out of Central Detention in Lyon, and where; you are to be the conduit." She smiled slightly at his silent nod. "Good, under no circumstances should I know who."

"Sister, *I* am not sure who it is," he replied dryly. *One of two drivers on the regular supply run, but that too shall remain confidential.* "Also, I did several monographs on secret societies during my academic career." He inclined his head toward the seat that Father Adelard had occupied. "You do not think we should recruit him?"

Marya frowned. "Forgive me, Professor Lebrun, but I would not tell you if I did. Nor approach him during a courier drop, in any case. But no . . ." A hasty gesture with one hand. "Father Adelard is . . . a holy man, a good priest. My superior in the religious life, of course."

She crossed herself. "I must risk the stain on my soul and not confess explicitly what we do, Professor. Understand . . . Father Adelard is a brave man, one always ready to take the crown of martyrdom for the Faith. But he thinks mainly of his flock—as is understandable. The bishop the Draka allow is duly ordained; we must obey his commands in spiritual matters, but . . . I suspect they selected him carefully. The Holy Father might feel constrained to agree, for fear of losing all contact with the faithful here in Europe. Likewise Father Adelard is fearful of who might be appointed to his care of souls if he were removed. And the people on this estate *must* have a spiritual shepherd whose first loyalty is to God. Best he not know of what we do.

"If we do anything of consequence," she added in what was almost a mumble.

Lebrun extended a hand that trembled with the misfiring of his nerves and rested it on hers; the nun's fingers closed around the professor's with careful force.

"Tell me, sister," he said gently. "If you cannot confess to a priest, let me help bear the burden of your doubts. I may not share your faith, but I have faith in you, at least. There was anger in your voice when you shouted—is that what is troubling you?"

"No," she sighed, looking up at him with a smile of gratitude. "She—not boasted, just mentioned, that they intended to . . . geld the Church, I suppose you could say. Over generations, alter its message into one of worship of the Draka, I suppose."

Another sigh. "God moves in history, my friend; if He sends us trials, they are no greater than we can bear. We must do our best, and the Church Militant will survive. Oh, it may fall into corruptions for a space— the Church is the Bride of Christ, but here on earth it is made of men, and all men are fallen. Satan speaks in their hearts, and chasubles and vestments are not enough to bar him entrance; the Borgia Popes, even—" A shrug. "For a moment I believed despite myself that they could do this thing, and my anger was the anger of despair."

"Something else troubles you, though, does it not?" he asked. She bowed her head.

"Another despair; for myself. All this time I have told myself that I had refused compromise beyond the point that my conscience could bear. The Holy Father has said that such religious as remain in Europe must minister to the needs of the people; they may render unto Caesar, so long as no specific action violates faith or morals. What I have done here . . . nothing beyond bookkeeping, and there must be records if people are to be fed, the sick tended, houses built, whether we are free or slave."

"And you have helped whenever you could," he reminded her. "Interceded, often at risk to yourself."

Marya laughed, and he was slightly shocked at the bitterness of the sound. "She . . . that woman, no, that *female Draka* . . . pointed something out to me. That all my work, even my helping of others, makes this *plantation* run more smoothly. They approve! She praised my accomplishments!" Sudden tears starred her eyes and thickened her voice. "So much for my careful distinctions. *This* Caesar demands everything, most certainly including what should be rendered only unto God. Have I become accomplice in abomination?"

The old man felt warm drops spattering on the liverspotted surfaces of his hands, and forced the faltering muscles to give an emphatic squeeze to the strong work-hardened palms between his.

"Sister." He waited. "Sister Marya Sokolowska!" She looked up at him. "Remember who invented lies, Sister. And that the best lie is a twisted truth."

The nun gave a shaky nod, returned the pressure of his hands and withdrew hers to find a handkerchief in the pocket of her skirt. "It would be simpler," she said with a slight twist of the lips that might have been called a smile, "simpler, if—"

"They were just brutes and monsters?" he replied, and gave a Gallic shrug. "The Domination is an evil that twists and poisons everything it touches, including the better qualities of its leaders. You have nothing of which to be ashamed, Marya Sokolowska." A grin. "Name of a name, I don't think she would congratulate you on what we've been doing here today."

She returned his smile. "Forgive me for pouring out my doubts and despairs to you, my friend; it seems I'm nothing but a thundercloud today."

"You carry too much of a burden yourself. Chantal was involved in such affairs in Lyon; couldn't you bring her into this?"

Marya frowned and shook her head, once more in command of herself, and her tone had a professional's objectivity. "No, professor, I think not. She was with another organization, to begin with; one we felt was compromised. She herself I have no doubt of, as far as her loyalties go. But she is, you must know, under severe stress at the moment."

He nodded quickly to spare her embarrassment, and she looked aside as she continued. "I am afraid for her stability, and this is no business for one who may lose control of herself. In recklessness or otherwise. Besides which—" She paused. "I find myself reluctant to take *anyone* into this matter, the risks are so great, balanced against what we can accomplish, a little information passed along, perhaps a package hidden . . . I feel guilty at endangering you, my friend."

"Allow me to chose my own martyrdoms, my devout one. I am an old man, and will be gone soon enough in any case; let me die as something more than a Draka pensioner, at least in my own mind."

She hesitated, then pursed her lips and spoke: "You do have a daughter, and we may be endangering her as well, through you. Not to mention . . . well, I had hoped you might be the means of her . . . recovery."

It was Lebrun's turn to look aside. "Have no fears on that score, Sister. Or hopes. Solange . . . Solange is safe, whatever befalls me. The mistress would neither believe her capable of conspiracy, nor allow her to be punished in my stead. She is safe, even happy, regardless if I live or die. So I may operate with no fear except for my own, eminently expendable, life."

He turned his hands palm-up on the stone and concentrated on slowing the shaking. "The mistress is right, you see. My daughter would report me in a moment, if she knew." Marya made a shocked sound and reached out to touch his arm, knowing the comfort useless against a unbearable grief, but offering it nonetheless.

"I am the false idol, you see," he said quietly, looking off over the roofs of the chateaux. "She loves me still, but I am the god who failed to protect her." His hands clenched into fists, and despite the wasting and shaking they showed a little of the strength that had been his. "I *did* fail her and her mother, I did." He smiled. "I must have failed my daughter long before the War, for things to have happened as they did; I never wanted to be an idol in her sight. Only for her to be happy and secure, and then a woman who would remember her father kindly; one who could stand on her own feet, with no need of a protector-god. She was such a bright child, so full of life—" Jules Lebrun shook his head with slow finality. "I failed her, perhaps by seeking to protect too much. But you I shall not fail, Sister."

CHAPTER ELEVEN

DATE: 01/08/47
FROM: Cohortarch Eurydice Skinner
Stalker Sub Procrustes
Atlantic Exclusion Zone

TO: Merarch Delia Beauchamp
Third Fleet HQ
Le Havre, Province of Normandy

RE: Contact with Alliance submarine

Intermittent contact from 0700 to 1100 this date; sensor data compatible with fuel-cell submersible in the 2,000 ton range proceeding ESE my position at 120 meters + - 20. Estimate probable Alliance Benjamin Franklin class patrol boat. Subject's evasive action resulted in final loss of contact at 1100 hours.

Service to the State!

SEABED NEAR NANTES
ESTUARY OF THE LOIRE RIVER
AUGUST 1, 1947

Captain Manuel Guzman leaned against the periscope well of the *Benito Juarez* and felt the clammy sweat trickling down under the roll-top collar of his sweater. The control center was underlit by the eerie blue glow of the silent-running lights, and utterly quiet; even the feet of the crewmen were muffled in felt overboots, and when they moved at all it was with an exaggerated care. Natural enough, since their lives depended on it: the *Juarez* was grounded in the soft silt of the estuary and helpless if the Draka searchers found a trace of her. The passive sound-detection gear was in operation, but they could all hear the throbbing of high-speed screws through the hull, resonating in the closed spaces of the submarine.

Twin screws, the captain thought. He was a stocky brown-skinned man with the flat face and hook nose of Yucatan's Maya Indians, old enough to have been a sub commander in the Pacific during the Eurasian war, and there was sympathy behind the impassive brown eyes as he watched the younger members of the bridge crew. This was the hardest part: nothing to do but think, nothing to think about but the crushing weight of water outside the thin plating of the hull, and of drowning in darkness.

Twin screws, going fast, his mind continued. Boosting on peroxide turbines, much more powerful than the fuel-cell cruise motors but noisy. Over them, fading now. Probably one of the new *Direwolf* class stalker-killer subs, based on German research the snakes had captured, they had never been much at naval design. His mind drew in the details, long cigar-shaped hull, streamlined conning tower, cruciform control rudders with rear-mounted propellors . . . built to hunt other subs, but the Domination's sensor-technology was nothing like as good as the Alliance's.

And the *Juarez* was a fine boat for this clandestine work. Modified from a mid-War cargo sub design, slow but ultra-quiet, with a hold capable of shipping a variety of surprises.

"What do we do now?" the man from the OSS asked in a whisper, after the noise faded.

"We wait," Guzman said curtly. He did not like the Ivy League types secret intelligence seemed to attract; this one reeked of old-stock Yankee money and breeding. *Too many of that type at Annapolis*, he thought resentfully. The type who had made his first days at the Academy Hell Week in plain truth, back when *indios* were a government-mandated rarity and fiercely resented; when the only other Spanish-speakers there had been *criollo* bluebloods, the sort of hacienda-owning *maricones* his father had spent a lifetime working for.

"Consider yourself lucky, amigo, that this isn't one of the old diesel-electric boats," he continued. Fuel cells did not need exterior oxygen, and if necessary they could wait two weeks, with abundant energy to crack fresh atmosphere out of seawater. "Now we wait, run up the antenna every night. When we get the message, you can bring out that fancy folding airplane of yours. If we get the message."

The agent blinked back at him; the captain reminded himself that the look of mournful reproach in the man's deepset eyes was a trick of his features, not genuine expression. *Face like a horse with a receding chin*, he thought.

"Our man will make it," the OSS man said in his nasal twang. "He's been in there a long time, but he'll make it, and with the job done. He's . . . that sort of fellow."

Guzman nodded. It would take a man with real balls to survive very long among the snakes and make it back to the west. He looked up, imagining the destroyers putting out from Nantes, the patrol aircraft and dirigibles lifting from their runways and docking-towers. *It's going to take balls* and *luck to be here alive when he arrives*, he thought wryly. The Alliance and the Domination were not formally at war; hence the *Benito Juarez* was still *officially* in her homeport at Hampton Roads, or out on a training cruise.

That was the necessary fiction. And there would be, could be no action to save the non-existent *Juarez* here in the Domination's territorial waters. Nothing but a "lost at sea" telegram to their families if they did not return.

His eyes went to the picture taped to the guard-rail of the periscope well, a smiling woman with hair the color of cornsilk and a Hawaiian lei around her neck. Bonnie-Lee would wait, and not in vain.

"Secure to holding stations," he told his exec. The man nodded, none of that surface-navy nonesense about bracing to attention in pigboats. "Carry on," Guzman continued, turning to go. There were always letters to write, even if they could not be posted.

CHATEAU RETOUR PLANTATION, TOURAINE PROVINCE AUGUST 1, 1947

"Lookin' good," Edward von Shrakenberg said, stripping back the maize-cob's silk and biting into the milky kernels, before spitting them out over the left quarter of his horse. The taste was sweet and green, halfway between candy and a grass-stem, and the feathery touch of the cornsilk on his lips was as homelike as the scent of new bread.

"Another two months, Mastah," Mohammed said, reaching across from his own saddle to take the cob from him and weighing it in one hand. "We gets one-eighty, mebbeso two hundred bushels th' hectare."

The Landholder nodded; Mohammed was his senior

fieldboss, a steady and reliable buck from his father's estate in Nova Cartago Province, south of Tunis, son of a bossboy there.

"Told yo' we didn't need steady irrigation here," he said absently. Behind him the hedge rustled, new-planted *rosa multiflora* sending its spindly canes skyward; another year or two and it would be man-high and hog-tight, like organic barbed wire. To his left was another hedge and a board gate; beyond that a stretch of grass and trees leading to the levee that held back the Loire's winter floods. A car went by along the embankment road, a three-piston steamer trailing a plume of white dust and the crunching sound of tires on rock, louder than the engine.

It was a hot summer's afternoon, warm enough to stain the white cotton of his shirt across the back and under the armpits. The cornfield stretched out in front of them, fifty hectares of dark-green leaves, the lighter green of stalks and the green-gold of tassels just turning; there were streaks and patterns through the rows, marking the outlines of the tiny plots this riverside had been divided into before the conquest. The chest-high maize rustled and creaked, nodding in the slow humid breeze; the air felt silky-soapy on his skin, nothing like the moisture-sucking dryness of the south Mediterranean weather he had been raised in. Above the sky was different, too, always a little hazy, a tinge of white in the blue, with little clouds like puffballs.

Always thought those French paintings were innacurate, he thought. *Quite close, really*. He glanced aside at Mohammed, idly wondering if the man missed the old estate; the heavy-featured olive face was impassive, a polite mask. *Probably not*, he concluded. The man had volunteered, after all. Fieldboss was about as high as a buck could go, and on Chateau Retour he had reached it far younger than he could have in the Police Zone. A bigger cottage, two wives, the deference of others . . . hard to really tell, though. It had been nearly a century and a half since the Draka conquered the Beylik of

Tunis and made it their Province of Nova Cartago; six generations under the Yoke tended to teach discretion.

A pair of two-row horse-drawn cultivators was plodding through the last quarter of the field, tiny against the distant line of hedgerows and trees. The work-gangs were following, catching any weeds the skimmer-blades of the cultivators missed; Edward could see the heads of the hoes rising and falling over the bent backs of the workers in a steady ragged thrashing. Step-back-and-chop, the *sshk* sound of iron in sandy earth, breaking through the surface crust and turning up the damper reddish-gray layer below. Bossboys walked behind, one to each group of twenty, waving their long willow-switches with an occasional shout.

It was a scene familiar enough to be nostalgic, but Edward missed the rhythmic chanting of the field-songs. They made the work more efficient, too: these French were not yet accustomed to gang-labor under supervision. There was a *thwack* of stick on cloth and a yelp from the nearest gang, as if to counterpoint his thought.

Long day, they're tired, the Draka thought. Close enough to see individuals now, men in the French peasants' traditional beret and blue overalls, women in cheap mass-produced cotton blouses, skirts, straw hats of their own weaving. Sweat ran down their dust-caked faces, impassive with fatigue; he could see them darting an occasional glance his way, then bending back to their task. A healthy degree of fear, a realization that the master could do anything to anyone, anything at all. There had to be a degree of regularity, though . . .

Mohammed stiffened beside him. " 'Scuse me, mastah," he said, and spurred his horse forward to halt beside the nearest bossboy.

"Give me t' switch, Erast," he said. Edward had bought foreigners for his foremen, Germans mostly, with a few Greeks and this solitary Ukrainian; it made for a better start. Just as the workers were a scattered grouping from anywhere within a hundred kilometers.

The bossboy handed the two-meter length of willow

up to the fieldboss. He flexed it with an expert flick of his wrist, and it split the air with a sound like ripping silk. "Claudine, y' useless cunt, *get over heah!*" he barked. "Rest, keep workin'."

The hoes faltered and resumed; the woman the bossboy had switched turned and walked back to the foreman and the mounted fieldboss.

Mohammed waved the tip of the switch toward her. "Erast, y'shoulda touched her up ten minutes ago." The stick pointed back down the row. "Some a' them weeds is knee-high!" This was the last cultivation before the field was laid-by; the maize would shade out new weeds but not established ones.

To Claudine: "Shuck an' bend, wench."

Edward could see her eyes twitch slightly to either side in an unconscious search for escape, then droop as she put her crossed arms down to pull the blouse over her head. An unremarkable face and an unremarkable body, sweat and dirt above, wet-glistening white below the U shape of the garment's neck. She leaned over, eyes squeezed shut and hands on her knees; would have been invisible if Edward had not been at the head of the row looking down along its length. Mohammed heeled his horse a few steps closer, stood in the stirrups and slapped the willow-switch down fast enough to blurr.

Whack. The serf's eyes and mouth flew open in surprise. A sound escaped her, something between a grunt and a cat-mew, not very loud. The limber wood rebounded instantly, a red stripe springing out across her shoulders as if by magic, a horizontal line neatly bisected by her spine. Mohammed waited a slow thirty seconds for the first blaze of pain to subside into the ache that would last for weeks, then struck again.

Whack. Another stripe, a handspan lower and as parallel as if laid out by a ruler.

"My god!" Louder this time.

Whack. Joining the points of the shoulderblades.

"Please, God, please, *no!*"

"Stop," Edward said. His voice was not loud, but the fieldboss's arm halted at the top of its stroke. "Mohammed, how many were yo' plannin'?"

"Twice six, Mastuh."

The Draka heeled his horse over to the site of punishment. He could see the surface of the serf's back twitching like the skin of a horse trying to cast off flies.

"Up, wench," He said.

Claudine reached for her hat where it lay in the dirt, fumbled it, picked it up again with hands that shook so that it seemed she was fanning herself. She straightened slowly, face wet with tears and the mucus running from her nose as well as sweat, and dressed with slow, cautious gestures and a continous low *huh-huh* sound as she struggled not to sob aloud, lips puckered in.

"Bit excessive, Mohammed." To the serf. "Claudine, look at me." Hazel eyes, still leaking moisture. Edward smiled and leaned forward, resting his hands on the pommel of his saddle. "Yo' work wasn't satisfactory, was it?" he asked softly.

"*Non, monsieur mon maître*," the field-serf mumbled.

"Yo' don't like bein' switched, do yo'? Well?" A mute shake of the head. "I don't like seein' it, and Mohammed don't like doin' it."

"*Oui, monsieur mon maître*." A darting glance at the fieldboss, who was tapping the switch in the palm of his free hand. *Good*, the Draka thought. A traditional principle, that the bossboys should be thought harsher than the master; you had to use honey and vinegar both to get optimum results.

"So work bettah, and we'll all be happier. Is that sensible?"

"*Oui, monsieur mon maître*."

"I'm speakin' to yo' rational-like, wench. Yo' can listen to words, or to Mohammed's switch." A nod to the fieldboss. "Carry on, Mohammed."

The Tunisian used his switch to swivel the woman's head around; she shuddered at the soft touch of the willow-wand. He pointed down the row. "Now, git yaz useless ass back theah, clean up whut y'shoulda done the first time, an' catch up with t'othahs. Unnerstan? *Comprend?*"

"*Oui, Monsieur Mohammed.*"

"Then git to it."

The fieldboss nodded, then twisted in the saddle and backhanded the Ukrainian bossboy across the cheek. The Slav stumbled back, crying out in shock and clutching at his face; a thin dark man, wiry and tough.

"Erast, y'wantsta shovel shit instead of bein' bossboy, *it can happen, buck!*" He tossed the switch back to the other man. "Do-yaz-job!" he bit out. "Unnerstan?"

"*Da, gospodin,*" he said, bracing to attention.

Shaking his head in disgust, the fieldboss turned his horse and trotted back to the gate with the master, ignoring the flinch of the gang as he rode through the one-woman gap in their line. Edward von Shrakenberg opened his mouth to speak, then looked sharply down at the fieldhands; one of them was staring at him, there was no mistaking the prickling under-observation feeling. A Citizen knew it from earliest childhood, and a recon-commando even more: he had felt it just before the grenade that took his left eye landed; it had sent him turning and snatching before he was conscious of a threat.

The scar across the left side of his face throbbed: he stared blankly for a moment, seeing the smooth steel egg, the desperate speed of his catch-and-throw. The surge of exultation as it left his fingers on the arc that would have taken it safely far away, then a flash and blackness. He shook his head, shook himself back to the present with a stab of pain inward from his temples that settled behind his brow. One of the hoe-gang met his gaze; a man, round stubbled face under the beret. Nondescript hazel eyes, quickly shuttered and dropping back to the ground under his hoe.

Not old enough to be the wench's father, he thought. The familiar swelling ache brought a fresh itching of sweat across his forehead and scalp, clammy even in the summer heat, and his lips skinned back in a grin that made the long cords in his neck stand out.

Husband or brother. That's right, buck, attend to your work. His hand fell unconsciously to the coiled sjambok at his saddlebow, then dropped away. Punishment was an example to others as much as to the one the whip landed on; if you made it too arbitrary, the deterrent power was lost. Still . . . He focused his mind on the serf, memorizing the face and letting him feel it, watching as the man's movements became slightly jerky and he pulled at the hoe with unnecessary force.

That's right, remember what you are, Edward thought. *Otherwise you may lose what you have left, the skin on your back or your balls or your life, buck.*

"Mastah, they's like wild donkeys," Mohammed was saying as he reined in beside his owner on the grass strip at the field's edge. Edward's horse raised its head to the other with a flutter of lips, then resumed its steady *crunch-crop* at the long stems. "Prophet a' God, I—" He stopped at the sound of hooves on the laneway beyond the hedge, dismounted and ran to open the gate.

Tanya rode through, twisting in the saddle to call something over her shoulder. She was wearing much the same working-clothes as he, black chamois breeches, boots, gunbelt, floppy-brimmed leather hat with a leopard-skin band, cotton shirt. A grin divided the dark tan of her face as she saw him, and she brought the big crop-maned hunter to a gallop with a shift of balance and thighs. It covered the ten meters between them in three loping strides, and he had only the warning in her eyes as she flung herself off her mount and onto his; his arms caught the solid weight of her out of the air with an impact that rocked him back in the high-cantled Moorish saddle.

Edward's mount plunged, neighed and buck-jumped sideways in a series of twisting leaps that nearly sent them both into the waiting thorns of the hedge. She was laughing inches from his face as he cursed and wrestled the tall gelding into a nervous foot-stamping standstill; her hunter dashed half the length of the field with the empty stirrups drumming at its flanks and divots of turf flying. Her laughter turned to a slow lazy smile as the horse quieted and he freed an arm to encircle her waist. The muscles of his wife's back moved smoothly under his touch, like living shapes of hard indiarubber. The scent of her was around him, clean sweat-musk, leather and horse and the warm summery flower-scent of her sunstreaked bronze hair; the fingers that dug into the sloping wedges of his neck were strong as slender steel rods.

They kissed, and he felt the old familiar fire at the pit of his stomach, a wanting that a hundred soft serf wenches could not still. Tanya smiled again with that taunting grin as their lips parted, and spoke in a husky whisper, wiggling her eyebrows in a parody of seduction:

"Hi, handsome stranger. Wanna fuck?"

Edward snorted laughter. "Wotan damn it, you only use that line 'cause it worked the first time!" he said, kissing her again. "Besides, it's seven; dinner's in half an hour."

"Well, no law says I can't torment yo' with a two-hour wait," she replied, shifting to a more comfortable position sideways to the horse with a leg curled up around the low mound that served as a saddlehorn. "That first time your flight was leavin' in twenty minutes, yo'd had a whole week an' hadn't done mo' than blush at me, I had to rush," she continued reasonably. "An' it did work. Remembah the closet?"

He threw back his head to shout laughter, and halted with a wince. Concern darkened her smile, and she rubbed at his neck, kneading and frowning at the tension-knots.

"Eye again?" she said. "Want one of the painkillers?"

"Started with it," he shrugged. "Then the head. Nevah no mind, Loki take it iff'n I'm goin' to end up serf to a pillbottle."

"Yo' needs a soak an' a rub," she said, giving him a

final squeeze and dropping to the ground. Mohammed had caught her mount; she took a half-step and vaulted into the saddle as he led it past, nodded thanks and caught the reins he tossed.

"Finished up here, anyways," Edward said. "This was the last field I was overlookin' today. Arable crops turnin' out fine this year, but we're dead lucky the namin'-day holiday starts tomorrow. Goin' be locked-in fo' a while, next hay-cuttin' an' then the wheat harvest."

"Vines lookin' good too," Tanya replied, shrugging her gunbelt back into place; the niello-and-silver inlays on the hilt winked in the afternoon sunlight. The vineyards along the northern edge of the estate were her special care. "An' the tunnage is all lookin' sound. Tested the stemmer-crusher an' the temperature control; we won't have to turn any grapes into raisins this year."

"Praise Frigg," Edward said, running a palm down the neck of his horse and slapping it reassuringly. It snorted and rolled an eye and ear back at him, mumbling the bit and tossing its head in a quick up-and-down gesture of doubt. "We goin' need the wine, an' prices look like they're headed back up. Plus the League says they may have an export contract fo' our Bourgeuil if we can equal pre-War quality." The pain had retreated, a dull presence that seemed to sharpen vision with an edge of nausea. He wanted food in the stomach, hot water, then darkness and sleep.

"Pa!"

More horses were coming throught the gate; his children. *My older children*, he corrected himself. He looked aside at his wife, remembering the exhausted triumph on her face when the midwife laid the two yelling red forms on her stomach, his own wondering touch on the delicate black birth-fuzz of heads smaller than his hands.

Edward von Shrakenberg pushed the consciousness of pain aside with a practiced effort of the will to wave and grin at his son and daughter. *Ten already*, he thought. There was so little time, they were away at their schools for so much of the year, which was only right, of course, but . . . and then the War, robbing even more.

Tim in the lead, naked to the waist and nut-brown with summer, his hair a faded white-blond, a fishing rod bobbing over one shoulder and a dramatic-looking cleaning knife at his belt, bare toes showing through the stirrups. He opened a basket at his saddlebow and proudly held up a string of Loire pike, threaded together with a strip of osier through their gills. Gudrun followed, massively freckled with the late-season sun and wearing a huge-brimmed hat, her body still shimmering with river-water from her last plunge. Drying clothes lay across the saddle before her, and a bucket of javelins swayed behind, the honed points glittering. She waved to him, then turned back to talk to the young serf-girl beside her; Fleur, he remembered, the one his daughter had "bought" with her allowance money. The young wench was awkwardly perched on an ambling pony, strapped around with picnic baskets and bundles, smiling and chattering as she clung to the saddle with both hands.

Edward frowned slightly, then relaxed as Tom followed; the ex-Janissary rode with the easy competence of a man who had spent a good decade as a mounted infantryman, the butt of his T-5 resting on one thigh. *No need to worry with Tom about,* the Draka thought. The Loire was treacherous with riptides, which he could rely on Tim and Gudrun to ignore if left to themselves, but the old soldier was someone they would heed.

"Want me to send fo' a car?" Tanya asked. There was a military-issue handset on her saddle, but he shook his head.

"Thanks, love, but no. Jus' pain, is all." Leaning over to admire his son's fish: "Mighty fine; we can have 'em done up as *guenelles de brochet*, with dinner tonight."

Tanya was staring pointedly down at the boy's feet. "Yo've got just enough time to scrub down an' get dressed, too," she said.

"Ah, Ma, I spent half the day in the water, *n'est-ce pas*

suffisant?" he said, giving each of his parents the kiss of greeting on their cheek.

"No, it isn't. An' save the francey fo' the serfs, young man." She returned the kiss and twisted in the saddle to lift Gudrun's hat and inspect her skin. "Child, despite the fact that yo' appears to be turnin' into a giant freckle, yo' just goin' have to face the fact that yo' don't tan. Clothes on. Now."

Gudrun sighed, tossed the hat to her maid and began to struggle into her shirt as the von Shrakenbergs turned their horses toward the gate. Edward nodded to the fieldboss, then fell behind the children and servants to ride side-by-side with Tanya as they walked their mounts through the gate and north on the laneway that led toward the manor. They transferred the reins to their off-hands and linked inside fingers, exchanging a smile as they watched their children ride ahead; Tim waited until Gudrun was helpless with the pull-over shirt imprisoning her arms before reaching over to poke her in the ribs and spur to a gallop. She yelled, struggled free of the cloth and heeled her horse after his, snatching back her hat to thrash at him as he crouched jockey-style with his face in the windblown mane of his horse.

"Hellions," he said as they disappeared around a bend in the farm-road.

"But they ride like leopards," Tanya replied.

Edward nodded. The knots in his back and neck had relaxed a little, and he rolled his head to further the process. The cornfield lay to their left; to the right was a stretch of sunflowers, nodding orange and gold almost too bright to watch, seeming to turn their heads in homage to the masters of Chateau Retour. *The sun's in this direction,* he reminded himself dryly, but smiled at the thought as he took a deep breath. There was an intense spicy smell of vegetation, of dusty cultivated earth, wildflowers, the hint of wet from the river at their backs. Trees cast streaks of shadow over the sunflowers, where established growth had been left in the midst of the new field; young poplars trembled their leaves by the side of the lane. Muscles moved between his thighs, and hooves went *crunch-pop* in gravel.

He took off his hat with his rein-hand and wiped the back of his wrist across his forehead, feeling the slight tug at his salt-wet hair as the arm touched the thong of his eyepatch. His scalp turned cool for an instant as the wind ran fingers through the sweat-damp mass, then warmed as it dried. He laid the hat on the saddle and looked aside at his wife, admiring the strong chiseled curves of her face. The family likeness was strong, even though they were merely fifth cousins; his branch of the family had left the inland plateau of southern Africa only a generation after the land-taking, a younger son heading north to the territories wrested from the Turks during the Napoleonic struggle.

The blood runs strong, though, Edward mused. *Not just in looks,* his mind added, remembering the War. He had never risen higher than Tetrarch, never wanted to: Tanya had been a Cohortarch of the Guards before her twenty-fifth year. *So beautiful and so dangerous,* he thought.

He had still felt awkward around Citizen women when they met back before the War, both off their home ground, visiting the ancestral von Shrakenberg estate of Oakenwald south of Archona. Doubly so before this glamorous stranger, already with a prize from the Central Gallery for her paintings. A grin lit his face at the memory of that first wild coupling in darkness amid the clatter of falling brooms and buckets; emerging with clothes carefully straightened to find an amused audience alerted by the noise. Letters, visits . . . The coming of the War had been obvious by then, they had hurried to have their immortality, no time to take up land and build first—"Auric fo' yo' thoughts, love," she said gently.

"Oh, rememberin' our youth," he said.

She raised a brow, replied in a mock-aged quaver. "Ahh, yes, hand me m' shawl, sonny . . ." A return squeeze at his hand. "Good times, darlin'."

"Bettah to come," he said. "Leastways the War's over."

Tanya nodded around at the fields. "Good to have a place of our own," she said quietly. A chuckle: "Remembah that Fritz sayin', 'Happy as God in France'? I can see what they meant. One problem, though."

"Hmmm?"

"No Wayfarer-Guest fo' the namin' feast."

He frowned. "We could arrange it," he pointed out.

"No, no, it's supposed to be a genuine stranger. Some-one passin' by, representin' the Race in general an' treated as one of the guests of honor. First on the invited list arrive tomorrow, an' still no passers-by. Frontier problem."

That *was* the problem; Citizens were still a thin scatter of pioneer planters in the Loire valley, without the town populations that would provide through-traffic later.

"Put someone out on the road to flag down cars?" he guessed.

"Done, love, but all we've got so far today is passin' serfs and people on official business that won't wait."

"How old *is* this Loki-cursed custom, anyhows?" he said.

"Gods know, an' they don't tell. Frey's prick, my daddy was christened in a church, with a plain dinner-party afterwards," she said frankly.

Edward stared. "In a *church?*" he asked incredulously. "*That* yo' nevah told me, love."

Tanya shrugged in embarrassment. "Oh, not that they were *believers* or anythin', darlin'. Just, ah, con-servative, it wasn't all that uncommon then, 1890's, remember. I suspect this Wayfarer thing's not much older than yo' or I; custom has to start somewheres, though." Another shrug. "Someone will turn up; there's forty million of us, after all. *One* isn't too much to ask."

Frederick Kustaa braked the Kellerman mini to a halt on the embankment road, steering over to the verge.

The sudden quiet struck ears numbed by the rush of air past the open windows, the *pink-ting* of gravel thrown up by the wheels, and the dull roaring of the burner. Metal pinged as it cooled, and the fan sank to a gentle sough as the engine's feedback system signaled reduced demand for steam. He looked back over his shoulder; nothing on the long stretch of road behind him, nothing ahead since the two staff cars had whipped by fifteen minutes ago. Silently, he cursed the chance that had brought them up behind him just before the turnoff; under no circumstances did he want any Draka to see where his car had left the main road.

"We are unobserved?" the man in the back seat said. A thick Austrian-German accent; Professor Ernst Oerbach was a balding man in his forties, looking incongruous in a servant's livery of dark-brown trousers and high-collared jacket.

More at home in sloppy tweeds, Kustaa thought: the man was almost a caricature of a *Mitteleuropan* Herr Doktor of physics. At a pinch he could pass for a medical man swept up in the conquest and sold cheap to a crippled Draka veteran.

"I hope we are," he said aloud, pushing down the reversing-lever and turning the little car in a U. It handled well, very much like an American autosteamer of the same class, say a Stanley Chipmunk. More of a driver's auto, less in the way of auxiliaries, but it was solidly built and the standard of the machining was beautiful; the Domination had never developed Pittsburgh's liking for planned obsolescence.

The American flogged his mind to keep awake as they drove east once more; his eyes were sandy with fatigue, and his mind and tongue felt thick with it. He looked at his watch: ten to seven in the afternoon. *No, 18:50 hours*, he reminded himself doggedly, pulling the ragged edges of his cover-personality's protective blanket back up about himself. *You're a Draka, they use the twenty-four hour system all the time.* The Loire turned gently amid islands of warm gold sand and green willow, a hypnotic glittering as the sun sank behind them, soothing and lulling . . . He jerked his head up and wound down the window, letting the warm air blast at his face. Hot and a little humid, but nothing like a Midwestern summer, and the smells were different, more varied.

The fields beside the road were turning to the harvest; big fields of tasseled corn, sheets of sunflower and chrome-yellow rapeseed, wheat gold-brown and flecked with blue cornflower and red poppies. Grain rippled in long slow billows, dusty yellow sunlight catching the flowers so that they glowed like jewel-chips afloat on an ocean of molten bronze. Pasture was a faded green, until they passed a hayfield being mowed by half a dozen horse-drawn cutter-bars; that was a darker alfalfa color, and the scent struck home with a memory of warm barns and the weight of a pitchfork in his hands. There were orchards, cherries and peaches and others he could not identify, and vineyards, the grapes showing blue-purple among the big forest-green leaves, hanging from the trellis-wires along which the vines were trained. The land seemed more wooded than it was, the slow rise to the north hidden by lines of trees high enough to cut the horizon.

"How it has changed," Ernst said, and the American could feel the headshake in his voice.

"You were here before?" Kustaa said, grateful for the conversation; he had not wanted to force it.

"In the '20's; I was doing some work at the Curie Institute, and friends took me on a . . . pilgrimage. Just this time of year, as well." A long silence. "If it was not for the river and the lay of the land, I would not recognize it. All this"—he waved his hand—"was small farms, with scattered houses and little barns. Small fields, vegetables, and the flowers, so beautiful . . . little inns where we stopped, and had wine and crayfish soup and hot bread; there was Madeline, I remember, and Jules, he was a good friend, and André . . . We were young, the Great War was over and such madness

could never come again, we would make the world
anew with the power of Science. Jules would tell me
that first we must learn how to design a just and rational society, and I would say that no, first we must tap
the power of the atom to free men from the poverty of
nature so that they could *afford* to be humane."

He laughed. "And now all anyone wants of me is
means to destroy," he said. "Turn this"—he nodded at
the landscape outside the auto—"into a poisoned waste-
land. It is not my world, this place of fire and ice you
young men must inherit."

"Doubts, professor?" Kustaa said lightly. Unseen by
the man behind him, his lips tightened; this was only
bare-bones possible with the civilian willing.

"No. No doubts, my young friend; these Draka," and
his lips twisted at the word, "they have the souls of
reptiles and their Domination is a cancer. That they
have atomics is bad enough, but fusion . . . there is no
way to prevent them forever, nobody can declare secret
a law of nature, but yes, I believe your United States,
your Alliance, should have it first. If only because you
are less likely to unleash it."

Unfortunately true, Kustaa thought with bitterness.
There was a long pause before the Austrian spoke again.

"Yet you also used atomics on a city of men," he said
softly. "Human beings flashed to shadows on the concrete, children burned alive, cancer, leukemia, steril-
ity. The warlords of Japan were evil men, but can that
justify . . ."

"You have a better way, Professor?" Kustaa asked
sharply.

"No." A sigh. "No, I do not, if I did I would not be
here, *ja?* Ruthlessness drives out restraint, as bad money
drives out good, until we are left using madness against
madmen, with the death of all that lives as a prize; such
is this *Todentantz* of a century of ours." Another pause.
"I am glad to be old, my friend, very glad indeed."

Kustaa remembered his family in the primary target
zone; remembered the microfilm in his belt, and what

rested in the baggage trunk of the autosteamer. This time he slammed his hand against the pressed-steel panel of the car door, hard enough to skin a knuckle. The sharp pain jolted him back into alertness; how long had it been since he slept?—Christ, two days now. Fear returned with thought, the waiting between his shoulderblades for sirens and shots. He almost stamped on the throttle when the two figures stepped out into the road to flag him down by the tall stone gates. The men leaped aside with a yell as the Kellerman leaped forward with a spurt of dust, then slammed to a halt.

Kustaa heard Ernst's quick surprised curse in German as he shoved home the brake and the cylinders exhausted with a quick hiss-*chuff*! The older man's forehead thumped against the back of the seat, and his own nearly slammed into the padded surface of the wheel. He sat, shaken, staring at the sign that hung in chains between the gateposts:

**CHATEAU RETOUR PLANTATION
EST. 1945
EDWARD AND TANYA VON SHRAKENBERG,
LANDHOLDERS**

"That's *it*, by God," he mumbled. "That's the one." *Now* the problem was gaining entry to the household. The fabled planter hospitality would do him some good, his wounded-veteran status more, but . . . he remembered the notice in the local paper, this christening party or whatever it was. *Maybe they haven't got the last guest, yet.*

The two men with branches came cautiously to the driver's side of the car; French by their looks and dress, serfs certainly by the numbers on their necks.

"*Maître*," one said, and shifted into barely comprehensible English, obviously picked up from Draka or Domination-born serfs:

"Mastair, pleez to 'company moi, a l'Great House, to be guest?"

Kustaa croaked, and waved a suitably imperious hand at Ernst, who responded with accented but fluent French. The serf's face cleared from its frown of concentration, and he poured out a torrent of response accompanied by hand-waving.

"He says that you are bidden to the house as a guest, for a naming-feast, master," Ernst said.

Kustaa hid his grin; the nearest thing most Draka had to a religion was a belief in the destiny of the Race, but they had as much need for ceremonial as any people. There had been a Nietzsche-and-Gobineau-inspired attempt to revive Nordic paganism back in the 1890's, but it had failed even more dismally than the later Nazi efforts, only a scattering of swearwords surviving to mark it. Customs like this helped fill the gap; he supposed they also built communal solidarity. The Citizen caste was thinly scattered and would need some sort of structure to ensure a minimum of social intercourse. *Which makes them less suspicious of a passing fellow-Draka, which I will take* full *advantage of,* he thought.

The other serf suddenly slapped his forehead, pushed the first aside and bowed, presenting a square of cardboard pulled from his pocket. Kustaa took it with a grunt of relief, read the flowing cursive script. It was handwritten, in a neat old-fashioned copperplate penmanship familiar from his study-courses:

Edward and Tanya von Shrakenberg bid the passer-by to be Wayfarer-guest at the naming feast of their newborn twins, now to be welcomed to the Race. If your duties allow, enter for the sake of the blood we share and join in our celebration of kinship, standing as honored guest for all brothers and sisters of the Dragon breed. Let the bond of past, present and destined Future be renewed!

We expect the feast to last three days from tomorrow morning.
Be welcome; our house is yours.

"Shit," Kustaa whispered, remembering to turn it to a cough at the last minute. *Our luck is in at last*, he thought with hammering glee. The recognition-codes sounded through his head.

The manor house of the plantation was an old French chateau; he glanced indifferently at the bulk of towers, the eighteenth-century additions, more recent construction. There would be time to memorize the floor-plan later, he thought, climbing stiffly out of the Kellerman, time when his brain was functioning on something less than reflex. He slung the battle-shotgun from the boot beside his seat and looked about. They had halted in a gravelled yard in front of the arched entrance that cut between two round towers and through the bulk of the building; he could see hints of courtyard and garden through the dim arched recess and the wrought-bronze gates that closed it. His mouth tasted of chalk, and his feet seemed to float over the rock and dry dusty pinkish earth of the drive as he moved to unlock the baggage compartment at the front of the auto.

Ernst's small cardboard case. His own luggage, carefully faked by the OSS; two fold-and-strap bags of ostrich leather and aluminum framing with the gold stampmarks of Foggard of Alexandria. A marula-wood case for the shotgun; he took that himself as servant's hands reached for the other luggage.

"No," he croaked as they touched the other piece that filled most of the compartment, a box like a small steamer-trunk with handles at the corners, securely locked, plain steel freshly painted in dark green. His mind saw the markings underneath:

Technical Section: Weapons Research Division. DO NOT TOUCH—RADIOACTIVE AND TOXIC. With the purple skull-and-bones symbol to add emphasis.

Even without markings, it would provoke too much curiosity if the serfs tried to lift it; there were a dozen sealed tubes of raw plutonium oxide inside, each slotted into its holder. Plutonium is heavy, and the lead tubes and multiple lead-foil baffles of the shielding were even more so. The sight of it made him sweat, and he slammed down the lid with unnecessary force.

"L'auto a parkin', Mastair?"

He started and wheeled; the Frenchman jumped back with stark terror on his face, mouth working as if he was about to burst into tears. The sight of it turned Kustaa's stomach into a tight knot of nausea, adding to the sour taste at the back of his mouth.

I'm a strange Draka, he reminded himself. *I could blow his head off with this scattergun and get nothing worse than a fine and a tongue-lashing for destroying other's property.* More reluctantly: *No, not exactly. These planters are paternalists, in their way; they'd call out anyone who did that and kill them on the dueling field, the way an American might beat up someone who shot his dog. I'm a special case, with immunity to the usual sanctions.* And he would look wild, dusty and tousled from the drive, unshaven, eyes glaring and red-rimmed from lack of sleep.

The American straightened and forced himself to calm, plastering a smile on his face as he detached the control-locking key and handed it to the man. A garage would be as safe a place as any, for the next little while. He *had* to sleep. And the cargo would be ready to move.

Ernst came to his side. "Horses," he muttered.

Kustaa nodded jerkily, hearing the sound of hooves. Galloping; two half-dressed children leaped their mounts over a lane-gate on the west side of the chateau and pelted on behind it, yelling. He rubbed his eyes, wondering if he was seeing straight; then two adults followed more sedately, pausing to let a servant dismount and open the white-painted board gate before cantering over to him and dismounting. A man and a woman, he saw, both in planter's countryside garb. The man piratical with an eyepatch and scarred face; about Kustaa's own height, tow-colored streaks through short butter-yellow hair. Wedge-shape build from shoulders to hips, the usual Draka combination of startling muscle defini-tion and swift controlled movement. Dangerous-looking, even without the marks.

The woman stood with a hand on the man's shoulder, the riding-crop hanging by its thong from her right wrist tapping against one boot. Hard and mannish-looking to American eyes, like most Citizen women, bronze-blond hair cut in a short pageboy; gymnast's figure but long limbs and broad in the hips and shoul-ders, smaller bust than an American woman with her build would have had. They both wore the standard gun-belts with holstered 10mm automatics, pouches, long bowies at their left hips and slender daggers tucked into boot-sheaths. The weapons were finest-quality and custo-mized, inlay and engraving on the pistols, checked hard-wood knife-handles. But still eminently practical, and they both wore thumb-rings also, with surfaces chased to re-present the knuckles of a mailed fist: the Archonal Guard.

Don't underestimate them, Kustaa thought, stepping forward. *Nothing to arouse suspicion, nothing.*

"Ser-vice to the State," he said, in a rasping croak. *Damn, much more of this and my vocal cords* will *be injured,* he thought with exasperation. His left hand flipped back the crushed-velvet lapel of his jacket, show-ing a seven-pointed star of turquoise and red gold; his right waved Ernst forward.

"Glory to the Race," the two Draka replied in unison, their eyes dipping to the insignia, then back to his face with respect and sympathy. Kustaa's mind flicked back to his instructor, the Draka defector who had drilled him on basic etiquette.

"*Remember most Citizens don't just wear uniforms, they see combat,*" she had said, waving the cigarette for emphasis. "*Auxiliaries do the scutwork. A Category III disability is somethin' we all risk; everyone has a sub-conscious reason to follow the custom of treatin' yo' like*

*a tin god. Yo'll have to beat off the women with a stick,
an' men will buy yo' drinks an' listen to yo' war stories,
or leave yo' alone iff'n yo' wants. Y'can get away with
bein' considerable eccentric, too, 'specially with a
headwound.*

"Edward von Shrakenberg, Landholder, Tetrarch,
Archonal Guard, Reconnaissance," the man said.

Shit, Kustaa thought. *Recon-commando, close-combat
specialist, have to watch it.*

"Tanya von Shrakenberg, Landholder, Cohortarch,
Archonal Guard, Armor," the woman added.

Oh, goody, an armored-battalion major, he mused.
Well, she looks tough enough.

Ernst spoke for him. "My masters, my owner is
Frederick Kenston: traveller in art materials, private,
XX Mechanized Infantry Legion, Combat Engineers.
He regrets that his injury from blast and gas renders
speech difficult, besides damage to balance and hear-
ing. I am his medical attendant as well as his servant."

That had been the best cover available. A Category
III veteran got a pension of 5,000 aurics a year, equivalent to a steady middle-class income, enough for a
ten-room villa and six servants. "Traveller in art materials" meant loot-buyer essentially, a free-lance contractor who bought from individuals to resell in the cities of
the Police Zone, or to collectors and museums; it was a
plausible occupation for a restless man, one not content
to sit and vegetate. The injuries enabled him to avoid
an accent only years of practice could duplicate exactly;
when he *did* have to speak, the croak would cover most
of it, and the XX Legion was raised in Alexandria,
where the usual Draka slur was more clipped, a legacy
of l9th-century immigration.

And the balance problems . . . He recalled the defector: *"Yo' combat-style would be a dead giveaway in any
palaestra in the Domination, an' anyhows yo' cain't
fight worth shit.* Kustaa had bristled at the time, but a
few humiliating sparring-sessions had cured him of that.
Mo' to the point, yo' cain't practice, or do gymnastics,

*or even dance, and all of them is impo'tant socially.
This gets yo' off, an' nobody will pick fights with yo'.*
Impaired hearing would make others more likely to talk
around him, and the Combat Engineers accounted for
the workman's set of his muscles.

The two Landholders stepped back and saluted him,
fist to chest, then gave him the forearm-clasp Draka
handshake. "Honor our home," the man said. *Edward,
I'll have to remember that,* Kustaa prompted himself.

"Stay a day, stay a week, stay a month," the woman
added. "An' while yo' do, what's ours is yorn."

Kustaa nodded, failed to repress an enormous yawn.
His fingers signed at Ernst.

"My master thanks you, masters," he said. "And begs
your pardon, but he is very weary." The Cartwright
system, American, but that would arouse no suspicion,
the Domination had never evolved a full-fledged sign
language. Handicapped serfs went to jobs within their
capabilities, Draka born without hearing were sterilized
and sent to luxurious institutions calculated to shorten
their lives. For the few cases outside those categories, a
Yankee invention was tolerable.

"*Pas de problem,* as they says hereabouts," the mistress of the plantation said, clapping for service. "The
guest room is ready; dinner by yo'self, right away?
Good."

Kustaa hardly noticed the stairs. The bed was wide
and soft; sleep softer, deeper, more dark.

CHAPTER TWELVE

No better example of the hysteria and economic illiteracy of the Democratic-Progressive bloc in Congress could be found than the foreign-trade provisions of the Donaldson-Obregon Omnibus Trade Bill passed last week and currently undergoing debate in the joint sessions. First, the attempt to interfere with the political independence of the Federal Currency Board, already gravely limited by the Treaty of Rio, opens the way to further inflationary . . .

. . . and lastly, the ludicrous provisions of the so-called "embargo" on trade in advanced industrial machinery with the Domination deserve special condemnation. An unholy alliance between southern-state special interests determined to protect their high-priced sugar, cotton and coffee; trading blocs whose links with our South American allies open them to outright blackmail on tropical products and minerals; ideologically-blinded labor leaders, obsessed with fear of competition from so-called "slave-labor" goods—all are conspiring, in effect if not in fact, to raise producer and consumer prices at a time of serious shortages in raw materials, when capacity utilization is at unprecedented levels. The editors of this magazine urge President Marshall to veto this measure, or at least exercise his line-veto on the most objectionable clauses. The Domination, with its

extension in the Eurasian War, is an unpleasant fact of life with which sensible men must come to terms; trade is mutually beneficial, the best means of raising the standards of living of the suffering underclass; and contact with a free economy could be the most effective long-term means of softening harsh and archaic aspects of the Draka system. Besides these arguments, sufficient in themselves, it must be borne in mind that we hold no patents on the laws of nature; the Domination will develope its own rare-earth and transistor-manufacturing plants in due course. An embargo would harm nobody but our own American industries, already suffering from competition from a South America, Japan, Australasia rebuilt at our overburdened taxpayers' expense.

Editorial, Capital Monthly
Chicago Union Press
July 17, 1947

So what if they're technologically superior? What we can't steal, we can buy. When the time comes to geld the Yankees an' hitch them to the plough, we'll cut off their balls with a knife they competed to sell us; an' while we rape their virgin cheerleader daughters, they'll still be whimperin' about contracts.

Minutes of the Supreme State Council
Archon Edwina Palme Presiding
Archona, Executive Building
July 10, 1947
MOST SECRET: LEVEL XIX PERSONNEL ONLY

CHATEAU RETOUR PLANTATION, TOURAINE PROVINCE
AUGUST 2, 1947

"Mastaire, wake-up, plait," the voice said.

Kustaa's hand darted under the pillow to touch the butt of his pistol; the Domination's 10mm service-issue,

but he had practiced enough to be as much at home
with it he had been with the Concord .44's he carried
in Sumatra. Awareness came on the heels of the movement, and he relaxed into his yawn, catching himself in
time to stop his natural reflex to cover himself with a
woman in the room.

She had stepped prudently back after putting the
tray on the table beside the bed, and smiled timidly at
him as he sat up with another yawn and a stretch. *God,
it's difficult to be nonchalant with a hard-on*, he thought,
unconsciously glancing down at a morning erection like
nothing he could remember since he was a teen-ager.
Well, two months of celibacy doesn't help, he reminded
himself wryly. That brought other memories, and he
slapped the servant's hand aside with unnecessary violence when she followed his eyes and reached tenta-
tively for him.

"Sorry," he grunted, and saw confusion added to
alarm as she jumped back with a cry, cradling her hand.
Christ, what a bastard you can be, he thought at himself. Bad enough the momentary temptation, but to
take his self-disgust out on her in anger . . . *She's just a
kid*. Sixteen, he judged; slim, with long russet hair and
eyes the honey-brown color of water in a forest pond
blinking at him. Dressed in some sort of long knit-silk
shirt to just above her knees, and a tied-off cloth belt,
with sandals that strapped up her calfs. *She's probably
afraid of getting whipped if she doesn't lay you*. The
orange number-tattoo was obscenely evident behind
her ear.

Kustaa stood and let her put the caftan over his head,
sat while she poured him coffee. The smell was almost
intoxicating, and it was black and strong, enough to jolt
him into higher gear. The room was midway up the
taller square tower at the rear of the old chateau building, about ten feet by fifteen. Two tall narrow windows,
one looking east over the gardens and the other north
along the roofline of the new wing, with its neat black
slates and the balustraded terrace at the end. A small

lake beyond that . . . Both windows were open, letting in fresh green smells and early-morning light; it was about six, he estimated.

I could at least have fallen in among decadent *aristocrats who lolled in bed until noon,* he thought grumpily. The ones who owned this estate were probably up already, working at the famous Draka fitness. *No rest for the wicked,* he mused sardonically. *In this case, literally.* The coffee finished, he accepted a glass of orange juice and began prowling about the room; it was panelled in plain dark polished oak to thigh level, then finished in deep-blue tiles with silvergilt edges. The ceiling looked like translucent glass, probably some indirect-lighting system; the floor was jade-green marble squares, covered by an Oriental-looking rug that felt silky to his bare feet. He stopped by the east window, pointing east to a set of large striped tents half-hidden among trees, a thousand yards away.

"What a-re those?" he grated. Not quite so exaggeratedly as he had for the Draka—it was unlikely they would compare notes with the French girl.

"*Ces?*" she said, coming to stand beside him. "Pour . . . fo' les guests, maistre. No, how yo' say, room here fo' all."

A discreet scratching at the door; the girl answered in French and another woman entered, pushing a wheeled tray. This one middle-aged, dressed in blouse and skirt; there were razors, basins and towels on the metal-framed stand before her. With a sigh, Kustaa sank back into the chair, submitting to the routine of hot towels, a trim for hair that was growing a little shaggy by the standards of the Domination's military-style crop, a careful edging with tiny scissors at his moustache, manicure, pedicure, neck, face and scalp massage . . .

The girl kept up a stream of French chatter throughout, handing tools to the older woman in an apprentice-to-master style. Kustaa waited until his face was being rubbed with some astringent cologne before he pointed a finger to the ceiling.

"Up . . . there?" he said.

"Above us, master, is the armory," the woman replied in accented but fluent English; learned pre-War, he judged. "Above that is the communications room, for telephone and radio." A jolt of excitement ran through him at the news: perfect. There *had* to be a communications room, every plantation had one, there was a regular schedule of calls required by the Settler Emergency Network, to make sure no uprising went long unreported. But to have it right over his head—frustration followed; here he had an English-speaking informant, a legitimate excuse for curiosity . . . and a cover story which kept him dumb as a post. Nor could he simply say; "Where is Sister Marya Sokolowska?"

I can't count on having made it clean away, he thought. With returning vigor the fear was having its usual effect, sharpening wits and sight, making the world clearer and more real. *Nobody can throw sixes on every roll; Lyon was far too close anyway. It's getting tight.* The sub would be in place from tonight, for a full week. Waiting *that* long would be an invitation to disaster.

Patience, patience, he told himself. *One battle in a camgaign, one campaign in a very long war. More haste less speed.*

The plantation was not a very large community; he would have breakfast, and then wander. Sooner or later he would make contact, and he would just have to hope it was soon enough. One of the things the most gung-ho officer had to keep in mind was that men were going to stop to rest, eat and take a crap every so often, whether they had orders to or not. He had slept, and now—

"Thank you," he said to the manicurist.

"It is nothing, Master," she said, packing away her instruments with quick, efficient movements. "My name is Annette—Tom's wife Annette, anyone will direct you—if you require anything. This young wench is Madeline; she will show you the Great House, if directed." A stern glance at Madeline, who looked meekly

down at folded hands. "Although her English is not of
the best, Master. Breakfast will be served on the terrace for the family for the next two hours; your servant
has been directed there. Nothing more? A good morning, then, Master, and may you enjoy your stay on
Chateau Retour."

"I—will," he grated. To himself: *But Chateau Retour
probably will not.*

The terrace was a section of flat second-story roof at
the north end of the new wing. Inside, the recent
construction was still mostly empty echoing space, smelling of green concrete and strewn with ducts and wires,
no break in the sweep but the occasional structural
member. The far wall was stained glass; he gave the
design a quick cursory glance, the usual intertwining
vines and flowers the Draka were so fond of. Up under
the peak of the roof, in what would be the attic
crawlspace, he could see the mounts for an extensible
aluminum-framed glazed shelter that would run out
over the terrace in winter or bad weather. As he pushed
through the swinging doors, he noticed the metal rails
for more glass panels, running out along the sides; a
clear wall, to make the outdoor space a greenhouse-like
enclosure.

Now it was open to heaven, a stretch of warm yellow
honeycomb marble flooring, the cells separated by strips
of darker stone. The edges were fringed with a balustrade of some shiny reddish stone that looked semi-
transparent, carved into fretwork; the surface was
big enough to seat fifty or sixty when tables were set
out, not counting the space taken up by potted trees,
topiaries and flowers. Six tall cast-iron lampstands held
globe-lights about the perimeter in tendrils that looked
suggestively like tentacles; pots of brown earthenware
trailed sprays of impossibly red-purple bougainvilla.
Actually quite pretty, he thought.

Somewhere within him a puritanic Lutheran was asking where all this came from, and if he would ever find

bayonet marks on the furniture from the last moments
of the previous occupants. *Shut it off. Show some interest, man: you're a Draka, an aristocrat, aesthetics are
half your life.* Plus he was what passed for a lower-class
Citizen; mixing with Landholders wouldn't be all that
common for him.

He nodded appraisingly and turned in a circle, froze
with his back to the north and his face turned to the
stained-glass wall. The view from this side was better,
much, much better. The vines ran around the border of
the arched picture, and wove through the base of it. It
depicted a row of crouching figures, naked human forms
all enlaced about with thorn-vines and flowers no red-
der than the trickles of their blood; there were chains
dangling from collars about their necks as well, down to
pitted eyebolts in the ground. The faces . . . every race
and age of mankind, male and female, alike only in
their expressions of weary despair and endless strain.

Across their backs, supported by shoulders and knotted hands, was the bottom of a terrestrial globe; not a
solid sphere, but an openwork projection with outlines
for the continents. Overlaying the world, the Dragon.

Drakon, he thought. *I've met you before, oh, yes.*
Whoever had done this one was a real artist, of sorts.
The vast wings outspread, angled out and up in a flaring
gesture; scalloped like a bat's, and colored a dull crimson that experience reminded him was almost exactly
the shade of clotting blood. A skeletal ribbing supported the stretched skin, rendered in a glass halfway
between black and indigo blue. Taloned feet braced
against the outline of the globe, clutching symbols: a
slave-manacle, the glass somehow suggesting the peb-
bled black surface of wrought iron, and a sheathed
bushknife, the machete-sword of the Domination. The
body itself was the same dead-blood red as the wings,
with an underlying hint of darker color where the bones
would be. Enough to suggest a starved leanness to
match the eternal hunger in the yellow eye that caught
at his.

The face was a final masterwork, the bony outlines of the reptile visage curved and planed, not with any obvious mimicry of expression, yet still conveying something . . . a mockery that seemed to see within him and laugh at his defiance and his plans, an arrogance and cruelty vaster than worlds. *Power for power's own sake*, he thought, recalling the words of Naldorssen, the Draka philosopher. *Power as an end, not a means.* Power to crush the homes and hopes of men like him, to be used as building-rubble in this prison they called a Domination. Eternal tyranny.

With an effort that brought sweat to his face he stopped himself from emptying his automatic into the obscene thing. Hatred he had felt before, but it had always left him feeling a little dirty; like masturbation. *This* hatred felt clean, as if the thing on the wall before him was something that it was truly *right* to hate, the thing for which the feeling of hatred had been made.

You've been here too long and seen too much, he thought. *Control, control.* Then: *Come on, you're a Draka, you fucking love the shitty thing.*

He turned with a cheerful smile plastered on his face. *I was not cut out for clandestine ops, I truly was not. If—when I get back, I'm going to tell Donovan to go fuck a duck, and settle down with Aino so hard I'll grow roots like a barnacle. Re-up to Active in the Corps, even a line command, go back to university, hell, take the wife and daughter and head for the north woods and farm with Dad.* His false smile turned genuine and wry. *Who am I kidding? Every time I looked at Aino or the kid I'd be seeing these people here in Europe. Waiting for the bomb to drop.*

The family breakfast table was in the far left corner of the terrace, with a good view over the courtyard at the north side of the chateau and the lake beyond. A few serfs were sitting at a smaller table nearby. Personal servants, he supposed, required to be on call at all times. They rose and bowed to him, the hands-over-eyes gesture that always set his teeth on edge. Two caught his eye. One was a pretty colored girl who looked like a mulatto, with a mandolin propped beside her, and a smile that seemed genuine. The other was a Frenchwoman; *her* brief flicker of the lips had all the warmth of February in Minnesota, but her looks were enough to stop him an instant in midstride. *God, what a mantrap*, he thought. That brought a chill, as he considered what it probably meant to her life. *No wonder the poor bitch looks depressed.*

He seated himself where the house-servant indicated; the table was set for seven, with plenty of room, and he was the first there. Folded newspapers beside five of the plates, with neat stacks of mail on top for four, those must be the resident adults. He unfolded the paper, grateful for its cover, remembered Aino scowling at him while he hid behind it over the breakfast table at home. *Some men like to talk in the morning, some don't*, he'd said. *Me, I like to chew my way through the sports section while I eat.* Hands filled his coffee cup, began piling his plate. Little fluffy omelets stuffed with herbs and cheese, smoke-cured bacon and sausages, grits with butter, hot croissants . . . Kustaa waved them to a halt, propped up the paper and began methodically fueling himself.

The paper was the *New Territories Herald;* about sixty pages, and more like an Army field-rag than a civilian newspaper, say something on the order of the *Star-Spangled Banner* he'd read in the Pacific. Logical: most of the Citizens in the conquered lands would still be military, or on some sort of official business, administrative or economic. He scanned the leading stories:

FAMINE IN RUSSIA OVER

Command sources indicate that the food distribution program has now reached most of the remaining population centers; grain production should reach sufficient levels with two years to discontinue . . .

MEDITERRANEAN PROJECT AUTHORIZED

Energy Combine spokeswoman Marie Kaine to-day announced that preliminary studies have con-firmed the techno-economic feasibility of a large hydro-electric project in the straits of Gibraltar. "It will actually be more on the nature of a huge bridge rather than a dam, an arched structure that will be a virtual city in itself, supported by an openwork lattice descending to great depths. There are currents in both directions at different levels, and modularized power units, large low-speed tur-bines, will be added in series over a long period. The temperature differentials at various depths will also supply energy, and there are obvious aqua-cultural and industrial applications. The Dardanelles Project is a model, of course, but the Gibraltar complex will be of a new order of magnitude. We estimate a labor force in the 2,000,000–6,000,000 range, and thirty to forty years for the first phase alone. While the general concept is undoubtedly sound, I expect to spend the rest of my career troubleshooting this one."

BUSHMAN ACTIVITIES IN LYON

Kustaa tensed, hid his reaction with a cough. *Two days*, he thought. *I would have expected them to keep it quiet longer*. On the other hand . . . yes, the Citizen population was simply too *small* to keep the ordinary sort of secret well. Too stubborn as well: they were disciplined enough but lacked the sort of meekness that obeyed bureaucratic dictates without question. He read quickly; just an acknowledgment that sensitive materials had been attacked in transit, the safe-house of a resis-tance cell raided, and . . .

. . . suspicion of Alliance involvement. "We caught some of them," Strategos Felix Vashon of the Security Directorate assured our reporter.

"Right now they're telling us everything they know and some things they didn't know they knew. Soon we'll catch the others—this meddling Yankee, too, if that turns out to be the truth—and they can join their friends. My people are experts; we can keep them all alive, sane and screaming for weeks. By the time we impale them, they'll consider it a mercy."

The editors of the *Herald* wish Strategos Vashon all success in tracking down the last of the Bushmen, and making Europe a place fit for the Race's habitation.

Not as bad as it could have been, he thought with relief. *Thank God for the cell-system and Resistance paranoia.* Of course, the ones who had survived this long, first the Gestapo and now the Security Directorate, *had* to be paranoids. Blinking his way back from his thoughts, he noticed the flavor of the omelet on his fork; superb, a little too spicy but very good. The bacon was not smoked with anything like hickory, and the sausages had a trifle too much garlic, but both would do.

A grim smile; the spy heroes of the films he had seen rarely enjoyed breakfast on enemy territory, they were too busy dodging the invariably stupid machinations of the villains. His experience of clandestine operations was rapidly confirming that espionage fiction bore about the same relationship to reality as the war films he had seen in the Corps. And he fondly remembered joining a mob of enraged Gyrenes at a rest center wrecking a projector and screen after those USO morons tried to show what was left of an assault battalion Jason Waggen in *Hills of New Guinea*. Not that they would have appreciated a realistic war film—what they wanted was a nice light comedy with lots of leggy showgirls and music—but the heroic speeches and neatly photogenic casualties had been just too much.

Of course, those fictional heroes could also afford to spit in the interrogator's eye as the hot irons came out, because something always rescued them at the last moment, or their captors would stand cackling and spouting all their secrets before the dashing adventurer grabbed their gun . . . Kustaa took a last bite of buttered croissant, touched his coffee cup for a refill and leaned back with a slight belch. *I must have gained six pounds, even with all the running*, he thought. *Funny, you never see a fat Draka.*

There was a sharp clacking from the courtyard below. *Then again, not so funny.* Two of them were practicing there, stick-fighting on the tiled stretch just in from the colonnade that ran along the inner edge of the building. Not the ones he had been introduced to, so they were probably overseers. A short squat dark-haired man and a taller woman with reddish-brown curls cut close to her head; both stripped to trousers and singlets, the thin fabric clinging to their sweat-slick bodies. Swinging fighting-sticks in each hand, meter-long ebony rods with rounded steel tips. Swift flicking strikes, thrusts and darting slashes that blurred the night-colored wood and would have crushed bone and ruptured organs if they had landed.

Fast, God, but they're fast, he thought enviously. Another form dashed out from the exercise-room beneath his feet. Anonymous in unarmed-combat armor of brown leather and padding and steel; it dove forward on its forearms and kicked back with both feet. The one following was only a flicker before it flew back out of sight with a crash. He recognized Tanya as she went into a forward roll and twisted back the way she had come; just barely in time, as her husband followed in a huge bounding leap that ended with a side-kick and his heel driven into her midriff. Their feet and hands were thickly padded, the armor over the stomach strong, but Kustaa was still surprised to the edge of shock to hear no more than a *hufff!* of exhaled breath as the woman was knocked back half a dozen feet.

She backrolled half a dozen times and came to her feet to meet Edward's attack; for twenty seconds they fought almost in place, hands, feet, knees, elbows, blocking and striking almost too fast for the American's trained attention to follow. *Pankration* was what they called it, the classical Greek term for all-in wrestling-boxing, although it was an outgrowth of Draka contacts with the far east in the 1880s. He could see the origins of the style in the Oriental schools he had studied, but this level of skill could only be learned by continuous training from babyhood. *And we have better things to do with our lives,* he thought. Furthermore, the Way of the Gun beat the Way of the Empty Hand every time, in his opinion. *Automatic weapons at two hundred paces, that's my preference.*

It was functional, though, he supposed. Serfs rarely confronted their masters with weapons in hand, and on a subconscious level a demonstration of personal deadliness was probably more daunting than weapons, no matter that the firearm was so much more objectively destructive. Just as a rifle with a bayonet could drive back a crowd better than the rifle alone, even though the blade added little to actual combat effectiveness. A fresh clatter broke into his thoughts; the owners of the plantation were down on the ground now, rolling, close-quarter work, driving knuckles at pressure-points and trying for choke or breaking holds. Weight and strength told more in grappling style, and Edward called victory with clawed fingers in a position that would have ripped out his wife's windpipe in true combat.

They pulled off their helmets of padding and steel bars and kissed.

"Not bad fo' a turtle-minded tanker," he heard the man say.

"Pretty dam' good fo' someone who trained to crawl through ditches an' listen at windows," she replied, as they both shoulder-rolled to their feet.

"Mistah Kenston!" she called up to him. "Good mornin'; see yo' in half an hour!"

The two Draka were shedding their padding and clothes, tossing them aside with the casual unconcern of those raised to expect things to be picked up, cleaned and neatly replaced by ever-attentive hands. Kustaa remembered his own mother's weariness after he and Dad came back from the fields, keeping house for a family of six far from electricity and the sort of money that bought appliances. *Bastards*, he thought. They were trotting down to the marble beach; Edward swept the woman up in his arms and began to run, clearing a stone table with an easy raking stride. At the edge he halted and threw her; Tanya twisted in midair and hit the surface with a clean dive, her blurred form swimming out underwater for a dozen yards.

The overseers joined Kustaa at the table, freshly washed and dressed in long robes. *Any more of this and we'll look like a Southern Baptist's idea of the Last Supper,* Kustaa thought irritably. The man was wearing an earring and bracelets, too, one joined to his thumbring by a silver chain; it still looked unnatural to see men wearing jewelry. A rueful glance down at his own clothes; loose indigo-blue trousers with gold embroidery down the seams, ruffled shirt, string tie with a jeweled clasp, black silk-velvet jacket with broad lapels edged in silver-gilt, buckled shoes. He had drawn the line at the diamond ear-studs the outfitting section back at OSS HQ tried to insist on, but there was no alternative to the floppy-brimmed hat with the side-clasp and spray of peacock feathers; the only really comfortable item was the gunbelt. At least he didn't have to wear *that* to breakfast.

I look like the most dangerous goddam pansy in the world, the thought. The overseers were making conversation among themselves, tactfully including him when replies could be limited to yes-no. Making conversation about this party coming up, and the impending harvest; it was late this year, evidently the spring had been cold and the summer delayed. Once he was jarred by a question about Alexandria, his supposed hometown, but the Draka answered it herself after his noncommital grunt. They were going to *have* to get more agents trained in Draka speech-patterns; the trouble was that the ones who could pass even casually for Citizens were so few. The dialect was not really all that much like American Southern, either: derived from the same roots, but a hundred and fifty years made a *lot* of difference. Not to mention the regional variation; he could tell the two overseers came from separate areas, but . . .

Two of the von Shrakenberg children joined them, a tow-headed boy and a girl of the same age with freckles and red braids; disturbing—it was easier to think of Draka as adult monsters. Then the master and mistress themselves . . .

They halted by the servants' table, Edward only long enough to sign Ernst over to his "master's" chair; Tanya stopped and spoke to the French girl. *Girl?* Kustaa thought. She *looked* young, with that clear porcelain skin, on the other hand . . . The conversation was in French. His own command of the language was rather good, and he strained unobtrusively to hear over the sounds of wind and water.

". . . lonely, Mistress," the serf was saying. "My bad dreams again."

Tanya ruffled her hair. "I *do* have to sleep with my husband occasionally, you know, my sweet. Tonight, then; the day will be a busy one."

Does that mean what I think— Kustaa's thought began. Then they kissed, and he managed to avoid staring. *Jesus, they're french-kissing,* he thought, halfway between fascination and disgust. Reaching for another croissant, he used the movement to glance aside at Edward; the Draka had looked up from his newspaper and smiled, proud and fond, before glancing down again.

"Glad they've approved that Gibraltar thing," he remarked to his wife. Then: "See yo've got yorn mo' enthusiastic about domestic duties than I've ever managed on mine."

"That's because yo're a man and therefore crude,

love," she said with a grin. "But keep tryin', by all means." He laughed and kissed her fingers, then turned to Kustaa.

"We 'spect to be rather busy, today, Mr. Kenston," he said affably. "Guests should be arrivin' any minute—"

"Speak of the devil," the male overseer remarked, and jerked his head to the east.

Two black dots coming in low and fast: twin-engine small planes. Engine-roar grew swiftly, and they flashed by overhead; one began to circle, while the other drove across the chateau again at barely rooftop level and began a series of wild-looking acrobatics, looping and turning.

"My cousin Johanna," Tanya said. "Ace pilot durin' the War, an' never lets yo' fo'get it." She snapped her fingers and the mulatto girl came running. "Yasmin, up to the radio room an' have the operator tell 'em where the landin' field is."

Kustaa signed at Ernst. "My master asks," the Austrian said, "if you have landing facilities, Masters."

"Why yes," Edward said. " 'bout two kilometers north, there were some buildin's suitable fo' light hangars. Up near our primary wine-cellars an' the shelter."

"Shel-ter?" Kustaa asked in his own gravelly "voice."

"Oh, the War Directorate's insistin'," Tanya said with an expression of distaste. "Good idea, I suppose, but . . . shelter from radioactivity, in case o' war with the Yankees. Underground, industrial strength fuel-cell, air filters, food an' water, so forth. Jus' fo' the family an' some key serfs to start, eventually fo' everyone. Hopes to God we nevah have to use the damn thing."

"Amen," Edward said. "Though at least we didn't have to put it in ourselves. Public Works Directorate did it, nice neat job, reinforced concrete shell an' doors from an old French cruiser. Pretty well all local materials an' labor, come to that."

Kustaa signed. "My master says you seem to be making rapid progress, Masters," Ernst said.

"Very," Tanya replied, taking a second helping of the

grits. "Almighty Thor, but I missed these while I was expectin'. Mo, coffee, François . . . Yes, very rapid. Troublesome, conquerin' an advanced area like Europe, but there are compensations. Got the road net intact, fo' one; that saved us ten years. Local supplies of skilled labor, an electric power grid needin' only a little fixin' . . . well, yo' know."

Kustaa nodded and accepted a slim brown cigarillo. A nursemaid had pushed out a double stroller with the youngest von Shrakenbergs, to be dandled and appropriately exclaimed over; the American carefully shut his mind to how much the wiggling forms resembled any children.

"Now," Edward said. "As I was sayin' we're goin' to be ferocious busy, Mr. Kenston. But Tanya has volunteered to give yo' a quick once-over of our art collection, if yo'd like."

The woman sighed, opening a cablegram. "I'm the resident appraiser, fo' my sins. We got a fair bit in Paris; that's another benefit of conquerin' wealthy countries, they have more worth stealin'." That sally brought a general chuckle; Kustaa managed to join in.

"Darlin'!" Tanya exclaimed suddenly, the hard tanned face turning radiant. "It's from Alexandra! They can make it!" Politely, she explained to Kustaa: "Yo' know, the Alexandra from my 'Alexandra Portraits,' my lover in school, the exhibition I won my first Archon's Prize with?"

The American nodded, his grin going fixed. *Christ, these people are strange,* ran through him. And: *I'm supposed to be an art expert!* with a trace of panic. Running into what was evidently a well-known painter was just the sort of lousy break in his luck that was due, by now.

"And she's been pesterin' me ever since the war to do a new portrait, one so people won't think of her stuck at seventeen fo'ever, after all she's older than me an' a responsible official with four childer, but we've never had time to do another study." A sigh, and she looked down at the paper with a slightly misty-eyed smile. "Ah, youth, sad an' sweet.'"

Kustaa coughed, and signed again. "My master says, thank you very much," Ernst followed fluently, almost a simultaneous translation. "But he has several crates of selected pictures ready for shipment in Paris. Presently he is rounding-off this trip by acquiring antique jewelry?"

"Hmmm," Edward said doubtfully. "We're anxious to cash in some of the paintin's fo' want of space. The jewelry, what we're not keepin', takes no space to mention an' can only appreciate, market's glutted right now." Tanya nodded; they both glanced at him, concerned to make his visit a productive one.

More signs. "My master says, thank you, a few days relaxation is what he principally needs, he grows tired more easily these days." Nods of sympathy. "If, perhaps, you could show him some of the estate—particularly the winery, my masters, he would appreciate the kindness?"

"No problem 't all," Tanya said decisively. "Goin' up there now anyways." She rose, dusting off her hands and chamois breeches. "Glad of yo' company, Mr. Kenston."

They were almost to the main doors when the stout blond serf stopped the Landholder of Chateau Retour.

"I have those seating plans you wished, Mistress," she said. The accent was unusual, not French or even German, despite the transpositions of "w" and "v"; singsong and heavy at the same time. Kustaa's mind struggled to place it, the automatic filing process that kept covert-ops personnel alive; languages were his tools as a spy, as much as his rifle had been as a Marine, and he was good with both. He snapped mental fingers. Kowalski had the same accent! The big coal-country Polack, the one who'd gotten the Bronze Star on Bougainville for taking out the Nip machine-gun . . .

Polish. His eyes snapped back to her; in her thirties, about one-fifty pounds, five-three, built like a Slavic

draft-horse, flat face and ash-pale Baltic hair . . . and
something about the eyes that reminded him of Kowalski,
or Sergeant McAllistair, or even himself, sometimes.
Longer skirt than any he had seen here, long sleeves,
rosary and cross at her belt . . .

"Not now," the Draka was saying, when Kustaa
touched her on the arm.

"Ex-cuse," he said, jerking a suitably casual thumb
toward the serf woman. "Po-lish?"

Tanya stopped, swung round to nod. "Yes, though
we picked her up here. *Met* her in Poland . . . long
story, tell yo' later, Mr. Kenston. Nun, oddly enough;
name's Marya, Sister Marya. Bit set in her ways, but a
good hard-workin' wench; my head bookkeeper an' clerk."

Jesus fucking Christ, my contact! ran though Kustaa
like a song of exultation. Patience evaporated in a fury
of calculation: perhaps his luck had *not* quite reached
the turning point. Radio, airfield, hiding-place . . . and
his contact, who could put them all together. *Wait a
minute.* He rearranged his face, conscious that at least
something had shown; they were both looking at him a
little oddly. *I've got to* talk *to her, somehow.* Privately,
with no possibility of interruption, so that he could give
her the recognition-code that *must* be kept secret. The
way occurred to him; he almost gagged, but it was
necessary. The Sister would have a bad time of it, but
only until the door was closed, after all . . .

"Ex-cuse," he said, taking the Pole by the arm. Ernst
interpreted his signals, his eyes going wide in surprise.

"My master says . . . ah,excuse—" Kustaa signaled
further and the Austrian's eyes narrowed in understanding. "My master says, could he have the use of
this wench?"

The nun's arm went rigid under his fingers, and she
wheeled around on him with a look of pure hatred in
her eyes before they dropped in the worst imitation of
meekness he had ever seen. Tanya stared at him, began
a peal of laughter and ended it in a cough.

"No offense, Mr. Kenston, no offense, yo' don't know

her. Ahhh . . ." She looked at the nun: Kustaa could see her evaluating the stocky figure, graceless in its thickset strength. Not what a Draka looked for in a wench, at all, or comely by the separate standard a Citizen male used for women of his own caste, either.

"No offense, but this'n isn't trained or suited fo' erotic service. Really, iff'n yo' don't like the one sent to attend yo' this mornin' "—so his guess had been right—"there's a dozen others, prettier an' mo' enthusiastic."

"Pu-lease," he grated. Sweat had started out on his forehead, and his smile was more of a rictus. Perfectly genuine desperation, if the cause was one the Draka could not suspect. "Pu-lease, thu-is one." He put a hand to his throat, as if the effort had strained his damaged vocal cords.

Tanya stepped closer, put a firmly sympathetic hand on his shoulder and steered him a few steps away. He was suddenly, surprisingly aware of her scent, a mixture of fresh-washed body and some slight violet-based perfume. "I'm ashamed to admit it," she said with low-voiced sincerity, "but that one won't answer yo' bridle, sir. Stubborn an' we haven't broken her to it, a work horse an' not a playpony."

"*Pu-lease*," and a rasping cough.

"Mr. Kenston, suh, if it's a nun yo' has to have, well, there's one on our neighbor's place down the road a spell, I'll phone over an' borrow. They've got a Carmelite, nice bouncy little thing, they might have her original robes 'round someplace an'—"

He shook his head vehemently; from what he had heard he was straining the limits of hospitality, but a Class III veteran could push pretty far. There was a sickening fascination to it, as well, a realization that this could actually have been happening. Nobody knew but him . . . No need to hide his emotions now, just the opposite.

"Suh, I warn yo', she'll have to be subdued, an' even then once yo're into her she'll be dry an' refuse to move." A sigh, at his obdurate face. "Yo' might need help gettin' her stripped and spread, do yo' want her drugged or a couple of hands to help? No?"

Another sigh. "Well, Mr. Kenston, I'm tryin' to be mindful of a host's obligations, but I really can't spare her any time today, in fact she'll be workin' overtime until after dinner. So, if yo'd like somethin' in the meantime?" He shook his head again. "Well, if yo' insist, suh. *I* must insist that she not be marked or injured. We don't allow anythin' too rough here, I'm givin' yo' fair warnin' of that. Clear? Then I advise yo' to tie her legs to the bedstead first thing."

Tanya turned, a puzzled and half-angry frown on her face; she shrugged at Marya, who was standing with her hands clenched at her sides. "Well . . . this mastah seem's determined to have yo' fo' a mount, Marya. Attend his room aftah yo' finished work, and serve his pleasure. And no slackin' today. Understood?" The nun continued to glare at the ground before her feet, until her owner barked sharply: "*Is that understood, wench?*"

Marya's head came up slowly. For an instant Kustaa felt an eerie prickle of *déjà vu* as the fresh-cropped hairs at the base of his skull struggled to stand upright. Then he remembered where he had felt it before: Java, when the "disabled" pillbox had come back to life, and the turret-mounted cannon lifted its muzzle with a whine of gears. The Polish woman nodded once, with a curt snap, her square pug face held like a fist, then turned on a heel and stalked away. Her heels clicked like gunbolts closing on the marble floor of the vestibule, amid the statuary and the downslanting rays of crisply golden summer-morning light.

He became conscious of a hand under his elbow and shook himself loose again, turning to follow her out into the bright sunlight with its smells of garden and dusty gravel and the slightly oily smell of distillate. A six-wheeled car waited at the foot of the stairs, and the driver sprang down to open the doors.

"Well, well, yo've turned out to be a man of . . . interestin' interests," Tanya said to him.

"Th-ank you," he said, anxious to choke off curiosity.

A shrug. "I'll have restraints an' some oil-cream jelly sent up," she said. "And a silk switch." A snuffle of laughter. "I warn yo', though, the last man to get anythin' into that one got scant joy of it. I'll tell yo' the sad story of Horn-dog on the way up." She rapped on the back of the driver's seat. "The winery, Pierre. An' maybe yo' could tell me a little 'bout what you saw in Lyon, been a while since I was there."

Lyon? Kustaa mused. *Somehow I don't think so.*

CHAPTER THIRTEEN

WANDA THE WELDER TO KEEP JOB, EXPERTS SAY

Sociologists and economists at the Department of Labor say studies recently completed have refuted the common expectation that large numbers of women who took up the jobs of absent men during the Eurasian War—the "Wanda the Welder" phenomenon—will go back to homemaking now that peace has returned.

"Too many women have become used to the independence provided by the healthy weekly paycheck," said Maribelle Aquino, statistician and spokesman for the Department, "especially in areas, such as the southern Hispanic states, where such opportunities were rare before the War. This income has become part of family income, essential to the perceived standard of living. Not to mention the example of the armed services, where women are now employed in all non-combatant roles, and some, such as flying transport-aircraft, which would have been considered impossible before the war. Very little now remains of the traditional concept of a 'man's job.'"

Dr. Aquino said that the only factor which could have reversed the trend would have been a substantial increase in the birth rate, which some preliminary figures during the War seemed to indicate. "But the so-called 'Baby Boom' turned out to be more like a blip," she commented, noting that a slight increase in the northern states was more than overmatched by the continuing decline in births among Americans of Hispanic and Asian backgrounds. The ever-increasing labor shortage, due to the general economic boom, the enormous demands of post-War reconstruction, and the continuing high defense spending necessitated by the confrontation with the Domination should extend and consolidate the trend, she predicted.

> *From: "Women and the Post-War World"*
> Ladies House and Garden Journal
> *Suarez Publishing Corp.,*
> *Havana, July 28, 1947*

LYON, PROVINCE OF BURGUNDIA
AIRSHIP HAVEN
11:00 HOURS
JULY 28, 1947

The *Issachar* was approaching Lyon from the north. Kustaa let his eyes drop from the pale turquoise haze of the sky to the land droning by six thousand feet below. The Savoie Alps were passing by to the east, dark-blue with distance and higher than the airship itself; below, the Rhone trough was widening out, a patchwork of varicolored orchard, vineyard and field and the russet-brown of ploughed earth. Vehicles moved insect-small along the long straight roads, trailing dust-plumes like the white-gray feathers of sparrows; the river itself was blue-brown, with hammered-silver patches downstream where banks of pebbles broke the low level of the summer waters. An aircraft passed, climbing, a swift flashing of combined velocity, and there were two more dirigibles in sight, long whale-shapes laboring north against the backdrop of mountain.

The American took another sip of the single beer he had allowed himself; Danish, excellent, mellow amber with just the right hint of bitterness, biting at the back of his throat. Methodically, he probed at his nerves. *Not bad*, he thought. *Still a little shaky*. Hamburg had been bad, very bad indeed; he was running through cover-identities faster than Donovan had planned for. The danger was different from combat-strain, more like a night-ambush patrol; less intense, but it didn't *end*. Worse than the danger was the effort of simply *being* a Draka for so long; having them hunt him through the Finnish woods had been simple by comparison.

He'd been skipping a good deal of the multiple tasking Donovan had planned for, as well; it was even worse tradecraft than he had anticipated. Endangering the indigenous networks that were all the OSS had to build on, until it could somehow infiltrate the Domination's own organizations.

Shit, endangering me, too. Now I know too much; I've got to get back. Straight to Lyon, but the delays had put him right back on schedule. With any luck, the coded messages had been sent out for the last week. With any luck, there was still someone *there* to pick them up. *With any luck and a day at the races, I'd be rich*, he mused.

"Docking in ten minutes," the voice over the intercom said. "Docking in ten minutes. All passengers please be seated until docking is complete."

Kustaa finished his beer and waved to the stewardess, staring out the slanted window beside him. The airship lurched as she reached across him to pick the glass off the veneered aluminum table, and a half-full bottle on the tray in her other hand toppled, sending a stream of amber-colored Tuborg splashing off the rim of the birchwood platter and into his lap. He began a yell, remembered to turn it to a strangled grunt and sank back into the seat.

The girl was on her knees beside his chair, reaching out with a cloth that trembled in her shaking hands to mop at the stain on the front of his fawn-colored trousers.

"Oh, Master, I'm *sorry*, I'm so *sorry*, please, let me help, please, master—"

The lilting Swedish accent was raw with fear as he irritably snatched the towel and hastily wiped off the worst of the mess. Looking down he saw huge cornflower-blue eyes starring with tears, and a mouth working with terror.

"A-ll right," he grated, keeping to the strangled grunt that his cover allowed. "G-o."

She righted the bottles on the tray with frantic speed, wiping the floor plates. Froze again when she saw who was looking her way; the senior stewardess, a born-serf in her thirties with a hard flat Kazakh face and a leather razor strap on a thong around her wrist. They were both in the same livery, a smart tailored jacket with a long V neck and a pleated skirt of indigo blue, but the older woman did not have the Swede's look of vulnerability in it. She came over with a brisk stride, her low-heeled shoes clicking on the roughened-metal planking, muffled over the rugs.

The offending woman (*No, girl,* Kustaa decided. *Seventeen, maybe eighteen*) stood and held the tray before her; there was a slight rattling from the glasses and bottles, a quiver she could not suppress.

"Yo' wish punish this slut yo'self, Mastar?" The Kazakh's English was Draka-learned, with the hint of a barking guttural beneath; Kazakhstan had been the northernmost of the Domination's conquests in the Great War, a generation ago. About when this one had been born, he estimated. Her face held no more than her voice or the posture of her well-kept body: precisely trained deference.

"N-o," Kustaa said, waving a casual hand. "Is nothing." As much as he could say, as much as he could *do. You're here to observe and report,* he reminded himself savagely, behind a mask of detachment as perfect as the serf's. *Follow orders, dammit!*

The Kazakh nodded. "Rest assured, Mastar, she no sit fo' week." A jerk of the head, and the blond girl walked staring past them, through the cloth-curtain door behind the bar. There was a murmur of voices, one pleading it had been too little time since the last strapping.

The American rubbed at his eyes. *I thought I was tough*, he thought wonderingly to himself. *Every little bit pushes you a bit further. Fuck it, I want to be home, away from these people!*

"Not a bad little piece," the man across the table from Kustaa said idly.

He was an exec from the Dos Santos Aeronautics Combine, up from the Old Territories to oversee conversion of European facilities. A square-faced man in his fifties, conservatively dressed by Draka standards, down to the small plain earrings and Navy thumb-ring, smelling of expensive cologne. It mingled with the leather-liquor-polish scent of the long room along the lower edge of the dirigible's gondola; this was a short-range bird, shuttling between the larger European cities, not equipped with overnight cabins. No rows of bus-type seats, as there might have been on an American equivalent, though. Scattered tables for four, and freestanding armchairs, and a long bank of canted windows giving a view of the ground below.

"Not bad at all," he continued, with the air of a bored man making conversation. There was a flat *smack* of leather on flesh from the curtained alcove, thin yelps of suffering giving way to a low broken whimper. "Wonder how she strips."

"Black an' blue, now," the Air Corps officer beside him said. "Yo'd have to let her get on top."

She laughed at her own joke, more than mildly risqué by the Domination's standards, began stuffing files in the flat attaché case before her, then frowned. "That's a bit much," she said, and raised a brow at Kustaa. He nodded vigorously.

"Enough, there," she called, and the sound of blows

ceased. Yawning, the pilot glanced idly out the window and exclaimed:

"Look! *Just* what I was talkin' about, Mr. Sauvage."

The exec followed her pointing finger, and Kustaa's eyes joined his. They were over the military section of the airhaven north of the city, the usual tangle of runways, hangars, workshops and revetments. The usual expansion-work going on as well, the iron ordered standardization of the Domination being overlaid on the more haphazard pre-War foundations. Long modular buildings, a chaos of dust as the road-net was pushed out. Neat rows of fighters, older prop-driven models and sleek melted-looking jets. Strike aircraft, twin-engine Rhinos mostly, grim and squat and angular with their huge radial engines and mottled paint; they had been known as the "flying tanks" during the Eurasian War, for their ability to absorb punishment. Kustaa's OSS antennae picked up at the sight of the electrodetector towers, but they were basic air-traffic control phased-pulse models; no real need for air-defense here, he supposed.

And a row of helicopters, gunboats; that was what the Air Corps tetrarch was pointing at. He remembered the smell of burning woods, and the chin-turrets' blind seeking . . . There were wings on the breast of the officer's uniform tunic, and the Anti-Partisan Cross below that. Probably she flew the choppers; his ears went into professional mode again. He had convinced them that the cripple did not want to be included in a conversation he could not fully share, convinced them to the point that they ignored the human recording system sitting across the table.

"Look!" she said. "An' tell me those are cost-effective."

The exec cleared his throat. "Precision firepower," he said stolidly. "Entirely new application, an' barely a decade since we turned out our first single-seater scout model. Fo' once, we're completely ahead of the Yankees. We have to concentrate on capital-intensive weapons, we're—"

"—not a numerous people," she finished. "Look again," she continued. "How many of those are on-line, an' how many yanked fo' maintenance? Serious stuff, not jus' cleanin' fuel lines."

Kustaa checked . . . yes, three out of seven with the dismounted assemblies that told of more than routine care. Interested, he glanced back at the Draka woman; she was small for one of her race, thin-featured and dark with a receding chin and big beaked nose pierced for a small turquoise stud. For a moment he wondered what had moved her to emphasize her worst feature. Naivety? Defiance?

"An' that's the problem. Sho' yo' got them to us fast; *too* fast, they're the best thing since the hand-held vibrator when they *workin'*, but the whole beast is a collection of prototypes, every subsystem experimental. An' the power train is too highly stressed. An' the servos fo' the weapons systems is tempramental; and either they works *wonderful* or they don't work *at all*."

The man examined his nails. "Technical Section—" he began.

"TechSec doan' end up in the bundu with the bush-men breathin' down they necks an' only those things to save they ass! Yo' should 'a taken another four, five years makin' sure of things, in the meantime produce mo' Rhinos. They can't hover, but they *works*.

"*And* yo' should be simplifyin' maintenance. As *is*, we keep the squadrons goin' by keepin' preassembled subsystems on hand, jus' jerkin' anything that doan' work and sendin' them back to the factory." She thrust a thumb at the stewardess, who had emerged ashen-face from the bar cubicle and was walking stiffly about her tasks. "Look, it *easy* to train the cattle to pour drinks an' fuck, or to dig holes an' break rock. Maintainin' high-speed turbines is anothah matter!"

The exec rubbed his jaw. "Tetrarch," he said, "my own children are pilots, we *are* doin' the best we can. There are just so many engineers, aftah all, and any number of projects. As fo' maintenance technicians, that's always been tight. I'd've thought with all these Europeans comin' on the market, fully or partly trained already . . ."

"That another thing, we gettin' spoiled by Europe. Richest place we've ever took, an' skills the best part of it. Trouble is, we're livin' off loot; an' consider the social costs of maintainin' that level of trainin' over generations."

The man glanced from side to side in an instinctive gesture of caution and leaned forward, lowering his voice. "Mo' right than yo' know, tetrarch. We had some bad trouble in South Katanga, just last month." She duplicated his either-way and leaned closer herself; that was one of the important industrial subregions of the central Police Zone, mines, hydro-dams and a huge complex of electrical-engineering and motor works, mostly owned by the Faraday Electromagnetic Combine.

"Took a lot of the serf cadre out of the plants there fo' the conquered territories, promoted from their under-studies, an' shipped in Europeans to do the donkey-work."

"Uprisin'?"

"Serious. Citizen casualties, mob of 'em nearly bust out of their compounds into the free zones, turned them back with vehicle-mounted flamethrowers." The pilot winced; there had been nothing like that in the Police Zone in living memory, the sort of measure used in newly-conquered areas. "They had to gas a whole mine. Decided to lobotomize an' ship most of the survivors; three big factory compounds out of order, jus' when demand fo' industrial motor systems is gettin' critical."

The two Draka shook their heads; the woman seemed about to speak when the *Issachar* jolted. Kustaa looked up, and saw that they had docked. The dirigible quivered as her steerable tiltmotors held the nose threaded into the anchor ring of the tower; then there was a long multiple clicking sound as the restraining bolts shot home into the machined recesses. Another quiver as the engines died, the sudden absence of their burbling whine louder than their presence. More clicks and jolts as the anchor ring moved to thread the docking cable through the airship's loops, then cast them loose.

The American looked out the window, saw the horizon sinking as the winches bore the dirigible down below the level of the surrounding buildings, down to the railed tracks. A final quiver as the keel beneath them made contact with the haulers, and a whining of pumps as gas was valved through the connectors into the haven's reservoirs, establishing negative buoyancy. The observation deck was only five meters up, now; he could see the cracked concrete surface, the interlacing rails, the huge silver-gray teardrop shapes of the other dirigibles, most locked at rest, flocks of nose-in circles around their terminals. Groundcrew swarmed about, little electric carts flashed by tugging flatbed trailers loaded with luggage; a train of heavy articulated steam drags was passing under an anchored airship, unloading cargo-modules that clipped down on their backs with prefitted precision. The scene moved, creeping by as the haulers dragged the *Issachar* to her resting place, and there was a bustle as the passengers moved to fasten jackets and assemble forward.

Kustaa remained in his seat as the disembodied voice came tinnily through the speakers; just as fast to stay in comfort for a minute as wait standing at the end of the line. "Prepare to disembark. All passengers to Lyon prepare to disembark by the forward ramp, please. Through passengers to Marseilles, Genoa and Florence, please remain seated."

He was alone when the stewardess came by again. Her eyes flicked aside at him, returned to the table she sponged down. Her face was gray, with a bleak pinched look that aged her ten years, or a hundred, and she moved with the arthritic care of an old woman. Against his will, Kustaa felt his hand go out to touch her sleeve. She came to a halt, instantly.

"Sor-ry," he croaked, standing and taking up the heavy

leather case that never went out of arm's reach. "Ve-ry sor-ry."

The stewardess's face crumbled for an instant at the words, then she shot a lightning glance around and began to speak, her eyes flickering up to his face as she whispered fiercely and scrubbed at the veneer:

"Oh, Master, you look like a kind man, please here's my number"—a slip of paper, palmed and tucked into his jacket pocket in an invisibly swift movement—"please, I can't *stand* it any longer, buy me, please, I know it can be done, someone bought Inge out just last month because their children liked her, I'm a hard worker really I am, I can cook and look after children and type and drive a car and play the piano and I'm good in bed, very very good, buy me and I'll be the best worker you've ever had always, master, only 75 aurics, *please*."

She scuttled away to the next table and Kustaa stood for a moment, fingering the slip of paper in his pocket. Then he turned and walked calmly along the gallery, out into the passageway and down to the ramp that dropped from the nose of the airship, forward of the control deck. The last of the passengers were still there, checking out their firearms from the counter-clerk, smiling and laughing in unconscious relaxation as they shed the subtle tension Citizens felt when deprived of their weaponry. The American watched his hands strip the clip from the automatic, reinsert it and chamber a round and snap on the safety before holstering it. The battle-shotgun was handed to him still in its black-leather scabbard, with the harness wrapped around it. An auto-shotgun, basically, with a six-round tube magazine below the barrel, the butt cut down to a heavy pistol grip. He jerked it free, popping the restraining-strap, and checked the action; six rounds, alternate slug and double buckshot.

How many could I kill? he thought calmly, estimating the placing of the dozen Draka around him as his fingers caressed the chunky wooden forestock of the weapon. *You for sure, Mr. concerned-Citizen airplane maker who wonders how little girls look stripped. Maybe you too, bignose pilot, you'd be meat just like the two-legged cattle you killed to get that medal.*

More calmly still: *I am going insane.* A few of the Citizens were glancing his way, feeling the prickle of danger without knowing why. *When I get back to my family, will I still be fit for them?*

His hands put the shotgun back in its sheath, slung it over his back with the butt conveniently behind his right ear, buckled the harness around his chest; while his mind painted the varnished metal red and pink and gray with blood and shattered bone and brains. *Not enough*, he decided. *Not nearly enough.*

"How may I serve yo', Mastah? Kellerman two-door? Here keys, yaz sar, Mastah, right this way—"
Where had that been?
"Street St. Jacob? Right that way, suh; my respects to one who gave so much fo' the Race. Nothin' more I cain do? Service to the State!"
What had he replied?
"Drink? Certainment, maistre, you wish perhaps other entertainment—yes, maistre, I go—"

"Yes, this is certainly the place," he said to himself. Then started to his feet, the snifter of brandy in his hand. A frantic look at the bottle reassured him: only two drinks. He strode over to the table beside the bed; 25 Rue St. Jacob, Transit Hotel #79, room 221. Precisely right.

"My god, I nearly lost it," he muttered to himself, raising the blinds. An ordinary European street, a little broader than most, five-story brick buildings. A few autosteamers going by; sunset behind the buildings opposite, streetlights winking on, the branches of the chestnut tree outside tapping against his window. Ordinary hotel room, bed with white coverlet, nightstand, desk, carpet, bathroom. "I nearly lost it, my subconscious is a better fucking agent than I am."

He threw up the windowpane, letting in a breeze cooling with evening and fragrant with city-smells, coalsmoke, dirty river, acre upon acre of summer-warmed brick and stone, burnt steamer distillate. A few deep breaths and he took up the phone. "Dinner," he rasped. "Stan-dard." Now to wait for contact.

Well, well, fancy being back here so soon, Andrew von Shrakenberg thought, looking around the office of Lyon's Security chief. *Not just shopping, this time, unfortunately.* The room was much as he remembered it, really quite nice murals, the two glass walls with their tinted panes swiveled open like vertical venetian blinds to let in the cooling evening air. Westering sunlight sparkled on the broad surface of the Saone where it swung south and east to join the Rhone, forming the Y shape whose tongue of land had been the original site of Lyon. *Celtic*, he remembered. *Called Lugdunum, originally.* After the Gallic Sun-god; then a Greek settlement, followed by a colony of Roman veterans. Burgundians, later, an east-Germanic tribe related to the Goths and Vandals. French, of various types . . . *and then us, which is the end of the story everywhere.*

He took another draw on the cheroot, a sip of the coffee, touched his lips to the Calvados in the goblet in his right hand; he had always enjoyed the scent more than the taste. Strategos Vashon was at his desk, checking through a report and making notes on a yellow pad with his left hand. Ignoring the Security Cohortarch standing at parade-rest in front of his desk, who was probably earnestly willing a suspension of her vital functions behind the blank mask of her face. The bruise that was turning most of its left side an interesting shade of yellow-purple helped, of course. The Strategos continued his methodical labors, with a detachment which was certainly an effective demoralizer for the officer on the carpet before him.

The problem is, does he really want to demoralize his subordinates? Andrew asked himself, laying down the eau-de-vie and fingering the gold hoop in his left ear. *The headhunters were set up to play that sort of mindfucking game; the problem is, they become addicted to it, even with each other.* Which raised the interesting point, frequent at the higher levels of the War Directorate, of whether they were being too paranoid about the paranoids . . . *I wonder what the headhunter is thinking, I really* do.

Strategos Vashon scowled slightly at the report before him, stripped the handwritten notes off the yellow pad and peeled the foil-paper off a wax seal to attach it. *The development people are letting their enthusiasm run away with them again*, he decided. Pages of hyperbolic notes on how addiction to pleasure-center stimulation produced complete docility in even the most refractory subjects . . . Of course it did! So did lobotomy! This new treatment degraded performance levels almost as much, and to boot they had to leave a bloody great *electrode* sticking in the subject's skull; most of them developed infections and *died*, and the remainder had to have intensive medical care.

"Note:" he wrote on the bottom of the paper, "The Race's need is not for a breed of hospitalized idiots to serve them." So far, this new approach was no better than the standard electroshock–sensory deprivation–pentathol chemoconditioning methods; a little more sure to stick, but with even more unfortunate effects on their capacities. The Holy Grail of a safe, quick method of ensuring absolute obedience without affecting intelligence or ability would have to remain a dream a while longer; and serf-breaking would have to remain a primitive craft industry, not one conducted on modern conveyor-belt principles.

He closed the folder, wound the cord around the fastener, sealed it with another prepackaged wax disk and tossed it in the "out" box for his assistant to take in the morning. Morning . . . he glanced out the windows. After seven again; perhaps he should go home . . . *No*, he decided. Home was an empty shell; his wife was six years dead in a traffic accident, his children off at school, nothing to do at home but prowl about, reread Psych and Organization texts, mount his concubines . . . dull, compared to work. He took a sip at his coffee; decaffeinated, like eating deodorized garlic, but he had to watch the stimulants, the doctor said. *Sometimes I wonder who's the one who works like a slave around here . . .* That was the price of power; the serfs down on the lower levels were the ones with nice regular ten-hour days.

He transferred his gaze to the officer from the . . . research facility, better keep it at that level even mentally . . . research facility at Le Puy. The medical report said she hadn't been exposed to more radiation than would result in some nausea and purging. *Which was less than the bitch deserved.*

"Well, Cohortarch," he said pleasantly, looking at her for the first time and steepling his fingers. "How do yo' account fo' yesterday's events in Le Puy? Is it treason on yo' part, or simple incompetence?"

She did not move her head, but he could feel her attention move to the War Directorate officer in the lounger. "Don't worry, Cohortarch Devlin, our comrade-in-arms here is involved." *Slightly*, his mind added, but he could see another film of sweat break out on her face at the hint of yet higher levels of interest.

"Now, Devlin," he continued, leaving out her rank with deliberate malice, "I'm waiting fo' an explanation."

"Suh." Her eyes were fixed on the window behind his head. "The new link fixtures fo' the reprocessin' of the enriched uranium were shipped from the Kolwezara facility, in the Police Zone, an' checked as adequate because the machinin' matched the older European parts. Incompatible alloys, leadin' to possible corrosion—"

"*Shut up.*" Vashon's voice returned to its even, genial tone. "That's in TechSec's preliminary report, Devlin," he continued. "And TechSec sees the world in terms of engineerin' and physics, but we know better, don't we?" Another bark: *"Don't we?"*

"Yes suh. Mah own prelim'nary survey indicates that there could have been a manual override on the standard valve shunts, allowin' explosive mixtures of gases in the precipitatin' tanks."

"Oh, very good, very good. An' who would have had the required access?"

"Ahhh . . . suh, apart from mahself, the personnel with the required access levels are all among the casualties. Suh."

"Buggerin' marvelous!" He leaned forward over the axeblade of his steepled hands. "Devlin, we lost *four hundred dead*, an' twice that injured in this little accident of yorn. I'm not talkin' about field-cattle or broom pushers, Devlin, I'm talkin' about the most highly trained scientific an' technical personnel in the Domination, Devlin. A hundred of them Citizens, Devlin; their skills an' heredity lost to the Race, Devlin. Includin' ten European scientists so good we gave them an' their families *Citizenship* in return fo' workin' fo' us, Devlin. Not to mention we've lost facilities crucial to the . . . new weapon project, which we're runnin' neck-and-neck with the Alliance in even *befo'* this happened—they *may* not take advantage of a one-year lead, *but would yo' care to bet on it?*"

Vashon smiled and tapped his fingers on the blotter of his desk; tip-tap, tip-tap, and the Cohortarch gave a nearly visible flinch at each sound. "Anythin' mo', Devlin?"

"Suh . . . yes, suh. Nothin' certain, but . . ." She glanced at his eyes, returned hers to the windows over his head and continued hurriedly. "We haven't found some of the bodies . . . well, the acids used fo' refinin' the plutonium out of the spent uranium slugs . . . but Professer Ernst Oerbach was completely missin'. He's over on the . . . new weapons side, but was visitin', some conference on trigger-timers an' deuterium processin'. No trace 'tall, an' . . ."

"Tell me the joyful news, Devlin."

"Well . . . twelve cylinders of first-stage plutonium oxide from the recovery process are unaccounted fo' as well. They could have been ruptured an' scattered in the original explosion, but—"

"Joy." Vashon dropped his head, supporting his forehead on the splayed fingers of one hand. "Explain, please, Cohortarch, how a man *supposedly* under twenty-fo'-hour surveillance fo' the rest of his *life* would get out. If he wasn't just dissolved in a bath of acid an' suspended particles of uranium-238, that is."

"Suh." The Cohortarch came to attention. "Suh, the responsibility is completely mine. The, the explosion released radioactive an' toxic material extensively suh, and the fires would have released mo'. Extensive contamination outside the restricted area was barely avoided. I authorized all personnel undah my orders to aid in the containment efforts." More softly: "A numbah of them died doin' so, suh."

Vashon was silent for a full minute, then lit a cigarette and considered the glowing tip; it had become dark in the wide office, as the sunset-glow faded. "I agree, Cohortarch. And will so note on my report."

The woman in Security Directorate green managed to convey surprise and relief without movement of face or body. Vashon smiled once more, unpleasantly. "Agree *reluctantly*, Devlin. Emphasis on the *reluctantly*. Yo' know the code; there is no excuse fo' failure, yo're responsible fo' everythin' yo' subordinates do, *and so am I*. Skull House is on my ass about this; so is Castle Tarleton an' the Palace . . . shitfire, every agency of every Directorate is formin' line on the left, tappin' lead pipes into their palms an' smilin' in anticipation!"

He paused. "Yo' know, they're diggin canals to join the Ob-Yenisey system southward to the Aral Sea? Irrigate Central Asia. Need administrators fo' the labor camps: nice simple work, no technical problems, just plain diggin'. In West Siberia province. Fo' the next thirty years. *If I go there, yo' join me!* Now get yo' ass back to Le Puy, and *find out what happened*. I want to *know*, I want the report on my desk by *yesterday*. Is that *clear?*"

"Yes, suh!"

After she left, the two Draka sat in silence while servants came in with a fresh tray of coffee and a cold supper. Vashon moodily buttered a piece of *baguette* and spoke to the younger man:

"Well?"

"Well, I was beginnin' to think yo' were the sort of commander who keeps his subordinates so scared of failure they're unwillin' to take risks. Glad to see I'm not"—*entirely*, his mind added—"right," Andrew said.

"Thank yo' kindly," Vashon replied dryly. "Try the anchovy salad, they do it well here. What I *meant*, do yo' think the Yankee yo've been chasin' is involved, Merarch?"

"Hmmm." A moment of impassive chewing. "Not unless he's an amoeba who can split in two; besides Finland"—for a moment a hungry carnivore looked out through the handsome aquiline face—"we're pretty sure he was involved in the Hamburg incident. Sparked it, rather; the local bushmen stuck they heads out to impress him, wanted a Yankee link real bad." A grin. "Foolish of 'em, we chopped a good few off an' turned the prisoners over to yo' people there. This hunter-team thing Castle Tarleton came up with is workin' out surprisin' well; thought it was a boondoggle, at first, but it's becomin' real interestin', integratin' and gettin' the best out of a mixed force. We got real close to him there."

"Close only count with fragmentation weapons," Vashon said. "What trail?"

"Dam' little, the ones we caught unfortunately doan' seem to know much. Last seen at the airship haven."

"Which is right next to the port an' the heavier-than-air station; could be anywhere from Archona to Beijing, by now." He pulled over a file. "Got a physical description . . . tall, fair hair, muscular build, blue eyes, moustache."

Andrew laughed, a deep chuckle of unforced mirth. "Oh, wonderful; accordin' to my recollections of the Eugenics Board survey, the average height fo' an adult male Draka is 183 centimeters, and about 40% are blond. Leaves about six million possibles, 'less'n he's dyed his hair; 83% have light eyes, that ups it a bit." He snapped his fingers in mock enlightenment, then swiveled his forefinger inward. "I've got it! It's me!"

A sour smile. "Well, at least we know he's travelin' alone." Vashon slapped his hand on the desk. "Loki's balls, we've got to have more checks on Citizen movements."

Andrew shrugged. "Strategos, we already restrict movement of people an' information about as much as practical. We start runnin' that sort of surveillance on each other, there'd be no time fo' Citizens to do anythin' *else*. 'Sides, Draka don't like bein' gimleted all the time, what's the point of bein' on top, then?"

"True, but . . . anyway, this thing at Le Puy—provided it isn't jus' an industrial accident, the gods know quality-control is always a problem—it's out of character fo' the local bushmen."

"They tamed down?"

"Contrary, sneaky-subtle. Good leadership . . . that's why I smell yo' Yankee. It's even worse than the Hamburg thing, which is goin' to delay launchin' that aircraft carrier six months to a year."

"Blessin' in disguise." At the secret policeman's raised brow, Andrew continued: "We're never goin' to have a navy to beat the Alliance, not while we're forced to maintain a large army, too." More meditatively. " 'Sides, Strategos, look at the Alliance powers. Yankees, Britain, Japan too now. Island nations, history of naval war an' seaborne trade. We Draka, we could build the Domination because steam technology lowered transport costs and times enough to make it possible to unify and develop the continental interiors. We're a land beast. And finally, aircraft carriers are yesterday's weapons, in my opinion, like-so battleships thirty years ago.

A big surface fleet would be a total waste of scarce personnel; should concentrate on subs and coastal defense. We're only launchin' that damned carrier on account the Fritz laid the keel."

Vashon ground out his cigarette. "Maybe. Anyhow, Merarch, I do have one asset inside the local bushman net."

"Ahhh, good. Impo'tant?"

"They pretty tightly celled, but not bad. I've been usin' him fo' information only, makin' him look good. But this Le Puy thing is crucial, 'specially if the Alliance is involved."

"How'd yo' turn him?"

Vashon laughed. "Fritz technique; y'put the subject and maybe a close relative—we used his father—in opposin' chairs. Gag the passive subject. Active subject has a switch under his hand; every time he presses, the current goes through the passive one, an' every time he lets up, it goes through *him*. In increasin' increments, until the passive subject dies. Great fo' crushin' the will; the subject's convinced right down deep that he'll do *anythin'* to save his own skin. We've got this one's momma and sister, too; he's quite the family man, an' anxious to avoid their bein' the next passive subjects."

"I can imagine," Andrew said dryly, lifting the goblet. Vashon shot him a quick glance.

"Squeamish, Merarch von Shrakenberg?"

Andrew pursed his lips as he rolled the apple brandy around his mouth. "Fastidious, Strategos, only fastidious. Still, to get the stable clean yo' has to step in horseshit, as the sayin' goes. 'To desire the end is to desire the means necessary to accomplish it,' " he amplified, quoting Naldorssen. He hesitated, then continued: "Had any subjects refuse to push the switch on they nearest and dearest?"

"Some," Vashon admitted with a reminiscent smile. "Which provides us with one corpse an' the valuable datum that that serf would rather die than submit. Neat an' tidy . . ." He pressed a buzzer. "I'm controllin' this particular double myself. A man has to have a hobby, an' it's good to go hands-on sometimes, after spendin' all day readin' reports."

A serf stumbled through, pushed by two Order Police who saluted and left him kneeling on the carpet. He blinked about the darkened office, winced as a light speared down from the ceiling; the chain-and-bar restraints holding his arms behind him clanked. A young man with a thin stubbled olive face and an uncontrollable twitch beneath one eye, in a rough gray overall stained with oil and stenciled with the wheel-and-piston insignia of the Transportation Directorate.

"Why, good evenin', Jean 55EF003," Vashon said in a voice of mellow friendliness. The serf would be effectively blinded, of course; that was the reason for having the focused spotlight in the ceiling. His hand nudged the control up slightly, to keep the two Draka looming shadows in a deeper darkness.

"Master . . . Master, if they suspect I'm being held, please, I won't be trusted any more, I'll be no use—"

"*Do* credit us with some intelligence, Jean," Vashon said, chuckling at his own pun. "But yo' haven't been much use to us, anyway. How old is yo' sister, Jean?"

"Nine, Master." The Frenchman jerked as if struck. "Oh, Mary Mother of God, not the chair, not her, please, master, I'll do anything, *anything!*"

Vashon considered him; the buck was transparently sincere, but also crumbling. *A pity if he goes insane*, the Security officer thought. *I was hoping he'd make good in this little bushman network, before we activated him and snapped them up.*

"We know yo'll do anythin', Jean," he continued, in the same friendly tone. "Even kill yo' own father. Tsk, tsk." The Frenchman began to sob. "Pull yo'self together, serf, iff'n yo' don't want to add two more to the list!" A pause. "Nothin' from yo' but a few times an' places fo' courier drops, an' two names from yo' own cell."

The ragged breathing slowed. "Master, I tell everything I know, everything! Henri is cell leader, he gets the orders, Ybarra and I just do as we're told, believe me," Jean said with desperate earnestness.

"Yo' know, Jean," Vashon continued, "I'm goin' to do yo' a favor. Tell yo' something about me, personal. I *don't* like seein' little girls fucked by dogs. Have a friend who *does*, though." He slid a glossy color photograph the size of a placemat from a stack-rack on his desk and flipped it to land face up in the puddle of light by the serf. The young man looked down, then screwed his eyes tightly shut, so tightly that his face trembled, as if he sought to squeeze the information his optic nerves had absorbed back out through the lids. His throat worked convulsively.

"Puke on my carpet an' yo'll regret it, *skepsel*," the secret policeman said with quiet deadliness, using the old word for two-legged beast. Then in the friendly tone once more: "That isn't yo' sister, of course, Jean. No, yo' momma an' sister are safe, workin' in a canteen. Jus' washin' dishes, buck, that's all."

The serf was panting, eyes still closed. "Such altruism, from a creature who'd torture his own pa to death. Of course, yo' family *could* be better off. Maybe a trip to the sunny Western Hemisphere?"

Jean's eyes snapped open. "You . . . you would let us go?"

"Well, I'm not promisin' anythin', but . . . we *do* need people ovah there as well, yo' know. Send yo' an' yo' sister, maybe; nice cover story and a little nest-egg."

"God, Master, thank you, thank you!" The serf's tears were like a dam bursting this time, of relief and gratitude; his face shone with it. Unseen in darkness, Vashon smiled like a shark.

"But yo've got to *earn* it, Jean. Yo' understand that, don't you, Jean?" A frantic nod. "Now, we have othah sources in that pathetic little group yo' call the Resistance," Vashon continued. "So we know somethin' . . . of unusual size may be a-happenin', soon."

He reached into the desk and tossed a cylinder the

size of a single-cigar case toward the serf; it struck him in the chest and fell on the photograph.

"Look at that, Jean." The buck obeyed, although Vashon could see him blurring the focus of his eyes to avoid looking at the picture beneath. "It's a fancy little gadget. Yankee components, actually. Radio, inside the case, with attachements so's yo' can wire it onto somethin'. If yo' was to take that along, next time there's a meetin' at higher than cell level, I'd be mighty pleased when it was switched on. Or if yo' could get me somethin' *really* useful, like-so a Yankee we feel may be comin' through, that would make me very happy. Yo' *does* want to make me very happy, Jean, don't yo'?"

"Oh, yes, Master, of all things I want that most in the whole world, *believe* me, yes, certainly. Master . . . how shall I carry this?" His voice shook with a crawling eagerness to please.

Vashon laughed again, as he flipped the switch on his desk. "They'll take you down to the clinic an' show yo' right now, Jean. I'd have thought it was obvious."

The two Order Police troopers came back in, silent helmeted shadows; saluted, picked up the serf and radio with similar lack of effort, left. As the door soughed shut, Andrew rose and stooped to take the print between thumb and forefinger.

"Feh," he said, studying it for a second with a grimace of disgust before sliding it back onto the Strategos's desk. "Strange friends yo' has, Vashon, no offense."

"None taken," he said, keying the room lights and holding it out at arm's length. "It's a standard print from *Gelight's Erotic Art Sampler*. Minority interest, but *de gustibus*, eh? Actually, I think this is simulated."

Andrew chuckled reluctantly. "Strategos, yo' are one evil son of a bitch," he said.

"Goes with the job, Merarch. Taken as a compliment . . . Your hunters are here in Lyon, aren't they?"

"Mmmm-*hmmm*. Ready fo' stand-down; experimental unit, aftah all. Castle Tarleton"—*meaning my new aunt*—"wants to do an evaluation, befo' they decide on the program as a whole. I'm goin' to lay-over at my sister's plantation; there's a namin'-feast fo' her new-borns comin' up in a few days." For courtesy's sake: "To which I've been asked to invite yo', of course."

"Ah. Why, thanks kindly, I think I could find the time," Vashon replied blandly, hiding his amusement at the other's surprise; it might be interesting to mingle with the Landholders for an evening, and once the full consequences of the disaster at Le Puy avalanched down there would be little free time in the Lyon office. "Care fo' a little huntin', first?"

"Huntin'? I take it yo' don't mean wild boar?"

"Another type of swine altogetha. If the local bush-men are involved—still mo' if it's yo' Yankee—we'll have somethin' from young Jean, and soon. Hell, maybe tonight!"

"Agreed," Andrew said, finishing the Calvados. "I'll alert the watch officer at transit barracks, if yo' can get us transport fo' insertion in-city." The secret policeman nodded briskly. "We're supposed to be developin' closer liaison, anyhow, it'll be good practice."

He stood, slipping on his gloves and smoothing the thin leather over his fingers. His eyes met the Security officer's, and Vashon felt a slight sudden impact along his nerves, like a cold brush over the face. "And I hope we meet my Yankee. I sho'ly do."

The blindfold was snug, and Kustaa resisted the temptation to tug at it. It was sensible, simply the easiest way to make sure he could say nothing even if he broke under interrogation; the same reason he had torn up the slip of paper the serf stewardess hand handed him without looking at the number, and flushed it down the commode. With the address he had found under his souffle, during dinner. That he had to remember, of course, but it had simply been the point where whoever-they-were had met him. Since then he had moved on foot and in vehicles, indoors and out; presumably discreetly—an armed Draka Citizen being led blind-

folded by serfs was a trifle unusual . . . Once through a
sewer, he thought, but a dry one.

"*Arrête*," the voice at his elbow said.

Halt. He stopped obediently, obscurely glad of the
knife and pistol at his belt, the battle-shotgun across his
back. As irrational as the feeling of helplessness the
blindfold engendered, but a useful counterweight. He
could sense that he was inside a building from the
movement of the air, from its smell. Factory smell; it
reminded him of the summer he had worked at the
National Harvester plant in St. Paul, machine-oil and
steel and brass, rubber transmission belts and the lin-
gering ozone of industrial-strength electric motors, un-
derlain by a chalky scent like an old school's. Something
else as well, sickly-sweet, a hint of decay.

A hand turned him to his left; he could hear a faint
sound from that direction, a tiny wheezing and shifting.

"Take off the blindfold, American. But do not turn."

A new voice, an educated man's French, sounding
middle-aged. Kustaa obeyed, squinting his eyes against
the prospect of light. Even after an hour of blindfold
the interior of the great room was dim; he had been
correct: a factory. Dim shapes of lathes and bench-
presses around him, fading into distance and shadow, a
little light from grimy glass shutters far above. Enough
light to see what hung on the wall before him. A man,
standing with his feet on an angle-iron brace bolted to
the sooty brick. Slumped, rather; his weight rested on
the steel hooks through ribs and armpits.

Dead, Kustaa thought. *That's the smell of rot.* Then
he saw the outstretched fingertips flutter, the whites of
eyeballs move.

"Hnng-hnng-hnng," the pinned man said. "hnng-
hnnng-hnng."

The quiet, cultured voice came again from somewhere in the room; there was a hint of movement, but
Kustaa's eyes remained fixed forward.

"You see this thing," the man said. "And you think,
'Monstrous, inhuman.' Do you not, Mr. American?"

"Yes," Kustaa replied quietly. "At least that."

"Ah, no, my American friend. I will explain why that is an error. To think of this as the act of inhuman monsters is a step toward thinking of it as the work of devils. Toward thinking of the Draka as not human, as devils: which is a step in turn toward thinking of them as gods. That, my old, is what they themselves think, in the madness of their own hearts, that they are gods or devils, perhaps they care little which. This . . . A Citizen supervisor noted that the output of this plant was too low, or more likely the spot-checks showed too many defective parts. He informed a born-serf manager, who passed it on down the line to a gangboss, probably a Frenchman like myself. Who picked perhaps the least popular or most insolent of his gang, and the plant's serf-drivers came and took him from his machine one shift, and put him on the hooks. Men did this; human men."

Kustaa waited a few moments before replying, in a soft and careful voice. "Why have you brought me here, then, *monsieur*?"

"Did you not wish to make contact with the Resistance of Lyon? *Voilà*, we are here." There were rustling noises around him in the darkness. "More of us than have gathered in one place in some time, Mr. American. Ah, to this spot? Because it is as safe as any . . . and for the same reason that our masters put this man on the steel, as an object-lesson."

"Which is supposed to teach?" Kustaa continued. The pinned man's eyes might be open, but the OSS agent did not think there was much mind or consciousness left behind them.

"A different lesson, my old. This man, perhaps he is my brother, perhaps my son, perhaps my closest friend. Here am I, one of the leaders of the best organized Resistance group in all France, perhaps all Europe . . . and what can I do for him? Nothing, not even to end his agony, not unless some means can be found utterly untraceable."

"Why not?" Kustaa said.

"Because then, there would be *two* men on this wall. You see, Mr. American, Mr. Secret Agent, I think you seek to make contact with us for certain reasons. To call us to valiant action, perhaps? This man here, he was active: now he is less so. There were other groups here, in the beginning, more daring than we. Some of them believed, for example, that we could deny the Draka the fruits of their conquest with the weapons of class struggle. Strikes." There was an ironic wonder in the man's next word: "*Strikes*. Can one believe it? Others thought of sabotage, assassination, very active measures. Now these other groups are corpses, or lobotomized in chain-gangs . . . and very much less 'active' than our network. Like the *maquisards* in the countryside, the last of whom are being hunted down like starving animals."

"The Finns—" Kustaa began.

"Ah yes, the heroic Finns. The *extinct* Finns, very shortly. Mr. American, there are always those who would rather die on their feet than live on their knees; if you seek to make contact with such, you had best hurry. If there is one thing under heaven at which our masters are experts, it is for arranging for such to have their wish, and die."

"You are running a very considerable risk by *having* an organization," Kustaa said. "If you don't *do* anything with it, what is the point?"

"Very true . . . Mr. American-whose-family-is-far-away, we *do* take this risk. Because we are not content to live as cattle, between our work and our stalls and our fodder, to be bred and sold as cattle, slaughtered when it suits our owners with as little thought as a chicken is killed and plucked. Why does this organization exist? For memory's sake. To preserve that discontent, not simply as sullen beast-hatred, but as knowledge. That once there was something different, that there may be again. That we are a nation . . . perhaps no longer the nation of France, but still a people.

"Thus we organize, we recruit, we organize . . . in tiny groups, with cut-outs at every stage. We pass on information; occasionally we can help individuals who suffer more than the common lot. Simply to tell a kinsman where his family has been sent, that is victory. Very occasionally we take direct action, against a foreman perhaps; even the Draka cannot make massacres at every accident. And we wait. We were conquered by an enemy more patient than we, more far-sighted, more ruthless; by conquering us they offer lessons, and we learn. Do you know how many Draka there are in Europe?"

"We estimate no more than a million."

"Too high, I would say . . . many times that many born-serfs, of course. The great strength of the Draka is that they are skilled at using others; thus they accomplish feats far beyond their own raw power. Their great weakness, exactly the same, that they must use others. These born-serfs, the Draka bring them to teach us obedience. They are just beginning to suspect, I think, that such learning can be a two-way process . . . Always before they have smashed the societies they conquered, killed their elites and reduced the survivors to isolated human atoms, to be refashioned as they wished. Here as well, to a certain extent, but not completely. *And that is the central purpose of this organization.* To *exist*, simply to exist. So long as we do, their victory is not complete.

"What we have done—are trying to do—is build a brotherhood that they can wound but cannot kill. Strong and hard they are; if we try to match their strength, we will be smashed. Instead we must be as soft as water, and as patient. Enduring, that wears away the rock slowly, but, oh, so surely. Perhaps you Americans and your allies will come and liberate us; if that is so, we will welcome you with tears and flowers and as much gratitude as humans can find in their souls to give. But we are those to whom the worst has happened, and we must prepare for the worst, that they destroy you in the end as well. Then our quiet war must last, who knows, perhaps a thousand years, to ensure that their 'Final Society' joins so many lesser tyrannies in the grave."

"That," Kustaa said with a slight chill in his voice, "sounds very much the sort of plan a Draka might conceive."

"If they had the flexibility, my old, which they do not." A laugh. "Perhaps we become like that which we fight."

Perhaps, Kustaa thought, looking at the man on the wall. *Perhaps, if you have to fight an enemy too closely, too long, perhaps that is so.* "You refuse to help me, then?"

"Did I say this?" The same even, almost monotone voice. *Control would be something living at the bottom here would teach,* Kustaa thought.

"No, we will aid you, Mr. American, *on our terms.* Information, yes, provided it can be conveyed without serious risk. The Draka are no fools, but sometimes they forget we have ears . . . and sometimes they are too eager to believe a serf has knelt in his heart and accepted chains upon his soul. Although, God in His mercy knows, that is true often enough. Sometimes, rarely, *very* rarely, we will be prepared to take direct action on your prompting. None of us is essential; they could take everyone in this building, and what we have built will continue. Wounded, but that is the virtue of an organism so simple and diffuse as ours, it regenerates. And endures if need be, generation after generation, until . . . in the end, if nothing else, they will become lazy . . ."

"Information is what I'm mostly after," Kustaa said. *And getting. Not information that will make Donovan or President Marshall particularly happy, but then, just because these people are allies doesn't mean they have identical perspectives or interests.* "Specifically, here, information about the Draka weapons program at Le Puy."

A laugh startled him, full and mellow. "Well, after all

my eloquent preaching of the virtues of inaction, I must confess that something along those lines has already been done. The facility at Le Puy was largely destroyed a short time ago."

"Judas Priest!" Kustaa said, grunting as if a fist had driven into his belly. *Donovan will shit his pants.* "You did that?"

Another laugh. "No, no, *au contraire*. It was done by one of the scientists themselves; we merely took advantage of the confusion." More soberly: "And thousands were nearly killed, as well . . . remember that we *live* here, Mr. American; and our families. And atomics were used on our soil. Our feelings concerning the good professor are, how shall I say, mixed. You may turn, *monsieur*."

Kustaa swiveled, thankful for the opportunity to take his eyes from the thing on the wall. A man was standing close behind him, a tall cadaverous-looking man in middle age, dressed in badly-fitting servant's livery. *Still no sight of the Resistance people,* he thought. *Good.*

"Ernst Oerbach, at your service, *Mein Herr*," the man said, offering his hand and inclining his head with a gesture that somehow suggested a heel-click. The face was too expressive for a Prussian's, though, now showing mostly exhaustion and a bone-deep melancholy. "Late of the Imperial University in Vienna, physics department." Kustaa took the Austrian's hand, a dry firm grip.

"I'm going by the name Frederick Kenston, just now," he said in reply. "You were in a position to sabotage the plant? I'm surprised the Draka let a 'serf' that close to critical equipment."

"Ah, Mr. Kenston, I was not a serf, you see. I was given Citizenship after the war, in return for my services."

"*What?*" Kustaa managed to restrain himself from jerking back his hand, or wiping it on the side of his jacket. Ernst Oerbach smiled sadly.

"A natural reaction, Mr. Kenston. One I have felt

myself, often enough . . . but though my son was dead by then, my daughter-in-law and grandchildren were alive, and included in the offer." His eyes went over the American's shoulder, to the figure on the wall. "You can imagine the alternatives. The Draka considered me valuable enough, for my genes as well as my self." Another of those gently self-deprecating smiles. "I was fencing champion of Lower Austria in my youth, I suppose they decided my descendants would be desirable . . . The children were taken away, of course. Helge and I would be Citizens by courtesy, only: a sort of second-class citizenship, always closely watched. The children were to be adopted into Draka families who could not bear, and would forget."

Kustaa's eyes narrowed; it fit with what the OSS had been able to learn from European scientists who had made it out in the chaos toward the end; the Draka had contacted some of the ones who decided to chance a try for the Alliance instead. Not many—this would be a one-in-a-million arrangement—but there *weren't* that many first-rate creative brains. Others could be forced to work by more immediate pressures, but for a few Citizenship made sense. *Hell, it's only a generation since they stopped accepting selected immigrants,* he mused.

"Why did you change your mind?" he asked.

"I could not stomach it any longer," Oerbach said simply. "Even in luxurious isolation, I saw too much of what I was giving the power to destroy the earth."

Kustaa grunted again. *That bad, whatever it is,* he thought. "Your grandchildren?" The man winced, but it was necessary to be quite sure.

"There the Draka made a mistake," he said. "Citizenship would mean nothing if it could be withdrawn. Citizens can be killed, yes . . . but I have come to believe that a clean death might be preferable, even for little Johann and Adelle. And they will not kill them, because there would be nothing to gain from it once I am out of their power, and two members of the Race to lose." A shake of his head. "I have come to . . . understand them, somewhat."

Kustaa turned his head sharply. The faceless voice spoke confirmation:

"A major disaster. Hundreds killed; they have been flying in decontamination teams and doctors around the clock. This is being kept very secret, you understand, Mr. American. But continue, professor, you have not told our friend what other gifts you bring beside yourself."

"Ah, *ja*," he said, patting at his pockets like a movie-version absent-minded professor. "*Ja*, the microfilm of my research results on the threshold temperatures for deuterium-lithium fusion."

A spool of translucent tape, and a masked face wheeled a green steel box beside them on a dolly, let the standbar come down with a thump that told of considerable weight. "Well, it was not my department, you understand, the plutonium refining. Plutonium for the triggers, you see. But it was there. You must understand I had been thinking of doing *something* for some time, but the opportunity was fleeting." A bleak grin, over in an instant. "You might say Satan whispered in my ear, and I fell. It probably even looks like an accident, and this unprocessed material was there; plutonium is a considerable bottleneck, so . . ."

Kustaa took a half-step back and leaned against a lathe, heedless of metal angles digging into his back. "Judas Priest," he whispered again, this time almost as a wheeze. "Tempted by Satan? More like divine inspiration, Professor Oerbach! Maybe you should have been in *my* line of work."

"No." He looked up at the tone, and saw tears glitter behind the spectacles. "A temptation to mass murder, and I fell. Hundreds . . . *thousands* could have been killed, Mr. Kenston. Thousands of innocents, women, children. The earth itself for hundreds of square miles, *that* was what I risked. I am a murderer, Mr. Kenston, I who never harmed a living soul before that day. *That* is what the Draka have done to me!" Softly: "And the alternative was to give them a power for murder beyond conception . . . What I did will delay it, at least. If I have no part in it, perhaps some of the guilt will wash off me, perhaps . . . That I must believe."

Qualms later, Kustaa thought with a hard glee, and turned to speak to the faceless shadow-voice.

"*This* you have to help me with, by God," he said.

"We agree. For this, we agree. What do you need?"

"A place within a hundred miles of the Atlantic, where an aircraft can land and take off. A grass field a hundred meters clear would do. Some manpower, if possible."

"You have the means to signal?"

"In that leather case your man took from my car."

"Ah. Tell me no more, I may guess, but . . ." The voice withdrew, and there was a murmur of conversation. Footsteps returning. "Mr. American, another will come to stand where I am. Approach closely, but do not attempt to make out a face. A name will be given you, a location, a password. But first . . . Do you, by any chance, know the Cartwright system?"

"Sign-language? Yes, why?" One of a number of bizarre skills Donovan insisted his field men learn.

The Austrian looked up sharply, shaken from thoughts that his expression said were less than pleasant.

"Excellent; so does the good professor here. With your so-ingenious cover story—do not be disturbed, only two know of it and I am one—it will account for his presence. I suggest you pass him off as your servant in the medical sense as well; we have applied an appropriate tattoo. You will grasp that this is a facility useful to us . . . And now another will impart the information you seek. A place within the distance you specify; about guards and helpers, I will have to think. Perhaps."

Chateau Retour, Kustaa repeated to himself. *Sister Marya Sokolowska. The escargots of Dijon are very fine.* That last brought a slight smile; he supposed food-codes were natural in a continent that had been hungry for some time.

"Now, you will be returned to your autosteamer," the voice said. "Please, the blindfold—" A masked man had come to stand beside the dolly with its so-ordinary looking box of green-painted steel; Kustaa sensed he was young from his stance, could smell fear and another odor, fecal. He wrinkled his nose slightly. *What the hell, I hope he hasn't shit his pants,* the American thought. *Oh, well, they've been efficient so far.*

"Shit!" The green-uniformed serf technician ripped the earphones from her head with a violence that set the van rocking slightly on its springs, clutching at her ears.

"Report!" Andrew von Shrakenberg snapped from the map table, and the tech's spine stiffened, shaven head locking in eyes-front despite the pain that crinkled her eyes almost shut in an involuntary grimace. Above on the roof the motors of the directional loop-antenna whined, searching.

"Mastah, signal irregular, compatible with movement through built-up areas an' steel-frame buildin's, stable fo' the last fiv' minutes, then *ah, shit,* sorry Mastah, blast a' static an' lost signal."

The Draka's lips peeled back in a snarl, but his finger stayed steady on the map, resting on the last spot where the lines from the two vans crossed.

"Cause?" he barked.

"Power line, any'tin givin' off strong radio impulse, tha' thing would've shut down to prevent surge burnin' out circuits, Mastah I doan' *know.*"

Specialized training, Andrew thought bitterly. Necessary, but it did not give the sort of broad base of knowledge from which intuitive leaps spring. *Well, the creative intelligence is supposed to be your job!* he told himself as his hand stabbed down on the send button.

"All Shrike units, all Shrike units, *execute Downfall on last position posted.* Now! Do it people, let's *go.*"

His hand swept the Holbars from the table, and he dove through the open rear doors of the van, rolled, came up running.

"FREEZE! THIS IS SECURITY! DROP YOUR WEAPONS AND PUT YOUR HANDS UP OR YOU DIE!"

Kustaa dropped to the ground in instant combat-reflex as the amplified voice roared in their ears, like the shout of an angry god. Hard concrete thumped at him, ignored in a surge of adrenaline that brightened the murk as it flared his pupils wide. Multiple echoes, as if it was sounding throughout a complex of buildings, broadcast from half a dozen sources. The skylights shattered, and round objects fell through, to burst hissing. Tendrils of mist snaked through the gloom, then sprang into brilliant blue-white as searchlights played on the roof and reflected electric-arc glare within.

Voices shouted; there was a rapid thudding of feet, and Kustaa felt a swift tug at his heel as he snaked forward and yanked the Austrian off his feet and behind a lathe. Hands reached out and dragged the man away, and someone called in French, in Lyonnaise dialect:

"American! We have him! This—"

A stab of tracer went by above, the light bullets pinging and whining off metal and stone. The OSS agent's hand went over his shoulder and stripped the shotgun free with a surge of cold elation at the thought of targets. A Draka voice, shouting.

"Yo' headhuntin' fools! *Take 'em, boys!* Bulala! Bulala!"

Shots were flickering through the half-lit immensity of the factory shed, and Kustaa could see the flash and sparkle of ricochets running across the motionless machines like sun-flicker on moving leaves. Men and women dodged, fired, screamed. Boots slammed on concrete, and a shadowy figure loomed, helmet bulking, bulbous-nosed with its gasmask. Kustaa rolled up to one knee, snaked the battle shotgun around the drillpress which sheltered him, fired.

Crung. The heavy weapon bucked against the muscles of his wrists and forearms, lost. The solid slug hammered through the fleshy part of the uniformed man's thigh, spinning him around in a circle before he pitched to earth; the last wild burst sent rounds close enough to the American to sting with spalls flicked out of the pavement, nearly killing him by chance where aimed fire was useless. The wounded man thrashed in his small square of open space.

"Ah'se hit, Ah'se hit!" he screamed, the first half of the shout muffled by the mask he ripped off before pressing both hands to his thigh, as if trying to squeeze shock-shattered bone and flesh back together. His blood flashed from red to black in the strobing light, as the searchlights played back and forth above.

Bullets flicked at the prostrate figure, and struck; his second scream was shrill, wordless. Another man followed him, but this one leaped *over* the lathe the soldier had blundered into; head-first, landing in a perfect forward roll just beyond the writhing casualty. He was masked, but there was no helmet on the bristle-cut red hair, and he had a machine-pistol in each hand, firing them as if they were automatics at muzzle-flashes and glimpsed movement.

"Get him out, get him out!" the man shouted through rubber and plastic. *Branggg* and a burst hammered the machine by Kustaa's ear, *brangg* and a scream as a Resistance-fighter pitched back, *brangg* and another dropped without sound. Behind the Draka the thrashing Janissary was being dragged away, as the submachine-guns snapped their three-round bursts with killing precision and the hands behind them moved like oiled metronomes.

Kustaa's second round took the man in the stomach. At close range the heavy buckshot did not have room to spread much; it pulped a circle of chest and stomach the size of a small dinnerplate and rammed the man backward to fetch up against a lathe four feet behind him, legs outstretched like a sitting child. Even then, the muzzles wavered up toward the target that had killed him before the second charge let the Draka's intestines spill forward into his lap. *One*, the American thought, with a chill satisfaction, his mind seeming to move in layers like the leaves of a book. Behind the voice was shouting in gutter-argot.

"Jean, drop that dolly, *drop it*, Ybarra, you two, get that box and out, *American, this way!*"

Kustaa had never felt less like a berserker, or himself. There seemed to be an infinity of time for thought: *They are dying to buy me seconds*. On hands and knees, he followed the voice into the gun-shot dark.

"Well, here's our tracer," Vashon said, nudging the brown-streaked metal casing that was wired to the underside of the overturned dolly.

Andrew grunted reply, watching as the stretcher with the shrouded bundle passed by. "Always were a little reckless, Corey," he murmured. Around him the factory lights had been reconnected, and Security techs were swarming with their cameras, measuring cords, fingerprint kits. *Busy locking the door on the empty stable*, he thought.

"But why wasn't it functioning?" the Strategos asked the senior technician, who had opened the feces-streaked container with gloved hands.

"Damned if I know," the man replied, frowning at the circuit-board with its black transistor beads. "Have to take it to the lab." He spoke loudly to override the wailing scream of a field-interrogation going on a few yards distant.

"Don't—don't—don't—"

"Would close contact with a, oh, X-ray machine've done it?" Andrew asked.

"Hmmm? Yes, even a fairly light dosage, nothin' that would do a human bein' any harm. These-here bitty things is sensitive to any sort a' energetic particles. Scarcely likely here, Merarch."

Andrew locked eyes with Vashon. "Well. Pull in yo' double?"

The older man ran a hand through the dense sable cap of his hair. "Nnnno, Merarch, I don't think so. No, he'll try really hard; be difficult fo' him to make contact, of course . . . but worth waitin' fo'. They'll go to earth, of course . . ."

"And we'll dig them out." Andrew smiled. "Oh, Mr. Yankee, I'm beginnin' to *dislike* yo'." His eyes went up to the man pinned to the wall. The Holbars was across his chest on its assault sling; his hand found the pistol grip, squeezed. Two dozen muzzles pivoted toward him, then wavered away in puzzlement or indifference.

Andrew looked up at the slumped corpse with the neat line of holes across its chest, wondering why he had killed the serf. He felt the answer roll through the undersurface of his consciousness; it was there, but his mind refused to analyze it.

"Enough," he said. "Tomorrow, then, Strategos."

CHAPTER FOURTEEN

DATE: 03/08/47

FROM: Merarch Delia Beauchamp
Third Fleet H.Q.
Le Havre, Province of Normandy

TO: Chiliarch Argen Foddard
Commander, Task Force Beta
Atlantic Exclusion Zone

RE: Reported Contact by Procrustes, 01/08/47

Please to be informed that Third Fleet HQ
authorizes resumption of normal patrol patterns. Lack of subsequent contact indicates report was either due to a technical or the Alliance
vessel has left the Zone. Further diversion of
resources is, therefore, unwarranted.

Service to the State!

369

DATE: 03/08/47

FROM: Chiliarch Argen Foddard
          Commander, Task Force Beta
          Atlantic Exclusion Zone

TO: Merarch Delia Beauchamp
          Third Fleet HQ
          Le Havre, Province of Normandy

RE: Yours of this date

          With respect, please to inform the Strategos
          that I am detaching two destroyers and a pa-
          trol aircraft squadron to continue the search
          for at least another two days. I know Skinner
          and I know the Procrustes; a good commander
          and a taut ship. They weren't seeing bogeymen
          in the closet, and a possible clandestine incur-
          sion is more important than preparing for Yan-
          kee aircraft carriers that aren't coming and
          catching a few fishing-boats full of refugees.
          We need that network of detection-buoys!

                                    Glory to the Race

CHATEAU RETOUR PLANTATION,
TOURAINE PROVINCE
AUGUST 3, 1947
0200 HOURS

It was the quiet hours after midnight; the time of deepest sleep, the time when old men die and young ones lie awake and shiver with an emptiness glimpsed at the heart of things. The wind had died, and the stars shone soft and huge through the damp clear air; grass gave off its heavy scent as the dew beaded on stems, but the flowers were curled in on themselves, petal folded over petal. Mysterious creaks and rustles sounded through garden and field, stalks rubbing one on the other in the slow cellular swellings of growth and decay. A light went by on the river, drifting downstream silently; then others passed overhead with a quiet throb of engines and a long torpedo shape black against the moon.

Below, a dog-fox crouched and barked shrilly as the dirigible passed, then went about his rounds with swift paws that moved the leaves hardly more than his black questing nose. Green bush-crickets sounded, strident bursts of sound fading into the empty spaces, and a midwife toad pipped from the borders of the lake.

In the Great House of the plantation, this passed:

"Non."

Tanya woke at the stirring, from a dream where burning rubble collapsed again over the vision-blocks, and ventilators poured smoke. For a moment she was bewildered, expecting first the engine-growl and the thunder of the falling building, then the harsh feel of the sleeping-bag, starlight and the bulk of her tank above.

Home, she thought. *I am home*. Smooth silk against her skin, the near-absolute blackness of her own bedroom; underneath the wavy resilience of a bed whose mattress was water-filled cells. No prickle of dirt or sweat, clean smells of fabric and wood and the garden odors from beyond the curtains. No light except the radium dial of the clock on the table across the room. She sank back into a half-drowse, smiling to herself. It was a pleasure like waking up early on a school-holiday as a child, just so you could realize that you were free to go back to sleep. Her own home, bulking solid about her. Edward, the twins, the new-born pair, all near at hand.

"Non."

The bed was big enough that Solange's thrashing had not touched her, but the sound and the flowing trans-

mitted through the liquid mattress brought her fully
awake. With a sigh, Tanya slid over until her hand
touched the smooth warmth of the serf's back; the
Frenchwoman was curled into a fetal ball, and her
owner could feel the shudders of nightmare running
under her skin. A running mumble in her native tongue;
pleading, Tanya thought, and she could catch *Poppa*
and *Maman* occasionally.

Damn, thought this was tapering off, the Draka mused
to herself. Aloud: "Wake up." A firm, arm's-length
shake. "Wake up, Solange."

The younger woman convulsed, shot into a sitting
position and screamed twice. Shatteringly loud; Tanya
winced but kept her hand between the other's shoulderblades. The Draka could imagine it from times when
the light had been on, the serf's hands plastered to the
sides of her face, eyes owl-wide and unseeing. Her
quick shallow panting echoed through the room, slowing gradually as the rigid lock of her muscles relaxed.
When her hands sank from her face, Tanya pulled her
down and close; Solange pushed her face into the angle
of the Draka's neck and clung within the circle of her
arms, shivering quietly.

"I was—I was—" she began.

"Shhhh, shhhh, I know," Tanya whispered into her
hair, rocking her gently. "It's all right, all right, yo're
not there now." There were several places Solange
went during her worst dreams, and none of them were
pleasant.

They lay together in the darkness for quiet minutes;
Tanya could feel the serf's heart beating against hers,
fluttering in the cage of her ribs. It slowed, and the
warm breath against her neck, until Solange sighed and
moved her face so that their lips touched.

"Thank you, *maîtresse*," she whispered.

Well, I know what comes next, Tanya thought. There
was a complex wiggling beneath the sheets as Solange
slid out of her panties. *Do I want to?* She probed
mentally at herself; it was only three days since her

period had ended, which was generally a low point in her libido. Also she had only been asleep four hours, and . . . *No, I don't*, she thought. *I want to go back to sleep. On the other hand, she'll be hurt, she needs the reassurance, and besides, in a few minutes I will feel like it*.

They kissed, and she could taste the slight salt of fear-sweat on the singer's upper lip, the stronger mint from her toothpaste; and the natural flavor of her mouth, which had always reminded Tanya of apples and earth. A pointed tongue flicked at hers, ran lightly along the inside of her lips. The Draka nudged with her knee, and Solange welcomed it between hers, gripping with her thighs.

"You wish to make love, Mistress?" Solange asked breathlessly, a small catch in her voice.

Tanya murmured assent, running her fingers through the serf's hair, marvelling at the texture soft as ostrich down, how it was matched in the fine curls pressing against her leg. Solange's mouth was moving across her face to the angle of her jaw, feather-light brushes of petal lips and tongue-tip, while her hands stroked at Tanya's neck with only the pads of the fingers touching, just enough to brush the near-invisible hairs. The sensation was an unbearable mixture of caress and tickle; she heard her own breath catch as the pulse speeded in her ears with a long swelling.

Now I want, she thought, smiling silently into the darkness. *Now I want*. Their bodies moved for long minutes in a subtle mutual urging, and then Tanya rose to hands and knees, while the serf slid beneath her and lower. *Her hands are so soft*, the Draka thought, as they slid down over her shoulders to cup her breasts and then trace delicately along her flanks. They moved in slow gliding circles as the kisses floated down her throat. Tanya shivered as her skin grew tingling-tight, even her lips feeling swollen, like buds about to burst.

"Ahhh," she hissed aloud as the mouth closed around a nipple, and made a small convulsive arching of her back when small sharp teeth slid over it, nibbling. *All sweet goddesses, that's hotwired to my crotch,* she thought exultantly. Solange moved to the other breast, stroked her stomach.

"I—*want,*" the Draka said hoarsely.

Solange lay back, wiggling lower, and Tanya could feel hands gliding up the backs of her thighs. The serf's voice was still a whisper.

"Then ride this pony," she said.

Tanya reached up with her right arm to touch the ivory plaque that controlled the lights. They flickered once and shone dimly on the lowest setting, reflected through gaps between the frosted glass false ceiling and the wall all around the big room. Shadows remained, hinting at a few large pieces of furniture, desk and *armoire* and massage-table, hiding inlay and rare woods and even the colors of the glowing thousand-knot Isfahan carpet. There was a slightly brighter patch above the big bed, and the crumpled black silk of the sheets had a liquid shine around and across their bodies. The Draka lay back, examining the face in the crook of her left arm.

Spots of bright red high on her cheeks, that was familiar enough from their more usual times together, afternoons mostly. But not the tears that slid quietly from under her closed eyelids, pooling and beading and then running in slow tracks down the sides of her face. It was a contrast to her usual sleepy-smug-catlike expression of satiation, but common on these rare nights when she woke from the terrible dreams. *Amazing,* Tanya thought. *She looks lovely even when she cries, most people get red and puffy.*

She bent her head to kiss the tears, salt, the taste of melancholy and of life, stroked back the drifting wisps of black hair to join the fan that lay invisible on the pillow. A kiss on the lips, smelling and tasting the warm flavor of sex, her own and the lighter musk of the serf's, mingled on their mouths.

"Why so sad, my pretty pony, my butterfly, kitten?" Tanya said softly, pulling up the sheet and holding her closer. "Didn't I make you happy?"

A sigh, and the long curved lashes fluttered back. "Oh, yes, I felt marvelous."

"Thought so. Do yo' know, you *sing* when yo' come? Anyone awake on this floor is goin' know I did right by yo'." Solange smiled through the tears and snuggled closer; Tanya could feel the slow dropping warm on her arm, then cooling, a little chill where the serf's breath ran over the wet skin. "Still haven't said why yo' cryin', though. Happens whenever yo' get like this."

"I . . . don't know, Mistress. It was my dream, I was . . . alone, everyone had turned away from me. I wanted them to come back to me, because there were . . . things . . . and I called out to them to help me, to save me, but they wouldn't, they walked away without speaking, I ran from one to the other but my hands could not touch them. And then, just before I woke up, they *did* begin to turn towards me, and I knew suddenly that if I saw their faces it would be too terrible to bear, my heart would burst."

Solange gripped Tanya fiercely, hiding her face in the angle of shoulder and neck. "Isn't that a silly dream to be frightened of?" she said, muffled.

The Draka stroked her back. "No, it isn't," she said, resting her cheek on the other's head. "Not at all."

"And then . . . when I wake up and you are there . . . I want very much to make pleasure with you. Not like other times, but because it makes me feel—" A hesitation. "Real again, not alone. As if I am found, not lost." The tears dripped more slowly onto Tanya's shoulder, and Solange sniffed. A moment later she spoke again, almost too soft to hear. "I love you."

Never promise more than you will give, Tanya reminded herself, as she stroked the serf's hair. She stretched, feeling a delightful lassitude that was not quite sleepiness, as if every muscle had been individually massaged and soaked and returned painlessly at half its original weight. *And tenderness,* she mused, reaching up for a handkerchief and gently pushing Solange's shoulder down to the pillow so that her face was exposed. *Odd. Ah well, it's my feeling, why not?*

"I know yo' do," she said, wiping the streaks from the other's cheeks and putting the kerchief to her nose. "Here, blow." A tremulous smile, and the Frenchwoman obeyed. "There, isn't that bettah? I know, my sweet. I'me glad yo' do, and I'm . . . very attached to yo'. Yo' are wonderful and precious to me, yo' give me infinite enjoyment in a dozen ways."

Solange reached up and gripped her arms, eyes searching Tanya's. "You will never . . . send me away, Mistress?"

Tanya kissed her firmly. "What a thought! Nevah."

"Not even . . . not even when I am old and ugly?" More quietly: "I am twenty-one this Christmas, mistress."

The Draka chuckled. "Look . . . Solange, honeybee, how old were yo' the first time I took yo'?"

"Eighteen, mistress." An answering smile. "So frightened and ignorant . . . how did you tolerate me?"

"Easily, sweet." Tanya remembered the violet eyes watching her undress, huge and misted with terror and determination. "Yo' were tryin' . . . anyways, that's about as young as I care to go. She gave the serf a peck on the nose. "I don't fuck children, Solange, and I'm ten years older than yo', as is. Keep up yo' dancin', and yo'll still be breath-stoppin' beautiful at fifty."

She rolled closer and took the other's face firmly between her hands. "And," she said slowly, "I've said I care fo' yo'. That means there'll always be a home fo' yo' here, an' I've made provision in my will. Word of a von Shrakenberg."

Solange sighed again, took one of Tanya's hands and kissed the palm before pressing it against the side of her face. They settled to sleep, curled spoon-fashion in a warm tangle of arms and sheets.

"Oh, one thing," Tanya murmured sleepily.

"Yes, Mistress?"

"When we're sleepin' together alone like this, call me by name."

Solange inhaled sharply, knowing the rarity of the privilege, especially for one not estate-born. "Thank you, ma-Tanya," she said.

"Yo' welcome, sweet," the Draka said. *Twenty-one*, she mused. *Have to get her a present*. Perfume, probably, or more platters for her needle-player. Or another crate of those trashy pre-War romance novels, she devoured them like candy . . .

Dirigible, Fred Kustaa thought, leaning out the window and looking upward. *The Paris–Alexandria passenger shuttle*. Below, the grounds were washed in moonlight and starlight, only a low seeping of yellow somewhere from a curtain not completely drawn. There was a countryside quietness to the landscape; the sounds of merrymaking from the pavilions had ceased. The Draka were early-to-bed even in a party mood. The air smelled of dew but not rain, and he could tell that tomorrow would be another day of dry sun and heat. *Good for the crops*, he thought sardonically. The harvest of his plans was prepared, and needed only the cutter to bring it in. With a controlled impatience he turned and strode across the room, kicking angrily at the hem of his caftan.

Past the bed, which the servants had noiselessly stripped of the usual sheets and relaid with smooth linen, less likely to tear. The posts had soft cloth restraints fitted to them, laced to the wood and with quick-fasten loops suitable for holding an ankle or a wrist; there were other fasteners on a table nearby, hard pillows, a jar of what the label claimed was scented, flavored lubricating oil, a blindfold and a whip with a dozen cords of hard-woven silk. Kustaa looked at them for an instant, then turned to the window, hawked and spat copiously into the night; it was silent enough that he heard the tiny *splat* as it landed on the roof of the shorter tower below.

Childish, he thought. *But sometime's a man's got to . . . say what he thinks*. Then: *Where is she? It must be going on for two a.m.* There wasn't much time for what they had to plan; not to mention that the sooner she arrived, the sooner he could tell her the truth. It could not have been a pleasant day for her, and the news seemed to have spread rapidly. At least, there had been a couple of hard looks from the servants who arranged the room for his "pleasure"; he suspected that Sister Marya had made herself well-liked.

A knock at the door. He cleared his throat, grunted. It opened smoothly, and the nun stumbled through. The male overseer leaned his head in past the jamb for a moment.

"Found thishere wench still ditherin' in her room, 'stead of reportin' to be tupped, Mistah Kenston." He looked her up and down. "No accountin' fo' tastes . . . Anyhows, enjoy yo'self and maybeso yo' can pump some manners into her, too. Uppity inside her head, I kin tell."

Marya shrank back against the door. She was carrying a cloth bundle in her hands, probably tomorrow's morning clothing. Some perverse Draka sense of humor had had her dressed in a short silk peignoir, transparent, that lifted her heavy bare breasts and swept open beneath to show the round belly sagging slightly over her thickset legs. He had started forward to whisper reassurance when he saw that her crouch was not a cower; her eyes had gone to the bed and seen what awaited her, and the sound she made was a low growling as the lips curled away from her teeth. The bundle of clothes she held floated down, and time slowed as he saw what came free of it in her right hand. Knife, fighting knife, long and slender and double-edged with a round hide-wound hilt. Draka knife, she must have palmed it somewhere, Ildaren wrist-blade.

It should have been comical, the fat woman in the obscene silk nightie coming for him with the hilt clutched in a clumsy white-knuckled hatchet grip. It was not, not to a man who had seen and dealt violence as often as Kustaa, not with that face behind the seven inches of edged metal. He backed away behind the corner of the bed, and fear blocked his throat for an instant before he could stutter out words, quietly but in his own voice.

"American, I'm an American!" The woman kept coming, her eyes rimmed all about with white, the point of the knife moving in the gloom. "I'm not a Draka, the Resistance sent me." Even then, the absurd code-phrase almost stuck in his throat. "The escargot of Dijon are very fine. Goddammit, Sister, the escargot of Dijon are very fine!"

She stopped, as if a glass wall had come between them. The berserker look faded from her eyes as she began to straighten; it was probably the sound of his undamaged voice that got home, as much as the words and accent. "Not . . . American? Resistance?" The knife slipped from her hand, bounced once on the carpet, lay still with lamplight breaking off the honed edges. He was barely in time to catch her as she began to crumple.

"*Ah,*" Edward von Shrakenberg said. "*Ahhh.*"

He looked down. The wench Chantal had her legs about him as he knelt on the surface of the bed, thrusting steadily. Her back was arched, making her a bow with weight resting on her shoulders and neck. His hands were clamped on her hips, thumbs kneading at the edge of her bush and fingers moving her in rhythm with him; he watched the mingling of their pubic hair at the end of each stroke, dark coarse black and tawny down below the ridged muscles of his belly. Obedient, she gripped tighter with her thighs and pushed up to meet him each time, the full plum-nippled breasts jiggling. The air was heavy with sweat and sex and the fumes of strong Moroccan kif.

They were both sweat-slick, her body seemed to glisten with it, but her face was hidden. He leaned back slightly on his heels and let his head fall back also, looking into the pattern of silvered mirror-tiles on the ceiling. Tanya had laughed at that, calling it a symptom of encroaching vanity. He smiled at the memory, smiled more at the soft warm moistness clenching and un-clenching around his penetration of the wench. He could see her face in the mirror, although he doubted her open eyes were seeing much beyond the spray of black hair that lay across them. Her mouth was closed but her lips were wide in a teeth-barring grimace, half the hard muscular effort that was making her grunt with every straining breath, half fury at this steady intolera-ble invasion of her self.

But she's learned not to try that passive-resistance nonsense any more, he thought with satisfaction. Amaz-ing what a little pain, a few drugs and patiently ruthless will could accomplish. *By Frey,* he mused, in the inter-vals of lucid thought, *this may not be a serf-taming technique fo' mass employment, but it has a lot to be said for it in individual cases.* Though he doubted the odd Mr. Kenston was having as much luck with his nun; the two thoughts brought a snort of laughter.

Chantal broke rhythm; his fingers gave her a tweak, and they settled back. *Still, can't keep this up all night,* the master of Chateau Retour decided. *Might get boring.*

He turned his head to Yasmin, who was beside them on the wide bed. She was lying on her stomach with her chin in one hand, the mouthpiece of the water-pipe in the other; her feet swayed in time to the rhythm of the act that rocked the fluid-filled mattress beneath her. Edward nodded at her, and she smiled lazily, blew scented kif-smoke toward him through pouted lips, rolled closer. One hand went down to where the master's body joined the wench he was riding, caressing them both; the other settled on Chantal's fist where it clenched straining beside her shoulder. The brown girl's mouth went close to the other's ear, whispered: about how to bring him off faster and get it over with, Edward supposed.

He let slip the control that had kept his thrusts slow

for twenty minutes, increased the speed until Chantal's buttocks were slapping against the hard flat muscles of his upper thighs with the violence of their movement. Yasmin's long cool fingers stroked unendurably at him, and he could hear her calling encouragement to the wench; until everything was lost in the long exquisite moment of release and his own triumphant shout.

The Draka came back to himself with a long sigh and worked his hands down under the Frenchwoman, working his fingers into the slackened muscles and feeling the residual tremors deep within. Her head whipped back and forth, a sound halfway between a whimper and a cry of protest escaping her: there were words in it.

"No," he heard. "No, no, no, not with you, no, *never.*"

Pity she takes it so hard, Edward thought idly. There was a . . . what was the French word? A certain *frisson* to it, with her so visibly defiant; still, it would be better when her heart broke and she truly submitted. *Tanya was right*, he mused. *This one's hard but brittle. Not the type who can live without hope.*

He released her, and she moved away to the edge of the bed with jerky motions, curling her knees up against herself and reaching blindly for the mouthpiece of the water pipe, drawing on it as if it were air and she drowning. Drawing, coughing, drawing again. The Draka yawned hugely and stretched out his arms, the thick muscles sliding and bunching beneath the damp skin. Yasmin was looking at Chantal's hunched back, shaking her head with a frown; at his movement she shrugged, smiled and picked up the damp and dry cloths from the head of the bed.

"Pleasure yo' good, Mastah?" she asked politely and began to clean his genitals with gentle deftness.

"Just fine," he said, with another stretch and yawn, conscious of enormous contentment. *And of a full bladder. Damn.*

The dark girl had finished and was cradling him in

her hands. "Then maybeso yo' doan' need Yasmin no mo', mastah?"

He laughed and ran square strong fingers through her hair as she bent her head to take him in her mouth. "Yo'll see how much in a little while," he said, using the thick black curls to lift her away from his crotch and kiss her. "Wotan's balls, yo' do that good. But first I've got an errand. Back in a minute."

Yasmin watched him pad across the darkened room and then moved to touch the other woman's shoulder where she lay in a shuddering ball. Chantal slapped at her without looking around.

"Go away, don't touch me, go *away*," she said, in a hoarse thready wail.

Yasmin caught the hand that struck at her and held it in a grip as soft as her voice. "Chantal, honeybee, it's terrible to see yo' sufferin' so. Is there anythin' I can do t'help?"

"Help? You help *him*, bitch, slut, whore, go *away!*"

A sigh. "Chantal, we all does what we's told; me an yo' both, we's serfs, honeybee. I tries not to hurt anybody, I really does. Look, Chantal, it's just fuckin', that don't mattah nothin' at all, really it doan'."

Wide-pupiled black eyes came up to peer at her through matted hair and a face wet with tears and sweat. "So you serve him with a smile, you!"

"Well, I's born 'n raised to service, Chantal. He was m'first man, too . . . sometimes I'm not bothered by it, sometimes I likes it, an' if I could take all this on mahself an' spare yo', I would certain-sure. But I *cain'*. Jus' like you cain' say no, or lie still like yo' tried." She shook her head. "Sometimes they can be pow'ful cruel. . . ."

Patting the other's hand. "I knows yo' doan' want to end up like Solange, givin' them everythin'; well, *I* doan' give everythin', either. Somethin', yes, cain' be helped an' why bothah? It like the wind an' rain; no shame to bend to the wind, let the rain fall on yo'. Grass an' reeds, they mighty humble, bend right to the ground, but the rain and wind, they come an' go and the grass and reeds still there. Proud strong tree git tumbled ovah, broken."

"I want to die," Chantal whispered, letting her head slump back to the bed. "I want to die."

Yasmin gave an almost-painful tug on her arm, and there was real fear in her voice. "Now that jus' *stupid*, wench! 'Less'n yo' believes Marya's stories 'bout the place we go when we dies, which is too good t'be true, like-so them tales 'bout the Western Land where everyone free an' happy. Yo' die an' that an end to everythin', good as well as bad. No mo' eatin, drinkin', singin', tellin' stories, playin' with babies—" She stopped, struck by a thought. "Is that it? Chantal, is that it? Yo' quickenin'?"

A mumble almost too low to be heard. "I'm three weeks late. Vomiting in the mornings."

Yasmin's face lit in a smile as she leaned over the other serf. "Why, that wonderful! A chile of yo' own, an'—"

"It's *his!*" The Frenchwoman's face was a gorgon's mask as she reared off the resilient surface, hissing so that a drop of spittle struck Yasmin on the cheek. "*He* put it in me like a *maggot!*" She collapsed as if a string had been cut. "I want to die," she repeated, in the voice of a weary child. "I want to die."

"Oh, honey, doan' feel like that!" Yasmin said softly. "It only a baby, doan' matter whose seed, baby belong to the momma. Be your'n to raise, iff'n yo' wants. Jus' little an' helpless, needin' everythin'. Your'n to love an' to love yo'; everybody need that. Where we all be, iff'n our mommas didn' raise an' care fo' us?" A sigh. "Yo' feeling pretty bad, I knows. Doan' do nothin' foolish . . . but look, Chantal, when they knows, they leave yo' alone, doan' bed yo' fo' a year or mo'."

"Truly?"

"Mmmm-hm, that the rule." A hesitation. "They pro'bly let yo' get rid of it, iff'n yo' wants, but then yo' . . ." She patted the surface of the bed. "Say, honeybee, yo' go back to the room now. Only, first, go take a *nice* hot shower. I tell mastah yo' take too much smoke an' puke; ain' no man in creation wants a pukin' woman around while he pleasures hisself. Then I make him feel real good, an' I tells him yo' bearin', and gets him to say yo' doan' have to bedwench no mo'. Hey?"

Chantal nodded dully and pulled herself to her feet, groping along the wall in the detached lassitude that *kif* and despair together bring. *To be left alone*, she thought; it was like a vision of . . . of the Revolution. She touched her stomach and thought of the price, and almost doubled over with nausea in truth. *Shower*, she thought. *Shower first, long and hot.*

"I'm sorry, Sister," Kustaa said, as she sat hunched and shivering in the chair with the blanket wrapped securely around her, eyes fixed on the knife in her lap. "I just couldn't see any other safe way of managing it, without blowing my cover."

"I forgive you, Mr. . . . no, don't tell me. 'Need to know.' A day of fear is a little thing, compared with what so many others have suffered. And suffering is a great teacher: how did the Englishman put it, More, I think? 'God whispers to us in our thoughts, sings to us in our pleasures: but in our pain, He *shouts*.' I forgive you as I hope for forgiveness."

"Forgiveness?" he asked, puzzled. "Given what you thought was in store for you, it was . . . heroic." He glanced at the bed, with the dangling bonds he did not dare remove. "By the way, my first name really *is* Frederick. My friends call me Fred. And considering your, ah, vocation, Sister . . ." He paused delicately.

To his surprise, the nun laughed. "You are a Protestant, are you not, Mr. . . . Frederick? I know Americans use first names easily, but . . ." At his nod she proceeded. "I swore an oath of chastity, Frederick. Renouncing a good for a higher good; but when I became a Bride of Christ, I did not swear to be omnipotent, able always to prevent my body being violated and abused by armed and ruthless men. Chastity is a matter of choice, Frederick."

He blushed, and she returned her gaze to the knife. "So I ask forgiveness for the sins of pride, cowardice, despair . . ." At his startlement, she nodded to the weapon. "I thought all today, as I counted figures and solved problems . . . I thought, why has God let this thing come to me? To strike a blow and die? As I decided in the end, fully expecting to be killed, either tonight or later on the stake. Perhaps that was God's will, His test of me, as He tested Abraham when He commanded the son of his heart be laid upon the altar. I knew that there was purpose in this," she continued, with another of those astonishing smiles. "Vanity is not one of my sins, Frederick: I know why that particular trial has not been mine so far. I am not comely."

A slow shake of the head. "Or perhaps, I thought, God wished me to know—with my heart and soul, not merely my intellect—how it feels to be so compelled and used as the vessel of another's lust, so that I might better comfort others." She sighed. "This very night, on this very estate, others are experiencing that which I only feared. Some with complaisance or even willingness, no doubt; so staining their souls with sin, but sin may be forgiven. Others, more, in fear and pain. How better could I aid such, perhaps even lead them a trifle closer to the Truth, than if I could say: 'Sister in God, I know your anguish, it is my own?' If that was God's purpose, then I have failed Him, who said 'Be ye perfect.' "

A smile. "There are no end to my doubts and weakness, it seems. For I also thought, perhaps God wishes me to preserve my life for some small part in the greater work that you, Frederick, are also helping to accomplish, the overthrow of the Domination."

"Sister, I've wondered why—if there is a God—He permits it to exist. I was raised Lutheran, don't go to church much anymore, but I guess I still believe . . . but . . ." A wave of his hand. "Ah, hell—sorry—why are we talking about this?"

"Because it is late, and we have neither of us had a chance to talk openly and without fear for very long . . . and I think also because we are friends, is that not so, Frederick?" The smile again, and he wondered how he could have thought her plain. Beautiful, not in any sexual sense, but beautiful still.

"And as to the Domination, that is part of the Problem of Evil, bearing on free will—and I will not burden you with the theology of Aquinas tonight, my friend. Also a Mystery, which we can never completely understand . . . You see my problem, though? Every day the Domination exists, it causes evils far greater than the mere theft of my body's privacy; which if I truly do not consent is mere suffering, even suffering for the Faith.

"The Domination . . . it feeds on all the seven deadly sins, and engenders them. It robs men of everything. Of the fruit of their labors, making them despise the toil which is Adam's legacy; of the building of their own families and households, the source of right education and morals; of the chance to hear uncorrupted the Good Tidings; menaces Holy Church; crushes the ordered liberty in which men were meant to live . . . Its very existence causes millions to doubt God or His goodness; it is the masterwork of Satan." A long pause. "Not least for what it does to the Draka themselves. I often think of that."

Slowly: "So, if in any way my services could hasten its end, was it not my duty to endure all, even . . ."—she nodded to the bed—". . . for other's sake? And my reluctance mere pride, desire for death, my being *delicati*, fastidious? Or was that the voice of the Tempter, using Scripture for evil's ends, when my duty was resistance unto death and the martyr's crown?"

Kustaa looked at the square face, the pale brows set in a frown of thought. Opened his mouth, closed it, struggled to put a name to an unfamilar emotion, finally decided: awe. "You don't hate the Draka, then?" he asked.

"I *try* not to—to hate the sin and not the sinner," she

said with a wry grimace. "Father, Son, Holy Spirit, Mary Mother and all the Company of Saints know, it isn't easy, the Draka do their vile best to make it impossible." A quick glance up at him. "You know, Frederick, if you think about the implications, the most terrifying thing Our Lord ever said was: 'Judge not, lest ye be judged.' Draka children, at least: no more innocent than other children—we are all fallen—but no less so either. Then think: all their best qualities turned to the service of their worst. Natural love of homeland and family, twisted to idolatrous worship of a 'Race' whose philosophy is about as close as imperfect man can come to pure evil. Bravery and loyalty turned to brutality; every perversion of natural feeling which we are prone to encouraged . . . Socrates, who so often glimpsed doctrines of the Truth, said it was better for one's soul to suffer evil than to do it. Also a counsel of perfection . . ." She threw up her hands. "But on to practical things, Frederick. Tell me just so much of your plans as is necessary for me to accomplish them."

"Just for starters, Sister, you've increased my morale."

"What, by half-hysterical spoutings of the words of those greater than I? And burdening you with my doubts?"

Kustaa shook his head. "I don't know how or why, Sister, but just listening helped." A nod. "Now, here's what I need—"

She listened in silence, nodding occasionally. When he had finished she propped her chin in her hands and frowned.

"An old man, a scholar from the few words I had with him, and a heavy box," she said. "I think I can guess." A troubled sigh, and she spoke as if to herself. "This is a Just War if ever there was one, yet the Just War must be waged by just and appropriate means. Perhaps it is legitmate to use these weapons as a threat to prevent the Draka from using them, which they would . . . yet to be believed such a threat must be genuine, and no earthly cause whatever could justify . . ." The words sank away, and she stood up briskly.

"Frederick, you Protestants cannot know what a comfort dogmatic authority and the Magisterium of the Holy Father can be in cases of doubt. If all use of these instruments of destruction is evil, the Church will tell me. Until then, I may safely assume it is not.

"Our first item of business is to get this box of yours safely close to the place where your airplane may land; the shelter near the winery and airstrip will be ideal; nobody enters it, and I have the combination. Come."

She started toward the door. "Wait, Sister," he said. "Whoa a minute. Can we be sure nobody's going to stop us?"

Marya looked aside, then down at the blanket and visibly forced herself to unwrap herself and fold it neatly over one arm. When she spoke, it was to the wall. "It is a warm night, Frederick. Anyone who sees us will assume you—the Draka you pretend to be, rather—is simply taking his, ah, wench elsewhere for his sport. Outside, that is. We can drive to our destination quite openly. The message—that should be sent tomorrow, I think. The confusion of the feast will be at its height, and . . . yes, tomorrow."

Kustaa smothered a grin: the nun could be quite wickedly cunning, it seemed. He bowed her toward the door, then froze as two screams rang out from a window somewhere on the same side of the Chateau as his room. A woman's screams, desolate and piercing, full of pain and raw grief.

"What the *hell*—" he began.

Sister Marya touched his arm, her face sorrowful. "There is nothing you can do, my friend. That was Solange, Mistress Tanya's . . . body servant."

He remembered the elfin beauty of the sad-faced girl at the breakfast table, the hard strength of the Draka woman's face, and shuddered. "Poor bit—sorry, poor woman."

The nun looked at him with eyes full of reflected pain and pity; pity for him, he realized, for his innocence. "Poorer than you think, my friend. That was nightmare, not mistreatment." At his raised eyebrow, she continued. "Solange has . . . embraced her chains. With the zeal of a convert, I fear. At least, one of her has."

"One of her?"

"The one that rules her waking soul. I think . . . I think there is another; and sometimes, at night, it remembers what it was, and what it has become."

He recalled the scream and shuddered again. "Let's get going," he said roughly. "Get the hell out." *Of hell*, his mind japed at him.

The driver slowed, easing the long lever of the steam throttle back. The vehicle rattled and whuffled in protest, bolts groaning; it was an ancient Legaree that might have hauled supplies in the Great War, an antique with a riveted frame and steel tires. He dimmed the headlights and peered around; nothing, except a few distant houses showing yellow-soft through the trees, the blinking running lights of a dirigible high overhead.

"Now!" he called back through the window behind him, into the body of the truck. It was brighter tonight than he liked, and the stretch of road beside the Loire looked hideously exposed in the moonlight. A patrolboat had gone by a few minutes ago, and he could still taste the sour fear at the back of his throat from that moment when its searchlight had speared him, hiding the ready muzzle of the gatling-cannon behind.

There was a series of thumps from the road behind him, and he rammed the throttle back up with a nervous jerk and twisted the fuel and water intakes to the boiler.

A stop in a few kilometers, to lace the canvas tilt back up, and then on to Nantes ahead of schedule. The "feed-pump problem" that kept him from the usual daylight departure-time had already earned him ten strokes with the rubber hose from that swine of a foreman.

"Filthy Serb," he muttered, as the bruises shot pain through his back; the man couldn't even speak understandable French. The driver knew nothing of the men who had darted out of an alley into the briefly halted truck, wished to know nothing. It was better that way; an order came through, passed anonymously, and you carried it out. Never anything conspicuous—a driver with nightpass papers was too precious an asset to waste.

I am a highly valued man, me, he thought sardonically. The Transportation Directorate used him on high-priority transport like this load of parts for the naval shipyard at Nantes. Electronics, he speculated, then consciously washed the guess out of his head with a drift of no-thought. That was a habit they were all getting used to. The Frenchman reached down beside the frayed padding of his seat and carefully extracted a cigarette, pinching the end to prevent the loosely packed tobacco from falling out. A7 Drivers got a double ration, which opened up interesting trading possibilities, if one was abstemious. The match went *scrit* on the crackle-surfaced metal of the dashboard, a brief smell of sulfur and glow over the dim bulbs of the dials.

He used the opportunity to study the valve-pressure gauge: dark as usual, he must speak to maintenance about it. *No more cigarettes tonight,* he decided. The docking reception clerk in Nantes was an agreeable Breton widow; for half a carton, he might be able to get perhaps a bottle of Calvados as well as a meal in the canteen and a cot.

"Name of a dog, Jean, hurry up!" the team-leader hissed, pulling on his own dark knit ski-mask and thrusting the Walther 9mm through the waistband of his overalls. The young machinist was fumbling with his knapsack—that was the bricks of *plastigue;* Henri hoped to God the man hadn't forgotten to pack the detonators safely. You had to rely on others to do their jobs while you did yours, but sometimes he wondered about Jean, especially since his father was executed and his mother and sister were sold off in that big sweep this spring. You would think it would have toughened him . . .

Ironic, that the innocent father had been executed and the Resistance-worker son not even detained.

"Ready," came another voice. They crawled out of the ditch where they had lain to let the truck get out of sight, north into the dark-rustling hedgerow of old poplars and new thornrose.

That was Ybarra, the Spaniard; reliable, even if she was a woman and a foreigner and a communist. Their explosives expert, and very good with the long stiletto or the piano-wire garotte; she had learned them all during the war in Spain back in the '30s, when the Reds had taken over and defeated the generals; from what one heard, that had been almost as bloody as the Eurasian War itself, allowing for differences of scale. They were all serfs now, all on the same side, as she was fond of saying.

The three Resistance fighters lay on their stomachs in the shadow of the hedge, relaxing slowly. No sound, except the harsh rasping of the crickets and the slight water-noises from the river a hundred meters south; not even much wind, tonight. More light than he liked, but they were all in dark clothing, their faces covered, nearly invisible from any distance. The smell of sandy earth and green things overbore the traces of tar and oil-drippings from the road. A warm night, sweat gathered in his armpits and on his face, insulated by the wool. He was about to signal them to move when the faint whine of tires on pavement alerted him.

No need for words; they all froze in place. *Coming from the west*, he thought. *No lights*. Both bad, could they have stopped the truck, found something? Had someone seen it slow to let them off? The Frenchman controlled his breathing with conscious effort, remembering lying in the burning forest of the Ardennes, not moving while the Draka hunted yipping through the woods for the survivors of his volunteer company. Not moving as pitch melted out of the trees above his boulder and dripped down around the curve to fall on his back, not moving at the laughter and the screams as they bayonetted the wounded and collected ears. Not moving.

A military auto but not an armored fighting-vehicle, silent and steam-powered. Helmeted heads, difficult to tell the color of uniforms in the dark; he peered at the door insignia as it halted. A skull, black in a circle of red chain: Order Police. The doors swung open and four men emerged, stretching. One handed around a canteen, another did a few deep knee-bends; a third walked to the edge of the road and opened the fly of his trousers, and the team-leader smelled the ammonia of urine seconds before the spattering on the leaves at the bottom of the ditch. The talked softly among themselves; there was laughter, and the slap of a hand on a shoulder, then a quick order from their NCO.

Just a rural security patrol, he thought with relief. Out looking for plantation-hands off bounds without a pass, candidates for a working-over and a day in the local police pen until their owners came to take them home for the serious flogging. None of the Resistance fighters moved. They had a mission, and it was not to attack a few serf policemen; not that the odds would be good anyway.

My pistol, Ybarra's knife and Jean's Schmeisser, he thought. One and a half clips for the machine pistol, six rounds for the Walther, against four trained fighting-men with automatic rifles. They would fight if discovered, of course. Being found out of their pens at night warranted suspicion, a beating and interrogation. Being caught with weapons meant an immediate hamstringing slash across the back of the legs with a bushknife, torture for days, death on the stake or the hooks.

"Right," he said, after the police steamer had been gone a safe ten minutes. "We're . . ." He looked up at the stars, down at a pocket-compass flicked open for a moment. ". . . About two kilometers from the chateau." They would not go to earth anywhere near the plantation headquarters itself, of course. Far too much chance of a Draka out for a night stroll, and none of them had much illusion about their ability to silently dispose of a Citizen in hand-to-hand combat. Disaster even if they did; a police patrol that did not report in would bring Security and the military swarming about, but a dead Citizen would mean slaughterous reprisals all through the countryside.

"We'll head for Bourgueil," he concluded; safer to stick with the plan, although he had authority to vary according to circumstances. The town was on the fringe of the plantation, and their informants said it was unpeopled, heavily damaged in the fighting back in '44 and mined for building material since, only the winery in use. On the edge of a big forest area, too. "Lie low until daylight, then see about making contact."

It must be important, to risk his whole cell, whatever it was they were to help the American with. He reached over his shoulder to pat the radio set.

"You first, *madame*," he said. "I'll take the rear. Ten-meter intervals."

"Right, comrade."

"And don't call me comrade, Ybarra," he added with a slight smile. Better her insolence than Jean's sweating nerves; if he had known the man was this shaken, he would have left him behind.

"Then don't call me madame."

"*Merde* with that, get going."

She moved past him, less than a ghost presence in the blackness. "*Su madre*, yes sir."

"How's it work?" Kustaa asked, shivering slightly in the damp of the cave. Except for his shielded handlight, it was pitch-black, dank, smelling of wet rock and concrete. The surface was rough under his feet, still bearing the marks of pneumatic hammers.

The drive up from the chateau had been uneventful, barely two miles; nothing in the ruins of the town, nothing but piles of stone, the shattered ruins of the Gothic church and arcaded marketplace looking as if they had been desolate two generations instead of three years. Moonlight on tumbled rock and the serried ranks of the vines on the low hills; an open field with a windsock and a strip of darkened landing-lights and three light aircraft tied down with lines and stakes. Not even a watchman; in a countryside under permanant curfew, where the population had no access to money and rarely left the Quarters, there was little danger of theft.

Perhaps it was that which was depressing: the sheer confidence of it. *Arrogant overconfidence*, he reminded himself. *And you're the living proof of it*. Or perhaps it was what he and the nun had lifted in short jumps from the compartment of the auto; the thing always gave him the willies. He looked over at her, and she smiled back at him with serene confidence. *You've got it good, buddy*, he told himself. *You're getting out of here*.

"Well, this is the outer entrance, Frederick," she said, with that trace of dignified old-world formality that was already becoming familiar. She nodded back along the short sloping tunnel cut into the pale limestone of the hill. "You see the niches? Those will be command-detonated mines."

Ahead of them was a blank surface of smooth gray metal; in its center was a naval-type blast door with a dogging wheel inset in the center. "This is from the cruiser *Baboeuf*, sunk in Toulon by the English in '40, after the surrender to the Germans. A section cut out of one of her main turrets, I believe, and slightly modified." There was a ball-mounting beside the door on one side, with an armorglass vision block above it, tank style. "That is for a machine-gun."

Her hand fell on his wrist and guided the light to the other side. A steel box had been welded to the surface, and she undid the latch to show a safe's combination lock recessed into the metal. "This controls the locking mechanism from the outside, although it can be disabled from within." She began twirling the dial.

"How on earth did you get the combination, Sister?" he asked.

"Oh, it's kept in the office," she said, as the tumblers clicked. "The lock on that cabinet is childishly simple . . . here we are."

Something clicked and whined deep within, and the wheel of the door swung with oiled smoothness as he spun it. The bolts went *chung-chank* and the thick metal swung open, bringing a hint of deeper chill from within, and a stronger smell like stone after rain, mass-concrete poured within the last few months. They wrestled the box through and dropped it, panting, with a dull *chunk*. Kustaa shoved the door home, and heard the nun feeling in the dark for a switch. It ticked, and overhead fluorescent lights hummed, flickered, and shed bright bluish light on a square box of a room ten feet on a side, lined with metal closets. The air smelled stale, with paint and metal and rubber odors, like the basement of a construction site. In the center of the room was something he recognized.

"Periscope!" he said wonderingly.

Marya nodded. "German," she said. "More military salvage. Through there"—she pointed to another ship's watertight door—"are more rooms. A suite for the masters, dormitories for some serf cadre, storerooms. A control room for the power system; there is a fuel cell in a sealed unit, it utilizes exterior air. Water comes from deep wells; there are air filters, room for a year's supply of food, weapons . . ." Her finger pointed to the ceiling. "Five meters of strong rock, not to mention the concrete. Ventilating shafts, but they will be baffled and fitted with filters, later." He noticed the inlets around the room, covered with temporary grilles, steel cap-covers hanging ready to be bolted into place.

"Protection against a fairly close miss, and complete safety from radioactive debris. Only the shell, now; the furnishings and so forth are to be added over the next few years. Eventually a linked system for the rest of the serfs, and even sealed barns for breeding-stock."

"So they do plan atomic war," Kustaa said softly, glancing around the bare, well-lit, evil room.

"No," the nun said slowly. "No, I do not think so . . .
not without a chance to strike first and suffer little
retaliation themselves. I've heard them speak of it and
every one has had fear and hatred in their voice. At
least at the prospect of the land itself being laid waste;
they care for that more than they do for any number of
non-Draka lives. This is . . . a precaution. On the ini-
tiative of the State, you understand."

"It'll be safe here?" he said, nudging the box. "And
you'd better give me the combination, as well."

"Very safe. Only the Landholders and the overseers
have the combination"—she made an impish smile—
"officially, and none of them come here unless they
must. With the feast and their duties, virtually no chance
at all. And we are close to the airfield, relatively far
from the Great House. Where better?" She shrugged,
then pulled the door of one of the metal cupboards
open. "This will be decontamination gear someday . . .
in here." They struggled it over to the locker, Kustaa
repeating the numbers after the nun as he went.

As they swung the outer door shut, the nun stopped
as if struck, then gave a low laugh.

"What is it?" he said. The night outside was still
black, but it had the flat depthless quality of the time
between moonset and sunrise.

"This place, Frederick, it was designed to keep that
poison *out*. And what is inside it now?"

His own laugh had only begun when a word came
from just outside the tunnel.

"*Attend.*" Kustaa felt his mind click over into another
mode, another time and place; his hand moved silently,
cautiously through the darkness toward the butt of his
pistol.

"Wait," came the voice again. French, male, hoarse.
"What are your tastes in cuisine, Monsieur-with-the-
American-accent?"

Cuisine? thought the OSS agent blankly. Then: "O.K.
Well, the escargots of Dijon are very fine," he continued casually.

A gusty sigh, and the unpleasant metallic sound of an automatic pistol's action being eased back into place by hand. "That is true, *Monsieur*, very true. With some fresh bread to mop up the garlic butter, and perhaps a bottle of—"

"Wait, that isn't in the password," Kustaa said.

"No, merely being nostalgic, *Monsieur*." The man came forward, a knitted mask over his head, dressed in dark stained city-serf overalls; the woman beside him was similarly clad, but tapping the blade of a long slim knife on her knuckles. "Lyon felt," he added, "that it might be important to forward certain items you left behind in your haste." He removed his backpack. "Your radio, for example, my old."

Kustaa took the offered hand, feeling the hard strength of a manual laborer. "Damned nice of you, but as it turns out Sister—"

"No names, please," the man said, taking in the blanket and the wispy silk beneath with a slightly raised eyebrow. "Our contact, I suppose." He drew her aside, and they exchanged codes in voices too low for the others to hear. "And you do not need the radio, you say?"

"She has access to the one in the chateau. It's an authorized transmitter, less likely to attract attention."

"*Merde*. Well, we also brought twenty kilos of *plastique*—"

"*Twenty kilos?*"

A purely Gallic shrug. "It is easier to steal it than hide it; it had to be disposed of in any case; we thought that it might prove useful. As might three helpers—" he looked around, swore, strode out to the entrance.

"Jean!" he called, low but sharp. A figure by the raised hood of Kustaa's Kellerman started erect. "Jean, name of a name, what are you *doing*, imbecile?"

"Nothing, nothing, just looking at this auto," he said.

"You repair the accursed things every day; get inside and under cover!"

To the two beside him: "Even if we are not so essential as we hoped, there has been a great deal of effort to account for our absence for three days. A place of refuge is most essential . . ."

Kustaa and Sister Marya both began to speak at the same time; the American nodded to the Pole and let her continue.

"I think," she said, "we have a refuge available and one of . . . unique strength."

"And," Kustaa added, his eyes narrowing in the dim starlight, "I've just thought of a possible use for that *plastique*, boys. Just by way of a fail-safe."

Chantal halted, leaning in the corner of the corridor. Her skin felt raw with the scraping she had given it in the showers, but not clean. *Not clean for weeks*, she thought bitterly. At least the man's smell was off her, but she could still sniff the stink of it . . . She thought again, of what was growing beneath her heart and nearly heaved her empty stomach once more. Voices ahead drew her alert; Marya's, and a man's. She pressed herself back against the wall, leaned her head around.

It *was* Marya, wrapped in a blanket. The man with her, the Draka visitor they had sent her to . . . and he was speaking. Low, but without the hoarseness she had been told of. Chantal felt something cold crystalize inside herself as she pulled her head back; the nun was not holding herself like a woman speaking to the man who has just raped her. *I should know*, she thought savagely. And why would he bring her back here, to her own quarters? A master would use her, then dismiss her when he was done with her. The Frenchwoman risked another look: the tall man was handing something to Marya. Something that glittered . . . a knife. Something else as well, from his belt: a cartridge-case.

". . . eggs in one basket," he was saying. "You hold this for a while." *An American accent!* She recognized it from the radio and motion pictures, before the War.

Chantal pulled back again and sank to the floor, hugging her knees to herself, waiting for the closing of the door and the sound of the man's bootheels walking away. *Something* was going on. *Something that sanctimonious bitch hasn't been telling me*, she thought with a wild flare of rage that left spots swimming behind the closed lids of her eyes. *Her with her sympathy and prayers! Resistance work, it must be*. Something to *do*, a way to strike *back*. And the nun had left her out of it, left her in the misery of utter helplessness, a powerless victim, a *thing*.

"You're not leaving me out any longer," she whispered savagely. "Not any more."

CHAPTER FIFTEEN

PRESIDENT MARSHALL PROCLAIMS PEACE ZONE

[NPS] New York: In a statement delivered from the First Office of Washington House, President Marshall announced that the Alliance Grand Council had proclaimed a Peace Zone covering the Atlantic coast of North and South America to a 200-mile limit, the entire Pacific outside the Domination's self-proclaimed Exclusion Zone (of 125 kilometers) and the western Indian Ocean. No non-Alliance warships would be allowed within this Zone, or non-Alliance merchantmen except those proceeding under license from the Office of Shipping Control. Unauthorized ships will be treated as hostile intruders, and similar restrictions will apply to air traffic.

President Marshall denied that this was an act of war, or in any way modelled on the Draka Exclusion Zone regulations. He further categorically denied statements from the Domination's Information Directorate that Alliance submarines have been routinely violating the Exclusion Zone's limits. "The Alliance stands for freedom of the seas, as it stands for every other freedom," he stated in response to requests for clarification. "But in an era when a single bomb can destroy a city, we cannot allow vessels from a power which has demonstrated

*complete contempt for human life to approach our coastal
cities without prior inspection and control." In further
spontaneous remarks, the President heatedly denounced
allegations that the OSS was behind disturbances in
Europe and Asia. "Tyranny is the cause of revolt," he
said. "Liberty is the cure, not repression."*

*In related news, Washington House officials confirmed
that a permanent site for the Grand Council and Assembly of the Alliance is being considered. All of the cities
mentioned were in the Pacific Basin, and highly-placed
sources indicate the choice has been narrowed to San
Francisco, Lima and Sydney.*

> U.S. Weekly Chronicle:
> Nation's Bilingual Newsmagazine since 1912
> From "President Marshall's Plan for Peace"
> by Ulysses Sherman Sandino
> Managua, Nicaragua
> August 2nd, 1947

CHATEAU RETOUR PLANTATION,
TOURAINE PROVINCE
AUGUST 3, 1947
1100 HOURS

"Andrew! Yo' made it!" Tanya's eyes widened as the
long car with the Security skull-blazon crunched to a
stop by the steps. He was in crisp garrison blacks, with
nothing non-regulation but a tasteful ruby eardrop. The
warmth of her smile and embrace was still on her face
as she turned to formally clasp forearms with the Security officer who followed. "And Strategos Vashon," she
continued. "Yo' welcome to my House, sir. Make yo'self
free of it." A rueful shrug. "Bit crowded, I'm afraid."

To her brother: "Edward's up by the winery, lookin'
over our new Cub with Johanna and her Tom." She
turned to the waiting housegirl and took two greeting-

cups, handing them to the guests while harried-looking
servants swarmed down to take their luggage and direct
the *Orpo* trooper-driver to the vehicle park west of the
Great House.

They poured ceremonial drops and sipped at the
wine, eyes widening slightly in appreciation at the taste.

"Spicy," Vashon said. "Hmmm, hint of . . . flint,
maybe? Local?"

"From a friend's place, east of here: *Pouilly-Fume*.
Fo'give me if I don't join yo', gentlemen, but I've got to
get through the day standin'."

Andrew held out a hand to stop one of the serfs going
by with the luggage. "Not those two, boy, they're the
gifts."

The serf, a middle-aged fieldhand hurriedly kitted
out in house livery for the day, bobbed his head and
looked at Tanya questioningly. "*The table with the gifts,
Marcel*," she translated into French.

"*Oui, maîtresse*," he said, and trotted up through the
main doors.

"Yo' lookin' good," Andrew said to his sister as she
turned back to them. "And considerable less pregnant
than last time." Fresh and summery in a crisp white
linen suit, with no hint of color but the ebony butt of
the little Togren 9mm tucked into its holster inside her
belt.

"Never again," she shuddered, linking an arm through
his and courteously motioning the Security officer before her. They turned to the high arched gateway that
passed like a tunnel through the bulk of the chateau's
oldest section. Light showed at the other end, and the
soft lilt of a string quartet. "Through here; the main
court is out back . . ."

It was a bright noon, almost cloudless; hot and dry,
with a fitful breeze from the north. The courtyard along
the north side of Chateau Retour was a blaze of color;
from banks of flowers, from the silks and jewels, from
the dragon's hoard that sprawled along the long cloth-

draped trestles where the naming-gifts were exhibited, from the tile and stone of the courtyard pavement itself. A wooden bandstand draped in tapestries from Lyon held musicians in pre-War formal dress, contributed from neighboring estates for the occasion. In the cool shadow of the arcade along the court's eastern flank more trestle-tables held food; piles of scarlet lobsters, roasts, salads, fruit, with white-hatted carvers and servers standing ready. Housegirls in brief gauzy costumes circulated with platters of delicacies, dabs of crevet cheese on wafers, brandied truffles, savory morsels of fish or spiced sausage, wine coolers, juices, cigarillos and hashish.

Kustaa leaned against a pillar beside the buffet table and watched the crowd, taking occasional nibbles from a plate held in one hand. A crowd of Draka; he had never seen so many Citizens in one place on a social occasion. Forty adults, he estimated, and nearly as many children, from infants being carried by their nurses to the teams playing water-polo down at the lake; their shouts and splashing echoed back, and he could see their sleek bodies slipping naked through the clear water and flung spray. The guests seemed to fill the great yard without effort, though they were far too few to crowd it, and less noisy than this number of Americans would be.

I wonder what it is, he thought. They were in every combination of attire formal and informal, from one severely elegant woman in her sixties dressed in a Grecian-style gown of pure white, through uniforms of every rank in the Domination, to a few who had just come up from the lake in nothing but the glistening water on their skins. Sitting on the benches, strolling, talking, one even in a wheelchair . . . There was a sickness to them, he could feel it; a rot somewhere within, but it had not seemed to weaken them. Instead they fed on it and it made them strong . . . You could see it in their eyes and movements, a consciousness of power. Power of life and death over other human beings, power held since birth by hereditary right.

They believe, he decided. That was what gave them that air of absolute confidence and cold will. *They believe their own myth of what they are and, believing, confirm it to themselves every day of their lives.* Then: *Don't get spooked, they put their pants on one leg at a time like everybody else.*

When they wore pants, that was. He tried to imagine a similar gathering in the U.S., Social Register types and *haciendados,* with one in every ten of them down to the buff. A grin forced its way to his mouth; they probably wouldn't strip half as well. Which reminded him to be careful himself; he was circumcised, and he was getting graphic evidence that Draka men were not. Beside him Ernst w: ·ted, in a creditable imitation of a personal servant's combination of attentive waiting and don't-notice-me deference. *Hell with it,* Kustaa thought. *Can't be helped, so why should I feel guilty about it?*

Then the man stiffened, looking over Kustaa's shoulder. His fingers moved:

send me away. quickly!

why? He was officially nearly dumb without him, and it was a nuisance. Particularly since there were some here who might have valuable information, and they seemed reluctant to offend or directly deny him. He wished everyone in the States were as pleasant to disabled veterans, and that tall fiftyish man was a member of the Domination's Senate, just retired from the Supreme General Staff. A quantum opportunity . . .

because there's a Security general coming through the gate who's seen me before and probably read my file a hundred times. even without the beard and in livery he may recognize me.

Kustaa's fingers flew, and he made an imperious wave for audience effect, if somebody should be looking. *get your ass out of here. the shelter, if you can. back after dark and be careful.*

"Yes, master." A low bow and the Austrian hurried

away, weaving through the partygoers. Carefully, with left-and-right bobs of the head: Citizens expected to be avoided.

Kustaa turned, feeling his heart surge and slow with the brief rush of adrenaline, then subside into alert wariness. *He* was too conspicuous to run. A Citizen was noticed when he moved, not part of the continuous background flicker of life like a serf. He would have to take his chances; his tongue probed at the capped tooth at the rear of his molars, imagining the swift crunch, a brief bitterness and oblivion. That was a choice he had made his mind up to long ago. Not simply that he accepted that there was too much knowledge in his skull, but they had sent Rutherford *back*. Alive, in a dirigible shipping container to London, with glossy prints of his progress from capture to the thing that had made one of the bomb squad team that had opened the lid faint. With "Thanks for the lovely chat" carved in his forehead, above the lidless eyes.

The container had been correctly addressed to OSS clandestine headquarters in Britain.

For a moment, he thought of Sister Marya. Who would never use the tooth, never even consider it, even knowing what would follow . . . *and there are advantages to being a lapsed Lutheran*, he told himself. Somehow he was smiling as he completed the turn and saw Tanya von Shrakenberg walking through the archway. She waved and guided the two men with her toward him.

One in black, tall, with what Kustaa was coming to think of as the von Shrakenberg face, bony eagle-handsome features and pale eyes. Another, short, black-haired and green-eyed, in a Security Directorate uniform that matched the shade almost exactly, *Jesus, a Strategos*. About general—the precise level would depend on his posting; Domination rank was more flexible than Alliance and the police were not run on quite the same lines as the military anyway . . .

"Mr. Kenston, pleased to see yo' lookin' so well," she was saying; seeming to mean it, too. An odd pang of guilt, quickly suppressed: *This isn't the middle ages, Marine. You don't owe them anything because you've eaten beneath their roof. It isn't theirs, anyway.*

"I'd like yo' to meet my brother Andrew," she continued. "An' Felix Vashon, here. Mr. Kenston," she continued to the two, "is the Wayfarer-guest. Art-supply buyer, and a Class III veteran. Throat an' head injuries, unfortunately, but he's got a boy to talk fo' him . . . Where is he, Mr. Kenston?"

"Hel-o," Kustaa grated, exchanging forearm grips with the two men. *Christ, I'm glad I don't have to arm-wrestle for a living here,* he thought. "Se-nt . . ." he waved vaguely. "Er-rand."

"Andrew von Shrakenberg, Merarch, XIX—*formerly* XIX Janissary. Now on detached duty." Hard arm, direct stare, polite expression, expressionless eyes. No. Flat, slightly dead; thousand-yard stare, familiar as the cracked scraps of shaving mirrors on troopship bulkheads during the War. Combat man, and not from a bunker, either.

"Felix Vashon, Strategos, West-Central European district," the secret policeman said. Pleasant smile, well modulated voice. The sort who made you understand why the standard nickname for Draka was "snake"—or that might just be knowledge of what he did for a living. *Maybe this is the one that cut off Rutherford's eyelids and left him staring into a strobelight for a week,* the American thought.

Tanya was about to continue, halted, beckoned imperiously. Marya came up to the small group of Draka, bowed politely and stood with a clipboard in her hands, eyes meekly downcast.

"Report," her owner said.

"Mistress, all the scheduled guests have arrived. These masters are also to be staying?" She brought up the paper and produced a pen. "Masters, there is camp-style accommodation in the pavilions in the cherry orchard west of the maze, or rooms at the plantations surrounding. Here? Very good, Masters; the last pavilion on the right; your luggage will be laid out." To Tanya:

"The final check on provisions indicates more than ample, Mistress. Cook says the suckling-pigs are turning out very well. The extra servants and the personal retinues of the guests have all been settled in and familiarized with the floor plan and the events. The transport for the boar-hunt tomorrow is on schedule. Refueling arrangements for the aircraft at the landing field are complete, and the tanker-steamer is standing by. Repairs on the dock at Port-Boulet are complete and the yacht is at anchor. Yasmin and Solange are completing their rehearsals and Solange says she is satisfied with the musicians"—she inclined her head toward the dais by the old chapel building—"for a provincial group. No serious problems, Mistress."

Tanya patted her on the cheek and spoke to her brother. "Remember pickin' her up fo' me, back this spring? Yo' were kind enough to offer me the run of yo' pens back there in Lyon, Strategos."

"It's a festive occasion. Felix, please. The wench is satisfactory? I had my doubts, frankly."

"Mo' than satisfactory. Occasionally troublesome, but worth it; real mind fo' organization. New plantation, routines not set, Edward an' I have to concentrate on plannin' and getting the labor force goin', she's invaluable."

"Hmmm, thought she might," Andrew said. "Yo' get a feelin'. Type yo' have to watch, though."

"Yes . . . although she turns out to have unexpected talents as well. Mr. Kenston here"—she gave him a smile and a friendly squeeze on the forearm; her fingers were like slender metal rods, precisely controlled force—"took a sudden hunger fo' her yesterday. To tell the absolute truth," she continued frankly, "if there'd been a way of refusin' him compatible with manners, I would have." A favorite horse or a regular concubine was something only a friend could ask the loan of, as a favor;

ordinary household goods like Marya were a guest's to use, of course. "I've gotten to know the wench somewhat, an' I'd've sworn on the soul of the Race and the first von Shrakenberg's grave all her erotic juices were channeled into her superstitions, need a prybar and help to get her knees open. Pro'bly girl-only if she *were* beddable, at that. Instead—"

She put a finger under Marya's chin and lifted her face to the light. "Look at that. Yo' wouldn't notice, but the skin around her eyes is mo' relaxed. Set of the shoulders, too." A rueful shake of the head. "Happy! An' I was afraid she'd be sulkin' and poutin' off her work fo' weeks, at least. Turned out all she needed was a night-rider and she's purrin'. Shows, never be too certain about anybody."

To her guest: "Satisfactory fo' yo'?"

Kustaa smiled, looking at the three; their sleek strong bodies so expensively trained, the beautifully tailored clothes and uniforms, the cold predator eyes that never lost that speck of icy watchfulness. At the woman waiting patiently, dowdy in her long sleeves and the heavy wool that brought a glow of sweat to her face. Waiting with serene patience. *Filth*, he thought at the Draka, behind the mask of his smile. *You're all filth, none of you worth a thousandth the Sister.*

"Go-od," he said, nodding and smiling, knowing his face was flushing—but that was all right, they weren't going to guess it was with the intensity of his need to kill them all. *Out*, he thought. *If the world were ruled by sanity and justice as she believes, I could get her out. Introduce her to Maila. God, I'd send my kid to any school she taught in.*

The Draka's finger freed the nun's chin; her eyes met his for a moment before dropping into the proper downcast position. Level and very calm. *Do nothing foolish, Frederick.* No, he wasn't going to do anything foolish, no, there was an entire lifetime of work ahead of him. Until the last Draka was dead. *Do not let them damage*

*your soul with hatred. You owe your wife and child
more than that, and yourself.*

That brought him up cold. "Th-an-k y-o," he said.
The Draka woman nodded, taking the gratitude that
was not meant for her, as he had intended. And the
Sister would say this place was her cross, which she
would take up to follow Him.

"Hold yo'self at this mastah's disposal, when yo' not
workin'," Tanya said. "If yo'll forgive me, Mr. Kenston?"
He nodded, and the group moved on.

"Uncle Karl," he heard the voice say. "Cousin Eric;
yo' two aren't fightin' again? Sofie, yo'd better learn
how to keep this pair of bull rhinos—"

"It's the *Boche*," Jean said, when Henri finally called
from the other room. He inserted his head through the
hood of the vision block beside the door, pressing his
face to the padded visor. There was enough light in the
short section of tunnel beyond the armorplate for him
to see a distorted image of the man's face. Peering
behind him, so there was only a stretch of neck swollen
by the mirrors and thick glass that bent its image through
ninety degrees to bring to him. Turning around, mouth
working, he must be talking.

Whunk-wunk-whunk, a stone on the thick steel. So
far away. *Like father's face, when the switch was under
my hand and the pain*—No thought, no thoughtno-
thoughtnothought. White sound inside his head, soothing. Forget the shaking, the sweat, they could not
trouble him while he whitesoundnothought could not
remember the room and the chair and the whitesoundnothought—

"Well, let him in, you young cretin!" Henri's voice,
Henri's hands shoving him aside, spinning the wheel.
He turned, helped, the heavy door swung open. The
Boche stepped through, shaking his head, speaking in
heavy guttural French even as they strained together to
swing it shut again, quietly, quietly. *Shhhh-chung, and
the bolts were sliding home again.*

"What took you so long? I might have been *seen*. Ach, there's no possible excuse for my being here."

"Quite correct," Henri replied. "We are supposed to be *hiding* here." Suddenly he turned and gripped Jean by the collar. "*Merde*, what were you waiting for! You know we can't hear anything in the inner—" He turned suddenly, looked at the periscope. Jean felt a sudden stab of fear; it was up again.

Did I do that? Yes, he had; an impulse, in the hope that the Masters would see.

Henri's hand came around and hit him, across the face and back again. "Are you *drunk*, you little shit?" he said. Something seemed to snap behind Jean's forehead, and now he was seeing very clearly.

"Are you drunk? Have you been sucking that piss-smoke kif the snakes give us to rot our brains again? Or are you simply fucking insane? That thing's naked to the sky except for some wire mesh, anyone could have seen it move up there!"

Seeing very clearly, the strong jowly face of Henri Maloreaux, who had been like his uncle. His father's (screamingtwistedswitchchair whitenoisenothoughtno thought) best friend, old friend from faded pictures on the mantel before the War, old army friend. *God, how I hate you*, he thought, very clearly, as he smiled with the right degree of shakiness.

"Thank you, Henri," he said. "I've . . . well, I keep remembering little Marie-Claire, and—thank you." The man's eyes softened, not the hard clench of his muscles. Jean knew what he was remembering, he was seeing Marie-Claire in her white First Communion dress. (The photo, only it was his sister across the padded block and the dog was—whitenoisenothoughtnothought) The Draka had let him talk to her just last week, her and maman, hello Jean I love you no we are well the work is hard but nobody hurts us we love you when can you come to us—

"I understand," Henri was saying.

Hate you.

"It must be absolute hell, not knowing where they are." The Maloreaux family was in the same compound, three concrete bunks across the room. "I understand."

The Boche was looking sympathetic too. "Ach," he said. "It is always the families that make it worst." *Hate you.* Ybarra was in the room now too, looking at him. Cold eyes, considering. Filthy Red whore, she was the one they had picked to kill the foreman, the one who listened at the doors and asked questions. Got him into her bunk, they could all hear the wet slapping sounds behind the curtain, then the thin whining cry as she put the steel needle in under the hair at the back of his neck; everyone thought it was a heart attack. *Hate you, bitch.*

I will go to America, he thought with the same gleeful clarity. I and Marie-Claire will go to America, I don't know how I will get word to the Masters, but I will. Not the chair, not with her or maman, not their faces bulging around the gag and my hand pressing the switch and pressing and pressing and stopping the pain the pain pressing *whitenoisenothoughtnothought.* The Masters will come for me, and we will go to America and Marie-Claire will wear a white dress, and we will sail under the big bridge like the newsreel and never again the compound, she will laugh and clap her hands and not bend over the block with the dog *whitenoisenothoughtnothought.*

"It's that pigdog Vashon; he didn't see me," the German was saying. Jean felt another clear metallic thing go *snap* behind his eyes, because it was all working just right, just as the Master called Vashon had said it would, the voice that spoke to him from the darkness beyond the blinding light, it always did and the photo landed at his feet and he looked down, no he didn't.

"Probably just chance he's here, but we've got to be even more careful, Almighty Lord God but he's a cunning devil."

Not chance; the voice from darkness was strong, it was wise, it would lead him into the newsreel and the ship and the tall fountains of water and the thrown streamers and confetti, where Marie-Claire laughed and did not huddle beside him on the concrete bunk listening to the noises in the dark. The voice knew he was its faithful servant and had come to reward him.

"But there's one stroke of luck, as good as Vashon is bad: Jules Lebrun is here, he and I were friends in the old days, and he's in on it with the other, the nun. They've arranged to have him on radio-watch during the celebrations tonight, and with him I to 'play chess.' The American will slip away as soon as he can. When the message is received, we will flash the lights *three* times from the upper window. That gives us an hour before the airplane arrives; you must have the diversion ready, to draw all attention from this place. And the landing lights."

Henri smiled, nodded. *How ugly his teeth, why did I never see that before.* "Don't worry," he said, clapping the older man on the shoulder. *Disgusting, a Boche, maybe Henri just boasted of fighting them, he ran away and was a collaborator.* "We'll be employing our little *plastique* surprises, they'll be too busy attending to the transformer and their autos to notice a silenced plane. No killings, even, so it shouldn't mean more than a few sore backs among the locals, we'll all be far away in our different directions, no?" *He's a coward too, a coward.*

Vashon was here. It would be difficult to slip away, they were all watching him. Perhaps when they went to plant the explosives. The voice from darkness would take away all his sins as he knelt and begged forgiveness. It would wash him clean and it would all be clear in his head, like this.

"Sounds too good to be true, comrades." Ybarra's voice came from behind his shoulder.

His own mouth made sounds, and they were clear and good because Henri laughed and nudged him. *Die, bitch. Die.*

"Don't call me comrade," Henri was saying, an arm around Jean's shoulders.

Die.

"I think," the Austrian replied, resting a hand for a moment on Henri's arm, the woman's shoulder, "we can reclaim that word for all of us. It is a good word, *kamerad.*"

Jean smiled and said the word. *Die. Leave me alone in my head, stop talking to me inside, die.*

Tonight.

All of you. Die.

The picture was one of the middle series. Alexandra caught with the discus in her hand, leaning back against the wall with one leg propped up against it. Old stone wall, Mediterranean-white. Strong bare slender foot trailing toes in the white dust, just highlights of the rest, the scratched bronze of the disc, school-tunic, metallic-black of hair, face shadowed by the colored dark of the bougainvillea . . .

"I was always too fond of putting flowers in," Tanya said.

"No," Alexandra replied. They were sitting on the solitary couch in an empty echoing room in the new east wing, the picture propped up before them on a wooden chair. Their arms were over each other's shoulders, the free hands holding cooling late-afternoon glasses of beer. Light scattered through the windows, shafts into darkness, slanting hazy pillars of yellow crossed by the slow white flecks of dust-motes.

Gods, I'm glad to get away for a while, Tanya thought, and let her head loll back against the high scrollwork back of the seat. The tour of the Quarters had been deadly dull . . .

"Still thinkin' 'bout all those old fogies complainin' the serfs would be spoiled with four-room cottages an' runnin' water?" Alexandra said, with a slight teasing note in her voice.

Tanya turned her head. *She's aged well,* was her first thought. *Better than me.* Experience lines beside the eyes that were a blue deeper than indigo, almost black.

They kissed, drew back and laughed, turning to the painting.

"No, thinkin' of . . . back then."

"Gods bless, it's like rememberin' another universe . . . What were we goin' to do?"

"What weren't we? Conquer the world—"

"About half, it turned out."

"Paint the most beautiful pictures ever done, design planes to fly to the moon . . . love like nobody ever had or would."

"Ah, what happened to us?" Alexandra mused.

"What didn't? The war. Life. Love, death, victory, defeat, joy, anguish, children . . . time."

"There it is, captured fo'ever," the dark-haired woman said. "Not many can say that, Tanya. All the fire an' the sweetness and the old familiar pain . . ." A sigh. "While we, we're not those two any longer, are we?"

"No; we're older, sadder, and friends."

A door slammed and a small figure bounced through, cartwheeling, a flash of orange fire as the hair passed like a bar of flame through a patch of light.

"Ma, Ma!" Gudrun said, then stopped politely when she saw her mother had company. "Sorry, Ma, ma'am. I'll come back later."

Alexandra laughed. "Time takes, time gives. I'd best go see to my own, they've probably burned down half the province an' set sail on yo' yacht to play pirates all the way to Ceylon."

They touched fingers. "See yo' later, 'zandra," Tanya said.

"Sho'ly, Tannie."

Tanya held up her arm. "Not too old to snuggle with yo' momma?" she said.

The child settled into the curve of her shoulder, a wiry-hard bundle whose calm trust finished the task of relaxing the tension out of her back. *Not too old,* she thought. *Not yet.* Gudrun sighed and yawned, curling up, the bouncing energy suddenly flipping over into sleepy thoughtfulness. *How did I feel at her age? How did I think?* The effort to recall was maddening, slipping away from the fingers of the mind. A rage, a rage to do, to live, to *be* . . . Fragments of memory; holding a dragonfly's wing to the sun and seeing it suddenly as a vast plane of gold ridged with rivers of amber. Lying in her bed alone in the dark and feeling consciousness staggering as she comprehended death for the first time, realized that one day she, herself, the inner I would *cease to be.* Enormous unappeasable frustration with all-powerful adults who would not, could not *understand* . . . things that seemed so clear, but that she could never have put into words.

Her daughter was looking at the painting. "Did yo' love her, Ma?" she asked.

Tanya smiled and put down the glass, used the other arm to hold her daughter close. *Well, she's getting to the age when your parents' love-lives are troubling mysteries instead of boring grown-up stuff,* she thought tenderly.

"Yes, very much," she said.

"As . . . as much as yo' love Pa?" the girl asked.

"Different, child, different . . ." How to explain? "Remember what happened when we said yo' were old enough to drink yo' wine unwatered?" Tanya felt the beginnings of an embarrassed squirm.

"No, don't feel bad, baby, everyone takes a great big gulp just to see what it's like. Love's like that, carrot-top, yo' have to practice, an' the first real try makes yo' head spin. Makes everythin' wild an' strange-like, because it *is* the first an' the skill isn't there. Flares up like a bonfire, where yo' freeze and roast. Then yo' learn how to make the good warm coals that'll last all yo' life long, the way Pa and I've done. But ah! those first tall flames are a lovely sight."

A long pause. She looked down and saw the red brows knitted in thought, then a slow nod.

"Will I ever have a special friend like your Miss 'zandra?" she asked shyly. "The girls in the senior forms at school, they're always goin' on about who's fallin' fo' who, and it all seems so . . . silly, like a game."

"Sometimes it is, carrottop, and it'll all seem less silly once yo' body changes—I know it's hard when we say, 'wait until yo' older,' but sometimes it's all we can." She kissed the top of the child's head, feeling the sun-warmth still stored in the coppery hair. "Jus' have to wait, child; doan' ever rush into things 'cause others are doin' it and yo' want to fit in. When yo' time comes, listen to yo' heart; maybe in school, maybe later in the Army when yo' old enough fo' boys, maybe not till University. Maybe everythin' will work perfect right off, or yo' might have to try an' try again—most folks do."

"If . . . if yo' love someone like that, and it doesn't . . . work, does it hurt?"

A rueful laugh. "Sweet goddesses, yes, baby, worse than anythin' else in the world."

"Then why does anybody do it, Ma?"

"Can't help themselves, child, no ways."

Another silence. "Pa never had a special friend like Miss 'zandra, did he, Ma?"

Tanya squeezed a hug. "Freya, carrottop, yo' wants to find out everythin' in a hurry." A pause for thought. "No, though some do . . . Men are different from us, baby." A nod; Draka children learned the physical facts of life early, from observation and in their schooling. "Not just the way they're made, but inside."

She tapped her daughter's head. "They . . . come to the need fo' lovin' late, but need the pleasurin' part of it more, 'specially when they're young, and they can keep the two apart more. We're the other way 'round, the lovin' comes first, in general, and then the needin' grows on us. Not everybody's that way, yo' understand, but most. That's why the boys mostly start with wenches, because at first with them it's just this . . . blind drive to plant their seed."

Gudrun frowned again, and when she spoke it was in a quiet voice. "Ma, doesn't that mean . . . well . . ."

Tanya rocked her, smiling over her head. *That* was a

question all Draka children asked, sooner or later; important to give the right answer. "An' yo' wonderin' if that means he loves yo' less, with all those wenches' babies he made, makes yo' less special," she said. A quick nod. "No, never, darlin' of my heart," she went on, letting a note of indulgent amusement into her voice, showing that the fear was understood but not a thing to be taken seriously, feeling the momentary tension relax out of the girl's body. "Yo' see, Pa and I made yo' together; like he loves me special out of all the world, we love yo' and Timmie and the twins, because only yo' children of our blood are really ours. Y'understand, sweetlin'? Yo' the children we raised an' trained, and yo' our . . . well, when we're gone, you'll be all that's left of us.

"Know how we always say, 'Service to the State,' and 'Glory to the Race'?" A nod; civics classes would have taken care of that. "There's another meanin', and this is real important. Yo' are the glory of the Race, darlin'. Because of yo' and yo' brothers and sisters, Pa and I are joined to the Race, through the children yo'll have some day, and their children and children's children, forever. Just like we join y'all to the ones who went before, right back to the beginnin'."

"Oh. That's sort of scary."

"Mmmmm-hmmm. Big responsibility, carrottop, but it'll be a while before yo' has to worry about that. Never be in a rush to grow up, my baby; that's what 'zandra and I were talkin' about, before yo' came. Lookin' ahead, yo' see all the things yo' can do that yo' can't now; but lookin' back, yo' see what's lost. Take each year with what it brings, Gudrun."

"Ma . . ."

"What, mo' questions?" A laugh. "Go ahead, daughter, go ahead. Just remember, fo' yo' own when their favorite word is 'why.'"

"Why do Pa and yo' . . . I mean, I know yo' love each other, so why, ummm—"

"Aha, the wenches. Well, darlin', that's another thing

you'll understand better when yo're older, but . . . it's
like candy and real food. Yo' could live without candy,
fairly easy, but on nothin' but candy yo'd sicken. Nice
to have both, though."

"Why only, well, only wenches, Ma?"

"It isn't," she said frankly. "Fo' men so inclined,
there's prettybucks. Remember what I said about the
Race?" A nod. "Well, women can't mother as many as a
man can father, and it takes a Draka mother to make
Draka, child. Especially since we've other things to do,
like fightin' and helping run the estates and so forth. So
we have to save our wombs fo' the Race's seed." *We'll
leave aside the vexed question of whether contracep-
tion's made the Race Purity laws obsolete, and the even
more vexed question of the primitive male confusion
between penetration and Domination; that's for your
generation to deal with.* "Another thing that pro'bly
won't vex you for a good many years yet." More som-
berly: "When it does, remember, we're like iron, they're
glass; be careful touchin' them, yo' can shatter them
without meanin' to."

Gudrun yawned again, snuggled her head down against
her mother's bosom, squirming into a more comfortable
position. Tanya sat without words for a few minutes,
watching the near-invisible lashes flutter lower, the
near-transparent redhead's eyelids drooping down.

"But what did yo' come runnin' in to ask, my sleepy
baby?"

Another huge yawn, and a near mumble. "Beth said I had
to nap, but I'm too old to take naps in the afternoon, Ma."

"'Course yo' are, honeybunch. Yo' just lie there a
while, and momma'll sing fo' yo'."

Rocking, she began very softly:
*"Hush little baby, doan' yo' cry
Yo' know the spirit was meant
To fly—"*

". . .fiasco in Lyon," someone's voice was saying.
Kustaa pricked up his ears, bending over the gift

table. It was sunset, and the night's entertainment had begun. He glanced at his watch; Ernst and Jules would be in the radio room at 21:30, and for three hours after that. His scheduled transmission time started a half-hour later. Plenty of time, and it would be suspicious in the extreme if he absented himself; he could plead sickness but then his hosts would exercise their *damned* consideration and call for medical help, which he could not afford.

He smiled to himself as he edged nearer to the cluster about Tanya's brother and the Security general. The throat-story was bad enough, making elaborate explanations impossible; sometimes he felt Donovan had outsmarted himself there, the speech training had worked to *some* extent, a more moderate injury would have been better. The head injuries were even worse, because if he played sick they might override his objections to a doctor's examination.

Ah, well.

"Not quite a fiasco, sho'ly," Vashon was saying.

"Since I was there, and jointly responsible, I think I can speak frankly without givin' offense, Strategos. Fiasco I said and meant," Andrew replied.

Kustaa moved down again, past studbooks showing the pedigree livestock among the presents, past a da Vinci and a Cellini saltshaker. There was no formal organization to the viewing; you went and examined young Karl and Alexandra in their cradles, perfectly ordinary looking examples of two-month children, round squashed-looking faces and starfish hands. Then you drifted down along, giving each item the grave attention or amusement or comment it merited; the American took his cues from others. A pair of pistols caught his eye, and he lifted one out of satin lining of the rosewood case.

"We caught a good number of them," Vashon objected.

"Spearchuckers. That bunch is so tightly celled, even they contact-men don't know who their opposite numbers are, they just a voice in the dark."

"So they're claimin', to date."

"Strategos, yo' know as well as I do that it isn't impossible to lie while bein' castrated, blinded and bastinadoed, but it is impossible to lie *well* and *coherently* and *consistently*. We didn't get their leaders, or the American, or the scientist, or the . . . well, yo' know."

Kustaa turned the weapon over in his hands, hiding savage elation as the old oiled metal sheened in the lamplight. It was a six-shot revolver, but with a second barrel under the normal one; a massive weapon, the patterned Damascus steel inlaid with elongated leopards and buck, the butt with plaques of turquoise and ivory. He flipped it up to look at the white-metal plate on the end of the grip. "Le Matt, Virconium, 1870." Back, to examine the barrel. There was a slight pattern of randomly-etched pits around the muzzles; these had been used, and fairly frequently. He reached into the case for two of the cartridges; brass centerfire models, no corrosion so they must be made up to fit the antique. A standard revolver bullet, about .477, and what looked like a miniature shotgun shell. There was a faint smell of gun-oil and brass about the weapon, the patina of another's palm on the grip.

"Cobbler to the last, a fightin' man to weapons," a voice said by his ear. He turned, startled; the speaker was a tall gray-haired man in an Arch-Strategos' uniform. *That* was a rarity; there weren't more than a hundred or so in the Domination.

"Karl von Shrakenberg, Landholder, Arch-Strategos, Supreme General Staff, retired," the man said. Kustaa took his hand and gave the strangled grunt expected of him; another of the eagle faces, but this was an old bird, tired, face scored by years and pain; he moved stiffly, with a limp.

"Sannie von Shrakenberg, Landholder, Strategos, Supreme General Staff, Strategic Plannin', active." Kustaa blinked; the woman looked to be in her forties, a little old for the six-month belly, but it was still disorienting. *Like seeing one of the Joint Chiefs knitting booties*, he thought with a smile. The woman nodded to him again and moved off.

"I knew Charley Stenner, yo' commander," the retired general said. Kustaa turned his start into an appropriate grimace. "Good man, pity that strafin' got him."

Maybe Donovan was right after all, Kustaa thought thankfully. Following two conversations at once was another skill he had been taught; the secret policeman was still arguing.

" . . .*not an irretrievable disaster, in any case*. We were a little ahead of the Yankees on that project, now we're a little behind. Bad loosin' Oerbach, but the basic research is done an' recorded; the plutonium is really unfortunate, bottleneck fo' us and the Alliance both."

"It's the Yankee that sticks in my gullet," Andrew replied. "Much mo' of that and we'll have them runnin' wild. And Corey Hartmann was a friend of mine."

"Agreed. I want a film of him dyin' on the stake. After we've gotten what he knows, of course . . . still, in the long run, we gain mo' from espionage than they do."

Kustaa put the pistol in the general's outstretched hand. The older man snapped the action open with a practiced motion. "Le Matt," he said. "He did his best work in Virconium after the Yankees ran him out of New Orleans; sugar country must have been homelike to him. This was his first swing-out cylinder model, and the last black-powder sidearm authorized for regular use. Best close-quarter weapon of its day." He made another adjustment, and the thicker barrel beneath the main one slid forward. "Buckshot barrel, just the thing fo' a cavalry melee."

"*One thing, I'm glad we've still got his grandchildren*. Nice to have that tricky an' ruthless a set of genes in the Race." Andrew, in a tone of rueful admiration.

"I still say we should hold them ready to use as a lever, should, Loki fo'bid, he surface in Yankeeland." Vashon's voice was neutrally cold.

"No. Primus, he's shown he's ready to sacrifice them fo' principle; secundus, by grantin' Citizenship, we made them part of the Race. With all the protection that my sister's children have, or any other young Draka." Still friendly, but with an icy finality underneath. That would be reassuring to tell Ernst; as far as the OSS knew, the military were still more powerful in the Domination's hierarchy. Of course, the Party was stronger than either of the armed branches . . .

"These were my father's," the old general continued. Kustaa smiled and nodded. "Weddin' present; my mother's parents were Confederates. He carried them in the Northern War." The American racked his brain . . . yes, that was what they called the Anglo-Russian War of 1879–1882; the Draka had saved Britain from ignominious defeat, an important step in their progress to Great Power status.

"See the inset gold notches? Kills. Duels only of course, not countin' war. The last one was the one he remembered best. An Englishman, durin' the stalemate on the Danube. Dam' fool thought a duel was a game, fired in the air." Karl smiled, the warm smile of a man remembering his childhood. "Pa always laughed when he told us how *surprised* the Brit looked when he gut-shot him . . . Honor makin' yo' acquaintance, sir." He replaced the pistol. "Best ever . . . still take them ovah anythin' but a submachine gun . . ."

A liveried servant took stance by the doors that led into the palaestra wing and the stairs to the terrace.

"My masters!" she cried, rapping the staff she carried sharply on the flags. "The banquet awaits you."

"Oh, Poppa, are you sure you can't come?" Solange said, stepping back and turning her head a little to examine herself in the mirror.

How lovely, Jules Lebrun thought. *How much like her mother*. The image twisted with a pain worse than the growing lumps under his ribs, and he smiled to cover it and the tears that threatened his eyes. His daughter was dressed in a long form-fitting gown of platinum sequins, burnished until they glittered in a blinking, continuous shimmering ripple. Her hair hung loose down the length of her back, and thrown over it was a net of gossamer silver wire, the joinings of the mesh marked with tiny blue-white diamonds.

Solange turned to view herself from a different angle; her hands moved down from below her breasts and over her hips. "I look like a *princess*," she said happily, with a smile that highlighted the slight flush on her cheeks.

No, my child, you look like a very expensive toy, Lebrun thought with an aching sadness. The chamber that had been set aside as a dressing room was crowded, the quartet and their instruments, Solange and Yasmin, their friends. It smelled of cigarette smoke, clothes, brandy from the flask one of the musicians was handing around, faintly of the singer's jasmine perfume.

"Ernst is an old friend, child," he said. "Mr. Kenston will be leaving tomorrow"—*actually rather sooner*—"and we will never meet again, probably. I must spend some time with him, while his duties allow."

Solange sighed. He could tell why—only a few privileged house-serfs would be allowed to listen to the entertainment, from below in the courtyard, and she must have wheedled to get him included. Then he saw her cast off the shadow. *Determined to be happy, and allowing nothing to stand in her way*, he knew. She came over and embraced him lightly and he put his arms around her scented and bird-delicate shoulders.

"I love you, Poppa," she said, brushing her cheek against his. "Wish me luck—this could be the most important performance of my career!"

Career? he thought. "I love you too, my child," he whispered. *And it is true. We love our children as we love our country, not because they deserve it but because they are ours, and we must.* Angrily, he felt his weakened body betray him and the tears spill over his eyelids.

"Oh, father, don't be *that* sad, you will have *hundreds* of times to hear me sing!" She straightened, and gave her makeup a last check. "Yasmin, are you ready?"

The other serf girl looked up from her mirror. "Hold yo' horses, Solange-sweet," she said placidly. "Plenty of time." She was dressed in a white-silk fantasia loosely based on an Arab burnoose, a color that set off her crème-caramel looks. Satisfied, she nodded, rose, hummed an experimental note and opened the neck of her garment a trifle more.

"Goin' be some hungry eyes on us tonight," she said complacently, linking arms companionably with Solange.

"Only until we sing. Then they will be lost, and afterwards, it will drive them mad."

They made for the door, the musicians trailing, but it opened before they reached it and Chantal stepped through, followed by Marya.

"Why, hello!" Yasmin said to Chantal, then looked more closely. "Yo' lookin' bettah, honeybunch!" The Frenchwoman flushed at the faces turned toward her, but it was true; still haggard, but neatly groomed and holding herself erect.

Chantal's eyes passed over the serf with blank indifference, fastened feverishly on Jules Lebrun. Yasmin pursed her lips and turned to Solange with a shrug and roll of the eyes that said what-can-I-do more eloquently than words.

Solange's smile and nod to the nun had a trace of good-natured mockery, looking her up and down. "You are also looking . . . well . . . Sister," she said as the two singers passed through the door. "Good night."

Lebrun remained silent after the door closed, glancing warily from the flushed excitement on the young woman's face to the worried concern of his Resistance commander's.

"Well?" he said at last.

"Chantal . . . Chantal, unfortunately, has stumbled across our . . . enterprise, Professor Lebrun. Specifically, she has deduced that Frederi—Mr. Kenston is not what he seems."

"I saw him with you, last night," Chantal said triumphantly. "But *I* wouldn't have been fooled; I saw you all day when you thought you'd have to lie down for him. You hid it but you were looking into the grave. I'm not stupid enough to think you would change so quickly. He is an American, an *ami* agent, is he not? And that 'servant' of his, he is from the nuclear facility—"

"Quiet!" Lebrun said. Marya opened the door again and looked quickly up and down the corridor.

"And I know something that *you* perhaps do not. *Master* Edward mentioned it to that slut Yasmin, while he was violating me the other night. An Alliance submarine was spotted off Nantes just the day before yesterday, and the Draka cannot find it. *That* is how the American and the Boche are to escape. Well, *I am going too!* You thought you could keep me in ignorance, I who was arrested and tortured for Resistance work as well, leave me here to be a beaten drudge and whore, *I am going too.*"

"Oh, Chantal," Marya said softly. There was mourning in her voice, and Lebrun met her eyes with a like sadness. They nodded slightly at each other, one thought in their minds. *She knows too much.*

"Chantal, child of God, believe me, only the American and the scientist are leaving," Marya said. "I swear it by Father, Son and Holy Ghost, on my hope of salvation."

Chantal's fists clenched. "You may stay and be a martyr, I have done enough."

The nun closed her eyes in pain. "As you wish it, Chantal," she said. "We are to send a radio message; then you will come with us to the shelter in Bourgueil, where the . . . courier from the coast will take you to a boating dock, upriver."

Lebrun stiffened in shock, then looked at the sickened, weary face of the Pole and understood; away from the Great House, to where the armed Resistance fight-

ers were. Amid rubble where one more hidden body
would be a little matter. Marya crossed herself and
spoke softly in Latin. Which he understood and Chantal
did not, although he knew he was not the Person she
addressed:

"*And Caiaphas said, is it not expedient that one man
should die for the people?*"

Lebrun replied sharply, in the same language: "*And
if your eye offends you, pluck it out.*"

"Truly," she sighed, crossed and took Chantal's hands
with a smile. "It would be better if you had not tried to
force our hand so, Chantal. So much better. But I
understand, truly, and with all my heart I forgive you."

There was absolute sincerity in her voice, on the
square homely face. Lebrun looked at it and shivered,
knowing it was true, knowing it would be equally true
in the moment Marya pulled the trigger. *God protect
me from the truly righteous,* he thought, then almost
laughed to himself at the unintentional irony. There
were times when he congratulated himself on the sheer
convenience of skepticism.

"Do you understand, *Sister?*" Chantal said, the anger
still in her tone. She disengaged her hands. "What you
were afraid of *happened* to me, over and over, for
weeks, I had to . . . to do . . . and now I'm *pregnant*,"
she spat. "Pregnant by that swine, but I'll never bear it,
never stay here to be a sow farrowing little slaves.
Never."

For a moment Lebrun felt only a detached sympathy.
Then his eyes flashed to Marya's face, appalled, and
saw her go pasty-white beneath her tan. Inwardly he
was cursing himself for the quotation he had chosen,
remembering the first lines of it: Whoso shall offend
one of these little ones . . . it were better for him that a
millstone were hanged about his neck and that he were
drowned in the depths of the sea . . .' Knowing that she
would have thought of it herself, that no argument on
earth short of a direct pronouncement of the Pope
speaking *ex cathedra* would convince her that Chantal

was not carrying a human soul beneath her heart. And that she was as incapable of harming what she considered a blameless child as she was of defiling the Host or committing necrophilia.

Well, the one-time professor of anthropology and ex-soldier thought. His eyes rested on Chantal's triumphant form with detached appraisal. *She's stronger than I am in this state. It will have to be from behind, and quick, before the Sister can intervene. She'll accept it once done.*

Kustaa found himself surprised at how mild the banquet's entertainment was, nothing like the propaganda; of course, this was an important occasion, and a conservative family. The food was good enough that his first concern, how to force enough into a tension-tight belly to avoid being conspicuous, turned out to be misplaced. *Watch it*, old son, he told himself. Not good to be stuffed before action. He looked around the hollow square of tables, snowy linen, the glitter of crystal and silverware and bone china. More formal than the afternoon; the men in dark evening suits with lace stocks or uniforms, the women out of uniform all in draped classical-style gowns that left one shoulder bare.

Light from the globes and from burning crescents hung between, as well; the Draka liked to see what they were eating, not grope by candlelight. Seafood appetizers, soup, fish, a main course of roast suckling pig, salads, vegetables, while the chamber group played soft Mozart and he listened to the conversations; Andrew and Vashon rehashing their efforts to track him down, the female aeronautical engineer at his side explaining the long-term potential of hydrogen-fueled ramjets and lamenting the difficulty of modeling high-speed airflows; the Landholders and their close kin discussing weather and crops in words that might almost have been the ones he grew up among in the rural Midwest.

He raised a glass of wine and pretended to sample the bouquet; in fact, it all smelled and tasted like spoiled grape juice to him, he was strictly a beer-whiskey-and-aquavit man. He noticed nobody was getting more than mildly tipsy, or stoned on the kif that was also on tap. *Well, they are health fanatics to a man,* he mused. It might almost have been a very tony Long Island gathering at home, except for the costumed mime-dancers who enacted the legend of Leda and the Swan. They were dark women, with the bodies of ballerinas; professionals from the older territories, considering the length of time those skills must take to learn. The swan-wings and mask of the one playing Zeus transformed were really lovely, feathers and jewels and delicate goldwork; but then, this was not a society that went in for mass-production of anything but weapons and the cheapest consumer goods; it could afford artisanship.

The dance ended behind a covering of downswept ten-foot wings; the whole done with delicacy rather than gross explicitness, even erotic in a sort of eerie way. He noticed that Vashon had fallen silent to watch it with a burning intensity, and stacked away the datum for the OSS files. The mimes rose, bowed low, ran off in a flutter of feathers and long hair. That was after the tables had been cleared, set with coffee and liqueurs and nuts. Kustaa recognized the singers who came forward next, but was surprised by the sudden silence that fell as they stepped out before the musicians. He did not think it was for their looks, or not mostly; it was simply that they saw no point in having fine music unless they were going to listen.

Tasteful bastards, he thought, inhaling the aroma of the Kenia coffee, this time with genuine appreciation. *May they rot in hell.*

"My masters," Solange said with a graceful curtsy. "For your pleasure, we shall present a duet from the opera *Lakme,* by Delibes, with modified string and woodwind accompaniment of my own adaptation."

Kustaa had never enjoyed classical opera much; too many fat ladies in odd clothes screeching. Despite the valiant attempts of his mother, who had a dogged self-improving Scandinavian regard for capital-C culture, and Aino, who had dragged him to a fair number in New York after they moved to the capital. The Frenchwoman stepped forward and opened her mouth, and the OSS agent prepared for yet another run-through of the thousand ways the extraction could go wrong. Sound wove its way through the threads of his mind, unraveling. His eyes opened in shock, to see a face transformed into something beyond beauty, a purity of self-absorption as complete as the music that poured effortlessly from that quivering throat, wove around the deeper notes of the other voice, returned . . .

He blinked himself back to awareness as Solange and Yasmin walked the circuit of the table, hand in hand, bowing and flushing at the long sharp ripple of applause. Some of the guests even rose to clap as they went by, and a standing ovation was not something Draka did casually. At last the two came to the head table before their owners; there they sank gracefully to their knees and made the full bow, palms before eyes. The clapping continued, louder, directed to the Landholders now, congratulating them on possessions beyond price. *What a waste*, Kustaa thought angrily as the singers and musicians withdrew. *What a total, fucking waste*. It was obscene, far more than the unclothed dancers.

A deep breath, and another; he would have to listen to the first of the after-dinner speakers, at least. It was the retired Field-Marshal who rose, propping a cane against his chair. There was a murmur from the tables, then silence once more; he stood for a moment scanning them thoughtfully, a steady appraising stare.

"I am the eldest von Shrakenberg present," he said abruptly. "As we're here to celebrate the reinforcement of the Race by two of the youngest, it's appropriate that I speak." A smile. "Although I can't promise to be as melodious as what we've just heard." There was laughter, and a general settling-in rustle.

"I was born," the elderly Draka continued, "in 1882.

This would be a good occasion to reflect on the changes my lifetime has seen . . . When I received my commission, the Domination was still officially the *Dominion* of the Draka; part of the British Empire. We ruled all of Africa, but no more; the British still thought of us as a subject-ally. Europe," he added with a shark's smile, "was just beginnin' to worry about us. Many of the institutions yo're all familiar with were in their infancy; I can remember when the thought of women bearin' arms would have seemed fantastical. Why, I can remember old men usin' 'white' and 'black' as synonyms fo' Citizen and serf. A different world."

The scored eagle face swept around the tables. "*Now* everythin' since seems . . . inevitable. I can tell yo', we didn't think so at the time! We were afraid of the Europeans, fo' example. No, don't look shocked, it's fact. They were all openly set on subvertin' our institutions, *and they were stronger than us*. We were afraid." A grin. "The Yankees were just a cloud on the horizon. There were those, Draka among them, who thought our overthrow was just a matter of time. And they had a good case, on purely logical grounds.

"We all know what happened in the Great War; I was blown up over Constantinople, makin' it happen." He slapped the stiffened leg. "We saw our enemies' weakness, and we struck. *Then* words like 'world conquest' and 'Final Society' started to look more credible. The mo' sober worried that we'd be drunk with success, with victory disease. Europe was still the stronger, if only it would unite against us, despite the vast conquests we made. Japan, Germany, Russia threatened our new northern and eastern borders.

"And . . ." he held up his hands. "Here we stand, in the heart of Europe, here in France. Where are the children of the men who befo' 1914 calmly sat to debate how 'enlightenment' and 'reform' would be forced on the primitive Draka, how they could bring us 'democracy'? In graves from here to China, workin' in our fields and kitchens, laborin' in mines and factories to

build our power, singin' fo' our pleasure after this excellent dinner, and"—he crooked a sardonic eyebrow at
the owners of the plantation—"servin' pleasure in . . .
other capacities. Soon enough, fightin' and dyin' fo' us.
Doesn't this seem like the unfoldin' of Destiny, the
sacred destiny of the Race?

"Horseshit!!" The speaker's fist crashed down, and
Kustaa saw startlement replace bored agreement on
many faces. "We won because we were tough, and
prepared . . . because we were *lucky* enough to have
enemies who'd fight each other rather than us. This
land here is already a breedin'-ground fo' Draka; I
won't make the usual tiresome references to the repro-
ductive habits of digger wasps. If yo' young people plan
to extend *their* Domination, yo'll have to be *twice* as
tough, *twice* as disciplined as we were. *We can still lose
it all*. Never forget that, *never*. Every day we live, we
live on the edge of oblivion. It's up to yo', the young.
Rule or die, kill or be killed, *crush or be crushed*.
Always on guard fo' opportunity, takin' what we can,
never relinquishin' an inch.

"Destiny is what we make it. *Service to the State!*"

The guests came to their feet in a sustained roar.

"Glory to the Race!" It crashed out like thunder,
broke into a spontaneous chant that lasted for minutes
before dying out into self-conscious laughter and a rising buzz of conversation once more.

Short and to the point, Kustaa thought behind his
grin, looking up at the lights in the upper room of the
tower. *Let's see how you like being on the receiving
end, you evil old bastard*. He had a perfect excuse, too.
One hour more, and he could call. He rose, bowed to
the center of the head table. Tanya von Shrakenberg's
head came up, and returned the gesture with a wave.

"A good evenin' to yo', Mr. Kenston," she said. "Just
tellin' Uncle Karl here that he should go into politics,
but some things are even mo' urgent, eh?" Slyly: "And
don't let her convert yo'."

Good-natured laughter followed him. He smiled, nodded as he walked toward the glass wall on the inner side of the terrace. For a moment he halted beneath, stared up at the glowing backlit shape of the Drakon. *Fuck you, snake*, he thought, and pushed through. Behind him, the lambent yellow eyes stared sightless out over the darkened fields.

The sounds of the waters outside her hull were the loudest things that could be heard in the control center of the *Benito Juarez*. Whale-song, mysterious clicks and pings and creaks. Occasionally the distant throbbing of engines, once or twice the hard ringing of a sound-detection scanner.

"2100," the horse-faced OSS controller said.

The captain nodded to a tech-5 at a console. "Up buoy, stand by to monitor," he said softly. Theoretically a normal speaking voice was no threat, but pigboaters had a superstitious reverence for "silent running," and the attitude of mind was one valuable enough to encourage. The man nodded, depressed a switch.

Guzman strained his ears, but only imagination could supply the sound of the float inflating, rising out through the flooded hatchcover, rising with its spool of wire paying out carefully behind. Breaking surface with an inaudible splash, invisibly black against black water, no more metal than the cable itself and so near-invisible to electrodetectors, nothing for their microwaves to reflect from. Not much risk; the quick throbbing of destroyer screws had not been heard since they settled to the bottom.

The radio operator clamped on his headset, twisted dials. Time passed; Guzman brought out a stick of mint-flavored chicle, offered it to the agent, grinned to himself as the man refused with a repressed shudder. Not a *gringo* custom, but more comfortable for a submariner than tobacco; although he had to admire the way the *yanqui* waited without a twitch as the minutes dragged, most of the bridge watch were fidgeting and glaring at the unfortunate able-seaman like buzzards around a dying donkey. The captain himself planned to turn in as usual when his watch ended; this would be the first vigil of many.

Time passed. Guzman looked at his watch: 21:15. Ten more minutes until—

"Contact," the radioman whispered. "Contact on the assigned frequency, sir."

The OSS man crossed to the radioman's seat in two strides, took the headphones and listened; his face was still impassive, but the blue lights glistened across the wet skin of his forehead. His right hand went out, and the operator shoved the pad and pencil beneath it. He jotted without looking down, waited.

"They're repeating," he said. "Prepare to send confirmation."

The operator looked up at Guzman, unconsciously touching his tongue to his lip. The dark officer took the wad of chicle out between thumb and forefinger, considered it for an instant. *Now* the danger began. *The jaguar is in the jungle*, he thought.

"Do it, sailor," he said calmly, and replaced it, chewing stolidly.

The OSS man took the microphone, spoke slowly and distinctly. "The caa is in the paaak," he said, just once. A slow smile spread over his mouth as he looked up at Guzman.

"Two men and a treasure-chest coming back, Captain," he said in his nasal Bay State twang.

Guzman surprised himself; he saluted, and took the agent's hand. "He is a man, that one," he said quietly; then thought of this dry stick of a spy flying low and slow up the Loire, over the Domination's defenses, landing with nothing more than a sidearm and risking capture by a people to whom mercy was scarcely even a word. "And so are you."

To the exec: "Number two, maintain silent running drill; all hands to action stations, prepare to take her up." Ten minutes on the surface, to unpack and launch the bird. Two hours waiting at periscope depth for the return, and then the hideous risk of a radio beacon. *We're all going to be*, he thought. *Or dead.*

"Nobody here!" Solange sang, as she and Yasmin came out onto the terrace. The lights had been extinguished and the tables stripped; shadows washed across the yellow marble of the floor, and the air had begun to take on the cool spicy smell of late night in the dog days of summer. The Frenchwoman sang again, a wordless trill, and danced out into the open space, whirling the other serf by the hands until she pulled them to a halt, laughing herself in dizzy protest.

"They *loved* us, me, wheee!" Solange sang again, giggling. "Did you *hear* them applaud, did you see their *faces*, Mistress says I'll be in demand for appearances all up and down the *river*, maybe she'll even send me to the *city* for more training, maybe even to *Archona*, and they'll make *recordings*." She spun, arms high. "And I'll perform before the Archon, and people will offer Mistress *millions* for me and she'll laugh at them!"

"Solange, honeybunch, yo' drunk an' on more than wine 'n smoke. Calm down, maybeso it happen that way an' maybeso no—mmmmmmph!"

Solange had stopped her mouth with a kiss, and when she released her Yasmin was laughing again herself.

"That nice," she said. "But I've got anothah engagement, Solange-darlin', an' he impatient. See yo' t'morrow, and doan' dance the *whole* night away."

Yasmin left, and Solange laughed more quietly; she began dancing by herself, singing wordlessly under her breath, until she saw the glow of a cigarette-tip by the far end of the terrace, froze for a moment, then walked forward swaying toward the white outline of Tanya's gown.

"Don't let me stop the celebratin'," the Draka said. "You deserved it, Solange." She was leaning back against the angle where the head table met its neighbors, one hand under the other arm and the free fingers holding the cigarette. "I really may look into that trainin', that voice deserves to live."

"It was all for you, Mistress," Solange crooned softly, when they were at arm's length. "I was doing it all for you, couldn't you see it? I could feel your eyes on me, warm like hands." Her own eyes were wide, the pupils swollen until the violet color was a rim around pools of black, her voice slurred and husky. "Everything I am and do is yours, mistress. Everything."

Very true, Tanya thought happily. *But still nice to have it so enthusiastically volunteered*. The serf's swaying made her platinum sheath quiver in the night like a candle-flame of moonlight. *You are a treasure Solange, an absolute treasure*. She smiled, shivering slightly at the expression in the other's eyes, abasement and exaltation. *So much beauty, so much intelligence and talent and skill, and you are* mine.

"Oh, mistress, you give me so much, make me so happy," the serf said. "How can I thank—*oh!*" She giggled again. "Don't move, mistress, stay right there, I know just the thing." She skittered off, returned in an instant with a cushion from one of the chairs, dropped it at Tanya's feet.

"A cushion?" Tanya said. Solange was playfully crazy even when sober, but wild on wine and kif . . .

"*Mais non*, the cushion is for me, mistress, these flags are hard." Her open mouth was moist as she leaned forward to press a quick kiss on her owner's, and she smiled slyly as she dropped to her knees on the padded cloth. "I am for you, Tanya."

The Draka looked around for a moment to make sure they were truly private; it was dark . . . *Hell with it*, she decided. *Why not*. The cigarette made a minor meteor as she flicked it away over the railing and leaned back, resting her weight on her palms. *There goes my little half-hour chat with Tantie Sannie about the trials of childbirth, oh well, tomorrow*. She let her head loll upward; that brought the dim light of the tower's highest room to view.

Damnation, she thought with a frown, as Solange lifted the fabric of her skirt and tucked the front hem neatly into her belt. *We are visible from the radio room*. Not that that would bother her normally; serfs did not count much when it came to privacy, but Jules Lebrun was up there tonight, and making him watch this would be the sort of pointless cruelty she despised.

Tanya looked down; Solange was rolling down her left stocking with elaborate slowness, planting light kisses on the leg as it was exposed. The soft moist sensation was unbearable, and the singer was humming as she worked. *On the other hand, he can always look out the other window at the pavilions*.

"God, I though't I'd never get away," Kustaa muttered as he pushed in from the tube-like spiral stairwell; the efforts of the other partygoers to make the cripple feel wanted had been as entangling as glue-covered bunji cords. The radio-room door was a blank steel sheet like the armory one story below, but not locked in the normal course of things. He halted outside the panel; there was a murmur of voices from within. According to plan, then.

The American halted, drew his automatic and took in a deep breath. A glance at his watch: 23:30, right after the plantation's scheduled call-in, no alarm until the next was missed in four hours. The stairwell was redolent of old stone, with a faint underlying tang of ozone from the electronic equipment within; cables in metal conduits ran up the walls beside him, new metal and brackets drilled and bolted to the ancient tufa ashlars. This was the turning-point, the step that could not be taken back. He shook his head; that was cowardice speaking, as stupidly as it always did, the desire to buy safety for a few more hours or days at the expense of real escape after a brief risk. He firmed his lips and pushed open the door.

A square room, the size of his bedroom. Brightly lit, naked overhead fluorescent tubes. Small square windows facing east and north. Metal tables bolted to the walls, and banks of equipment: telephone switchboard, short-wave set, teletype. Five people: Ernst and Jules sitting stony-faced over a chessboard, Sister Marya, Chantal—*what in God's name is she doing here*—a nameless ordinary-looking serf with his back to the door, sitting in a swivel-chair and speaking to the nun.

"I know the visitor's boy is authorized up here to play chess with Jules, Sister, but you and the other lady will have to—"

"Don't look around," Kustaa said in French, in the flat emotionless voice that intimidated so much better than screaming. His hand had locked in the serf's hair, drawing his head to one side until the muscles creaked. The agent reached around to waggle the muzzle of the automatic in front of his eyes, just in case, then put it in his ear.

"One sound and you're all dead," he said for the watch-stander's benefit. "Down on the floor, hands behind your heads, *move*. Not you," he added, checking a scrambling movement to exit the chair and the hard cold metal grinding into an ear.

"Don't kill me," the man blubbered, but enough in control not to shout. "Please, Master, I'll—"

"This is the Resistance," Kustaa said. The man started violently.

"Oh, God, no, please, go *away*, you'll get us all killed, they'll impale us all, our families, *please*—"

"Shut up." You never knew what twisted paths courage might take, even in a rabbit like this. "I'm going to let go your hair. Keep your head pointed the same way or I'll blow your brains all over the wall."

Trembling silence, while Kustaa unclenched his left hand from the man's scalp and used it to pull the hypodermic from his pocket. The serf started once when the American plunged it home, then slumped.

"Out for hours," he said, as Marya rose and scrambled across to lay the man straight and peel back an eyelid for a check. The agent tossed her a roll of adhesive tape, and she began to bind the unconscious form,

hands and ankles, strips across mouth and eyes. Kustaa
dropped the hypo by his side. It was Domination-
standard with his own fingerprints on it. All that *should*
spare the bystander from anything too gruesome; serfs
were expected to surrender meekly to force. If not . . .

Toughski shitski, as they say in the Polish Marines,
Kustaa thought, gleeful under the hammering pulse of
action. His movements were crisp and controlled as he
sat before the shortwave set.

"What the hell is *she* doing here, Sister?" he asked as
he turned the dials, calling up the settings before the
eye of memory. His head jerked towards Chantal, as he
set pistol the pistol by his right hand and propped the
battle-shotgun by the chair.

"She is with us," the nun said, rising and coming to
lean beside him. Swiftly and very quietly, in German:
"She is the communist from my cell; she saw us together and guessed what you are. Be careful, we must
get her to the cave, the master has been forcing her and
she is pregnant and it has driven her . . . wild, she
thinks you can take her out and will not listen to reason."

"English or French!" Chantal hissed. "Don't think
I'm stupid. If I suspect you, I will scream."

The settings were as correct as he could make them,
and this was a big military-issue set, powerful enough
to punch messages across continents. He took up the
microphone, giving the young Frenchwoman a single
hard glance. *Par for the course*, always something to
fuck up at the last minute, he thought. There was a
certain detached pity in it, the girl looked close to the
edge, but . . . *Mission first, buddies second, your own
ass third and bystanders a distant fourth*, he quoted to
himself, the unofficial rule-of-engagement the Marine
assault battalions had operated by.

"Break, four-seven, four-seven," he began, repeating
it half a dozen times. You had to believe they were
listening, that no electromagnetic freak was damping it
out so that they got static and a ham operator in Patagonia
picked it up loud and clear.

"This is loganberry"—Donovan's perverse sense of humor again—"loganberry, with a friend, repeat, with a friend and a Christmas package. A package as big as two loganberries." The extraction aircraft wasn't very fast, but at least they'd factored in a wide margin on lift. "Co-ordinates follow." He read them off. "A grassy path bordered by light, repeat, a grassy path bordered by light." Let whoever they'd sent wonder how he'd gotten a marked runway for them. "Over."

He lifted his thumb from the send button and waited, suddenly conscious of sweat soaking his cotton jacket beneath the arms, crawling greasily out from around the rim of his hair; a hand squeezing up under his lungs. One broadcast might not catch some monitor's attention, but . . .

Hiss. Crackle. Wavering hints of words, spillover, this was close to a commercial frequency, an unused bit of bandwidth in a crowded neighborhood. Then: "The caa is in the paaak."

Kustaa grunted in sheer relief, suppressed euphoria; this was no time for it. He pulled out the yellow-edged Pan-Domination Map for the region, confirmed his earlier estimate. "ETA, not long, it's a good little aircraft," he said. "Hit that light."

He looked up, saw that the northern window that overlooked the terrace was shuttered, the one the Resistance people could see through the periscope. "What the fuck—sorry, Sister."

"I have heard soldiers before, Frederick," she said, rising to open it and giving Jules Lebrun's shoulder a silent squeeze on the way. "This is a battle."

The lights flickered three times, three times again. "Now, let's go—" he began, rising.

And there was a scream from the door, long and loud. Kustaa whipped around so quickly that the swivel-chair nearly dumped him on the floor, time slowing like treacle as he clawed up the pistol and staggered into some imitation of a crouch. The singer, the one from the banquet, standing in the doorway in some sort of pajama outfit, eyes wide and drawing breath to scream again. Chantal directly in his line of fire. His own legs driving, throwing him to one side, left hand slapping out for a breakfall, *too late too late*—

"Get the fuck out of the way!" he yelled, trying to get off one shot, but the girl was collapsing backwards; Chantal was standing with her mouth an O of surprise.

The face vanished as the girl threw herself back; there had been only the single scream, but he could hear the sound of tumbling and running footsteps going down that narrow stone corkscrew. *God, a single woman's scream is nothing here, if she just goes to ground we can still make it*—

"Quickly," Marya said. "Quickly, she will go straight to the mistress, *quickly*."

"Three lights!" Henri said, and slapped up the handles of the periscope. Ybarra and Jean sprang to their feet and snatched up their sacks. "You two, down to the cars; I'll get the lights. *Allons, mes enfants!*"

There was a smile on Henri's face as he led the charge out the opened door of the shelter, and up the short length of tunnel, and hurtled the green steel box they had placed on the lip where excavation met pavement. It would be quicker to load that way, and besides, being in the same room with it made even Henri nervous.

Moaning, Solange tumbled out of the stairwell into a main corridor; it was dimly lit, and for a moment she nearly screamed again, in panic at not knowing where she was. Blood was trickling salt-musky from her nose, and one eye was almost swollen shut where her fall had driven her face against the stone. She moaned again, seeing the horror of the room, the man bound, the gun coming up toward her, its black pit turning toward *her*, and father sitting there, looking at her, doing nothing while the gun came up to kill her, kill *her* . . .

She shook her head, whimpered at the pain but

almost welcomed it as her thoughts cleared. Tanya, she must get to Tanya at once, get out of this nightmare, get to safety. Hugging her bruised arm to her side, she limped down the corridor, tears of pain running down through the sheeted blood on her face, not conscious of speaking aloud.

"My God, Poppa, how could you, how could you betray me again, Poppa, Tanya help me, everything was so nice, Poppa, why did you spoil it—"

Figures, looking at her, jumping aside. House servants, common ones, asking questions. She ignored them, they could not help her, nobody but Tanya could help her. The door, the dear familiar bedroom, her pallet and nook, nobody *there*. *It isn't fair, it isn't fair, where is she, she must be here, she said she had to get to bed, the hunt tomorrow*—For a full minute Solange could only stand and stare, willing the empty bed full, seeing Tanya rising with concern and comfort, making the whole nightmare go *away*.

The Master. She must be with the Master. Panting through her mouth, Solange turned and plunged back into the corridor. *She must be.*

"Keep up, damn you!" Ybarra hissed. *That damned Jean, falls on his ass without a pavement under his feet*, she thought. There was ample moonlight for running, here with nice clear tracks between the vine-trellises. Easy compared with darkness in the hills above the Ebro, waiting to ambush the Fascist supply convoys. Her hand gripped the knife-hilt more tightly. It had been amazing how soft, how cooperative, how eager to please the toughest Fascist prisoner had become, when she showed him what she could do with the knife.

Jean got to his feet, brushing at the machine-pistol across his chest, clearing the sandy dirt from the action; he was still panting from the run down the long slope. Ybarra jerked him down into a crouch.

"The car-park is just beyond those trees," she said. It was actually a pasture, pressed into service for the celebration. "We'll go down to the end of the vineyard, low and quick. Through together to the first vehicle, they're parked in rows. You cover me, three cars behind, and I'll plant the little bomblets." A thumb-sized piece of plastique and a chemical detonator for each, not precision timers but reliable and good enough for this work. She sniffed the air; nothing but the rich damp earth-smell of this place, so different from the hard dry odors of her native Asturias, the bleak arid hills and the mining towns. A moment's fierce nostalgia siezed her, fueled her rage again. Asturias was no more, all the blood spilled in the uprisings against the mine-owners and the victorious war against the Fascist generals, wasted.

No sounds, except for night-birds and those accursed rasping crickets. No lights, except from the manor and the tents in its immediate grounds.

"Forward, Jean," she said.

"Why not you?" he replied. There was an unpleasant note in his voice, and her eyes narrowed. Perhaps his nerve had broken, that happened sometimes, men just ran out of whatever it was that kept them going. As well to remind him that there was no retirement from the Resistance.

"Because I have an uneasy feeling you might drop too far behind, *maricón*," she said, letting the honed edge of the knife show for a second; it was not blackened, like the rest of the metal. She could see his adam's-apple bob up and down. "And if this behind you makes you uneasy, Jean, *comrade*, remember I've never yet cut a man's throat unless I intended to."

Kill her now? Jean thought, fingering the trigger of the machine-pistol. *No, she's too close.* He shuddered, remembering again the sound the overseer had made. This one had eyes like a master, hard and flat and you were nothing, not even a cockroach . . . no, among the cars would be better.

Tanya sighed, and squeezed her husband's hand. *How nice just to lie here and talk over the day*, she thought drowsily. *Just the two of us, no distractions—*

The door to Edward von Shrakenberg's bedroom burst open, and Solange stumbled through. Tanya shot bolt upright; the serf's face was a mask of blood and bruise all down the left side, one eye a slit in the blue-shining swelling, and she was clutching at an arm whose fingers were limp. A low moaning trickled from her lips, turning to a sob of relief as she wavered toward the bed.

"Shit," Edward said with quiet anger and rolled out of bed and onto his feet, reaching for clothes and gunbelt. A flick turned the lights from dim to bright, and the serf looked even more ghastly then; Tanya was by her side immediately, an arm supporting-guiding her to a chair.

"Who did this?" she said, with low deadliness. *Somebody's going to die for this*, ran through her with cold conviction. Her fingers probed gently but irresistibly. No broken bones, the arm was just badly bruised; painful, but it looked worse than it was. Solange's arms shot up with an anaconda grip around the Draka's shoulders, and she began to cry hysterically.

"Who *did* this?" Tanya asked more firmly, nostrils flaring at the scent of blood and fear-sweat, overpowering the familiar cologne and musk of Edward's room. Solange gave a muffled cry, raised her head, jerked back a little in involuntary terror at the expression on the face of the Draka who held her.

"I'm not angry at yo', sweetlin'. Now, *tell* me." Firm but not loud . . . *Wotan's spear, if it's that swine Vashon, I'll call him out and gut-shoot the serfborn bastard.* Solange was far too well trained to have offered any provocation that would remotely justify this; even if somebody had the gall to ignore courtesy and take her, she would have submitted and complained later. This was wanton brutality for its own sake. "I don't let anybody treat my own like this, Solange. Was it Vashon?"

"No!" The serf shook her head, winced, continued. "It was that Kenston, the mute."

Tanya felt her face go slack with surprise. *Kenston,*

she thought incredulously. You could tell a serf-abuser, they showed it by a thousand mannerisms; Kenston she would have pegged as the type to spoil with sentimentality.

"He . . . he tried to *kill* me, Mistress, I went up to say good night to Poppa, to tell him how beautiful it was when I sang, and . . . and Raoul, they had him *tied up*, Chantal and . . . and Master Kenston, I screamed and . . . and Master Kenston tried to take his gun and, and *shoot* me and, and—"

"*Chantal?*" Edward bellowed, halting in the middle of stamping his foot into a boot.

Solange flinched, closed her good eye and continued in a breathless gabble. "Oh, it was horrible, there were Chantal and Marya and Poppa and the German and Master Kenston and they had Raoul tied up and they were talking—" She stopped, took a deep shuddering breath, visibly forced control. The eye came open again, and when she spoke her voice was shaking but coherent.

"Master Kenston was talking. Really talking. Like . . . like an American."

"Shit." This time it was Tanya who spoke. Edward's hand was flashing to the glass-covered alarm plate above the bed; there was a crunch, but not the expected shrilling of bells. Tanya lowered the bedside telephone in the same instant. "Out," she said. "Not even a tone." Which meant the lines were cut.

"Uprisin'?" Edward said bleakly.

"No. Smells wrong. Somethin' we weren't even meant to know about fo' a while." Aside: "Solange, yo' did well. Very well. Now, shut up." To her husband. "All right, twenty adults here overnight. Fifteen arms-bearers." That was not counting the crippled, very aged or severely pregnant. "Personal arms only." A hard mutual grin: the armory was just below the radio room, presumably in enemy hands. "It's night." Edward nodded; that made her commander, a one-eyed man was at a serious disadvantage without light.

Tanya had been pulling on trousers and shirt from a wardrobe as she spoke; several of her outfits were always here. "Edward, yo' collect the guests. We've got to collect an' guard the youngsters." Too much of the future of the Race was at stake, their own blood not least. "Once that's done, able-bodied an' any licensed armed servants assemble *inside the main gates*." Sheltered from possible snipers in upper windows. "Tom was in the armory, right? I'll scout there first, try an' make contact." The ex-janissary's loyalty also went without saying. "Let's *do* it, love, let's *go*."

Tanya hit the door running, ignoring the man behind her; she would not have married one she did not trust. A break-roll, looking both ways, painfully conscious of the light weight of the little 9mm Togren in her hand; it was the sort of token gun a citydweller in the Police Zone kept . . . down the corridor, vision hopping in a methodical skitter, another bubble of rage at having to go combat-mode in her own *home*, suppress it, count doors, *this* was Issac's.

She wrenched it open and slapped the light-plaque without ceremony. The narrow cubicle lit, and Issac rolled off his wife, reaching automatically with his good arm for the pistol he had been issued after the ambush this spring crippled a shoulder.

"Bushman trouble," she said.

"*Scheisse!*" he said, reaching for his clothes, throwing a rapid stream of Yiddish over his shoulder to the girl who sat with growing alarm on her face, pulling the sheet up around her as if that was a defense.

"'Zactly. Main entranceway, *fast*."

Back into the hall, swift cautious zigzag from cover to cover. Tom was in the armory; a good man, but he'd've been drinking tonight, it was traditional . . . *Freya, I hope he's all right*, she thought, then ground the words out of her brain. No time for words, hope, fear, anything but the automatic reflexes of war. She had a household to defend.

Behind her, unseen, Solange hesitated in the doorway, staggered, put her hand to her head. It *hurt*; somewhere she was conscious that she must have a concussion, things were showing double. She wavered again; she could shut the door, back there in the room. Shut it and wait for it to swing open again, the gun, like before, smashing glass and laughter and pain . . . *No*. The mistress, I must follow her. There is safety.

"*Fuck it!*" Kustaa hissed in frustration. The radio room had turned from a fortress into a killing box in a few seconds. His hands were on the levers of the junction-box, slamming them down into the "off" positions, insurance, a few extra seconds. "Come on, let's go."

"No," Jules Lebrun said. "I will stay, and disable the equipment." A smile. "There is no time to argue, and I am a dying man anyway. Cancer will give me pain even the Security Directorate cannot rival, and I will not be taken alive. Go!"

". . . an' then we pulled back to th' mosque," Tom rumbled, pleasantly aware of the glow of admiration on the face of Yasmin as she sat at his feet, arms wrapped around her knees. His wife Annette was a good wench, but she didn't appreciate a good story the way his daughter did. "Jus' five a' us lef', no officers, rag-heads a' yellin' an' screamin', hundreds of 'em. They din' know we wuz five *devil dogs*, 'n pissed as hell."

The armory about him was dim, the racked weapons and boxes of ammunition shadowy backdrops to his memory; the honest smell of his own sweat staining the thin cotton undershirt across his chest, beer and gun-oil and steel. Memories of warm nights in barracks and the casern, all his old friends, strong young men, laughter and dice, drink and the laughing friendly whores. He took another pull at the beer and belched, feeling a familiar humming in his ears. *How many?* Twenty, or only ten? Fuck it. 'Nuff storytellin', time to get back home and give Annette another youngun. He wasn't *that* old.

He dropped his hand to Yasmin's curls, opened his

mouth to speak. A scream interrupted him, loud even through the steel door, and *close*.

"Wha'?" he said, his chin rising from his chest. "Wha' that?"

Yasmin was on her feet. "Poppa!" she said urgently. "That Solange, it came from that-there radio room." Puzzlement fought with alarm on her slender features.

Tom lurched to his feet, waving her vaguely back. "Y' pretty fren'?" he said with bewilderment. "Wha' she doin' here?"

He walked to the door and pushed it open, glancing around. A slight hint of light and voices from upstairs, but nothing out of the ordinary. Tom shook his head, rubbed his hard-callused palms across his face. There was something wet on the step, at chest level, too dark to see color, only a blackness that glistened. He touched, raised his fingers to nose, lips. Utterly familiar, in a way that began to wash the fumes of alcohol out of his brain.

"Blood," he said wonderingly. "Gotsta' see whut happenin,'" he muttered, and began to climb.

This place is turning into a shitty railroad station, Kustaa thought disgustedly as the door swung open again. A conscious effort kept his trigger-finger loose. The last thing they needed was the sound of a firefight breaking out. Worth the time to gag and tie whoever it was.

A black. Big man, bigger than Kustaa, fifties, balding. Heavy muscle well padded with fat, beer belly and a bottle of beer clutched like a miniature in one ham-sized fist. Stained white T-shirt and baggy olive-green pants, splayed bare feet . . . eyes bloodshot and puzzled and mild in the heavy-featured African face.

"Silence," Kustaa barked. "Come in, lie down, put your hands behind your head."

The other great hand slowly squeezed shut into a fist, and the eyes were still bloodshot but anything but mild, thick lips drawn back from strong yellow teeth.

"Yaz no mastah!" he said in wonderment, glance darting to the bound form of Raoul.

"Janissary, *kill him!*" Chantal shouted, but Kustaa had seen too many fighting-men to need the warning; his finger was tightening even before the man finished speaking. The 10mm bucked in his hand, three shots merging into one, echoes in the small stone room, three soft-nosed slugs blasting into the black's solar plexus no more than a hand's width apart. The last so close the thin fabric of his shirt was crisped and singed, and that was the one that stopped him, stopped the bull bellow and huge hands reaching to kill.

Yasmin followed, and stood looking with utter disbelief at the heavy body lying jerking at her feet, blood pouring from overlapping exit wounds in the small of his back, a raw cavity bigger than her paired fists full of shattered bone splinters and things that glistened and moved. The dark girl's hands came up one on either side of her face, pressing palm-in as if to drive the knowledge out of her skull.

"Poppa?" she said, in a tiny voice, sinking down by his side. "Poppa?" A small shriek, and she was tearing at her clothing, shoving the scraps into the impossible gaping wound.

"Poppa, doan' die, doan' die, poppa, *please*, I love yo', poppa, doan' die, *please*—" She abandoned the hopeless effort and threw herself on his chest, clutching at his shoulders. "No, poppa, no!"

Kustaa turned his head; one of the others would know how to quiet her. That shift saved his life, Yasmin's clumsy thrust with her father's belt-knife scoring along the American's ribs down to the bone rather than sinking into his belly. Then she was a blur of white cloth and brown arms and heavy razor-edged steel, hacking with a berserker frenzy that lacked only knowledge to make it instantly deadly. Kustaa shouted, again as the edge jammed into his shoulder, clubbing frantically with the pistol as he tried to bring it round close enough to bear at pointblank.

"Yo' killed my poppa! Yo' killed my poppa!" Intolerably shrill, almost a squeal.

Christ, she's going to kill me! ran through him as he blocked and struck with elbows, knees, bone-shattering strikes but she would not *stop*, it's my own bloody fault shitshitshit—

The muzzle of his battle-shotgun reached around him and shoved itself into Yasmin's stomach. Chantal pulled the trigger, and the explosion was muffled by flesh and cloth. The result was not; the slender body of the serf girl catapulted back over the swivel-chair and struck the ground already limp. The Frenchwoman stepped over to the dead serf, looked down into the blood-spattered face frozen in eternal surprise.

"Bitch," she said in a voice that cracked, and retched dryly. The floor was running-wet, like a bathroom where the sink has overflowed. Or the toilet, for it stank, of salt, shit, the raw chemical smell of burnt propellant.

The scent of glory, Kustaa thought as he forced himself straight, vision returning after the grayness of shock; he felt the same brief irrational disbelief that always came after being wounded, compounded of *so fast!* and *I was all right just a second ago!* Neither ever helped . . . a long cut on the ribs, stab in the shoulder, superficial slashes, bleeding but no arteries cut, he could keep going for a little longer, he *had* to keep going.

"Come on," he said, and plunged down the stairwell. The others followed, all but Lebrun stone-faced before the radio and the bound and unconscious Raoul. Into the armory, across to the window that latched from the inside, only three feet down onto the low-pitched slate roof. He and Ernst helped the women through, and he gave the Austrian a tight smile.

"Not doing badly," he said.

"I fought on the Italian front in the Great War," he said. "It is nothing I have not seen before." He helped Kustaa through in turn.

*   *   *

Whore, filthy whore, Jean thought, frantically. There had been no opportunity, not down all the dozen cars and vans, not until now. The fuel tanks of the last two autosteamers were underslung, and Ybarra had to drop to her back and crawl beneath. *Now!* His finger began to close on the trigger, he could feel the cool metal against his skin and the tiny slack and the muscle would not close. It was very surprising, the way his head and body did not work the way they should, why couldn't he pull the trigger he hated her, she was going to put him back in the chair with his father screaming around the gag, pleading and—

whitenoisenothoughtnothought

Kill her, kill her, the Master will reward you. But the finger would not close, and if he did not then it would be Marie-Claire, bending over the block while the giant—

whitenoisenothoughtnothought and he could feel his arms and legs start to shake, and tears were running down his face. The clicking started again behind his eyes, but this time there was no sharp clarity of thought, nothing but the noise inside his head growing louder and louder, hissing like the sea. It reached a peak and he thought he would have to scream, to cry out to God for pity, for relief, but he knew that was nonsense, there was no pity and no mercy and pain was the only thing that was forever.

Jean turned, the machine-pistol dangling in his hand, turned and walked south. Not running until he was too far away for even Ybarra to catch, then at a shambling pounding trot; whitenoise was almost continuous now, but that was good, it kept the visions from his eyes, memories and fears, all too terrible to be borne. Vision came in glimpses, and thought; the Schmeisser dropping nerveless from his fingers in a field, they would shoot him down on sight, a strange serf with a forbidden weapon. The gardens at last, he was too far east, east of the house; everything was quiet, and he almost ran into the man standing fifty meters from the great tents.

"*Halt*," the man said, in bad French. "No serfs past here. I'm the bossboy; give me your name."

Jean leaned against him, hands pawing weakly for support as the knowledge of his own exhaustion came through the whitenoise. He made gobbling noises as his mouth tried to speak while his lungs could spare no wind for it, none, they were dry and tight and aching, and the gasping breathes did him no good.

"Drunk?" the bossboy asked. Short and dark and thin, with a long willow-switch in his hand. He prodded at Jean with it, as the Frenchman bent over and leaned his hands on his knees, rasping for air. "You drunk? You got drink with you? Our party's not until Wedensday. Nobody here but Masters and the wenches to pleasure them, that bastard Arab fieldboss posted me here where I can listen and do nothing."

"Vashon," Jean wheezed.

"What? What you say, boy? You belong who? Who your master?"

"Vashon, Master Vashon, Strategos Vashon, I have news, now, *hurry*."

"The greencoat?" Even in darkness Jean could see the fear on the serf foreman's face, the little start of recoil; he stood up, heartened. Even the Master's *name* was a thing of power. "Third door, he have wenches in there." The switch trembled as it pointed. "You lie, he kill you. Not Erast's business."

Jean walked forward, stumbling, pushed through the heavy flap, into the dimlit shadows. He could see the Master's face, at first he thought it was floating, all amid a froth of feathers and giant wings and the limp head of a great golden swan that lay and stared at him with eyes of tourmaline. Then his brain made sense of the pattern of line and movement before him; Vashon was on a woman, kneeling with her legs over his shoulders, embracing another who leaned back from her position astride the first's head. The Frenchman's mouth dropped open; the women were darkly beautiful, lithe as cats, the Master a study in power, his skin rippling, bunch-

ing, the whole human pyramid shaking with the power
of his thrusts. There was another clicking behind his
eyes and Jean fell to his knees, a vague wash of awe and
terror and worship submerging consciousness.

"*Who the Eblis*—" Vashon's roar cut off, and Jean's
eyes jerked open. Only seconds could have passed, for
the Master was just rising. His green eyes were like
jewels in the gloom, narrowed as he recognized the
double agent, came to stand before him like a squat
minotaur statue gleaming with sweat and fluids.

"Jean," he said. The voice was soothing, deep, all
that Jean remembered from—

whitenoisenothoughtnothought

"Master," he said, a choking in his voice. "Master."

"I am very pleased with you, Jean," the voice said,
and the serf felt an uprushing of joy. "Now, tell me.
Tell me everything."

A moment to marshal his thoughts. They seemed so
clear, once again, as if the noise in his head and the
shaking were all gone. *He is strong, He bears the
burdens of my sins*, Jean thought, and began, rapid and
precise:

"At the cave to the north, Master. Three of us. Here,
the American who calls himself Kenston, the nun, the
Boche; there is a box of the poison dust, and . . ."

Afterward nothing could bother him, not the shouting or the noises or the shots, the darkness or the
cramping of his muscles as he knelt, nor the whimpers
of uncomprehending terror from the dancers, who clung
together and stared at him with white rims around their
eyes. His strong Lord was pleased with him, and all
was well.

Tanya heard the distance-muffled shots a dozen meters before the stairwell entrance. She took the stairs in a
rush and flipped the gun into her left hand, leading
with it as she went up the steep spiral treads in a silent
crouching bound. The open door of the armory drew
her in like a magnet, coming up in a knee-roll and

quartering the empty room. Nothing, racked weapons and drained beer-bottles beside a cooler and an open window . . . she darted over, noticing the fresh blood trail without focusing on it. All her attention was out on the slate roof, on the figures at the far end of it, over a hundred meters, impossible distance with the snub-nosed toy she carred. A careful brace of the elbows against the windowsill, and all but one of them were gone, squeeze—*Crack-crack-crack,* and did he stagger or was that a wish and the distance and the starlight? *No time,* she thought, spinning back to the stairwell. No time for pursuit, she couldn't go haring off on her own. No telling how many there were, either. The stairs above the armory were wet, slow congealing trickles that were an old story to her. The astonishing amount of blood a human body carries and the swiftness with which it can escape through massive wound trauma as the heart itself shoots the pulse of life out to scatter and cool.

Jules Lebrun sat before the ruined equipment, watching it spark and refusing to turn. Even when he heard the pistol snap below, the light *tick . . . tick . . .* sound of bootsoles pulling free of what coated the floor stones outside. Instead his lips moved; surprising himself with the first genuine prayers since he had been an earnest middle-class chorister in Paris, all those years ago. Prayers for another.

"Ah, Tom," he heard Tanya's voice say behind him. The feet moved, to the dead girl's side. "Yasmin, sweetlin'. I should . . ."

They stopped behind him, and he waited for the bullet; wondering whether he would hear the click of the action first, and at how the pains in his chest seemed farther away, almost unimportant.

Even then the small hairs along his spine seemed to crawl and struggle to stand erect when he heard her voice. "Well, well, what have we heah?"

"A man who would rather die than be a slave," he

said quietly, proud of the fact that his voice did not quaver.

"No." The word was calm and even, but suddenly a hand spun him around and wrenched him upright with a force that jerked his limbs loose as a puppet's. The pistol was under his chin as Tanya held him off the ground, his eyes level with her own. She spoke, and now the killing was naked in the guttural snarl:

"*No*. That choice yo' made three years ago, Lebrun, it's too *late*. So what we have heah is a fuckin' rabid *mad dog*, that turned on its owners, an' now will be put *down* like one."

There was a faint sound from the Janissary, a mixture of grunt and sigh. Lebrun felt himself thrown backward over the desk and against the dials and hanging severed wires of the radio, felt them gouge into his back. The pistol remained unwavering on his face as she knelt beside the man who was incredibly not quite dead.

"Yas . . . min?" Tom said in a breathy whisper. His head had fallen turned away from her; Tanya looked up at the corpse, rested her free hand on his forehead, leaned close and spoke with clear conviction as the man's eyes wandered unseeing.

"She goin' be fine, Tom. Hurt, but not bad."

Another sigh, and a catch in the faint breathing. The next words were fainter still, almost a suggestion: "*Reportin' 's ordered . . . suh.*"

Tanya closed the lids with thumb and forefinger, rose, and gripped Lebrun by the back of the neck, until he could hear the tooth-grating sound of protesting vertebrae through the bones of his skull.

"No," she said. "Not quite like a dog; even at the risk of a few seconds, wouldn't be fittin'. We were discussin' what we have?" Suddenly she pulled him over to Yasmin's body in a slithering rush that sent him banging and twisting against unseen hard objects as they passed. The man found his face pushed down to within inches of the dead girl's.

"What we *had* here," she said, "was Yasmin. A pretty,

happy little wench, who loved music an' babies an' wanted most of all never to hurt anyone, anyone at all. What we have now is fuckin' *dogmeat*."

Another rush, over to the Janissary's body. Again the thrust nose to nose with the dead flesh. "What we have here, is a brave man an' a good soldier who died loyal to his salt. Who *should* have died thirty years from now, in his sleep, surrounded by grandchildren."

She spun him around, tapping the pistol-barrel against the bridge of his nose. "An' what we have here—here— here is the last thing yo'll ever see, yo' piece of vomit."

"Please," Solange said.

Tanya's head jerked around so quickly that her hair lashed across Lebrun's eyes before he could blink them closed, starring them with tears. His daughter was standing in the doorway, staring at the bodies with the backs of her hands pressed to her mouth.

"Oh, Poppa, what have you *done?*" she mumbled. Then her hands dropped, and she walked to the Draka. "Please," she said again, knelt. Pressed her cheek to her owner's foot. "It is your right, it is your right, we are yours . . . but he is my father, I beg, *please.*"

"No," Lebrun said, and looked up into the Draka's eyes. *She must know, know I am dying,* he thought. She smiled.

"I give yo' life, on her plea," she said. "Solange . . . Solange! He'll be out fo' a couple of hours, *tie him up* and then go back to my room and *wait.*" Her hand held his head while the pistol came down with precisely calculated force.

Ah, the peace and quiet of the country, Andrew von Shrakenberg thought. The leaves of the vineyard rustled as he strolled down the rows, enjoying the cool contrast of the air and soil still carrying fragments of the day's heat. *Am I being ironic, or not?* It was certainly more peaceful than the pavilion, now mostly occupied by the noises of vigorous fornication. Fresher, too, dew-damp leaves and turned earth.

Which is not displeasing in itself, but not conducive to thought either, he mused. Perhaps it was time to take his sister's advice and settle down. He looked up at the stars, smiling and remembering the night when he had first seen them with *depth*, not as lights in a dome but as tiny fires suspended in infinite space, feeling an echo of that elating, terrifying rush of vertigo. Wondering if somewhere out among the frosted scattering of light something was looking skyward at him.

And to them, all our loves and hates, wars and passions are so insignificant that they can't be seen, not even as a shadow on the sun.

"Jean? Is that you?" a voice said. French, accented . . . a woman's voice.

Peace held his mind in its embrace a moment longer. "No," he said, chuckling. "But if it's a man yo' lookin' fo', wench, I'm willin' to volunteer."

Starlight glittered on the blade of the knife as it drove toward his belly.

Smack. The edge of his left palm hit her wrist, and he felt the familiar jolt as the small bones of the joint crushed under an impact that would have broken pine boards. It was the measure of his bewilderment that his follow-through was completely automatic, a strike upward with the heel of his right hand that sent the woman flipping back with her nasal bone driven into her brain and neck snapped. The knife flew off, tinkling, but his fingers touched the piano wire garrote coiled within her belt before the body stopped twitching.

He stood, and the first of the vehicles blew with a huge muffled *thump* that struck his face like a soft warm hand. Light blossomed beyond the line of trees that screened the vehicle park, and explosions followed like a string of giant fuzz-edged firecrackers.

"I think," he said quietly to himself, "that a serious mistake has been made." Turning, he drove for the laneway at a steady loping run.

* * *

There was a bristle of guns under the arched entranceway to the central court of Chateau Retour. They lowered as the figure approaching halted and grunted out her name.

"Tanya," she said, shifting the body to a more comfortable fireman's carry over her shoulders, then dropping it in the midst of the crowd. "This one's necknumber was dye, not tattooin'."

The face sprawled upright as the body rolled, a small black hole between its brows. Tanya stretched, looked around, estimating numbers and weapons. Sixteen Draka, pistols, three submachine guns, two battle-shotguns, two assault-rifles. More in the armory, of course . . . Five armed serfs who would do to stand guard. The scouts had all reported back, and there was no sign of bushman activity beyond the one small band. *Which is enough*, she thought sourly.

"Oerbach," Vachon was saying, "by Loki and the soul of the White Christ, Oerbach." He looked up at her. "Congratulations." Back down at the body, and a murmur. "Because yo' may have just saved me from the Aral Sea."

"Dumb luck," she replied. "Hundred meters with a Tolgren, pure fluke." To her husband. "Situation?"

"Transport gone," he said calmly. "Power out. Communication out. Runners to the neighbors." Draka runners, nearly as fast as horses, but still a half hour there, more time to organize, transit time back . . . three quarters of an hour to an hour. "Children, sick an' bearin' mothers down on the yacht, Uncle Karl presidin'." A weight lifted from the back of her neck, a thing she had not been conscious of until that moment.

"Information from the Strategos here," Edward went on. "Three bushmen from Lyon, one a double who reported in to warn us. Two mo'—"

Andrew interrupted: "One, if the second was a woman with a knife," he said bluntly. "She's fertilizin' yo' vineyard, sister."

"One mo' up at the winery, with the Yankee callin'

hisself Kenston, an' the wenches Chantal an' Marya. Yankee plane comin' in, soon."

"And many, many kilograms of plutonium oxide," Andrew said.

"Bad?" Tanya said, as a fist clenched under her gut. She had seen the fallout-victim wards, the ones caught in the plume from the Ruhr strikes toward the end of the war. An image welled up in her mind, Gudrun, Tim, the newborns, their ulcerated skins sloughing away—

"The radiation isn't that severe," Vashon began.

"It doesn't *have* to be," Andrew cut in decisively. "Garbage is so toxic chemically yo' don't have *time* to die of the radiation sickness an' cancer that would kill yo' in days to weeks. It's worse than nerve gas, submicroscopic particles deadly almost immediately, the amount they've got could kill everythin' within light-artillery range of here, or *worse*. Dependin' on how it's scattered." He jerked his head toward the kilometer-distant glow of the vehicle park. "We *know* they've got explosive, and imagine how an updraft like that would scatter a finely divided powder?"

"Shitfire." Hushed awe in the word.

A thick silence fell. "We've got to attack," someone said.

"Sho'ly do! And quick. Befo' they can lose that stuff."

Tanya held up her hand, and silence fell. This was her land, and Draka were soldiers, they understood the need for teamwork down in their bones. She looked around, at steel and fugitive gleams from eyes and teeth.

"We can't just roll over them," she said slowly. "We may have to talk them out."

"No!" That was Vashon. "The Race doesn't back down from a threat! We take that plutonium back, and—"

Tanya nodded, and there was a multiple click and rattle. Vashon froze as the cold muzzles of weapons touched lightly on his skin. She walked close, held her face inches from his.

"Strategos . . . let us say, I'm not very *impressed* with the quality of yo' security work. Seein' as the position we're in."

Someone behind him spoke. "The *hell* we don't back down from threats, how do yo' think we got this far, by bein' bull-stupid like so yo'?"

Another: "It's our land and children, Vashon. I think the von Shrakenbergs are senior here . . . Hell, we *are* the Race."

Tanya continued, never taking her eyes from the man's. "Nobody here will do anythin' prejudicial to the interests of the Race or the State," she said. "Andrew, run it down fo' me."

"Bad if"—he kicked Oerbach's body—"had gotten away to the Yankees; he is, was, a genuine thinker, an experimenter an' theoretician in one. Unfortunate if they were to get his research to date, but no disaster, we've got it too. Mildly unfortunate to let them have the plutonium, it's rare an' expensive, but still just matériel."

Tanya nodded. "Against which we have to balance risk to the lives of two-score members of the Race. We're not a numerous people, Strategos; never start imaginin' yo' can spend our lives the way yo' might do serfs. That's not the way we've operated, ever." A pause. "I think it might be bettah if somebody else took care of this mastah's gun; the gleam in his eyes is a touch too fanatical fo' my taste." Hands reached out. Green eyes met gray, nodded. There would be feud, but not now.

Tanya looked around. "Yo', Sofie. Down to the dock an' tell Karl to cast off with the kids, downstream as fast as he can an' not run aground. The rest of yo' . . . *follow me.*"

They turned and ran toward the north, to the caves, toward the waiting poison.

"No, no, *no!*" Kustaa said, pounding his fist into the turf.

"He is with God," Marya said quietly. They were resting in the shadow of one of the disabled Draka aircraft, with the winking rectangle of the landing strip stretching away.

"That isn't going to do any good to the fucking Taos Weapons Research Lab!" Kustaa shouted, then mumbled apology as pain lanced through his wounds.

Marya examined them again, frowning; there had been bandages, iodine, sulfa powder in the aircraft first-aid kit, she had cleaned and bound as best she could, but he needed stitching and plasma, and complete bed-rest. Instead he had insisted on a stimulant, and he was right, but it made it so difficult for him to lie still. "Rest, Frederick. We have done what human hands can do, the rest is with God."

Her eyes went doubtfully to the steel box. It had been transformed into a lumpy gray mass by the ten kilos of *plastique* they had wrapped around it. The batteries and improvised switch rested atop it, wires spindling down to the detonator. *Such a simple thing,* she thought with a shiver. Their insurance. A deadman swich, so just a name. Grip, *so.* Press down sharply and now you must *keep* pressing or the contact will be made, contact, current through the detonator, detonator explodes, rapid-propagating shock wave provokes sympathetic reaction in the plastique.

And all this dies, she thought, looking around at the night countryside with another shudder. *Like wrath of God upon the cities of the plain, only this wrath is man's.* It all dies, the beasts and the humans, innocent and guilty, fathers and mothers and babes in arms for leagues around.

She signed herself, knelt by the box and began to pray; first seeking the intercession of the Saints, that they might stand between the her and the terrible necessities that God seemed to demand of her. Then asking mercy of Mary, the Mother that was the pattern of all mothers, human flesh united in nine months' inconceivable communion with the Word. Then at last to the heart of Mystery. The words ordained, and then her own.

Lord God, she begged, *let there be mercy in this hour. As you would have spared Sodom for ten upright men, spare those poor souls dwelling here, whose lives are humble and full of suffering yet still precious to them, as You intended. For indeed Your world is good, where we have not marred it. And if only through blood may there be remission of sin, let the sword fall upon me alone.* Wordless for long minutes. Then: *Lord, I am unworthy, full of pride and sin and conceit of my own righteousness, yet ever willing to be Your instrument. Give unto me not that which I ask, but what is best for me, though it be the thing I fear most. Not my will, but Thine be done.*

"Amen," she murmured, and took the switch in her hand, pressing down sharply.

The others looked up at the hard clicking sound. "It will not become easier to do if we wait," she said. "If we are successful, I can disconnect one of the wires."

Chantal glanced aside, then laid her head back on her knees, muttering under her breath. From this position, the nun could hear clearly what she had only suspected.

"I had to do it. She deserved it. I *had* to. She deserved it."

"Chantal!" Marya snapped. "I am losing patience with you!" The other's head came up, with anger in her eyes. "That is half a lie, worse than a whole one. It was necessary, to save Frederick's life. And she did *not* deserve it; the poor girl had been mistaught, grievously, since she was a little child. But of herself she was a gentle soul, who only acted from natural grief. You are trying to blame her because it eases your conscience, aren't you? So that you won't see her face and what you did to her? Remember it! Don't lie to yourself, and don't lie to me, either."

Chantal turned her back, but silently. Marya looked down at the bundle of steel and explosive again. *And it*

makes my temper still worse than it usually is, she
thought.

"By God, the plane," Kustaa said quietly. "The plane!"
he shouted, half rose, sank down again with a grunt.
Marya strained her eyes and ears: nothing. Then a hint
of something, a shadow against the stars, a muffled
purring drone. Circling, returning toward them, falling
featherlight in a steep slope out of the sky, and the nun
felt her eyes prickle with tears for the first time that
night. It landed, bounced, trundled toward them, a flat
complex wing with two engines buried in the structure
and thickly wrapped in shrouding cowl, a teardrop
fuselage.

"That's it, that's the Spector," Kustaa was saying in
what was almost a babble. "Isn't she a beauty, takes off
on a postage stamp, lands on a balcony, noisy as a
scooter, seats four with cargo—" He stopped, looked at
her. "And Ernst is dead," he finished in something
closer to his normal tone.

"But Henri is alive," she replied sharply, turning to
find the darker shadow that was the sole survivor of the
Resistance team. He was walking up the slope in a
crouch that rose toward a full stride, his impassive
stubbled face finally breaking into a grin of unbelieving
triumph as the cockpit window of the aircraft folded
back and an arm emerged, waving.

Marya smiled at the Frenchman in return, watching
as he grew solid in the darkness, as his grin went fixed,
his stride stiff-legged, as he toppled forward with the
glint of the throwing-knife's hilt winking from his back.
Thump went the body, limp as sleep, limp as death,
kicked twice, lay still.

"Down!" Kustaa yelled.

"Deadman switch, deadman switch," Marya shouted
out into the night, at the full stretch of her lungs. "The
plutonium is sitting on ten kilos of high explosive, and
we have a deadman switch. Think about that and hold
your fire!"

There was another shout of pain, mingled with rage

this time, from the encircling shadows. Then a brief burst of fire, a Holbars on full automatic, a dozen rounds that chewed into the left engine of the American aircraft, whapping thuds and sparks and a sudden metallic screeching as the internal parts seized hard. The prop slowed from its silent blurr, froze into four paddle-shaped metal blades. Then the stream of tracer waggled crazily up into the sky, went out, more thuds and grappling sounds.

"Wait, wait!" Tanya's voice. "That was a rogue . . . *no, don't kill him, yo' fools!*" The latter seemed directed at her own people. The hailing voice again: "There are twenty of us out here, we have enough firepower to cut that paper airplane into confetti, think about that!"

Silence, until Kustaa crawled to the airplane's landing struts; the effort left him gasping.

"No closer," Tanya called. "No packages!"

They were close enough for words, murmured too low for the nun to hear. He crawled again, to her side, and lay for a moment with fresh blood seeping through her careful bandages, his fingers digging into the soil as if it were his mother's body to which he clung.

"We're fu . . . we're in trouble, Sister. One engine completely out." The voice had the hard flatness she had come to know meant his deepest effort at control.

"It can fly. It can even carry a passenger . . . one passenger, preferably a very light one."

Marya prayed again, this time an utterly wordless appeal. She gasped sharply.

"What is it?" Kustaa asked.

"I think . . . I think I see what I must do," she said grayly. "Oh, Frederick, I had hoped . . . hoped so much you might return to your wife and daughter."

Aloud: "We have no time, and nothing left to lose. Will you talk, or do we all die?"

"I'll talk. Shall I come closer?" Tanya again.

"Agreed."

The Draka strolled into the dim glimmer of the landing lights, elaborately insouciant, her hands on her hips. Dark clothing, bright hair, the eyes throwing back the light like ice; she stood waiting for the nun to speak.

She is playing for time, Marya thought. Then: *Of course. They have sent their children to safety, the longer we wait the better. And the authorities will arrive at any moment.*

"No games," the Pole said. "The plane can take one of us out, only."

"Not the plutonium, of course . . . and not the Yankee. He stays; that's a matter of honor."

The OSS agent sighed, then looked up at Marya with a smile more relaxed than any she had seen him wear before. *There is a relief in acknowledging the race is lost*, she thought. *But there are more important things than life.*

"I won't let myself be taken alive," Kustaa said.

"Well, obviously," Tanya said with cool contempt. "Yo' a treacher who abuses hospitality, but not a fool. Yo' have that gun, don't yo'?" She grinned with bared teeth. "The one that yo' kill drunk old men an' harmless serf-girls with?"

"Enough," Marya said. "If you let the plane go with one of us, we will promise not to detonate this weapon."

"I made the mistake of underestimatin' yo', but please don't reciprocate with an insult to my intelligence," Tanya replied evenly. "Once it's out of sight, yo'd simply set it off anyway."

"To spare myself pain?" Marya asked. "Have you sent your children away?" Tanya nodded warily. "And those of your serfs?"

"Ahh, I see," the Draka said. "Then yo' will surrender anyhows?"

"No," Marya replied, meeting her owner's eyes in a steady glare as hard as the Draka's own. "Frederick knows too much. We will take it below, into the shelter. That can be sealed, and I will promise not to release the switch until it is. Quickly, decide, there is no *time*."

Tanya nodded, turned. "The terms are these," she said in a clear carrying voice. "We let the Yankee plane take off, with my wench Chantal on board. My wench Marya an' the Yankee go into the shelter an' we seal them in with they little hellbomb, after one hour's grace." There was a protesting murmur, and she held up one hand. "Listen! We lose nothin' by allowin' the plane back. Chantal's also nothin', unless the Yankees are perishin' fo' want of a so-so bookkeeper and bedwench." A mutter of unwilling laughter. "We keep the plutonium, it can be recovered, an' they lose their agent an' all his knowledge. I'd call that victory! An' I take full responsiblity fo' any repercussions from the State. Objections?"

"It's agreed," she said, turning to the American and the nun and raising her hand. "Word of a von Shrakenberg, by our honor."

Chantal had turned back to them, and watched Marya's face with an expression of thoughtful wonder. "No," she said, on the heels of Tanya's oath.

Marya looked over at her and laughed with a catch in her voice. "What a collection of martyrs we are . . . of course you must, Chantal."

"I . . . can't take your life!" the Frenchwoman said. "I want to, God, I want to, but how could I live with myself, remembering this? How could I owe you this, and never be able to repay?"

Marya sighed. "Chantal, nobody can give you their life. Only your own." More softly: "If you feel you owe me a debt, choose another and pay it to *them*, and I will be repaid in full and to overflowing." Chantal's face cleared; she touched her stomach involuntarily, then gave the nun an ashen nod.

"Will you give me the kiss of peace, Chantal?" Marya said, brushing her free hand across her face. The younger woman stood with sudden decisiveness, bent to offer her cheek, met the Pole's lips instead. Her eyes widened, and she swallowed convulsively.

Kustaa reached inside his jacket. "And would you take this to—" he began.

"No!" A voice from the darkness. "No papers, no chance to pass along microfilm, Yankee."

Suddenly Kustaa was on his feet, a big man bristling with rage, the lumberjack strength of his shoulders showing despite wounds and weariness. "*It's a letter to my wife, you bastard!*" he roared.

"Mah heart bleeds fo' yo'. Verbal only!" A dozen lights speared out to trap Chantal. "An' the wench has to shuck and bend, so's we can see she's not carryin'.'"

Kustaa turned to the Frenchwoman, who stood blinking and shading her eyes with a palm. "Tell Aino I love her," he said. "And Maila. Say"—he glanced back at the nun—"say she can be proud of the way her father died, and the company he kept. Tell her . . . tell her everything."

"I will. Rest assured, I will." When the cockpit door of the airplane closed on her, the nakedness was a lack of clothes only.

The single engine whined, stressed beyond its limit. Kustaa sank to the ground beside Marya, the shotgun clenched white-knuckled in his lap as the Spector took off.

"I know," she said. "I want to run after it shouting, 'come back, come back' myself."

"Good," he sighed. "I was beginning to think saints were too perfect to live around."

"Mr . . .. Frederick," she said, and he glanced around in shock at the cold anger in her voice. "You will *never* call me that again. Never!"

"Sorry, Sister," he said.

"I too . . . my temper was always bad . . ." To Tanya: "Mistress, it would be a courtesy if someone would fetch the radio for us, from the shelter."

The Draka nodded, and signaled with one hand; the parcel came, and Kustaa busied himself with dials and antennae, tuned to the Draka Forces emergency network. Time passed, and the night grew colder and more silent; in the distance, the fires of the burning vehicles guttered low. The headlights of a high-speed convoy flickered up to the main gates of Chateau Retour, and a runner went at Tanya's order to halt them. Another returned with a radiation detector, pointed it at the box with its leprous covering, and paled as the needle swung; there was a rustle from the darkness as the besieger's circle drew back.

Kustaa looked up, squeezed his eyes shut. "They missed it," he said softly. "It's full time, and they're going crazy looking for it. We won." A sour laugh. "In a sense, I suppose."

Tanya shifted her stance, the first movement in half an hour. "The Security people will be here soon," she said. "I've got influence, but not enough to stand off their rankin' people. My oath; I'm not answerable for them."

"It is time," Marya said. "Just one more thing." She raised her voice. "We need someone to carry this box; Frederick is wounded and cannot possibly do so."

Tanya snorted. "We'll send for a strong serf."

"No! Someone here, immediately. No time for tricks." *And I will not condemn an innocent. Any adult Draka is a murderer, fornicator, blasphemer.*

Another slight rustle in the darkness. "I can't order anyone to—"

Then a voice: "I volunteer."

"No," Tanya snapped, as her brother Andrew strolled up, paused to lay his weapon on the grass, walked toward the American's shotgun, which tracked him with a smooth turret motion.

"But yes, mah sister," Andrew continued gently. "Be logical, as yo' usually are. Here I am, thirty-two, unmarried, no children of the Race, a middlin' good Merarch among thousands . . . The Race can spare me."

"It can't, and neither can I!" Tanya said, and Marya

heard open pain in her voice for the first time that
night.

"Yes, yo' can," he said, stopping to confront her.
"Mo' than I could yo'. Furthermo' it's a risk of death,
not certainty. Furthermo' to that, it's my choice. Ser-
vice to the State, sister mine." Matter-of-factly: "Iff'n
I'm unlucky, would yo' see to my girls and my valet?"
She nodded wordlessly. "Glory to the Race, then."

"Yes, indeed," she said thickly. "I love yo', brother."

"And I yo', Tannie." Two more strides brought him
to Marya's side, and he crouched smoothly.

"Watch it, you son-of-a-bitch," Kustaa said, holding
his weapon close. "Slow and careful."

"Yankee, don't be mo' of an imbecile than nature
intended," Andrew said dryly, running his hands around
the box. "I'm squattin' next a live bomb, with enough
poison inside to destroy Archona, an' yo' puts a *shotgun*
in mah ear an' tells me to be *careful?*"

Kustaa flushed slightly, but kept the weapon pressed
against the Draka's back. "I know how you snakes train
by snatching flies out of the air without hurting them,"
he said. "You still can't grab her hand faster than I can
pull this trigger. Like I said, slow and careful."

Andrew's face went blank as he drew a deep breath.
"Now," he said, and exhaled with a long sustained
grunt as he stood. A seam parted along the rear of his
jacket, and they could feel the ground shake slightly as
he took the first step toward the shelter door. Tanya
stood to one side, eyes hooded. As they passed, her
hand came up in salute, held there. "I'll see there's a
priest to bless the ground," she murmured.

"Thank you," Marya replied. Their eyes met, but
there were no more words.

The shelter lights seemed painfully bright; Kustaa
blinked against them, and the ringing in his ears that was
growing worse. Andrew was whistling under his breath
as he bolted home the steel covers over the ventilators,
checking carefully to make sure the sealing-rings seated

square. Almost, the American missed the quiet sobbing sound.

"Sister, what is it?" he said anxiously, dropping down beside her with the shotgun trained across the room. Tears were dropping into her lap, onto the clenched knuckles of her right hand on the switch, onto the steel and dough-gray explosive.

"Fear, Frederick," she said, between catches of breath. A laugh through the sobbing, as she saw his face.

"Frederick, I fear death, so much . . . pain even more. You know what they can do, would do if they took me, they can make a hell on earth, less than Satan's only because it is not eternal. They would never believe I knew nothing of consequence . . . Oh, Frederick, I have had nightmares of that, ever since . . ." A shake of her head. "But if there was a way, I would walk out that door and right now and let them take me to the place of torment."

"*What?*" he said.

"Thank you for listening, my friend, when you too must need to speak . . . Frederick, I am in such fear that I cannot bear it, that this thing I am doing is self-murder. I tell myself it is not, it is as a soldier does when he charges the machine-gun or throws himself on a grenade to save his comrades, but . . . Self-murder, murder of the soul, damnation." The tears became softer, and her voice thickened. "Damnation . . . not the pains of hell, but never to to see God in the face . . . never . . . never to see the other Sisters of St. Cyril again, and Frederick, I am the last, they are all with Him in Glory, they were saints and martyrs, but sisters in truth, dearer than any earthly thing to me. Never to see them, never to share their joy, oh, I cannot bear it!"

I have gone crazy, Kustaa thought, as he heard himself speak. *But it's a pleasanter madness than the one before.* "I'll do it then," he said. "Here, give me the switch."

"No! Frederick, no! You may not believe suicide is

mortal sin, but it is for you as well, how could I buy
Paradise at the cost of your damnation? This is my
fault, Frederick, my weakness, if I were more worthy
God would have called to my heart, shown me a better
way . . ." The control and serenity were cracking out of
the nun's voice, leaving only raw pain and will.

Kustaa turned and drove a fist against the wall. "Dammit," he swore. "If only we could have gotten the
microfilm out. If only that, at least!"

"Oh, we did, Frederick," Marya said, half listlessly.
"Did you not notice—" She halted in mid-sentence,
and both their heads swung to the Draka. He completed the last bolt and dropped lightly to the floor,
dusting his hands on the black uniform trousers.

"Feh," he said, an exhalation of disgust. "I don't
suppose yo'd believe a promise not to tell . . . No, I
don't suppose so." There was no need to mention that
the Draka would mobilize every keel and wing to hunt
the Alliance submarine if they knew. He walked lightly
to the outer door, stood with one hand on the wheel. "I
could refuse to close it," he said.

"Your friends and relatives, snake," Kustaa said with
a grin of jovial hatred. "Much more limited spread,
from here."

"Yes, there is that," Andrew said, pulled the door
home with a clang, spun the wheel until the bolts went
shhnnnk-click into their slots, pushed the locking bar.
"Shit," he said meditatively. "Suddenly a long, dull life
becomes so much less wearisome in prospect." Suddenly he was laughing as he strode back to stand before
them, a low wicked snicker.

"What the fuck are you laughing at?" Kustaa glared,
glancing from the weeping nun to the scarred aquiline
face and the earring that jiggled in time with his mirth.

"Everything an' nothin', Yankee. Yo' bourgeois have
such a tiresome gravity about serious mattahs, takes a
gentleman to bring the proper levity to the grave. If it's
one thing I've learned in thirty-two years, it's that the
only thing mo' amusin' than this farce we call life is the

even more absurd farce known as death. If there was an afterlife, the sheer comedy of it would be too much to bear!"

"Have some respect," Kustaa said raising the shotgun despite his own sense of its futility.

"Oh, I do, an' that's the most comical thing of all, Yankee." His voice dropped. "Sister." She raised her head, startled to hear the title on a Draka's voice. "Sister, pardon me fo' listenin' to yo', ah, confession. But it occurs to me that while yo' belief is as absurd as anythin' else, yo' belief *in* it, is not." He spread his hands. "So, since if one is goin' anyway, one might as well go with a grand gesture—"

Kustaa screamed and fired, but he was too late, the fluid Draka speed had outmatched him; the boot-heel struck the nun with needle precision and pickaxe force directly above the nose. Sound merged, the snap of bone, the shot, the beginnings of a roaring blast as dead fingers unfolded like the petals of a rose.

CHAPTER SIXTEEN

"All victories are ephemeral. Only our defeats are final."
   Secret journals of Professor Jules Lebrun
   Last Entry
   Chateau Retour Plantation infirmary
   January 1, 1948

EPILOGUE I

CHATEAU RETOUR PLANTATION,
TOURAINE PROVINCE
OCTOBER, 1947

"Am I bein' sentimental, love?" Tanya von Shrakenberg asked, as they watched the captive priest bless the earth. It was a raw autumn day; they were the only Draka present, sitting their horses behind a screen of drab-coated serfs, while the world spread around them in gray cloud, wet earth, faded brightness of vine-leaves that whirled away down the wind like messages to yesterday.

"Yes," her husband replied. The gaping hole had been refilled, where the decontamination crews had pumped the shelter full of liquid concrete and taken out the block entire. Filled with good earth, and now consecrated as a graveyard. The vestments of the priest were a splash of color against the raw brown earth and the simple granite tombstone; but even before the ceremony, the serfs had begun to come with flowers and ribbons for the resting place of the one who had died for them.

"Yes," he said. "But we can afford a little, now and then." A squeeze of their gloved hands. "Andrew has his memorial, and it's mo' showy; let them have theirs." He took up the reins. "C'mon, love, dinner's waitin'."

They reined about and heeled their horses. The serfs bowed as they passed, but remained, kneeling to pray for her whose spirit surely abided to guard this place.

EPILOGUE II

HOSPITAL OF THE SACRED HEART
NEW YORK CITY
FEBRUARY, 1948

"Names?" The woman who looked up at the nursing sister was exhausted with the long labor, triumphant, but she had no slightest trace of the furtiveness the staff had come to expect of unwed mothers. Of course, there was some mystery involved; the nurse looked over at the godparents, a short Indian-looking man in naval blue with Commander's stripes on his arm and his blond wife with the soft Carolina accent. They visited often, and the quiet widow with her daughter, and the horse-faced man who your eyes never really seemed to rest on.

"Of course I've got names," the young woman was saying, in the French accent that had been considered exotic before the War and the refugee influx. She looked over to the cradle, the two sleeping pink forms still with their goldenblond birth fuzz.

"Frederick Kustaa and Marya Sokolowska Lefarge," she said, closing her eyes with a sigh. "I don't believe in making it easy for children. *That'll* give them something to live up to."

Excerpts from:
The Economy of the Domination: Historical and Regional Perspectives

by Sandra de Varga, Ph.D
Department of Economic Geography
San Diego University Press
1991

AREA ONE: THE OLD TERRITORIES

The initial conquests of the 1780s covered essentially the area between the Atlantic and Indian oceans and between the Cape on the south and the Zambezi on the north.

Capetown and Region - the Western Province:

Capetown was the original urban center of the Crown Colony of Drakia; the capital until 1820, the largest city until the 1830's.

Date	Population	S(serf)	C(citizen)
1783	10,000	S50%	C50%
1800	50,000	S67%	C33%
1830	100,000	S64%	C36%
1880	250,000	S70%	C30%
1914	350,000	S75%	C25%
1942	500,000	S77%	C23%
1990	725,000	S76%	C24%

As the population figures indicate, the initial growth spurt was followed by a long period of relative stagnation, as the main focus of economic expansion shifted north. Capetown remained an important educational center (Universities of Capetown and Starwood, Marine Sciences Institute, Simonstown Naval Academy), and a cultural one as well, with a number of important galleries, two orchestras and the famous Starwood Dancers. Tourism and entertainment became and remained important after the railroad to Archona was completed in 1829.

Besides serving as a marketing and processing center for the surrounding agricultural region, Capetown has considerable light industry (food processing, furniture, interior decoration, fashion), shipbuilding and ship repair, fishing, canning and fishmeal plants and woollen textiles, and exports iron ore, copper, manganese and colored marbles. The 1960's saw expansion in the computer, microelectronics and software fields, with many small firms setting up in Starwood and the other small towns north and east of the Cape, attracted by the universities, cultural facilities and climate.

The Domination's first commercial nuclear-energy plant was built northeast of the city and commenced operation in 1949 (the Silvercoast complex now generates in excess of 1,000 megawatts). There are storage facilities for liquefied natural gas, which is imported from the Gulf provinces in a fleet of 250,000-ton purpose-built tankers. An experimental 60-megawatt deep-ocean convection plant came on-line in 1979; the first of the Domination's microwave receptors for space-generated solar power is under construction as of 1990.

The Domination's XV Fleet (60 vessels, including 38 *Timur*-class nuclear attack submarines and two *Hengist*-class VTOL-jet carriers) is based out of Capetown; there is an extensive naval/air base with facilities for servicing orbital-capable scramjets (1966), laser-launch facility (1980) and airship yard.

Agriculture

The southwest Cape was intensively developed as the only area of Mediterranean climate in the British Empire; labor was brought in from the north, and an extensive network of hard-surfaced roads driven through the mountain passes to connect the valleys and basins.

Agriculture is, as usual for the Domination, organized on a plantation basis, but for historical reasons many of the units are unusually small, with only 100–300 serfs. The region of reliable winter rainfall within 120 km of Capetown is intensively cultivated, with a good deal of irrigated land; the wetter mountainsides are under planted forest of conifer and hardwood, mainly eucalyptus and oak. Deciduous fruit is grown under irrigation in the higher, cooler basins; vines, Mediterranean fruits (apricots, figs, nectarines, etc.) and tropical species are produced in the lowlands, with out-of-season fruits being shipped to the northern hemisphere.

The Karoo drylands beyond the winter-rainfall zone are divided into large grazing plantations of up to 200,000 hectares; the deep Kalahari desert is a 250,000 sq. km. State Reserve for wildlife and !Kung bushfolk. The ranching areas originally produced dried meat, leather, tallow and enormous quantities of fine-grade merino wool; in recent decades game-ranching of oryx and other desert antelopes has supplemented or even replaced the introduced sheep. Capetown University's *Aridland*

Management Project has been instrumental in efforts to preserve and increase the carrying capacity of the marginal lands. Scattered irrigated areas are mostly devoted to fodder crops such as alfalfa.

Eastern Cape

Settled in the 1780's, this region is transitional between the winter-rainfall zone and the Natalian subtropics. Inland are the Maluti Mountains, cold and wet; these are largely State Reserve and forest land, extensively planted with European and American species of forest tree and otherwise unused save for water-control and hydroelectric projects. Agriculture varies between intensive mixed farming on the better-watered plateau surfaces, irrigated specialty crops (vegetables and citrus) in the river valleys, sub-tropical crops such as tea and kenaf along the coast, and extensive grazing in the mountain foothills. Population density ranges from medium to sparse; plantation size from 2,000 to 20,000 hectares depending on crop and area.

Principal products: beef, mutton, pork, wool; tobacco, maize, fruits, horses, exotic hardwoods.

Venta Belgarum [East London, South Africa] is the largest (1990 pop. 450,000) city, a river-port midway between Capetown and Virconium. General manufacturing, shipbuilding (esp. ocean-going trawlers) and chemicals.

Natalia

Stretching from the Eastern Cape northeast to the valley of the Limpopo river, and inland to the mountains. Climate ranging from humid subtropical on the coast, to semiarid in some river valleys, to moist temperate and cool in the interior plateaus and mountains.
Settled during the 1780's, initial development focused

on the coastlands, which quickly became the world's largest sugar-producing zone, and on the corridors leading to the gold and diamond mines of the interior. By the 1790's, the intermediate benchlands were brought under cultivation to supply grain, meat, leather, timber and working stock for the mines and sugar plantations. Irrigation developments and swamp drainage (especially along the Pongola and Limpopo rivers and in the area around Shahnapur) permitted diversified orchard farming, and extensive production of indigo, rice and cotton. Inland, the coal and iron deposits around Diskarapur [Newcastle, South Africa] and Shahnapur [Swaziland area, to Maputo] were put to use in the decade 1790–1800. The coastal cities also served as bases for the drive up the East African coast, and the conquests of Ceylon, Madagascar and Egypt. For most of the 19th Century this remained the most thickly settled and richest zone of the Domination, and a source of surplus Citizen population for frontier settlement.

The coast remains a major sugar-producing zone, although there has been a good deal of conversion to pasture (for dairy farming) and market-gardening, to feed the huge urban populations. Elsewhere, mixed crop/livestock farming remains the rule, with many local specialties; several million hectares are under irrigation. Large reservoir and pumping projects to supply urban water needs; water shortages are the primary constraint on further development.

A major afforestation project (1800–1850) covered most of the steeper and colder mountain slopes along the plateau edge with forests of northern-hemisphere trees (predominantly oak and pine). Australian wattle trees are extensively grown for their tannin-rich bark.

Major Cities:

Virconium [Durban, South Africa]: founded 1784. 1990 pop. 5,500,000

Major port; handling and warehousing facilities. Food processing, diversified consumer manufacturing, shipbuilding and repair, chemicals, engineering. Major resort areas north and south along coast. Entertainment, record, CD, movie, video studios. Marine Research Institute. Deep-sea fishing base.

Shahnapur [Maputo, Mozambique]: founded 1799. 1990 pop. 7,600,000

Domination's largest port; handling & warehousing facilities. Primary naval shipbuilding center; very extensive artificial extensions to harbor facilities. Drydocks and floating docks, etc. Naval air and orbital scramjet bases; several large nuclear power facilities at 100–200 kilometer radius. Construction and assembly of marine nuclear power systems, fuel-cell submarine and industrial systems. Rail nexus. General manufacture. Iron and steel, heavy engineering (power-plant turbines, castings and forgings, ordnance), explosives, petroleum storage and pipelines to interior. Shahnapur Institute of Tropical Medicine.

Diskarapur [Newcastle, South Africa]: founded 1798. 1990 pop. 3,500,000

First, and for 100 years largest, heavy-industrial center. Located on inland plateau near headwaters of Tugela river. Iron and steel (1990 output in excess of 6,000,000 tons yearly); castings and forgings; locomotives; machine tools; general engineering, esp. heavy, mining machinery, large mine ventilation systems, power systems, nuclear reactors. Ordnance factories; tank assembly plants; turbocompound engines; autosteamers, esp. military-logistics vehicles. Basic chemicals. Headquarters of Ferrous Metals Combine, Trevithick Autosteam Combine. Metallurgical Research Institute

Archona/Central Province

Covers central plateau between eastern mountains and Kalahari desert on the west, Orange river on the south, Limpopo on the north.

The discovery of diamonds and gold in the 1780's forced early settlement. The landscape south of the Whiteridge [Johannesburg area, South Africa] is essentially a flat plain sloping to the west; the eastern third is subhumid, shading off into semiarid and then the arid, sandy bunchgrass savannah of the Kalahari and the absolute desert of the Namib on the Atlantic coast.

Large-scale mixed farming in the east, shading off into sheep/cattle/antelope ranching on the west and south. Local irrigation where possible, with arable areas fattening stock shipped in from drier ranching territory. The areas north of Archona [Pretoria, South Africa] are rougher and usually drier, and warmer due to lower altitudes; fairly extensive irrigated areas supply the cities with fresh produce. There are numerous local specialties, eg. tea in the wet foothills of the Northern Malutis, or cherries, apples and peaches in the mountain valleys of the southeast [Lesotho]. Despite intensive production, this is a food-deficit area due to the unusually large urban/industrial population.

Principal products: maize, wheat, potatoes, oilseeds (esp. sunflowers), sorghum, fodder crops, livestock (sheep, cattle, antelope), fruit (citrus, other tropical, temperate-zone), market gardening.

Minerals: Besides precious metals and diamonds (both gem and industrial), the area proved to be a treasure-house of industrial raw materials; coal in the thousands of millions of tons; iron in unlimited quantities, copper, zinc, platinum, manganese, rutile, titanium, chrome, uranium, and others too numerous to mention.

Major Cities:

Archona [Pretoria, South Africa], founded 1784. 1990 pop. 12,780,00

National capital; the original city was in a bowl-like depression, just north of the rather bleak Whiteridge gold-mining settlements, and near a major diamond mine. Later proved to be near iron deposits, reasonably close to major coal mines, and in the center of the mineral zone described above. The residential/administrative core remains in the old city, with the industrial developments and serf barracks to the north and suburban developments climbing the plateau to the south, east and west.

Civil service/bureaucratic staff of several millions. Military headquarters. HQ of most major industrial combines. Several universities and research institutes. Tourist traffic. Entertainment industries and luxury manufactures (eg. silk textiles).

Industrial research and development. High quality alloy steels, precision machine tools, ball- and roller-bearings. Ordnance and small arms. Final assembly of nuclear weapons. Computers, components, software. Sensor-effector systems, quality optics, electronics of all types. Word- and data-processing equipment of all types; office supplies. Fiber optics and transmission cables. Scramjet and laser-launch base; space-manufacturing research and support center. Exotic materials, eg. carbon and boron-fiber matrix composites.

Industrial development: the entire central and northern portion of Archona province is dotted with industrial cities in the 100,000–250,000 range, with mines and isolated installations stretching out into the Kalahari (e.g., breeder reactors and plutonium refineries). The aggregate population of the province in 1990 was almost certainly in excess of 30,000,000, over 90% of it urban; the concentration of industries is as great as the Midwestern complex in North America or the Tokyo–

Kyoto corridor in Japan, with only rigorous zoning and planning preventing a conurbation stretching unbroken for hundreds of square miles. The gold mines alone still employ over 500,000 serf workers, and vast sections of the central plateau south of Archona are honeycombed with tunnels stretching down over 15,000 feet—many of them now converted to clandestine military use, or stocked as shelters. The individual industries are too numerous to list in a paper of this size, but encompass the full range of modern manufacturing (with the partial exception of the petrochemical group, which the Domination prefers to localize close to the sources of supply). Minerals, even after a century of intensive working, are still abundant; energy was originally supplied by the extensive and easily accessible coal deposits, now supplemented by a massive complex of remotely-sited underground nuclear power plants, and increasingly by powersat microwave receptors. The primary limit to industrial expansion after the first 50 years or so was the water shortage; this was solved first by the Orange–Tugela schemes, and then in the 1900–1920 period by the huge Zambexi–Kunene–Okovango project, which brought in water from distances of up to 1,500 miles away.

Since the Eurasian War the Domination has restricted growth in this core area, for reasons ranging from aesthetic/environmental to military. There has been an increasing shift in emphasis, with highly-skilled and high-value-added industries being substituted for the basic process and production sectors, which in turn were relocated in other areas. The force of industrial inertia, however (the vast pool of skilled labor, the dense road-rail-telecommunications network, etc.) will ensure that this remains the core area of the Domination's economic machine.

Northmark [Zimbabwe-Rhodesia]

Conquered and settled in the 1790's; northward extension of the Archona-Central Province industrial zone.

Katanga . . .

Northwest . . .

Luanda . . .

Kivu . . .

Lakeland . . .

Northwest Rift . . .

Kenia . . .

AREA ***: MESOPOTAMIA AND THE GULF

Conquered and pacified in 1917–1919.

Defined by the Arabian desert on the west, the Zagros-Taurus mountain chains on the north and east, and the Arabian Gulf on the south. Site of the world's largest oil and natural gas reserves.

The oilfields of the lower gulf were discovered by Draka exploratory parties in 1910–12, and developed by the Hydrocarbon Combine from 1919; the Persian and North Mesopotamian fields, developed by German capital before the Great War, were taken over and expanded at the same time.

The first six-year plan (1920–26) saw output reach 10,000,000 barrels a year; a series of cities, from Basra to Muscat, was founded to handle, process and export the product. Pipelines were also constructed for overland export; the huge reserves of natural gas served as a limitless source of heat and electrical energy. By the

1940s, the conurbation at the head of the Gulf had a
total population of over 6,000,000; by the late 1980s,
12,000,000. (91% serf).

Major industries: petroleum refining, petrochemicals
and plastics, electrochemical and electrometallurgical
(aluminum, copper). Mechanical engineering, generators, turbines, turbocompound internal combustion engines, jet turbines, scramjet engines, military aircraft
and helicopters, airships, shipbuilding and ship repair,
locomotives, rolling stock, textiles (mainly cotton and
synthetics), food processing, fishing.

Agriculture

The Tigris–Euphrates lowlands were revolutionized
by a series of large dams on the headwaters of both
rivers, and control and check dams, settling ponds,
irrigation and drainage channels and saline-water pumping stations. Over 700,000 laborers were at work from
1919–1948 on water control; tens of millions of hectares were brought under cultivation, and the ancient
problem of soil salinity eliminated. Labor was provided
by drafts from Turkey, Bulgaria and China; a dense
road-rail net provided instant communications.

The areas to the north of Baghdad were partially
irrigated, and partially used for dryland cultivation. The
mountain areas were swept clear of their Kurdish-Turkish
populations and afforested; the desert likewise depopu-
lated, with a fringe of ranches and the deeper areas left
as State Reserve parks.

Products: wheat, barley, rice, dates, cotton, citrus,
sugar cane, truck crops, fodder crops, feedlots (southern lowlands); grains, vineyards and fruit-orchards, livestock, wool, nuts (pistachio, walnut) (northern foothill
zone).

Cities: Basra (2,500,000, 91% serf); Baghdad (600,000,
89% serf); Mosul (250,000, 88% serf).

Excerpts from:

Postwar Military Trends:
by Colonel B. Anderson
San Francisco Press, 1966.

At the conclusion of the Eurasian War in 1946, the Alliance for Democracy and the Domination of the Draka were left as the only two military powers on earth. The Domination, occupying the whole of Africa, and continental Eurasia except for India and Indochina-Malaysia-Indonesia, was the supreme land power. The Alliance, its navies enormously expanded in the course of the long struggle with Japan, ruled all but the enclosed seas, the Western hemisphere, insular and peninsular Asia, with India as an associate member.

Domination

Demobilization of the Citizen Force from its wartime peak of 4,200,000 began immediately before the end of formal hostilities in 1946. By 1948, Citizen Force strength was down to about 1,150,000, normal peacetime level with a free population of 40,000,000. The Janissaries were kept at their war strength of 6,500,000 on an indefinite basis.

The Supreme General Staff defined the postwar military tasks of the Draka armed forces as follows:

1. Pacification of the conquered territories and internal security.

2. Deterrence of an Alliance attack.

3. Preparation for the final war with the Alliance.

Pacification required a drastic switch in the "mix" of the ground forces. The armor-heavy mechanized Legions which had fought the open-country battles of the

Eurasian war were as unsuited to guerrilla warfare as a sledgehammer would be for swatting mosquitos.

The Janissaries were, as had been the case after the Great War of 1914–1919, tasked with the primary responsibility for garrison and routine patrol/counterinsurgency work. For these purposes the motorized-rifle format was retained by most units, with an increase of the infantry component and some modification of equipment; eg. a shift from gun-howitzer to more mobile rocket and mortar support weapons. Chemical weapons—mostly nerve gases—were given increased emphasis, as insurgents rarely had the capacity to retaliate in kind or use counter-measures. A number of Legions were converted to specialist mounted infantry, mountain or other configurations.

The standing units of the Citizen Force were also partially restructured. A core of armored formations was maintained; many others were converted to airmobile configurations. The perfection of transport helicopters (1940s) and tiltrotor VTOL transports (1950s) was given high priority, and they were used to form integrated "air-shock" legions. These were all-arms formations oriented to the speed and mobility of air transport, as the armored legions had been to the protection and cross-country capacity of the tank; they included organic helicopter-gunship and ground-attack aircraft units.

Areas of high-intensity counter-insurgency operations were under War Directorate control, although Security Directorate liaison and specialist units would also be present, particularly for intelligence, infiltration and interrogation work. Measures were based on intensive patrolling, reconcentration of civilian populations for easier control, relentless pursuit of organized guerrilla units and in really difficult areas (e.g., Finland) creation of "death zones" by mass deportation and sterilization of the evacuated areas. Sterilization involved the destruction of all structures, removal of all food sources and roundup and slaughter of any groups or individuals who resisted relocation. Quieter areas, and those slated

for immediate settlement, were under joint War and
Security Directorate authority, tending towards the lat-
ter as conditions improved, pending inclusion in the
Police Zone, the area of civil government. Security
Directorate forces included:

Intervention Squads: cohort (battalion) sized rapid-
deployment forces [Roughly analogous to our timeline's
SAS]. Used for brushfire operations, suppression of ter-
rorism and Alliance infiltration, etc. No fixed configura-
tion; some are tasked for urban counterterrorist work,
others for border-patrol, etc. All armed personnel are
Citizen volunteers; serf auxiliaries for routine clerical,
support functions. Total (Citizen) strength, c. 35,000.

Order Police: a militarized police force or gendarmerie, organized in units of up to merarchy (regimen-
tal) size. Serf personnel under Citizen officers and senior
NCO's, recruited on the same basis as the Janissaries,
equipped mainly as light infantry but including some
heavy-weapons units for emergencies. Used for perimeter guard, patrol and general policing duties; units can
be detached as labor-camp guards, for dealing with
Compound unrest and so forth. Total strength c.
1,250,000.

Regular Police: the police proper; again, mostly serfs
under Citizen direction, although there are some all-
Citizen units—only a Citizen may arrest another Citizen. Armed with light weapons and organized regionally;
has authority over private security forces such as Combine compound-guards, etc. Includes detective components, central record-keeping operations etc. and carries
out a number of functions (for example, neck-tattooing
and registering serfs). The Regulars handle ordinary
maintenance of law and order and "civilian" crime.

Compound and Camp Guards: Much of the industrial
work force of the Domination is "compounded," permanently enclosed in compounds, walled residential enclosures. These are usually owned by the industrial
combines, or by government administrative directorates (eg. Transportation or Land Settlement). Organiza-

tions which maintain compounds have their own internal police forces, usually not armed except for their Citizen directors; however, the Security Directorate provides training and performs a general supervisory function. (Ex-members of the Order Police are commonly "rented" as cadre for these organizations.) Policing measures can range from the quite formal (in the larger mining or factory compounds, which may have up to 10,000 inhabitants) to the makeshift (e.g., in a 20-man forestry "compound" in the Ituri).

Punitive deportation to labor-camps is a common measure in the Domination; prisoners of war, political suspects, hardened criminals, people found to be inconvenient, and anyone not quite troublesome enough to kill outright. Private owners may sell troublemaking serfs to the camps, or ordinary laborers may be levied/ bought for special projects and housed in mobile camps— this is the common pattern for large-scale road/railway/ irrigation works. Punitive camps are generally in remote areas, and the laborers are either worked under direct Security Directorate control or rented on a per-head basis to the relevant civilian organization, being delivered and picked up daily. Internal security in the camps is provided by "trustees," auxiliaries usually recruited from the criminal-prisoner elements and armed with truncheons and whips. Order Police units, or individuals on detached service, provide cadre and supervision, and guard perimeters. (Most camps are surrounded by razor wire and guard towers with automatic weapons.)

Krypteria: the secret police proper, and the "senior service" within the Security Directorate, entitled to commandeer and direct units from any other Security organization. Different divisions of the Krypteria are tasked with foreign and domestic intelligence (in cooperation with the War Directorate), covert operations abroad, countersubversion and counterespionage. Employs both Citizen and serf personnel, the latter especially as infiltrators, informers etc. The Krypteria has absolute powers of arrest, torture and execution over all serfs not in Janissary uniform, and broad powers of arrest over Citizens as well (although arbitrary treatment of Citizens can result in political repercussions; however, evidence of genuine political disaffection—e.g., dissent over the serf issue—repeals all protection). Enforces censorship and handles disinformation campaigns. Agents of the Krypteria may be found anywhere; the diplomatic service is a Security Directorate "cover" and under Krypteria control.

Note: There is very little in the way of special "riot control" equipment or training. Any overt resistance is treated as rebellion, for which there is only one punishment—death. Truncheons, electroprods and whips are only used to enforce obedience and for minor punishment; rioting would be suppressed by indiscriminate use of automatic and heavy weapons. A "succesful" revolt in a compound, mine or factory would usually be dealt with simply by gassing or napalming the area in question, and impaling any survivors. The ultimate example of this attitude was the city of Barcelona, where a revolt succeeded in temporarily overrunning the police HQ. All Citizens within reach were evacuated and the city destroyed with a nuclear weapon.

Land Tenure and Plantation Life . . .

There are essentially four types of land in the Domination:

1. *Urban*

Urban land tenure is closest to what Western civilization understands by private property, although Municipal governments own extensive areas and have strong zoning authority.

2. *State Reserve Land*

National parks, State forests, wildlife reserves. About 15 percent of the Domination's territory before the Eurasian War, rather more thereafter. The whole complex is managed by the Conservancy Directorate, which also oversees forestry—forest land is leased out to "private" firms on a sustained-yield management basis. Most desert and mountain areas are State Reserve; agriculturally marginal areas in the territories conquered in 1941–46 are generally turned over to this category.

A sub-category is land used for State installations—schools, military bases, firing ranges, research installations—which is leased and administered by the institution in question.

3. *Settlement Reserve Land*

Land suitable for plantation or urban development but not yet so distributed. Granted (in newly conquered areas) or auctioned (if physically reclaimed, e.g. through irrigation or drainage). Until then usually run by the Agriculture and Land Settlement Directorate.

4. *Rural/Agricultural Land*

The countryside in productive use is split into what are formally known as "plantation landholdings." These are technically leased from the State rather than owned; they may be sold (although there is a heavy sales tax when this is outside the family of the landholder) but are subject to certain restrictions on use:

a. The landholder must be resident at least 3/4 of the year, unless on State service (e.g., in the armed forces). Persistent violation will result in the property being adjudged "abandoned" and it will be released or put up for compulsory sale, usually to another member of the family.

b. The land must be properly managed; this implies first careful prevention of soil erosion, salination etc. Second, it must be managed as a single productive unit and the serfs kept "in order"; mostly confined to a single Quarters village and not allowed to wander abroad, etc. Penalties for violation as above.

c. A certain ratio of free to serf inhabitants must be maintained, and a plantation (except in emergency situations) can never be left without a free adult to oversee it; wages and working conditions of overseers are also State-mandated, and this is enforced by the Overseers Guild (informally known as the Brotherhood of the Lash). The effective maximum number of serfs per plantation is around 1,000; the average is between 600–1,000.

d. No individual may lease more than one plantation landholding; attempting to do so is a serious offense. Subdivision is forbidden except with government authorization; this is allowed in cases where changes in land usage (e.g., irrigation or conversion from pasture to arable) make the original units unwieldy.

Plantation Life—general.

Plantation size varies considerably with geography, soils, climate, predominant crop etc. The general rule is to adjust size to allow for full employment of a labor force of average numbers; thus a ranching operation in the sub-Saharan zone or Mongolia might be hundreds of thousands of acres, while an irrigated plantation in the Nile delta growing fruit and vegetables might be as little as 1,000–2,000 acres.

Whatever the product, the estate is run as a single large farm controlled from the manor or "Great House." The central settlement is divided into three parts:

i. The Great House proper, containing the living quarters of the landholding family and free staff (overseers, etc.), administrative serfs (bookkeepers, etc.), the domestic servants, the armory, kitchens, laundry, House stables and garages, and so forth. Two- to three-story buildings around a series of courtyards are the most common, with adjustments for climate. Any well established plantation will include park-grounds (up to 20–30 acres), kitchen gardens, a bath-wing (on the Roman model but with embellishments), libraries, sports facilities, a salle d'armes, etc. Domestic staffs are usually between 30 and 70.

ii. The Quarters, or serf village. Individual family cottages are grouped around a central green; piped water, sewage (linked to methane-generation systems), electricity and gas (methane-generated) have become increasingly common. Around the common will be the communal facilities: a bathhouse (daily bathing is usually compulsory), bakehouse (for breads and roasts), laundry, infirmary and lying-in clinic (with a trained nurse's aide and midwife), storehouse, and possibly a small church, mosque, or temple depending on the region.

   Normal cottages are (with variations) four-room with attics; building materials vary widely, and are usually locally-produced. The headman, priest, gang-foremen and skilled serfs (blacksmiths, mechanics, livestock specialists, vintners etc.) may have larger houses; unmarried wenches and bucks past 18 are often separately housed.

   Small kitchen gardens, and sometimes chicken-coops and rabbit-hutches are attached to the cottages. Cats are common, but only privileged serfs are allowed to keep dogs.

iii. The grange, or working areas. This would include barns, storehouses, machine and blacksmith's shops, possibly a methane or hydro power system, the sewing-shop where plantation clothing is made, equipment stores, holding pens for live-stock and any other necessary establishments. Very large plantations (ranches, for example) may have outlying granges, and groups of serfs may be assigned for periods of up to several weeks; however, permanent residence away from the Quarters is very rare.

Primary processing, such as crushing grapes or olives, drying coffee, shearing and sorting wool, crushing sugar, etc. is carried on in the grange; there are also facilities for bulk storage. Final processing—grain milling, cotton ginning and baling, meat-packing—is usually carried on by the Landholder's League at central points; the raw or semi-processed products are picked up by League steamtrucks, and graded, and the Landholder's account credited.

Labor Management

Workers (hands) are graded as full (healthy adult) or partial, in increments of 1/4. Worknorms are set by time-and-motion study methods, sometimes by professional consultants furnished by the Landholder's League. Dossiers are kept on each individual serf (this is required by law) with a full medical and disciplinary history, ready for quick reference.

Routine work is "tasked," usually by the week, to serf-gangs or combinations of gangs. Each gang (usually 10–20 hands, for field workers) has a driver or bossboy, appointed by the overseers, who is responsible for output and immediate discipline. Section bosses may be appointed to superintend larger operations; a pen-boss for the sheep pens, for example, a winery-boss for the grape-pressing sheds, a herd-boss for a group of animals; they would have a permanent staff and gangs of unskilled labor assigned as needed. Output for a particular task may be set individually or by gang—a certain area hoed clear of weeds, for example, would be done by gang, while picking cotton or fruit would be individually graded against the preset norm.

Skilled serfs, such as smiths or carpenters, are usually employed in or at least based out of the grange and work alone or in small groups; training is by apprenticeship.

Permanent gangs exist, sometimes with specialized functions. For example: building gangs, fence-repair gangs, stock gangs etc., although for harvests or emergencies everyone is mobilized.

Hours of labor are seasonal. The usual procedure is for a bell to be rung at dawn; hands have an hour to eat, dress and assemble in their gangs for the day's work; fieldworkers either walk or are trucked to their tasks. An hour is provided for the midday meal; those working about the settlement eat in their homes, while lunch is carried to those in the fields. At harvest or in emergencies the evening meal may also be eaten in the fields and work continue into the night; usually the day ends after about 10 hours of labor, the hands return to the Quarters, bathe, eat the evening meal and have until about 11:00 for private activity. At "lights out" all serfs must be in their cottages, and no movement outside is permitted except in urgent situations (e.g., sickness, fire, a woman going into labor). Most plantations give Sundays and half Saturday off, with other holidays at customary intervals—after harvest, Christmas, and on occasions such as a marriage or birth in the Great House.

Food rations are usually issued weekly, although some perishable products are kept in refrigerated storehouses and handed out more frequently, and some staples (e.g., dried beans) less often. Bread is issued prebaked. Diet varies according to local crops; grain or other carbohydrates are the basis, with meat or fish at about 5 lb. per adult per week, dairy products and fruit in season. Vitamin supplements are becoming increasingly common. Spices, coffee, tea, sugar and wine or beer are also issued; skilled serfs and supervisors receive more, and more high-status foods such as meat.

Clothing, bedding and household utensils are issued four times yearly; undergarments, shoes and socks are now (1990s) generally factory-made, while clothing proper is run up by plantation seamstresses. Individuals may earn thread, ribbons etc. as "extras" and decorate their or their family's clothing.

Discipline is maintained by a complex system of rewards and punishments. Rewards include extra rations, clothing or other luxuries; promotion (e.g., to a skilled position or domestic service) or public recognition. Punishments range from deprivation of privileges (eg. having to work during holidays or spend them in the *ergastulum*, the serf jail), to extra hours of daily labor, to physical punishment. Light physical punishment—not more than 10 strokes with a cane switch—may be administered by serf supervisors, such as gang-bosses and the headman (who is responsible for general discipline and cleanliness in the Quarters). The overseers or the landholder may administer heavier punishments, in rare or extreme cases up to mutilation or death. There is generally a semi-formalized system of plantation courts, held weekly or monthly, to deal with offenses between serfs—fighting, stealing, etc.; the landholder or overseer hears testimony, takes the advice of the headman and gang-bosses, and pronounces sentence; at these times, ordinary serfs may also make complaint against the serf supervisors, although they would be well-advised to have multiple witnesses. Sentences for other offenses —e.g., shirking work or insolence—will also be pronounced on these occasions.

Sentences (other than deprivation of privileges) may be flogging, time in the stocks, or working in chains. Floggings are administered in public, usually with medical help standing by. Mutilations such as gelding or ear-cropping fell out of general use (by the 1880's) but may still be used on occasion, especially in newly-settled territories. Incorrigibles may be branded and sold as such, and will in that case end up in a destructive-labor camp, mine or other such terminal location. At-

tempted escape, assault on a free Citizen, possession of
weapons or forbidden literature, etc. are crimes against
the State and may involve the Security Directorate
(usually the *Orpos*, the Order Police); the usual punishment for these offences is breaking on the wheel (the
offender is tied to a wheel and the major bones broken
with an iron rod) and then impalement. Death sentences are carried out in public, usually in the nearest
town, but some serfs from the offender's plantation are
brought in to be part of the compulsory audience.

Non-productive Individuals

Pregnant women are put on light work, and excused
from any but light sedentary labor from the fourth
month. Infants are born under the supervision of trained
midwives, or when necessàry doctors; mother and child
then usually remain in the infirmary for up to several
days. Nursing mothers are employed (at gradually increasing intensities) in work around the Quarters or
nearby fields, and given regular intervals to feed their
infants; continuous supervision is provided by full-time
child-minders. Barring medical complications, weaning
is usually complete within 6–12 months; bottle feed-
ing is available when breast milk is insufficient.

Infants are formally registered and neck-tattooed at
the age of about one year; this is usually done in the
plantation infirmary, with a Security representative
present.

Children are left to their parents (and their creche-
supervisors during the working day) until about age six.
After this, they are assigned light chores around the
Quarters for a few hours a day, and sometimes allowed
to accompany parents to the fields or workshops, where
they may do small helping-out tasks. Those who show
exceptional aptitude may be given basic schooling, literacy and numeracy; children of skilled workers and
especially clerks tend to be selected for such training.
Hours of work gradually increase until roughly puberty,

at which time the young serf is enrolled as a quarter-hand and assigned to a gang, or assigned as a full-time helper and apprentice to an artisan, or selected as a domestic (many ordinary maidservants serve in the Great House for a few years prior to marriage and then return to the Quarters). Most hands gradually learn the necessary skills during adolescence, and graduate to "full hand" status in the early twenties.

There is a daily sick call, at the infirmary; although there is usually no formal provision for sick leave, a limit of a day or two per month with no obvious symptoms is generally allowed. Beyond this, a doctor may be called in—and punishment administered if no real cause for complaint is found. Those with obvious symptoms (e.g., fever, nausea, severe headaches) will be treated either at the infirmary or at home; serious cases will again bring a doctor, and possible hospitalization. Doctors are generally Citizens, employed by the League and on call for plantations in a given area; serf hospitals are maintained by the League and possibly by Combines and private owners in the area, and available to all League members. Preventitive medicine is emphasized, vaccination and innoculation are compulsory, and the plantation population is generally physically healthy.

The chronically ill and crippled are given maintenance care and work suitable to their limitations—e.g., basketry or dishwashing for those who cannot walk, etc. As serfs age and their strength and physical stamina decline, they are reduced from full to three-quarter hands and so on; by late middle age they will often be transferred from field work to child-minding and other light tasks (supervisors and skilled workers retire later, and a headman is often elderly). The aged are not required to work and are generally looked after by their families; if this is not sufficient, the headman will assign their care on a rotating basis to provide cooking, cleaning, etc.

Agricultural Marketing and Technique

The Domination's agricultural sector might be described as semi-market farming, with semi-mechanized methods. Some areas of high-value, high-productivity land are under specialized crops—e.g. the market gardening of the Nile Delta, the rice and date plantations of southern Iraq, etc.; such areas import their staple foods (through the bulk-sales division of the League). Most areas produce a mixture of food crops and possibly one or more cash crops (e.g., cotton, sisal, coffee, wool); the surplus left once the labor-force is fed is sold through the League, along with industrial crops. The industrial labor force is fed by its Combine owners, who buy in bulk from the League and distribute the product to their compound messhalls; the League also sells to smaller-scale private owners in the cities, sometimes in the form of preprocessed ration-packs, and of course to the State and the armed forces. Higher-quality foods for Citizen consumption are marketed through either private stores and restaurants (which may buy from the League or direct from planters) or by purchasing co-operatives, often run through free-employee guilds.

Most regions are roughly self-sufficient in basic foodstuffs, importing only products which the local climate cannot grow, such as wine in the tropics, sugar in the temperate zone, etc. Large-scale processing industries such as textiles, leatherworking etc. are where possible located near the producing areas, although industrial inertia and other factors such as energy supplies sometimes play a part. Alexandria, Egypt, is still a textile center even though the lower Nile valley is no longer a cotton-producing area; the factories and ancillary manufacturing were there, and it was not worthwhile to move them. While serfs usually live on the staple products of an area (sorghum in West Africa, rice in Iraq, wheat in Kazakhstan, etc.), Citizen diets are more uniform and hence involve more long-distance trade; for example, in air-freighted fresh fruit and vegetables.

Agricultural techniques emphasize long-term stability (practices which undermine soil fertility are regarded with horror), productivity per acre rather than per man-hour (since labor is cheap and abundant), and ease of management. Farming is deliberately kept rather over-manned, to act as a labor reservoir in times of stress, such as a long war. Mechanized cultivation—tractors, combine harvesters—is not used where animal traction is possible, for a number of reasons. First, it would place an unnacceptable strain on the supply of skilled labor and require a huge infrastructure of fuel, repair and supply. Second, it would divert manufacturing capacity from more important aims, e.g., producing tanks. Third, while industrial productivity is considered desirable both for military reasons and to keep the urban working class as small as practicable, plantation hands are considered the most desirable source of Janissary recruits.

Cultivation is by hand labor and animal-powered machinery; within these limitations, tools are abundant and well-designed. Careful attention is given to field layout, for example to placing the more labor-intensive activities close to the Quarters. Power-driven machinery is extensively used for processing, pumping of irrigation water and other work where hand methods are inappropriate. All estates have a number of steam trucks and "drags," often used for transporting workers to outlying sections of the plantation, and great care is devoted to keeping the plantation's internal roads in order. Draka agronomy and biology are excellent, and continual research is done by the League and the Institutes on the development of improved strains of plant and animal, and on pest control. Emphasis is placed on biological controls rather than pesticides (which are occasionally used but distrusted), especially by habitat control—e.g. by avoiding monoculture of a particular crop. Several species of African animal have been domesticated and are used for meat and hide production; eland, a number of antelope, zebra. Wherever possible plantations will include woodlots for timber, fuel and wildlife production, and farming practices are adjusted to enhance wildlife habitat, e.g. by using live hedges rather than metal fences where possible. Aesthetics also plays a central role, and Draka will go to considerable expense to make a landscape look agreeable. The general motto is "Live as if you're going to die tomorrow; farm as if you're going to live forever." A plantation (which requires generations of management to achieve full potential) is regarded as an inheritance to be cherished, not a resource to be exploited.

JOHN DALMAS

He's done it all!

John Dalmas has just about done it all—parachute infantryman, army medic, stevedore, merchant seaman, logger, smokejumper, administrative forester, farm worker, creamery worker, technical writer, free-lance editor—and his experience is reflected in his writing. His marvelous sense of nature and wilderness combined with his high-tech world view involves the reader with his very real characters. For lovers of fast-paced action-adventures!

THE REGIMENT
The planet Tyss is so poor that it has only one resource: its fighting men. Each year three regiments are sent forth into the galaxy. And once a regiment is constituted, it never recruits again: as casualties mount the regiment becomes a battalion ... a company ... a platoon ... a squad ... and then there are none. But after the last man of *this* regiment has flung himself into battle, the Federation of Worlds will never be the same!

THE WHITE REGIMENT
All the Confederation of Worlds wanted was a little peace. So they applied their personnel selection technology to war and picked the greatest potential warriors out of their planets-wide database of psych profiles. And they hired the finest mercenaries in the galaxy to train the first test regiment—they hired the legendary black warriors of Tyss to create the first ever White Regiment.

THE KALIF'S WAR
The White Regiment had driven back the soldiers of the Kharganik empire, but the Kalif was certain that

he could succeed in bringing the true faith of the Prophet of Kargh to the Confederation—even if he had to bombard the infidels' planets with nuclear weapons to do it! But first he would have to thwart a conspiracy in his own ranks that was planning to replace him with a more tractable figurehead . . .

FANGLITH
Fanglith was a near-mythical world to which criminals and misfits had been exiled long ago. The planet becomes all too real to Larn and Deneen when they track their parents there, and find themselves in the middle of the Age of Chivalry on a world that will one day be known as Earth.

RETURN TO FANGLITH
The oppressive Empire of Human Worlds, temporarily filed in *Fanglith*, has struck back and resubjugated its colony planets. Larn and Deneen must again flee their home. Their final object is to reach a rebel base—but the first stop is Fanglith!

THE LIZARD WAR
A thousand years after World War III and Earth lies supine beneath the heel of a gang of alien sociopaths who like to torture whole populations for sport. But while the 16th century level of technology the aliens found was relatively easy to squelch, the mystic warrior sects that had evolved in the meantime weren't. . . .

THE LANTERN OF GOD
They were pleasure droids, designed for maximum esthetic sensibility and appeal, abandoned on a deserted planet after catastrophic systems failure on their transport ship. After 2000 years undisturbed, "real" humans arrive on the scene—and 2000 thousand years of droid freedom is about to come to a sharp and bloody end.

THE REALITY MATRIX
Is the existence we call life on Earth for real, or is it a game? Might Earth be an artificial construct designed by a group of higher beings? Is everything an illusion? Everything is—except the Reality Matrix. And what if self-appointed "Lords of Chaos" place a chaos generator in the matrix, just to see what will happen? Answer: The slow destruction of our world.

THE GENERAL'S PRESIDENT
The stock market crash of 1994 makes Black Monday of 1929 look like a minor market adjustment—and the fabric of society is torn beyond repair. The Vice President resigns under a cloud of scandal—and when the military hints that they may let the lynch mobs through anyway, the President resigns as well. So the Generals get to pick a President. But the man they choose turns out to be more of a leader than they bargained for. . . .